image comics presents

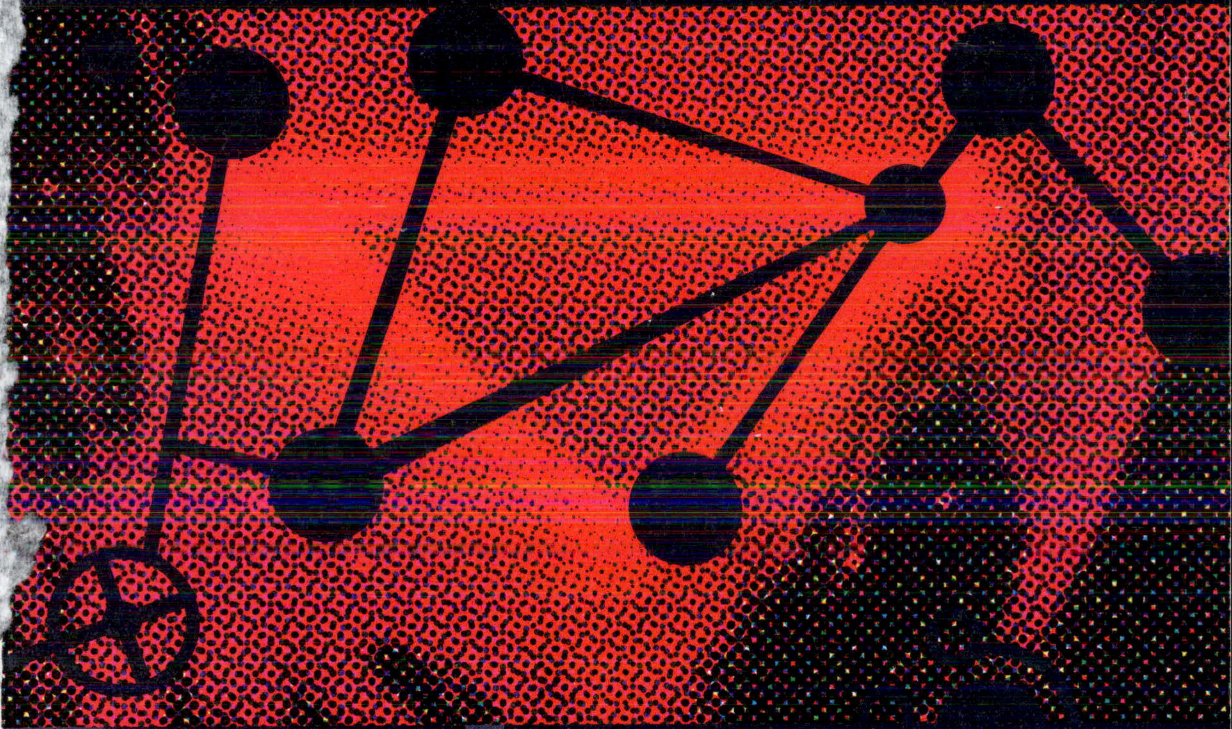

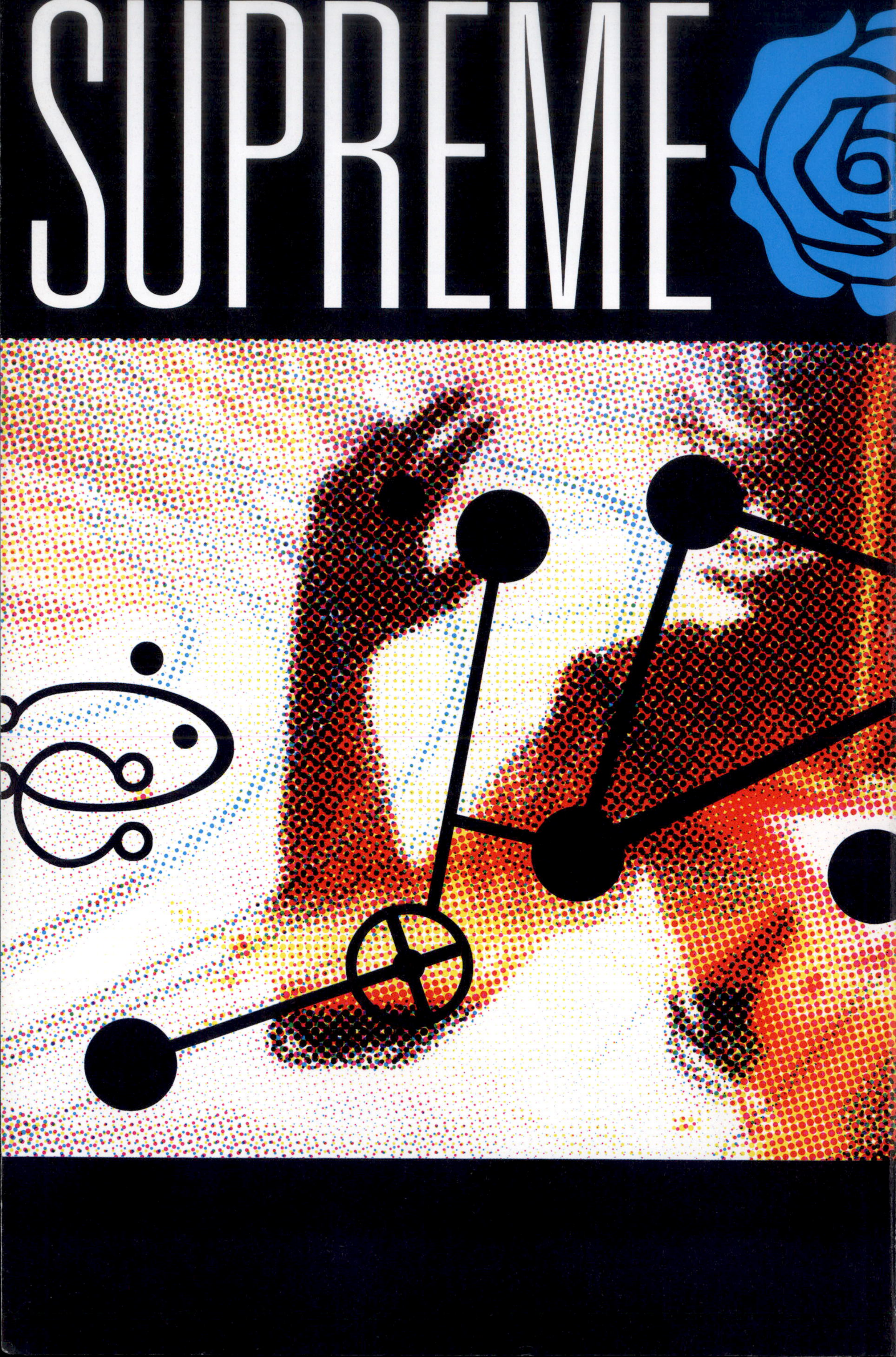
SUPREME

BLUE ROSE

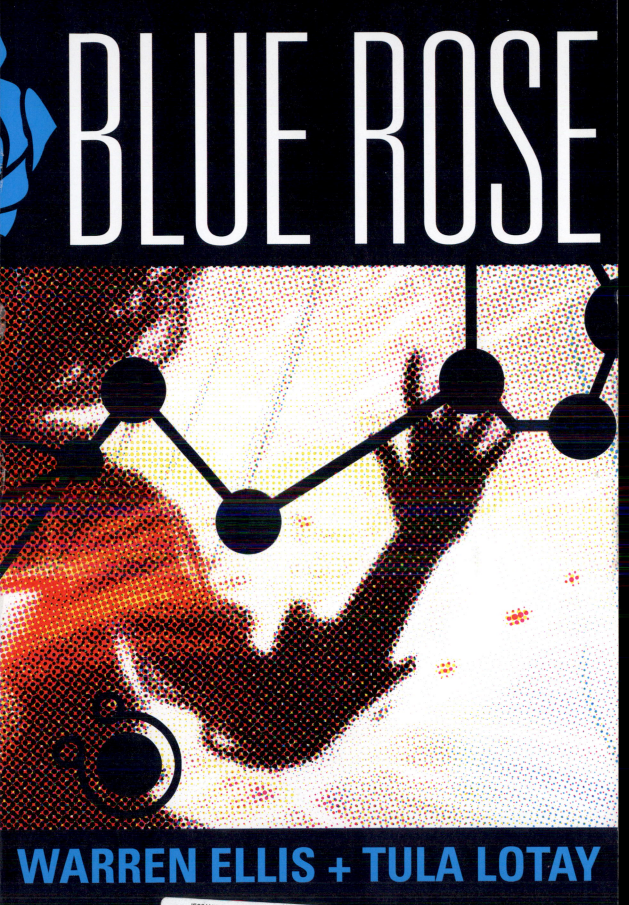

WARREN ELLIS + TULA LOTAY

for **COMICRAFT:**
RICHARD STARKINGS lettering
JOHN ROSHELL design

coordinated by **ERIC STEPHENSON**

SUPREME created by **ROB LIEFELD**

IMAGE COMICS, INC.
Robert Kirkman – Chief Operating Officer
Erik Larsen – Chief Financial Officer
Todd McFarlane – President
Marc Silvestri – Chief Executive Officer
Jim Valentino – Vice-President

Eric Stephenson – Publisher
Corey Murphy – Director of Sales
Jeremy Sullivan – Director of Digital Sales
Kat Salazar – Director of PR & Marketing
Emily Miller – Director of Operations
Branwyn Bigglestone – Senior Accounts Manager
Drew Gill – Art Director
Jonathan Chan – Production Manager
Meredith Wallace – Print Manager
Randy Okamura – Marketing Production Designer
David Brothers – Content Manager
Addison Duke – Production Artist
Vincent Kukua – Production Artist
Sasha Head – Production Artist
Tricia Ramos – Production Artist
Emilio Bautista – Sales Assistant
Jessica Ambriz – Administrative Assistant
IMAGECOMICS.COM

"And then it all changed."

ONE

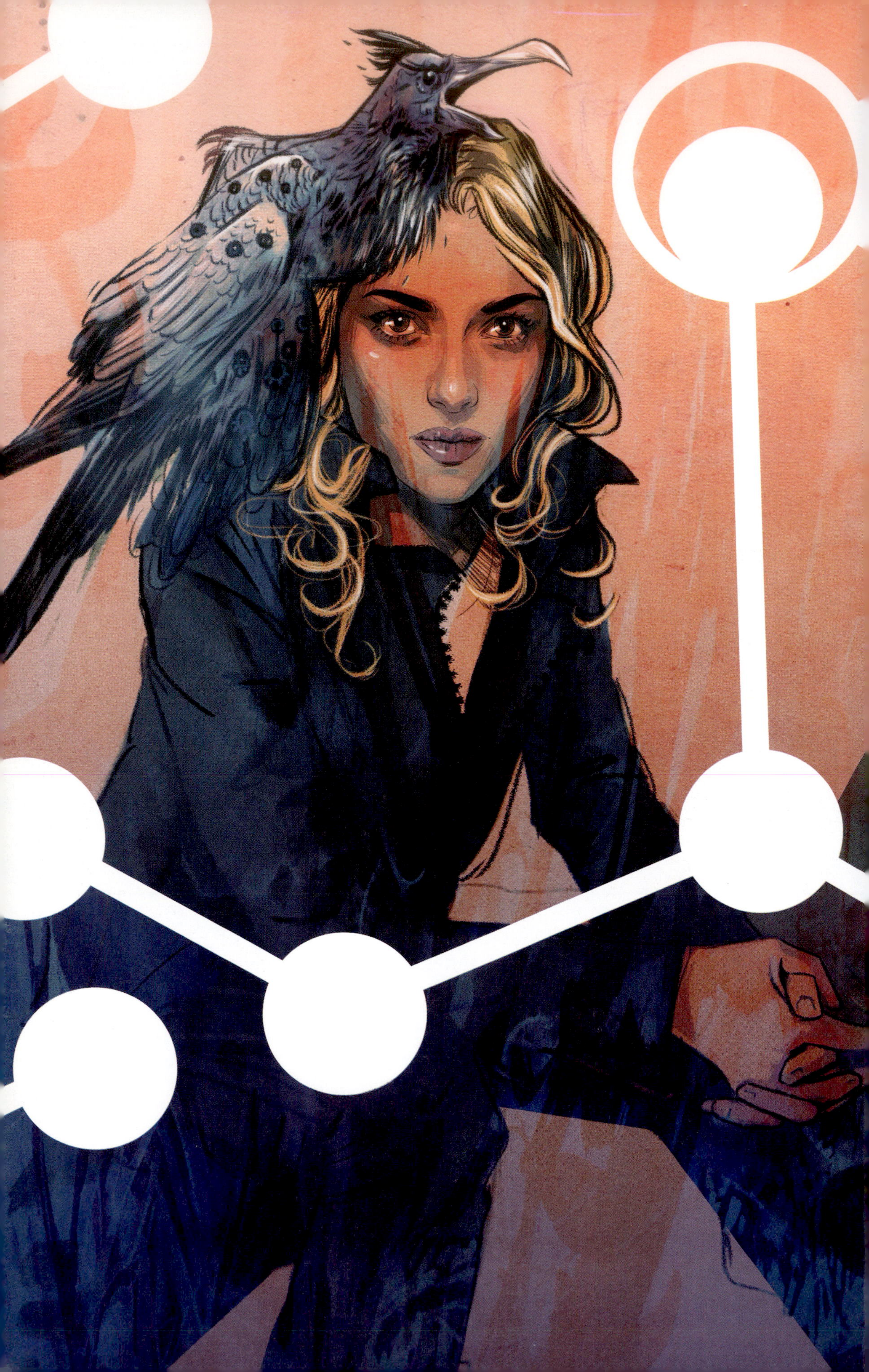

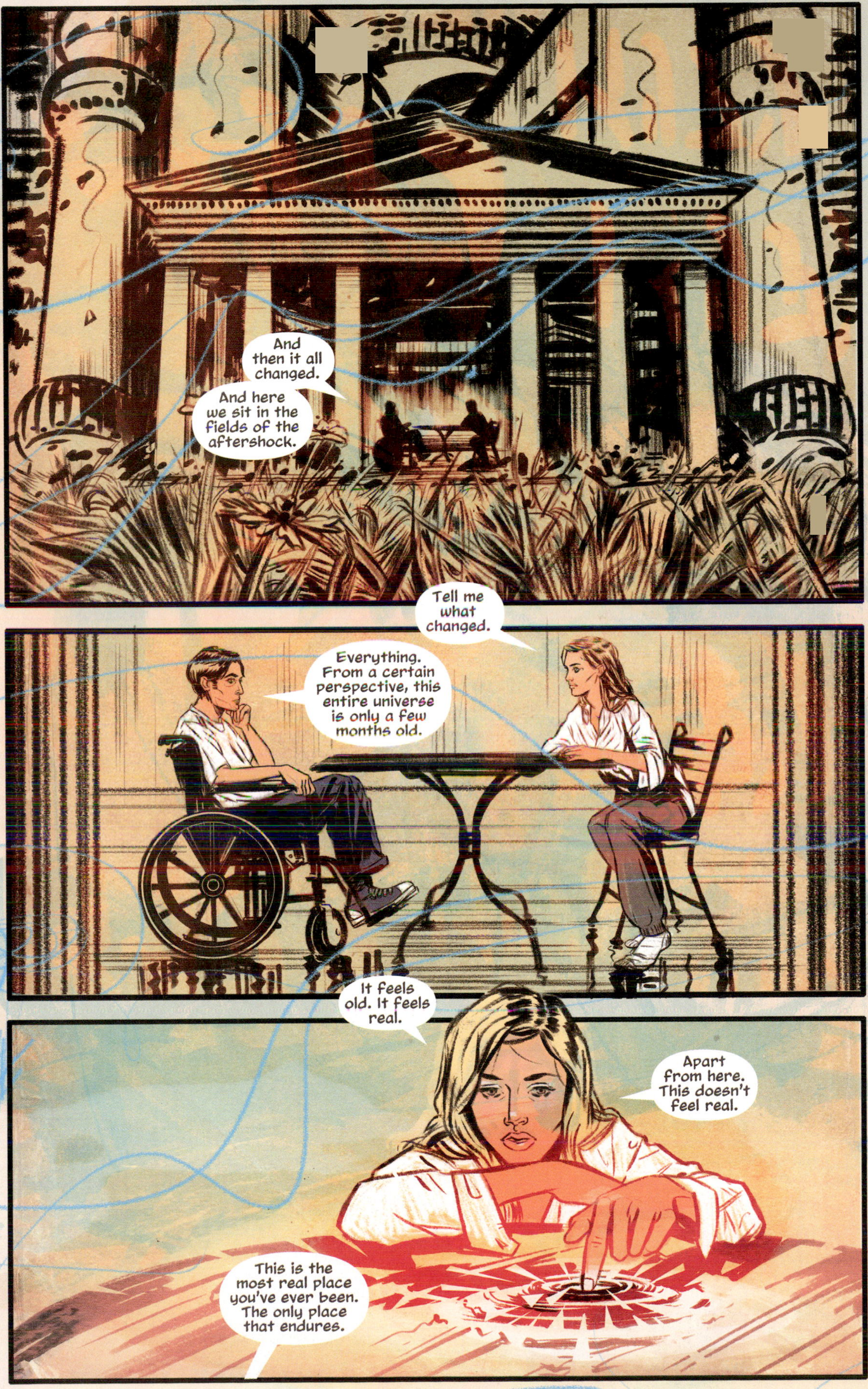
And then it all changed.
And here we sit in the fields of the aftershock.
Tell me what changed.
Everything. From a certain perspective, this entire universe is only a few months old.
It feels old. It feels real.
Apart from here. This doesn't feel real.
This is the most real place you've ever been. The only place that endures.

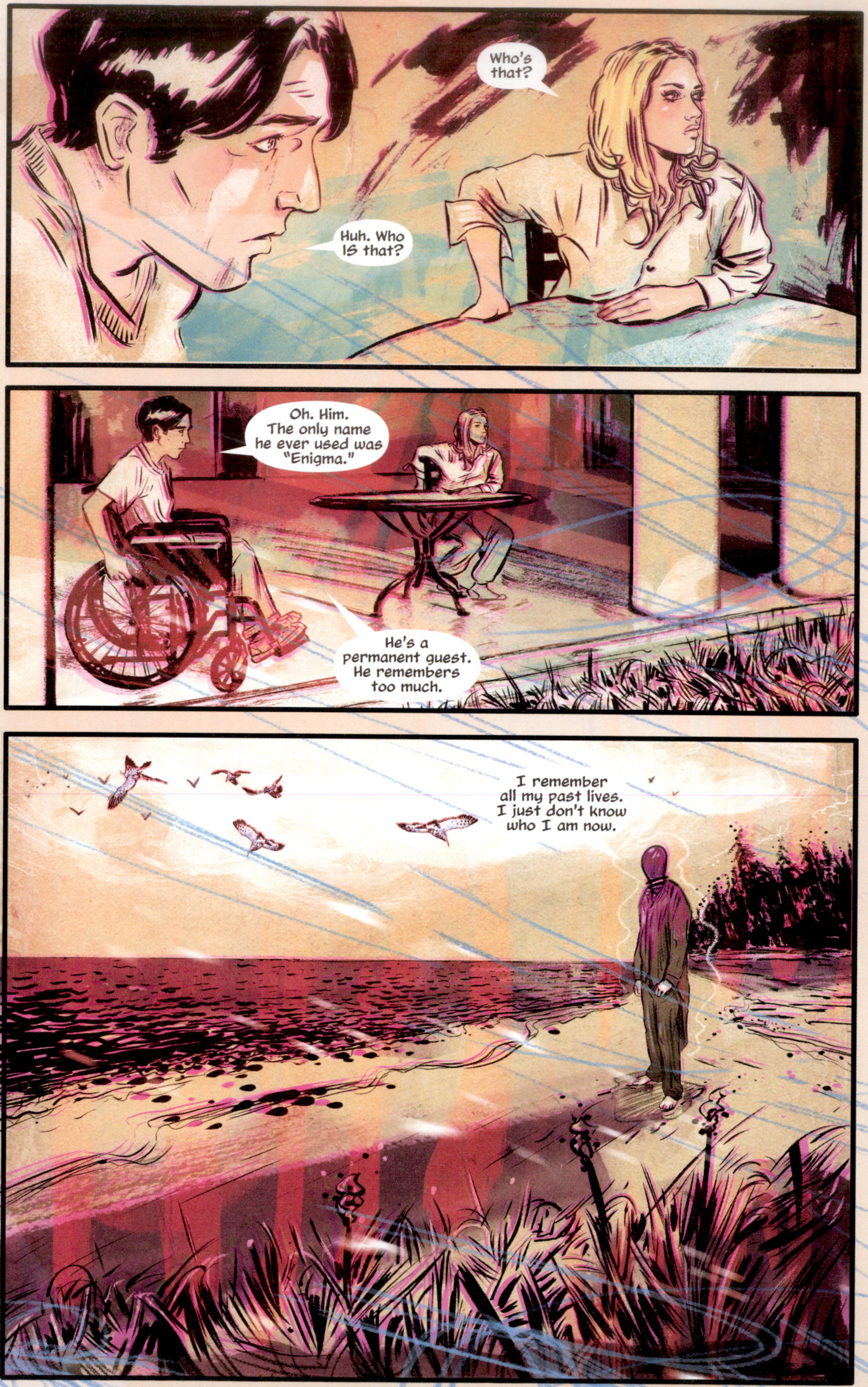
Who's that?
Huh. Who IS that?
Oh. Him. The only name he ever used was "Enigma."
He's a permanent guest. He remembers too much.
I remember all my past lives. I just don't know who I am now.

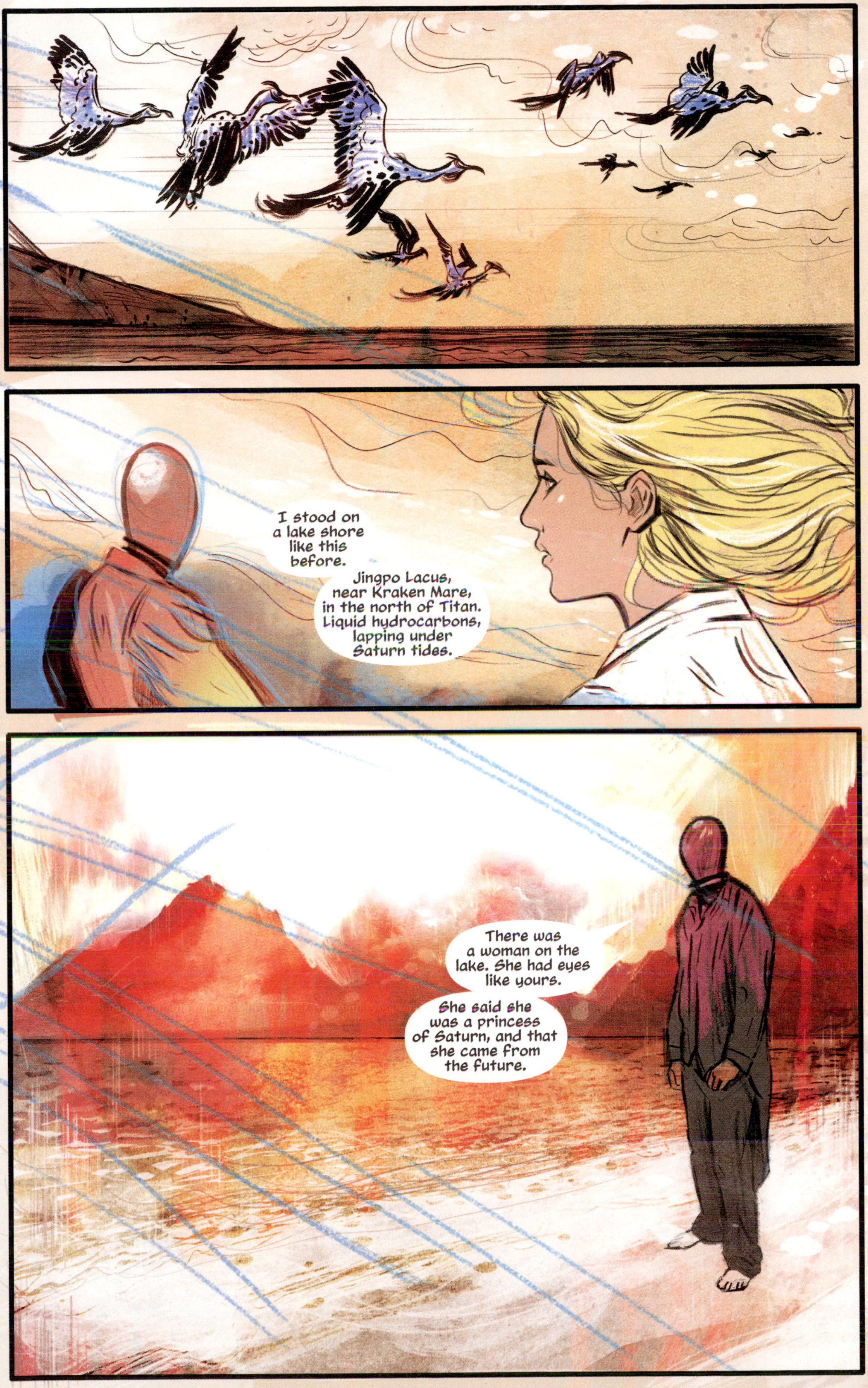
I stood on a lake shore like this before.
Jingpo Lacus, near Kraken Mare, in the north of Titan. Liquid hydrocarbons, lapping under Saturn tides.
There was a woman on the lake. She had eyes like yours.
She said she was a princess of Saturn, and that she came from the future.

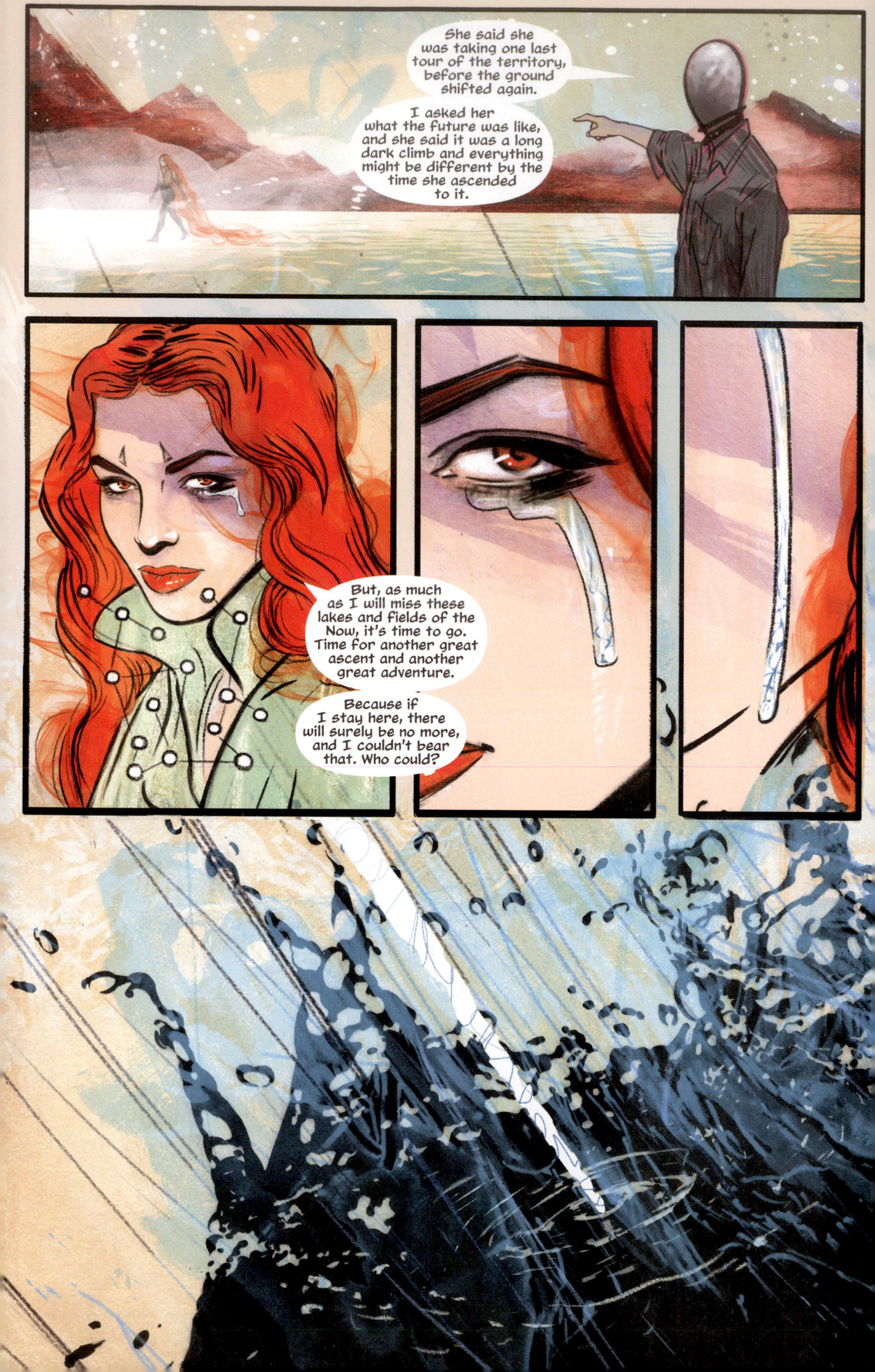
She said she was taking one last tour of the territory, before the ground shifted again.
I asked her what the future was like, and she said it was a long dark climb and everything might be different by the time she ascended to it.
But, as much as I will miss these lakes and fields of the Now, it's time to go. Time for another great ascent and another great adventure.
Because if I stay here, there will surely be no more, and I couldn't bear that. Who could?

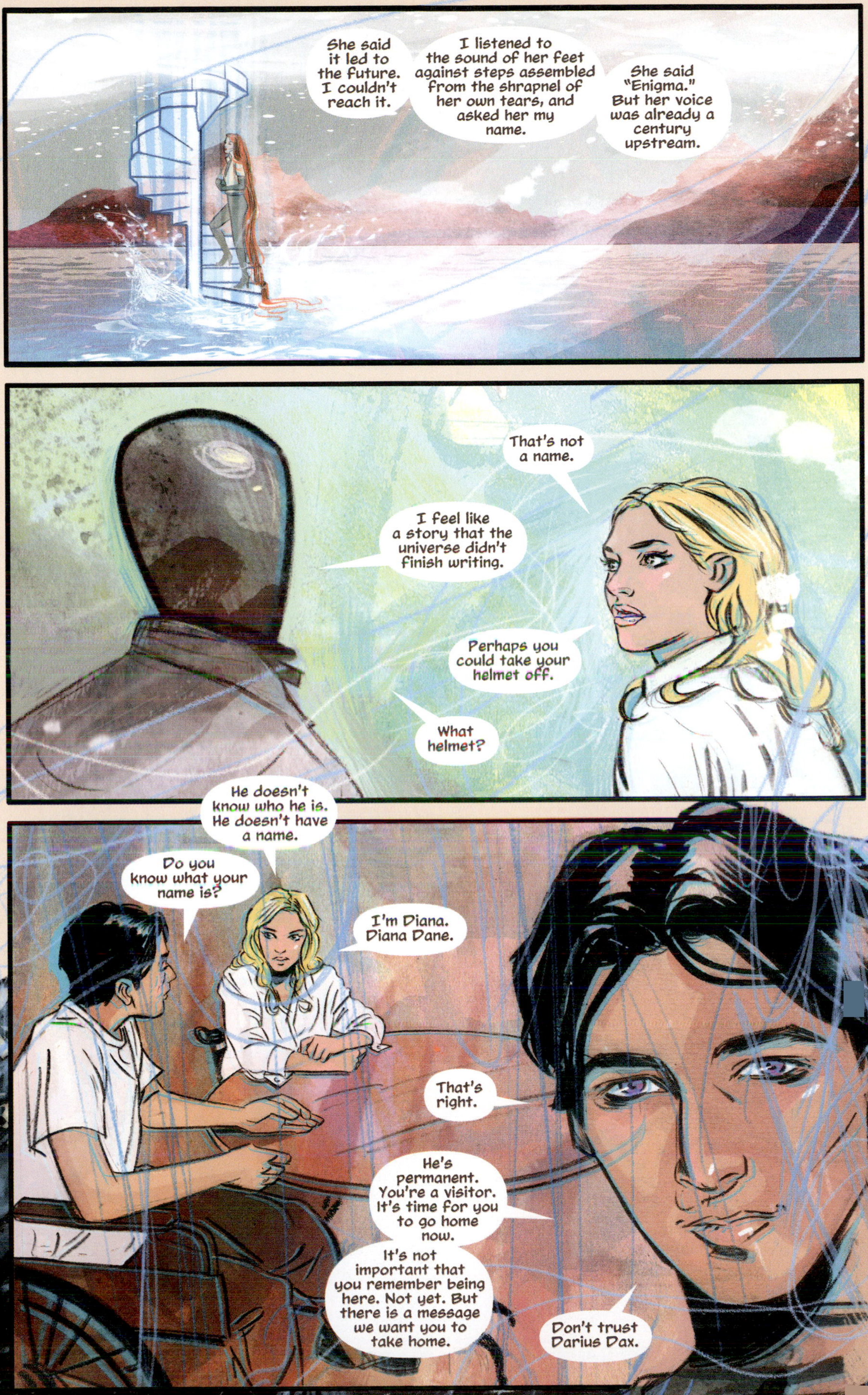
She said it led to the future. I couldn't reach it.
I listened to the sound of her feet against steps assembled from the shrapnel of her own tears, and asked her my name.
She said "Enigma." But her voice was already a century upstream.
That's not a name.
I feel like a story that the universe didn't finish writing.
Perhaps you could take your helmet off.
What helmet?
He doesn't know who he is. He doesn't have a name.
Do you know what your name is?
I'm Diana. Diana Dane.
That's right.
He's permanent. You're a visitor. It's time for you to go home now.
It's not important that you remember being here. Not yet. But there is a message we want you to take home.
Don't trust Darius Dax.

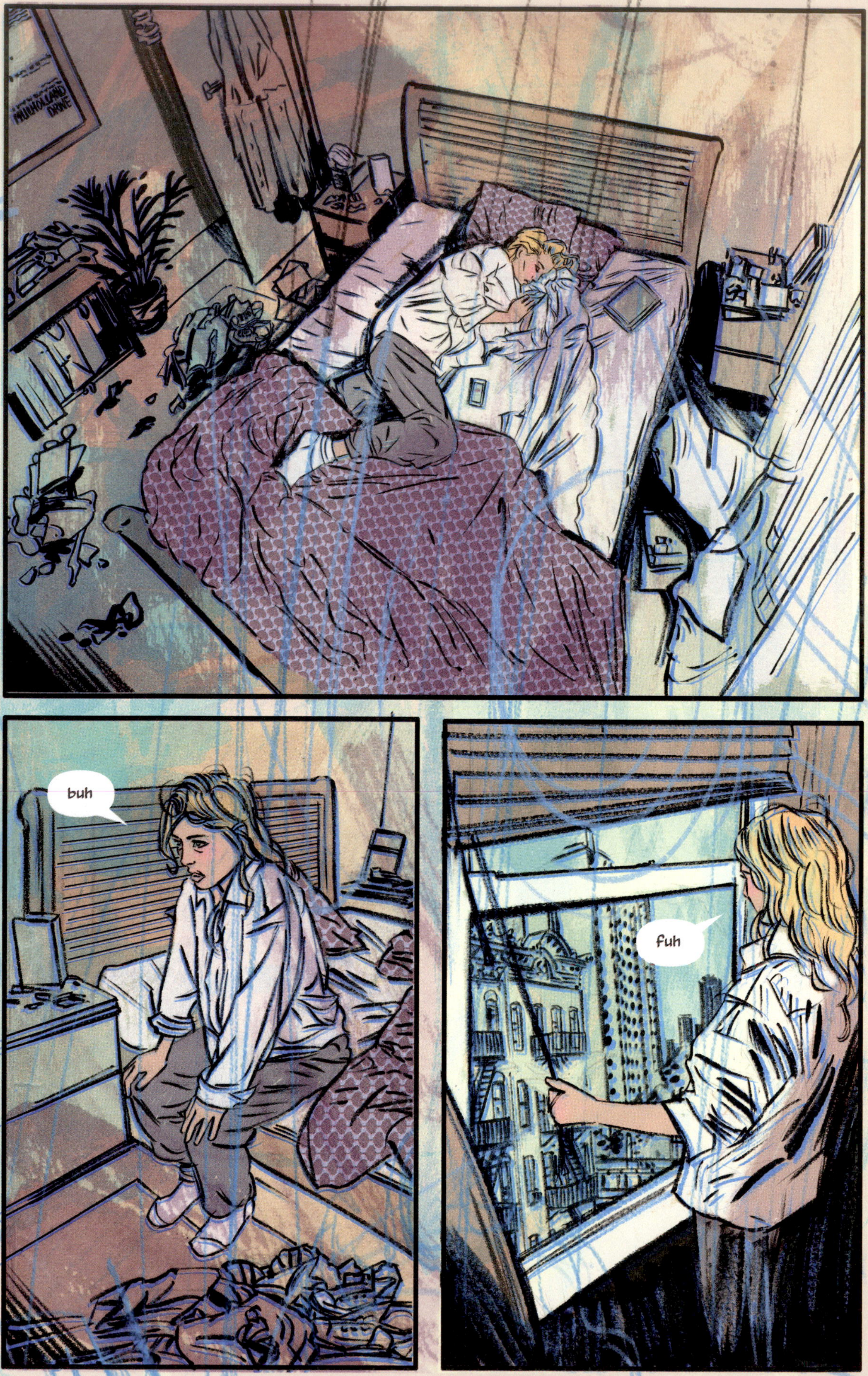
MULHOLLAND DRIVE
buh
fuh

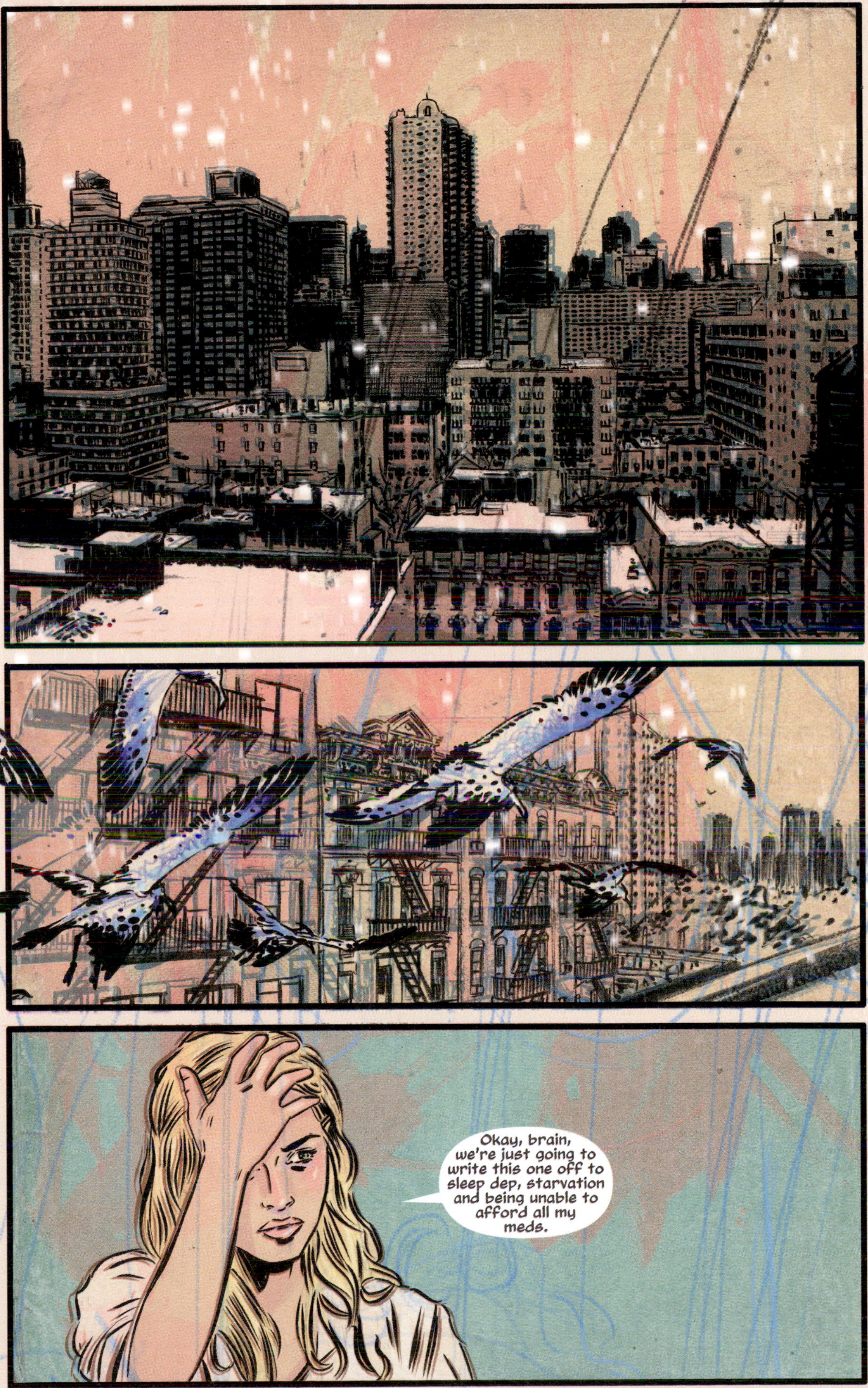
Okay, brain, we're just going to write this one off to sleep dep, starvation and being unable to afford all my meds.

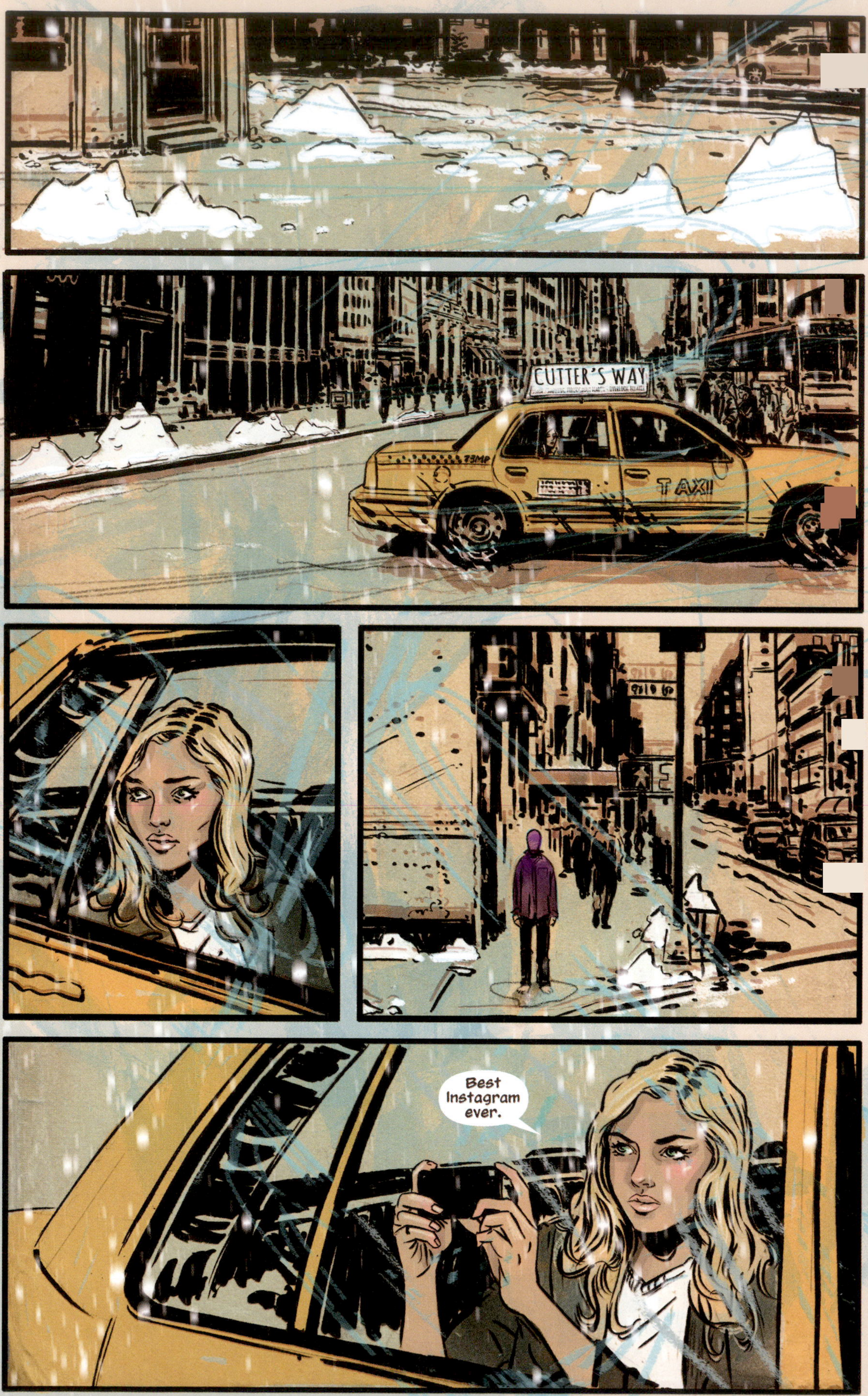
CUTTER'S WAY
TAXI
Best Instagram ever.

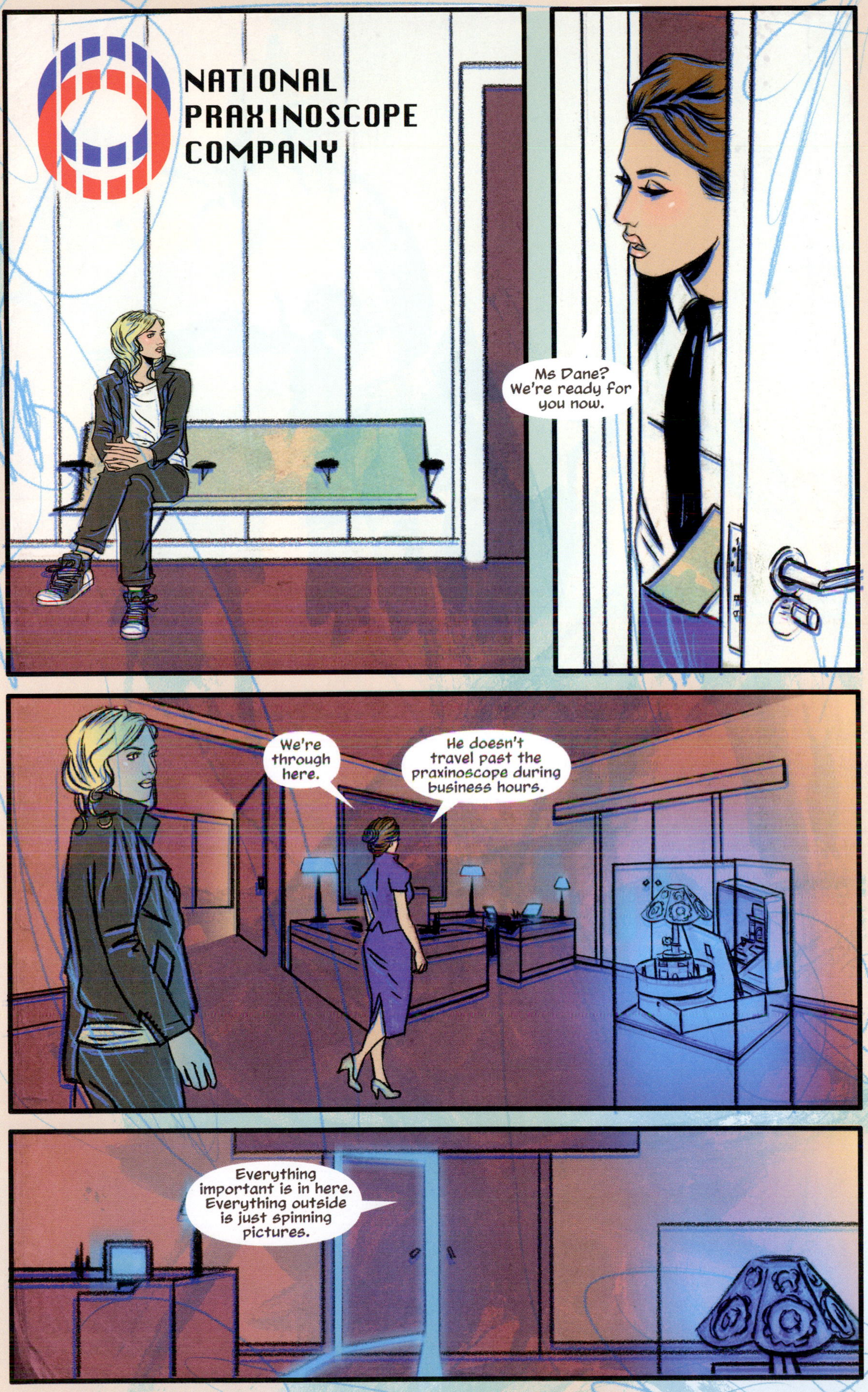
NATIONAL PRAXINOSCOPE COMPANY
Ms Dane? We're ready for you now.
We're through here.
He doesn't travel past the praxinoscope during business hours.
Everything important is in here. Everything outside is just spinning pictures.

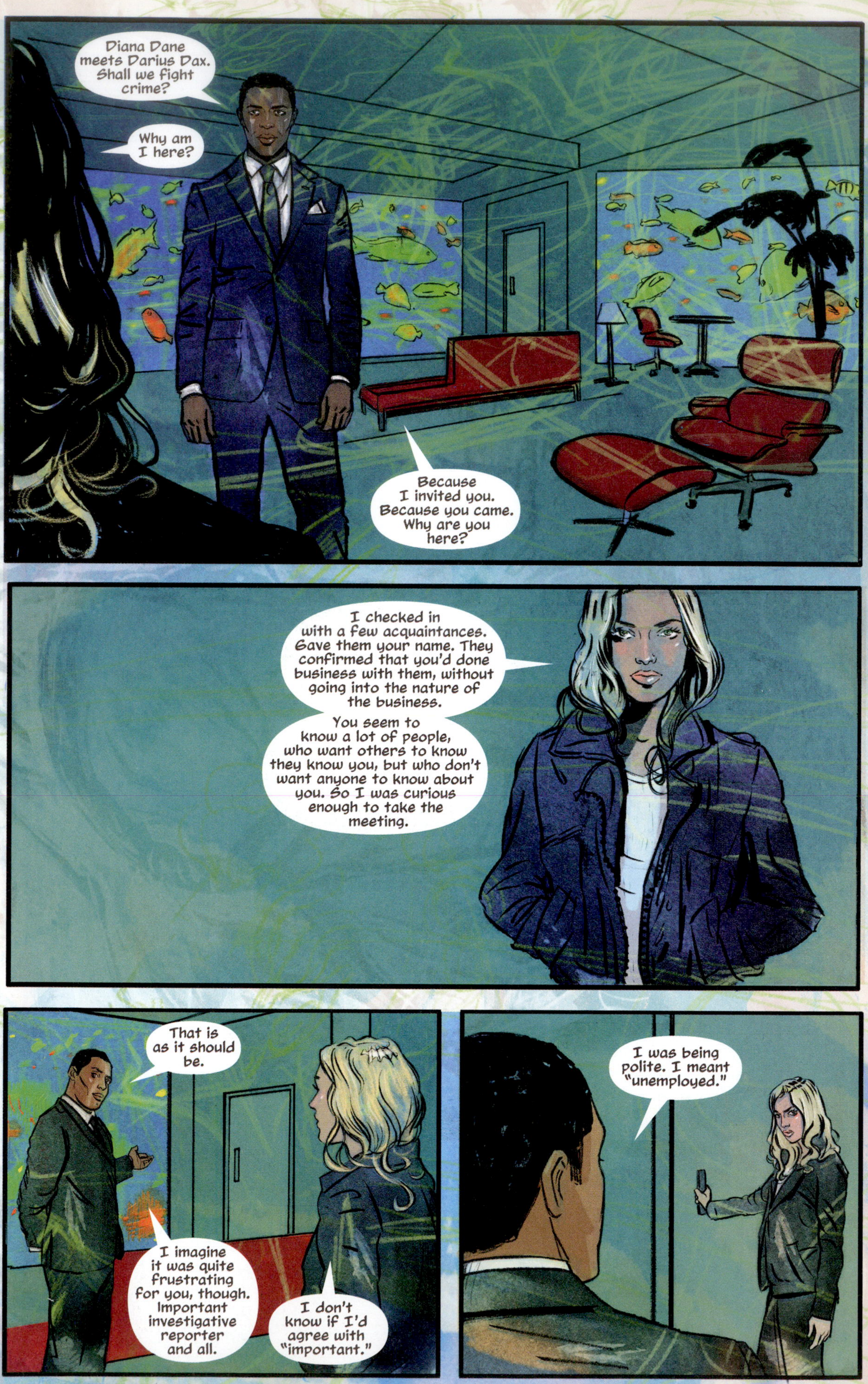
Diana Dane meets Darius Dax. Shall we fight crime?
Why am I here?
Because I invited you. Because you came. Why are you here?
I checked in with a few acquaintances. Gave them your name. They confirmed that you'd done business with them, without going into the nature of the business.
You seem to know a lot of people, who want others to know they know you, but who don't want anyone to know about you. So I was curious enough to take the meeting.
That is as it should be.
I imagine it was quite frustrating for you, though. Important investigative reporter and all.
I don't know if I'd agree with "important."
I was being polite. I meant "unemployed."

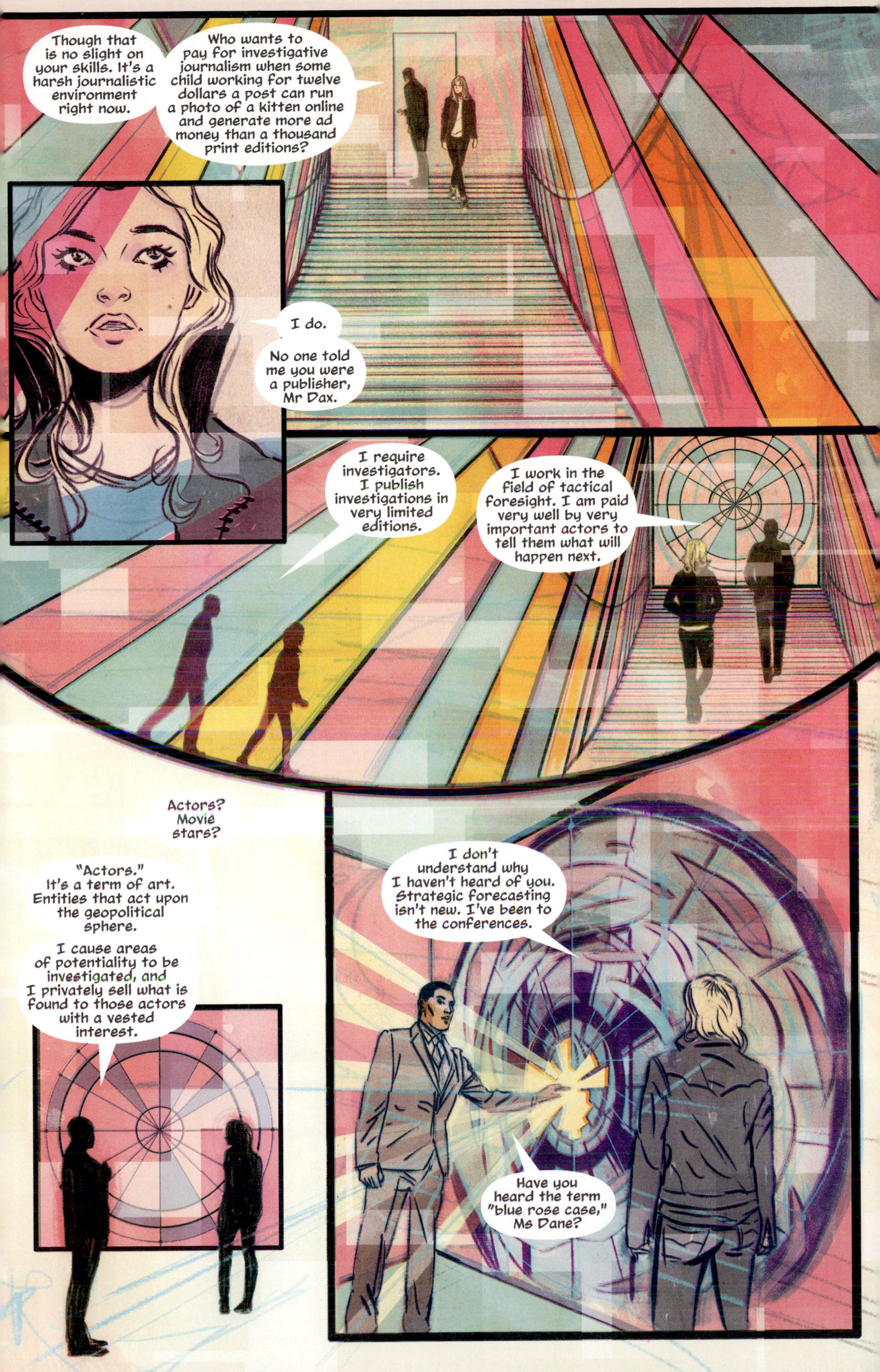

Though that is no slight on your skills. It's a harsh journalistic environment right now.
Who wants to pay for investigative journalism when some child working for twelve dollars a post can run a photo of a kitten online and generate more ad money than a thousand print editions?
I do.
No one told me you were a publisher, Mr Dax.
I require investigators. I publish investigations in very limited editions.
I work in the field of tactical foresight. I am paid very well by very important actors to tell them what will happen next.
Actors? Movie stars?
"Actors." It's a term of art. Entities that act upon the geopolitical sphere.
I cause areas of potentiality to be investigated, and I privately sell what is found to those actors with a vested interest.
I don't understand why I haven't heard of you. Strategic forecasting isn't new. I've been to the conferences.
Have you heard the term "blue rose case," Ms Dane?

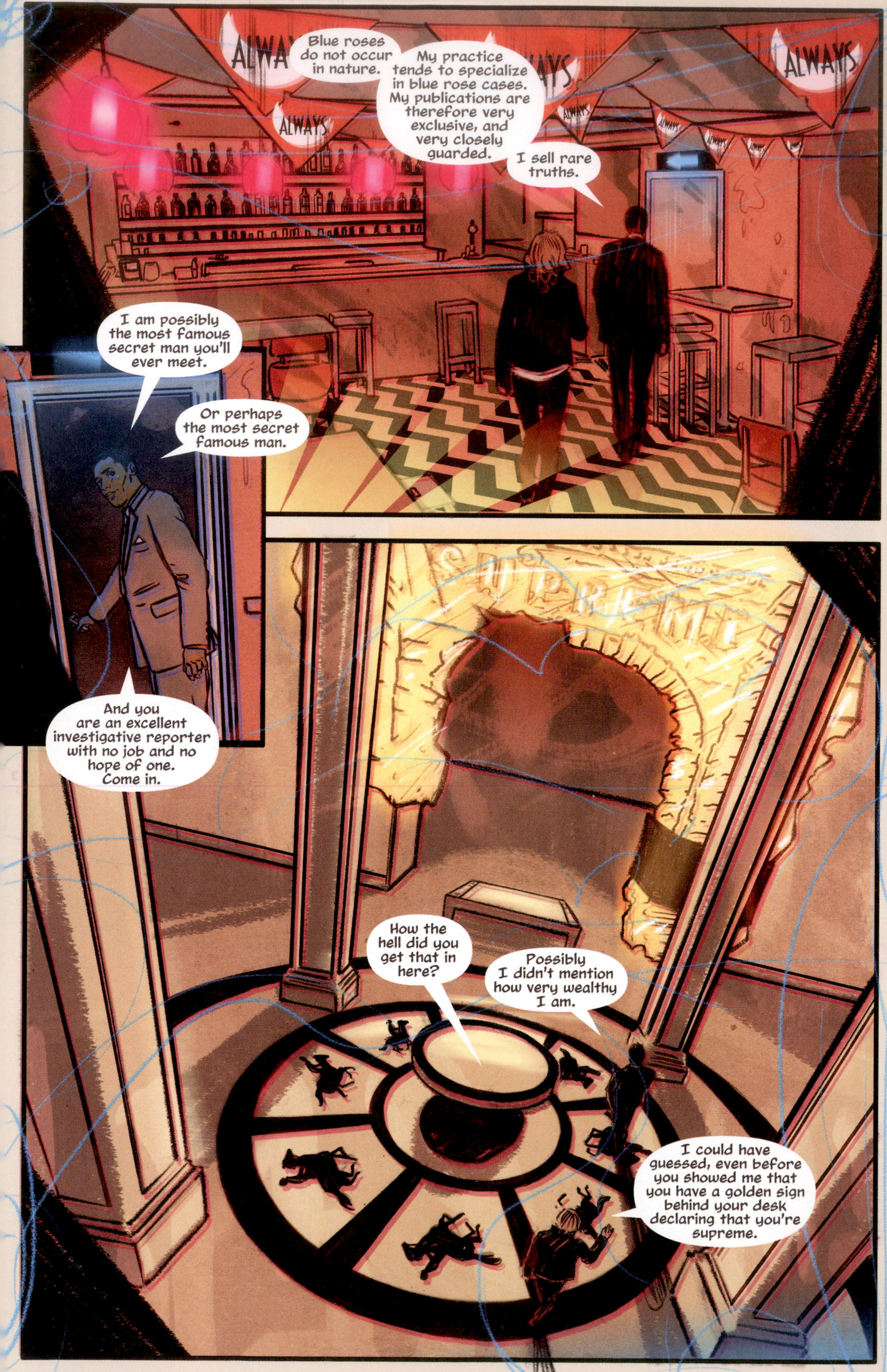
ALWAYS
Blue roses do not occur in nature.
My practice tends to specialize in blue rose cases. My publications are therefore very exclusive, and very closely guarded.
I sell rare truths.
I am possibly the most famous secret man you'll ever meet.
Or perhaps the most secret famous man.
And you are an excellent investigative reporter with no job and no hope of one. Come in.
How the hell did you get that in here?
Possibly I didn't mention how very wealthy I am.
I could have guessed, even before you showed me that you have a golden sign behind your desk declaring that you're supreme.

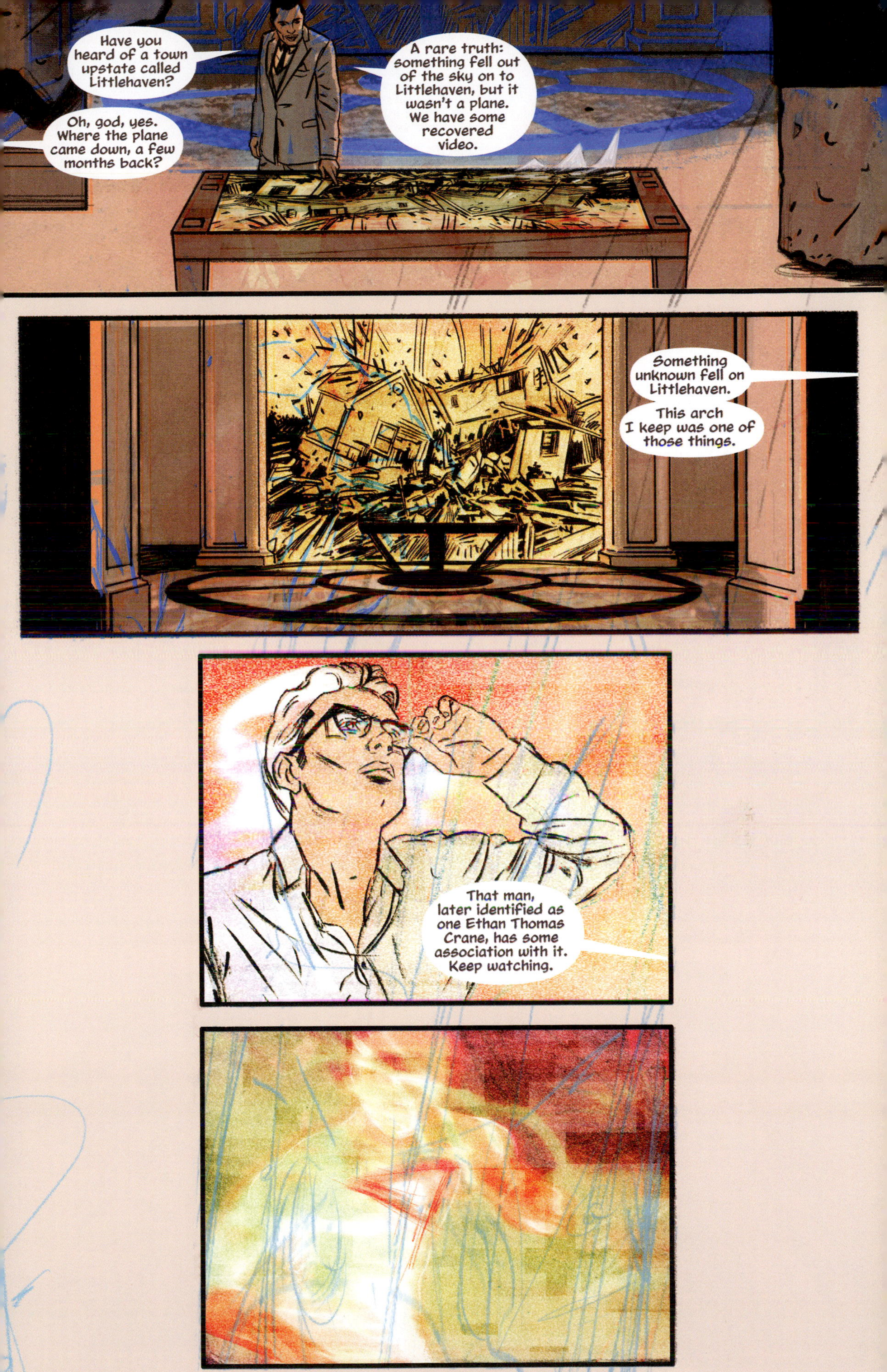
Have you heard of a town upstate called Littlehaven?
Oh, god, yes. Where the plane came down, a few months back?
A rare truth: something fell out of the sky on to Littlehaven, but it wasn't a plane. We have some recovered video.
Something unknown fell on Littlehaven.
This arch I keep was one of those things.
That man, later identified as one Ethan Thomas Crane, has some association with it. Keep watching.

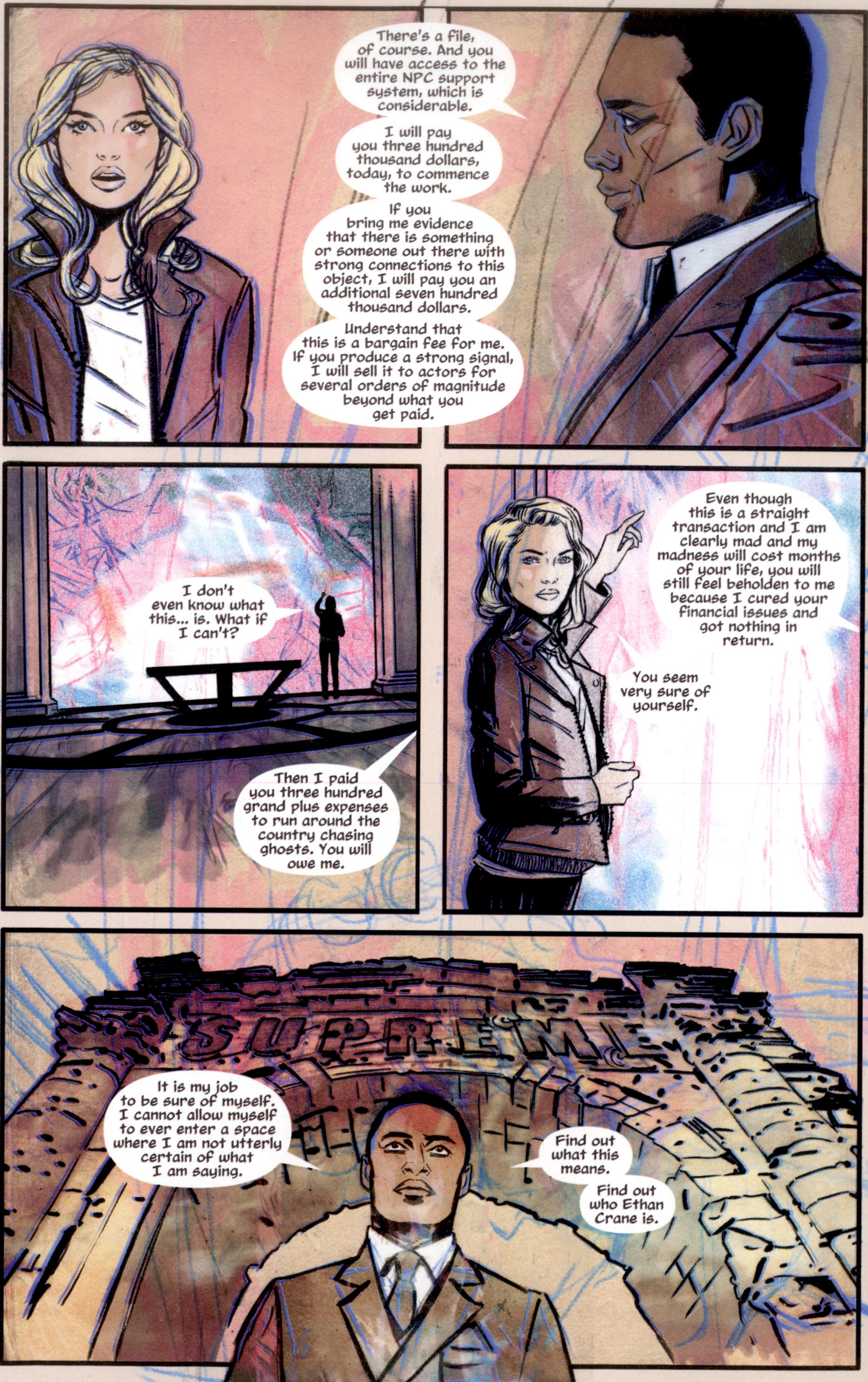
There's a file, of course. And you will have access to the entire NPC support system, which is considerable.
I will pay you three hundred thousand dollars, today, to commence the work.
If you bring me evidence that there is something or someone out there with strong connections to this object, I will pay you an additional seven hundred thousand dollars.
Understand that this is a bargain fee for me. If you produce a strong signal, I will sell it to actors for several orders of magnitude beyond what you get paid.
I don't even know what this... is. What if I can't?
Then I paid you three hundred grand plus expenses to run around the country chasing ghosts. You will owe me.
Even though this is a straight transaction and I am clearly mad and my madness will cost months of your life, you will still feel beholden to me because I cured your financial issues and got nothing in return.
You seem very sure of yourself.
SUPREME
It is my job to be sure of myself. I cannot allow myself to ever enter a space where I am not utterly certain of what I am saying.
Find out what this means.
Find out who Ethan Crane is.

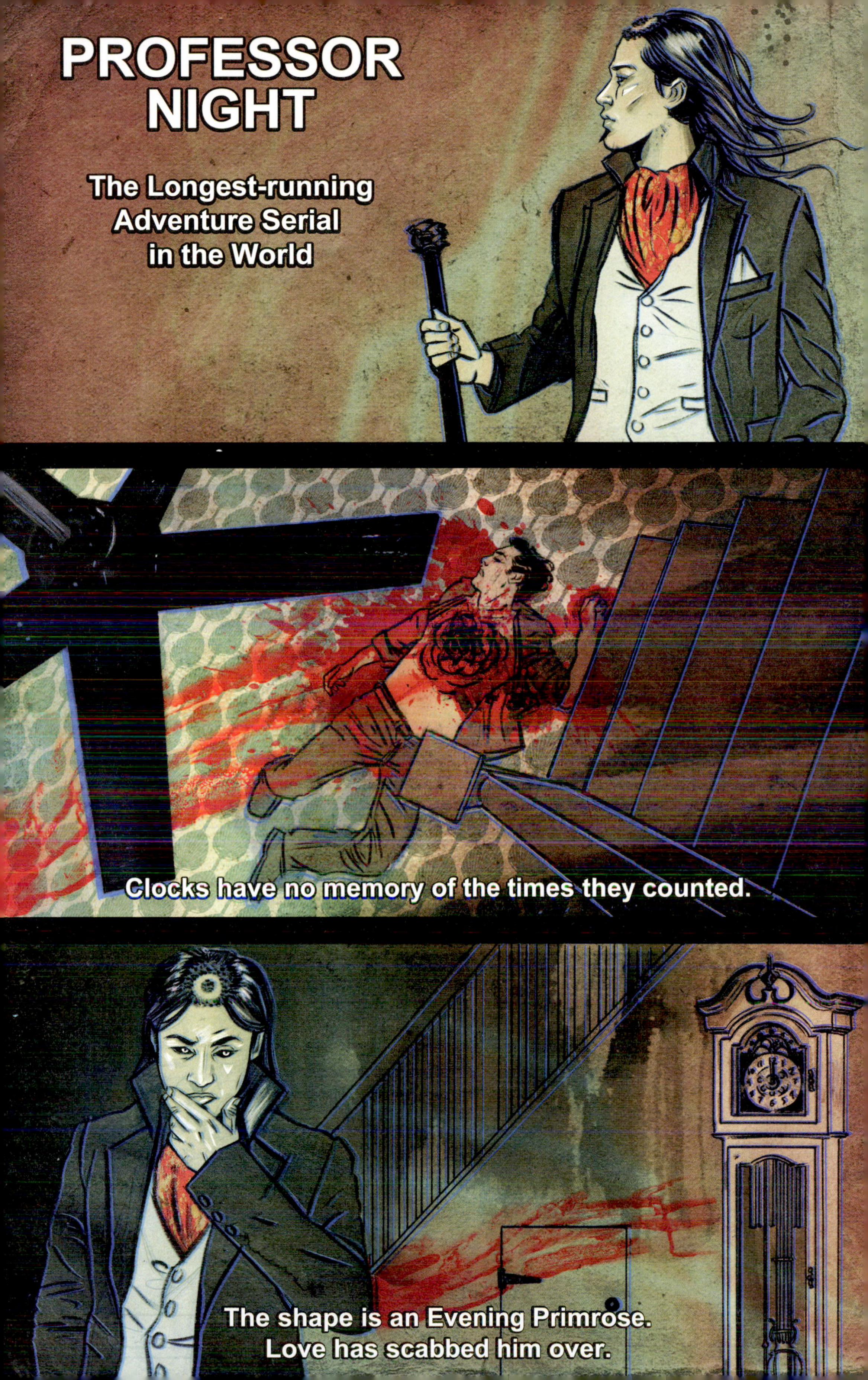
PROFESSOR NIGHT
The Longest-running Adventure Serial in the World
Clocks have no memory of the times they counted.
The shape is an Evening Primrose. Love has scabbed him over.

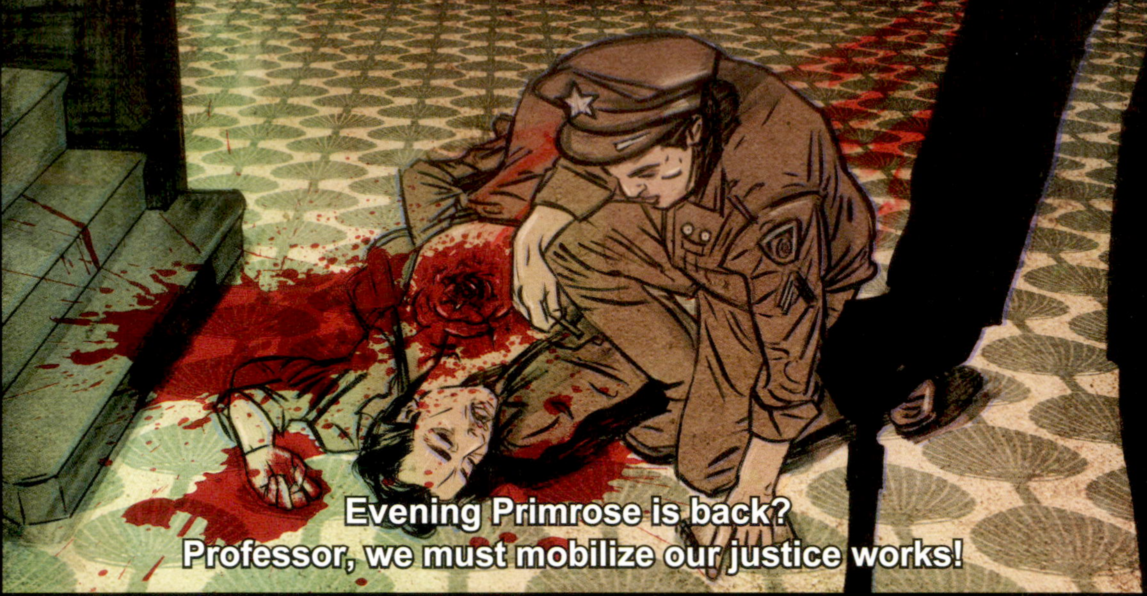
Evening Primrose is back?
Professor, we must mobilize our justice works!

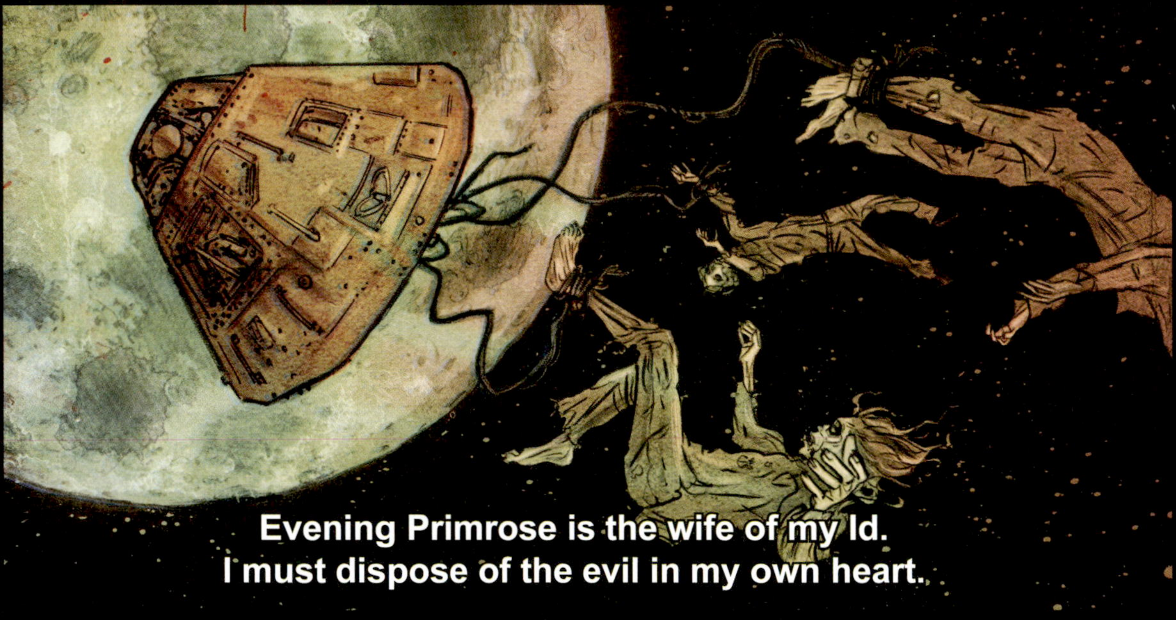
Evening Primrose is the wife of my Id.
I must dispose of the evil in my own heart.

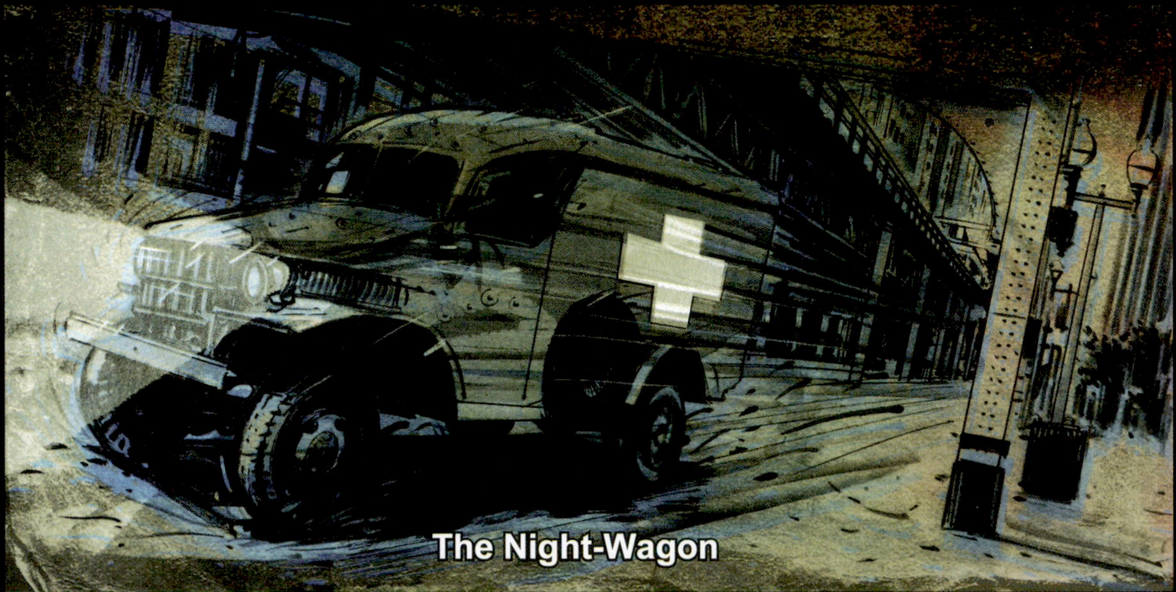
The Night-Wagon

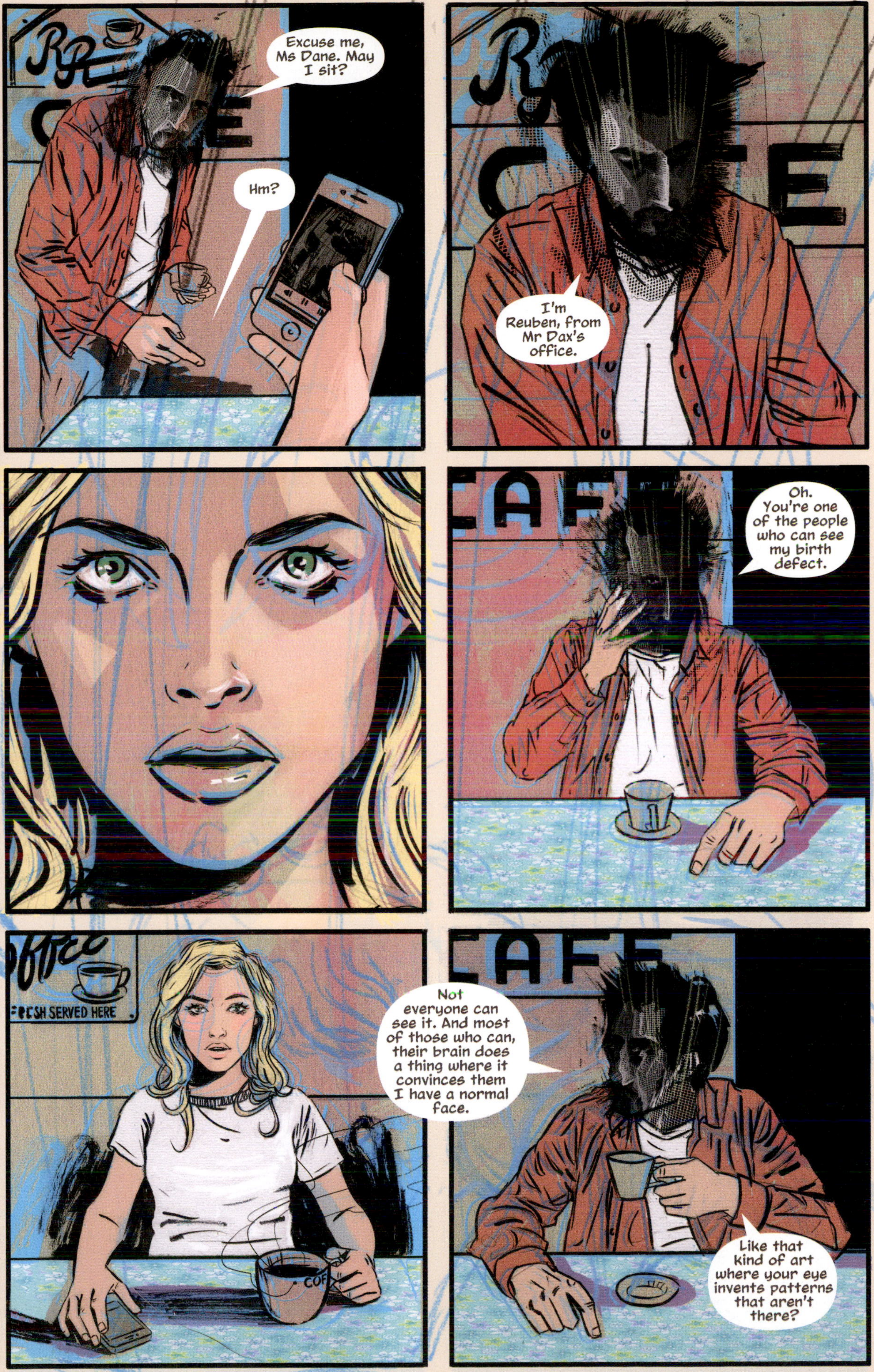

Excuse me, Ms Dane. May I sit?
Hm?
I'm Reuben, from Mr Dax's office.
Oh. You're one of the people who can see my birth defect.
Not everyone can see it. And most of those who can, their brain does a thing where it convinces them I have a normal face.
Like that kind of art where your eye invents patterns that aren't there?

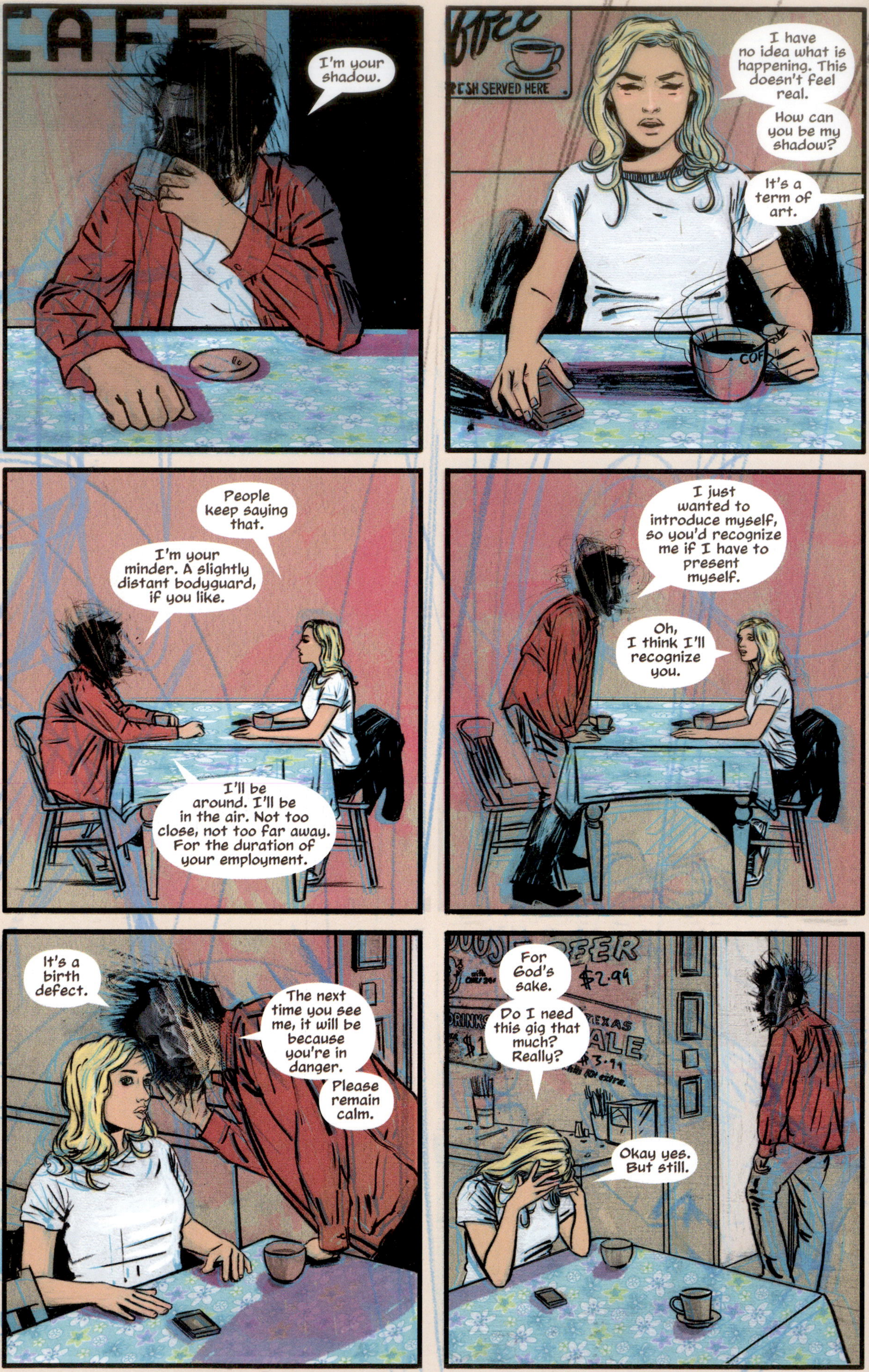
CAFE
I'm your shadow.
I have no idea what is happening. This doesn't feel real.
How can you be my shadow?
It's a term of art.
People keep saying that.
I'm your minder. A slightly distant bodyguard, if you like.
I'll be around. I'll be in the air. Not too close, not too far away. For the duration of your employment.
I just wanted to introduce myself, so you'd recognize me if I have to present myself.
Oh, I think I'll recognize you.
It's a birth defect.
The next time you see me, it will be because you're in danger.
Please remain calm.
For God's sake.
Do I need this gig that much? Really?
Okay yes. But still.

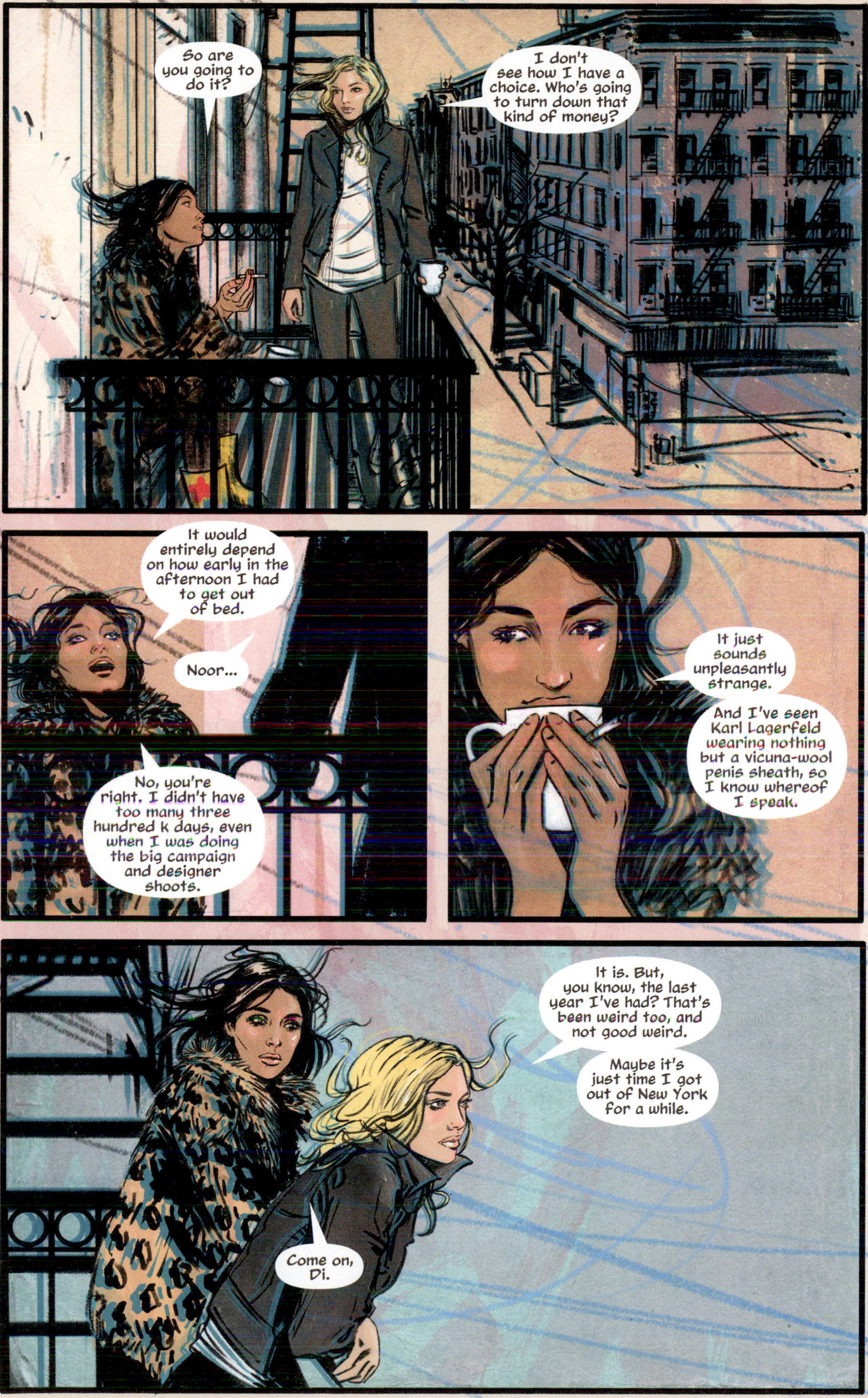
So are you going to do it?
I don't see how I have a choice. Who's going to turn down that kind of money?
It would entirely depend on how early in the afternoon I had to get out of bed.
Noor...
No, you're right. I didn't have too many three hundred k days, even when I was doing the big campaign and designer shoots.
It just sounds unpleasantly strange.
And I've seen Karl Lagerfeld wearing nothing but a vicuna-wool penis sheath, so I know whereof I speak.
It is. But, you know, the last year I've had? That's been weird too, and not good weird.
Maybe it's just time I got out of New York for a while.
Come on, Di.

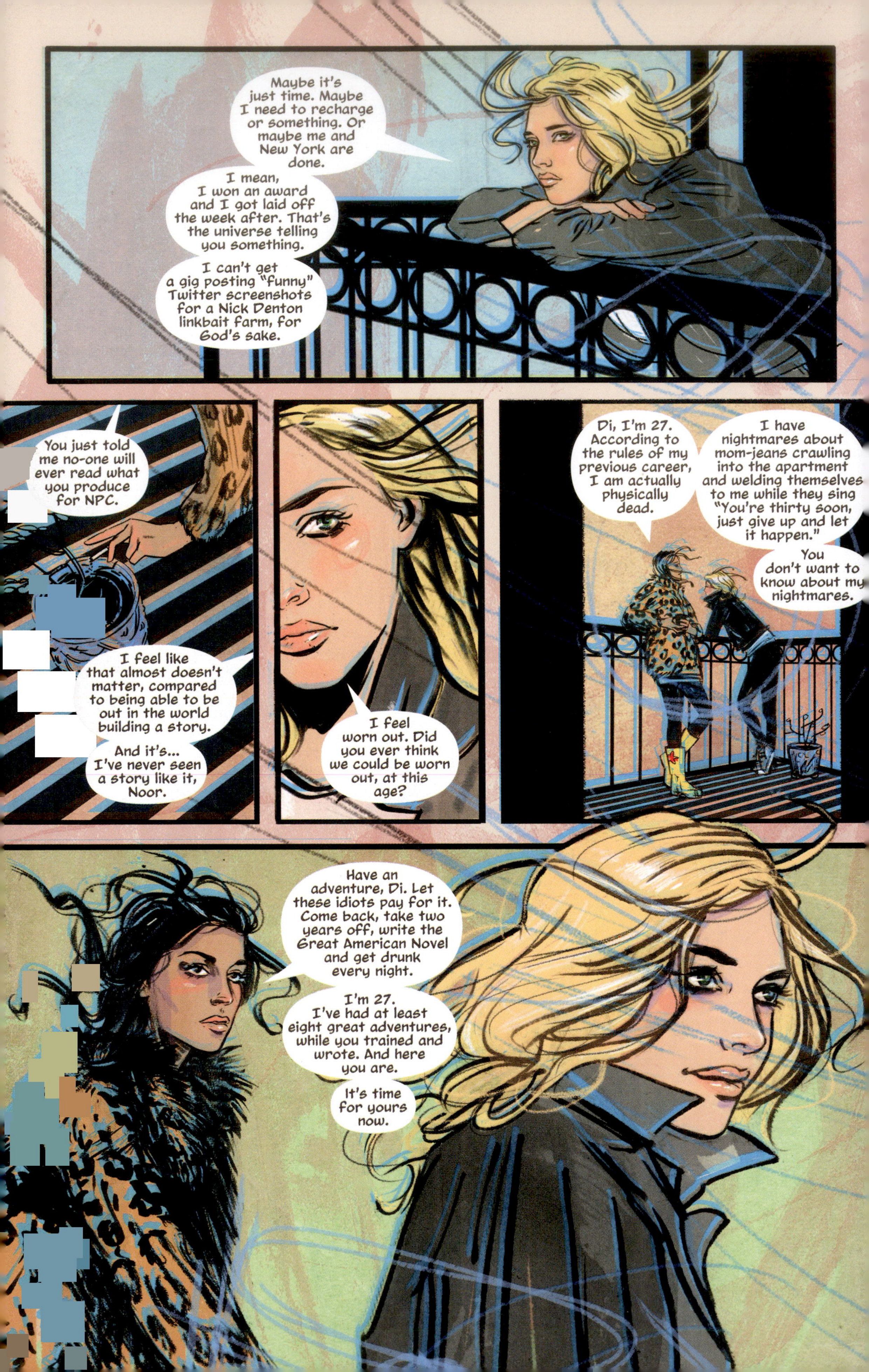
Maybe it's just time. Maybe I need to recharge or something. Or maybe me and New York are done.
I mean, I won an award and I got laid off the week after. That's the universe telling you something.
I can't get a gig posting "funny" Twitter screenshots for a Nick Denton linkbait farm, for God's sake.
You just told me no-one will ever read what you produce for NPC.
I feel like that almost doesn't matter, compared to being able to be out in the world building a story.
And it's... I've never seen a story like it, Noor.
I feel worn out. Did you ever think we could be worn out, at this age?
Di, I'm 27. According to the rules of my previous career, I am actually physically dead.
I have nightmares about mom-jeans crawling into the apartment and welding themselves to me while they sing "You're thirty soon, just give up and let it happen."
You don't want to know about my nightmares.
Have an adventure, Di. Let these idiots pay for it. Come back, take two years off, write the Great American Novel and get drunk every night.
I'm 27. I've had at least eight great adventures, while you trained and wrote. And here you are.
It's time for yours now.

"It is like a bullethole in the world."

TWO

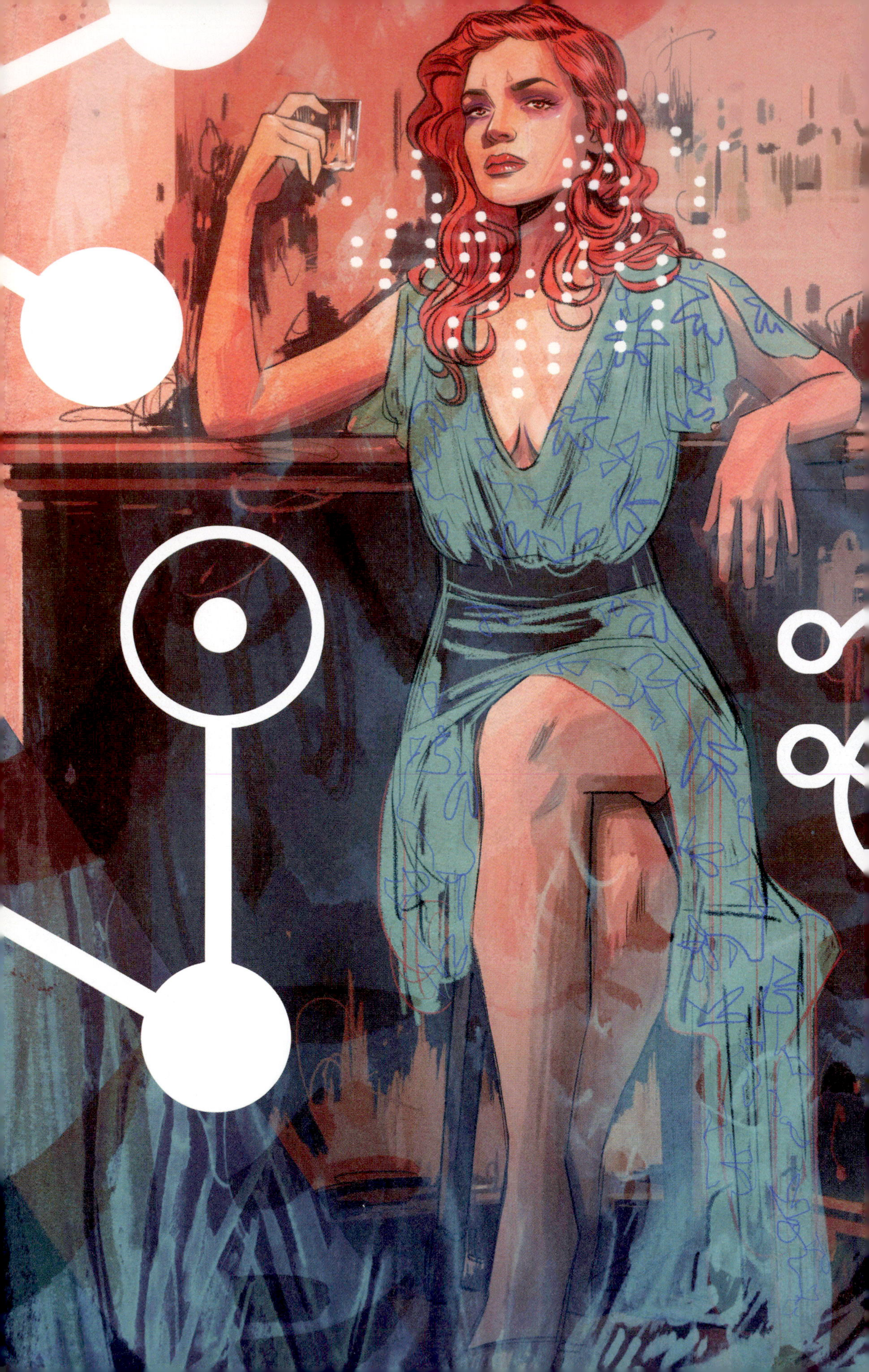

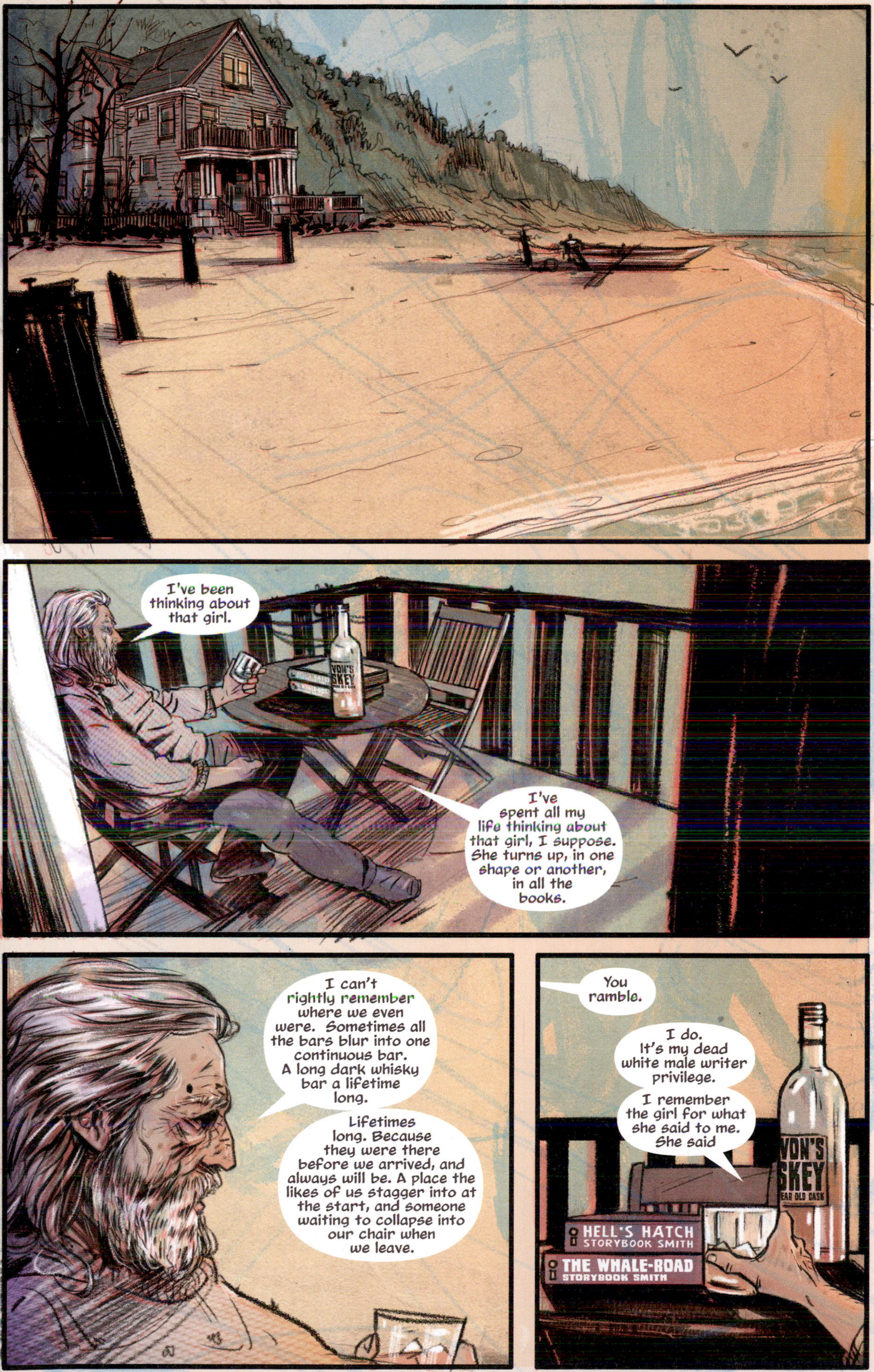
I've been thinking about that girl.
I've spent all my life thinking about that girl, I suppose. She turns up, in one shape or another, in all the books.
I can't rightly remember where we even were. Sometimes all the bars blur into one continuous bar. A long dark whisky bar a lifetime long.
Lifetimes long. Because they were there before we arrived, and always will be. A place the likes of us stagger into at the start, and someone waiting to collapse into our chair when we leave.
You ramble.
I do. It's my dead white male writer privilege.
I remember the girl for what she said to me. She said
HELL'S HATCH STORYBOOK SMITH
THE WHALE-ROAD STORYBOOK SMITH

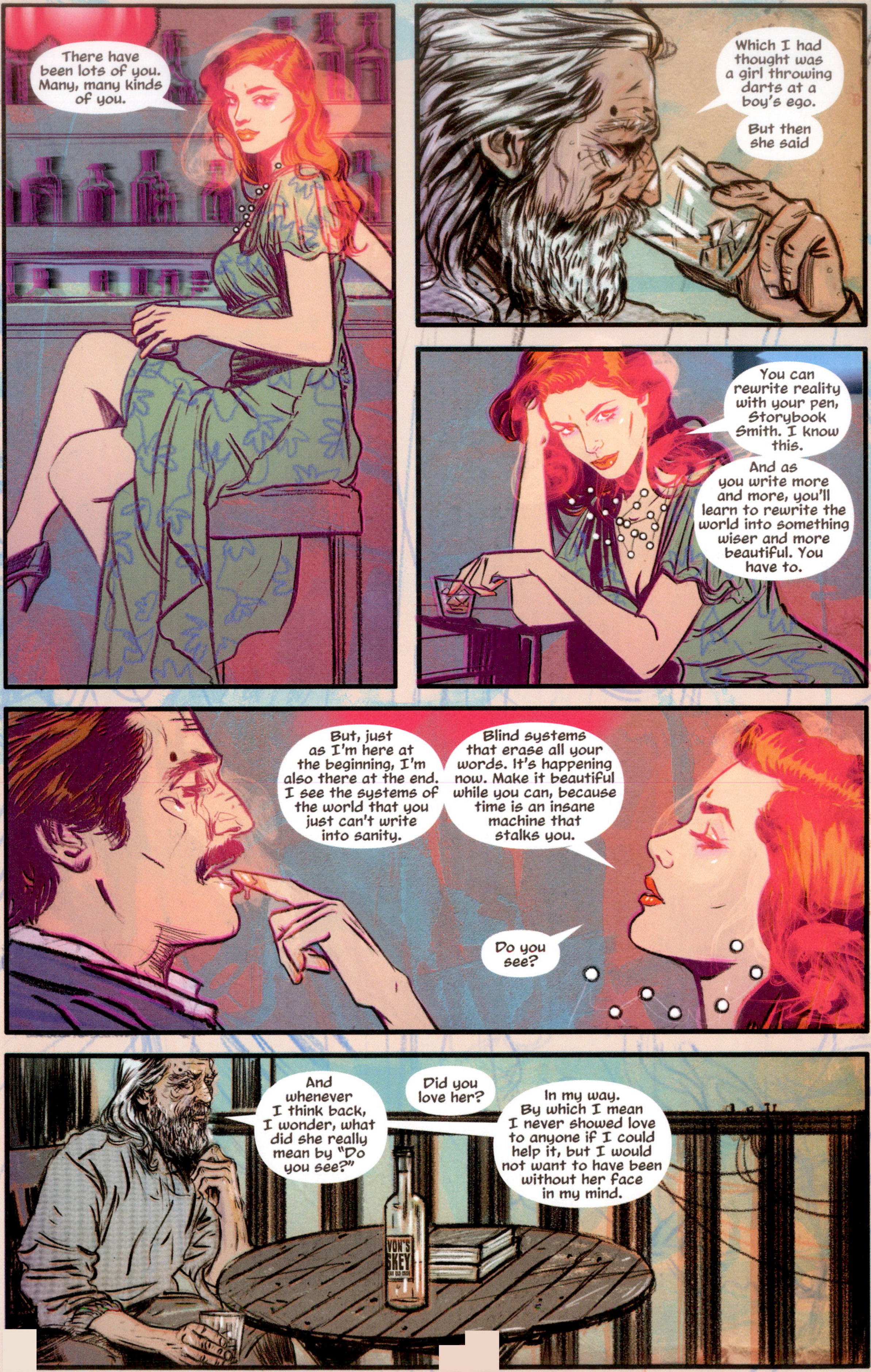
There have been lots of you. Many, many kinds of you.
Which I had thought was a girl throwing darts at a boy's ego.
But then she said
You can rewrite reality with your pen, Storybook Smith. I know this.
And as you write more and more, you'll learn to rewrite the world into something wiser and more beautiful. You have to.
But, just as I'm here at the beginning, I'm also there at the end. I see the systems of the world that you just can't write into sanity.
Blind systems that erase all your words. It's happening now. Make it beautiful while you can, because time is an insane machine that stalks you.
Do you see?
And whenever I think back, I wonder, what did she really mean by "Do you see?"
Did you love her?
In my way. By which I mean I never showed love to anyone if I could help it, but I would not want to have been without her face in my mind.

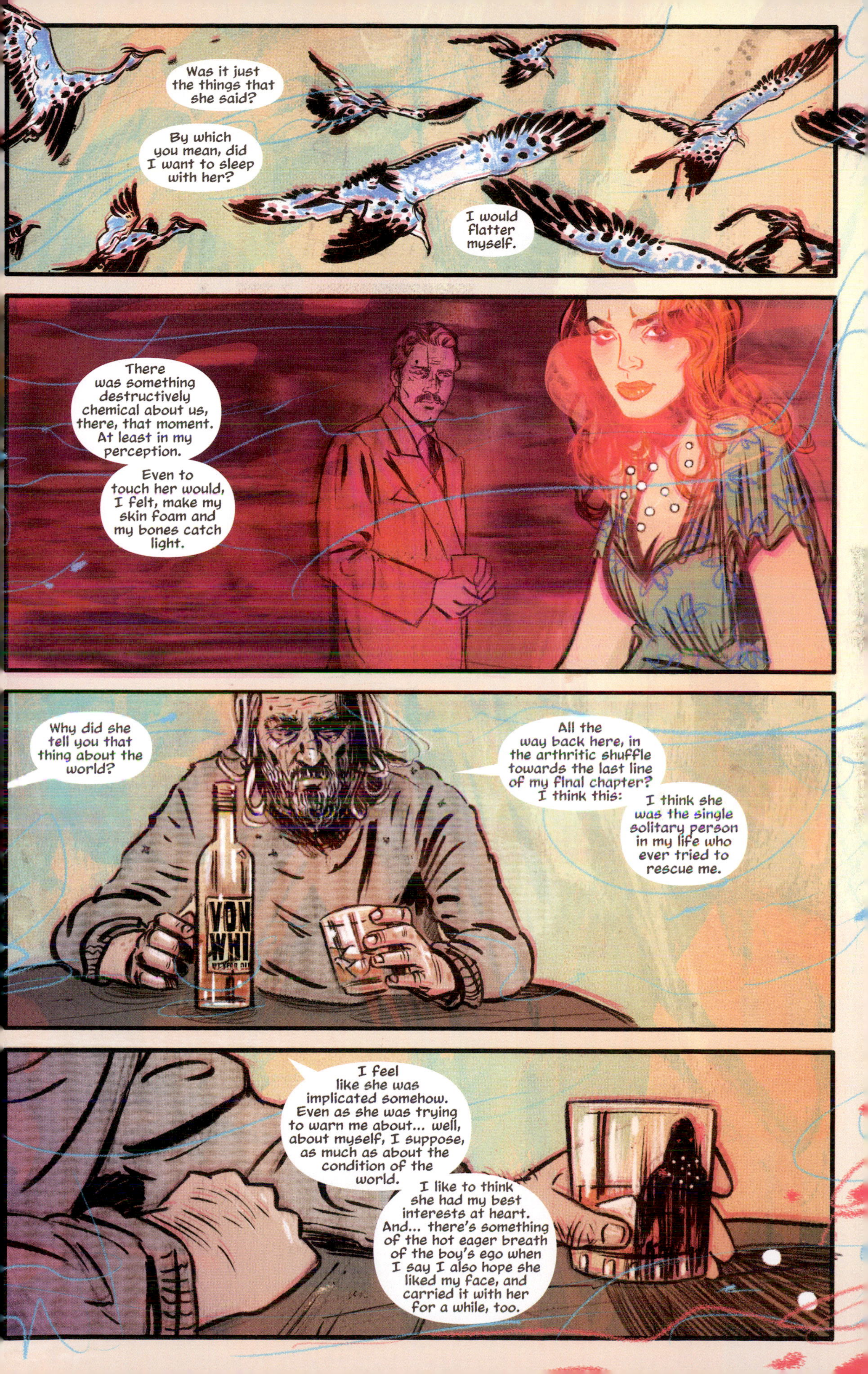

Was it just the things that she said?
By which you mean, did I want to sleep with her?
I would flatter myself.
There was something destructively chemical about us, there, that moment. At least in my perception.
Even to touch her would, I felt, make my skin foam and my bones catch light.
Why did she tell you that thing about the world?
All the way back here, in the arthritic shuffle towards the last line of my final chapter? I think this:
I think she was the single solitary person in my life who ever tried to rescue me.
I feel like she was implicated somehow. Even as she was trying to warn me about... well, about myself, I suppose, as much as about the condition of the world.
I like to think she had my best interests at heart. And... there's something of the hot eager breath of the boy's ego when I say I also hope she liked my face, and carried it with her for a while, too.

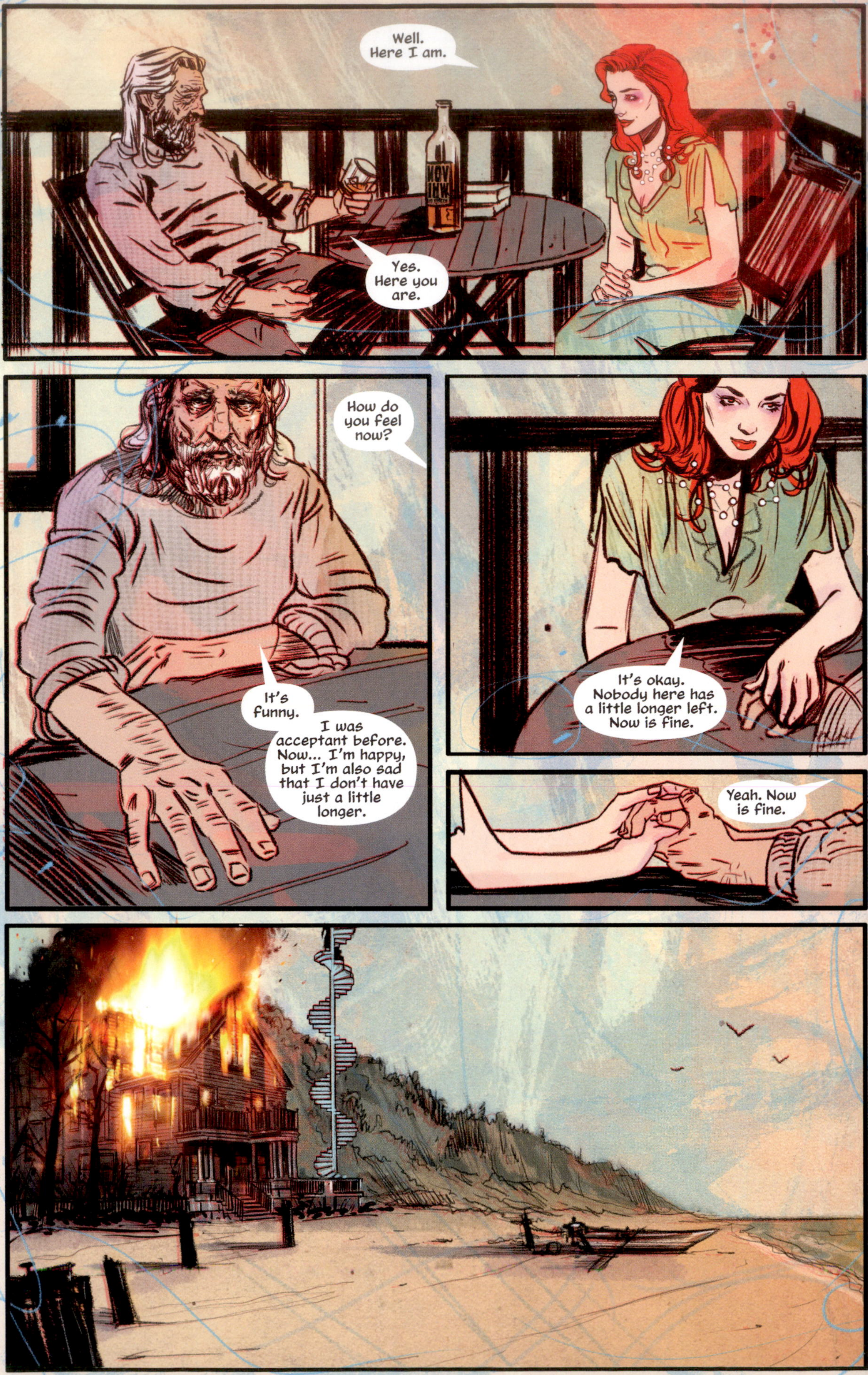
Well. Here I am.
Yes. Here you are.
How do you feel now?
It's funny.
I was acceptant before. Now... I'm happy, but I'm also sad that I don't have just a little longer.
It's okay. Nobody here has a little longer left. Now is fine.
Yeah. Now is fine.

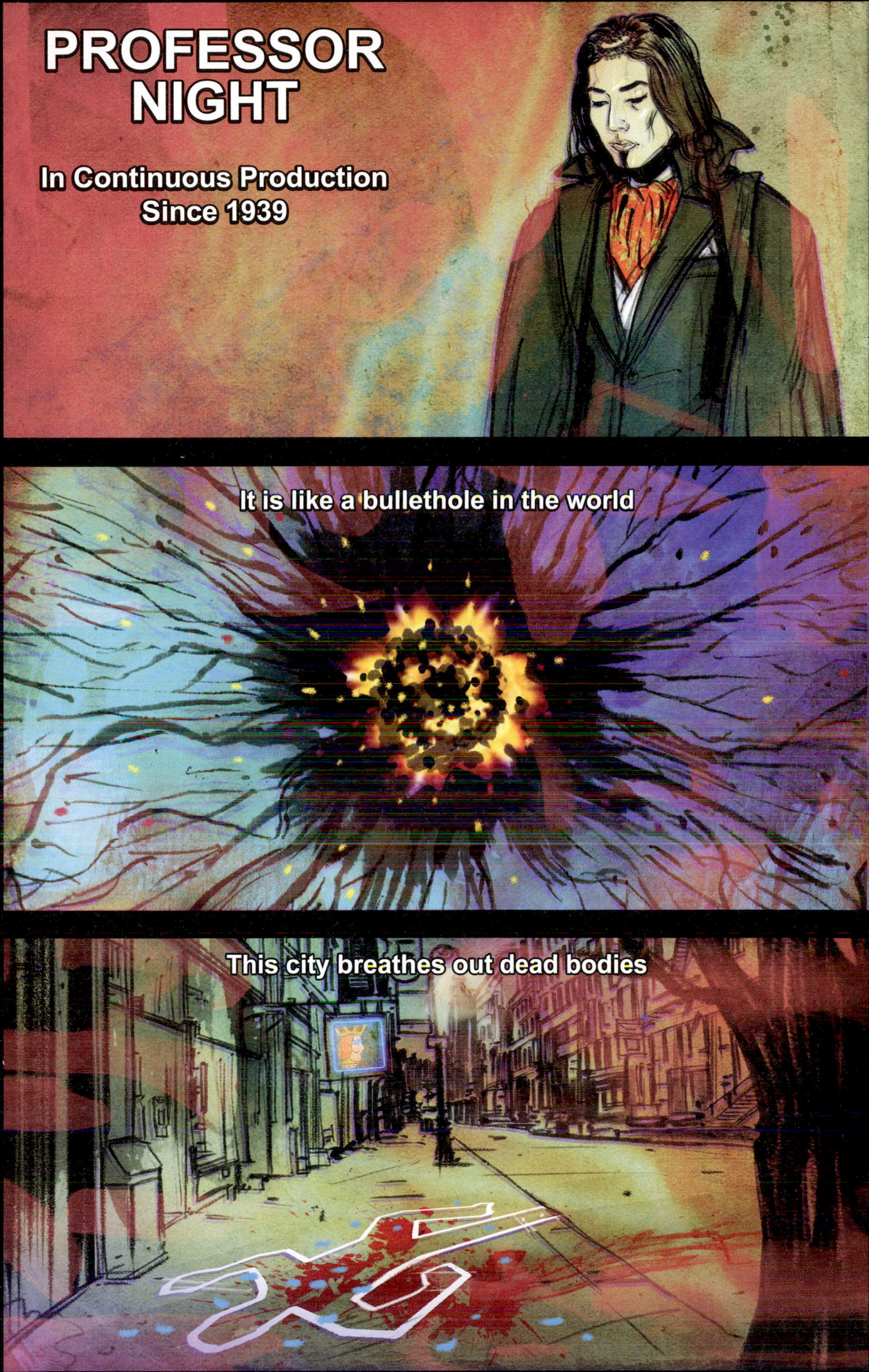
PROFESSOR NIGHT
In Continuous Production Since 1939
It is like a bullethole in the world
This city breathes out dead bodies

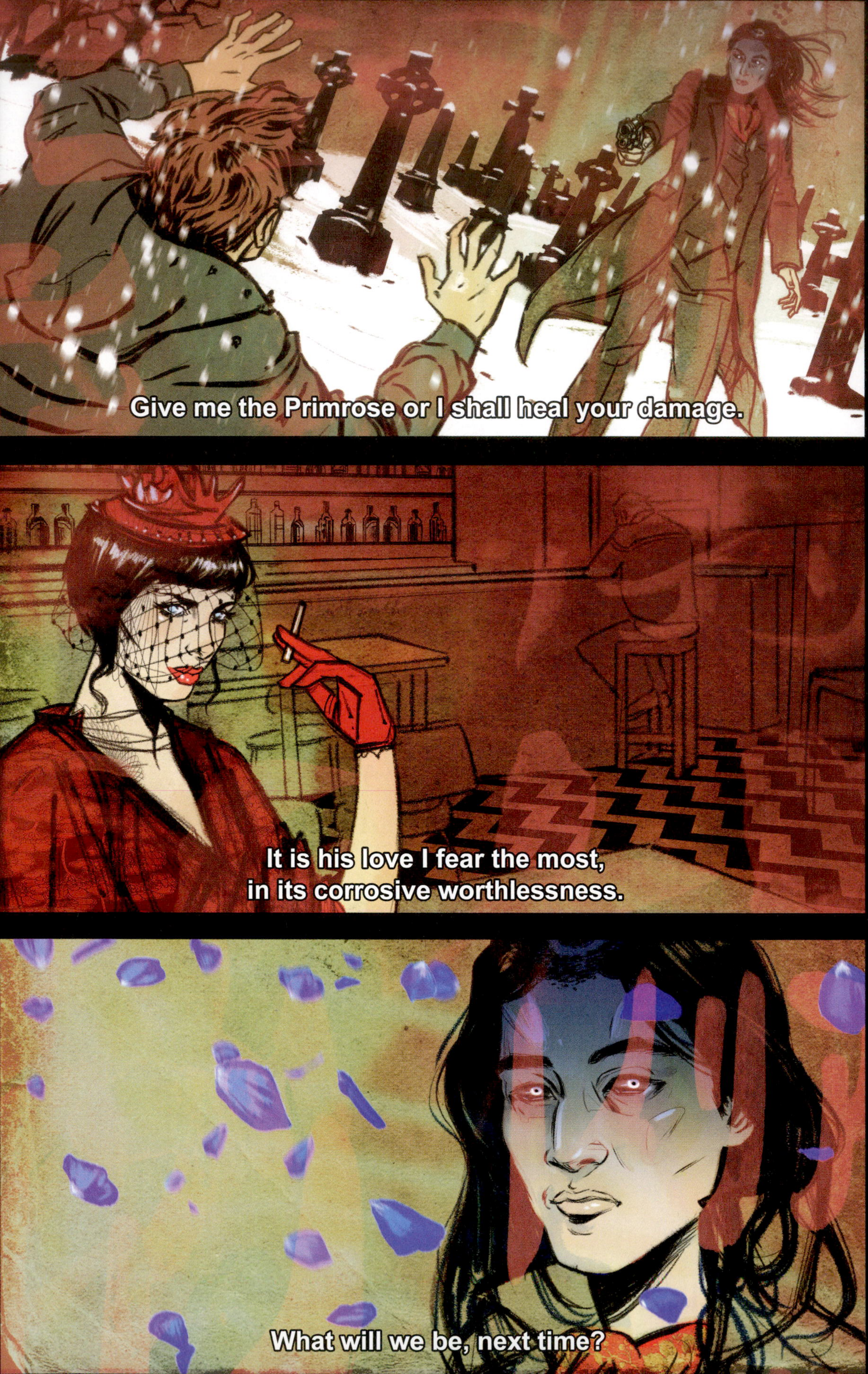
Give me the Primrose or I shall heal your damage.
It is his love I fear the most,
in its corrosive worthlessness.
What will we be, next time?

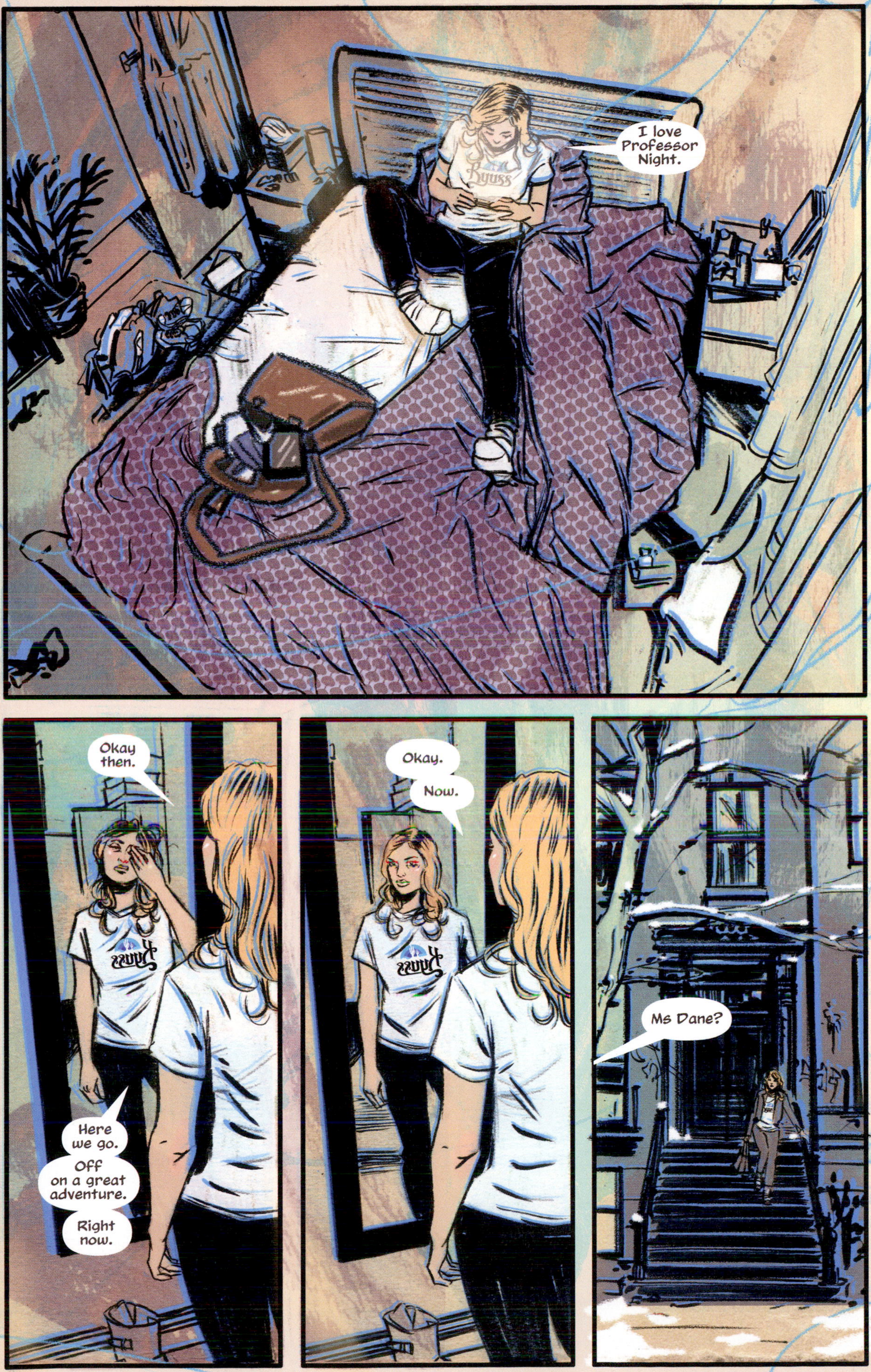

I love Professor Night.
Okay then.
Here we go.
Off on a great adventure.
Right now.
Okay.
Now.
Ms Dane?

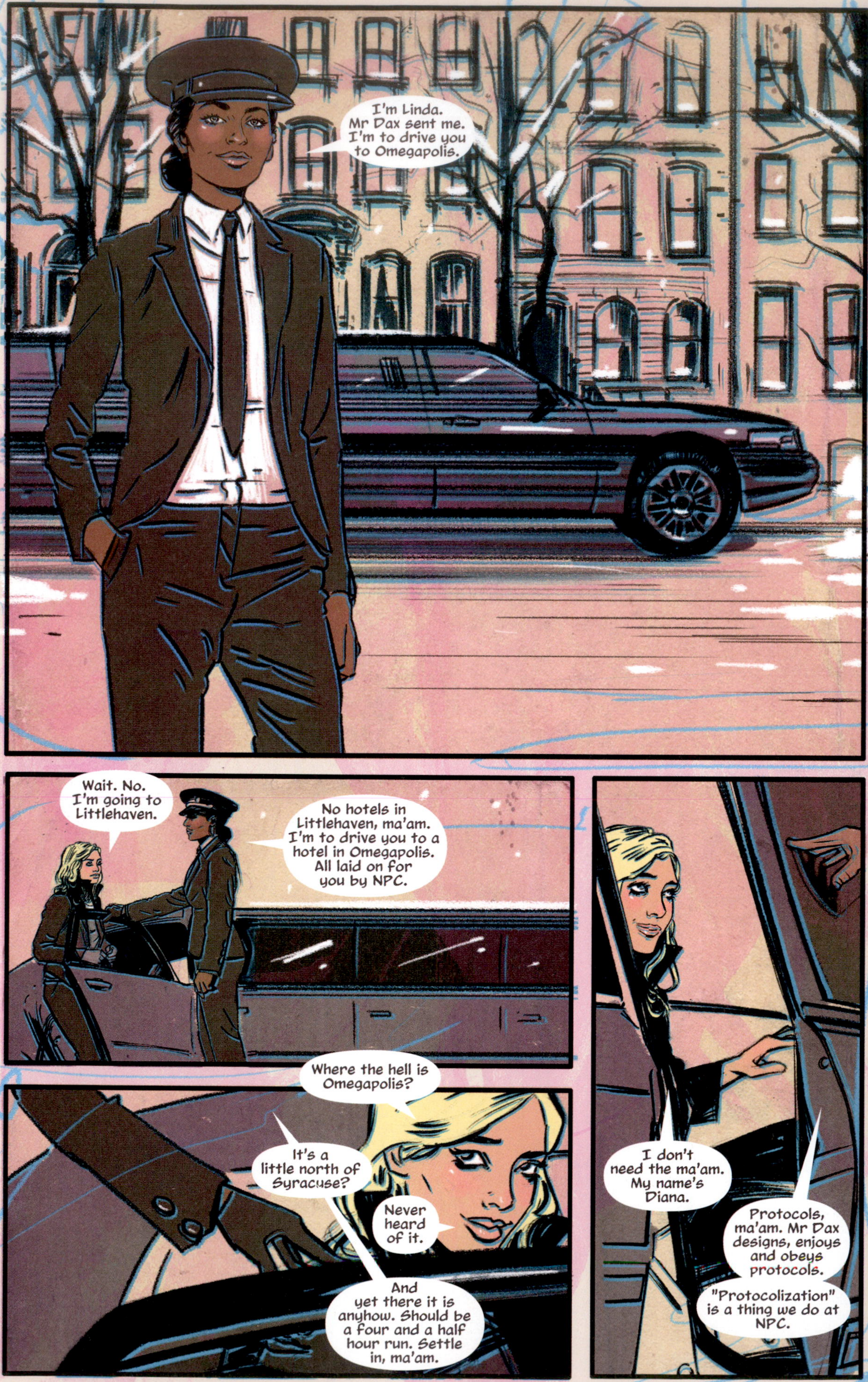
I'm Linda. Mr Dax sent me. I'm to drive you to Omegapolis.
Wait. No. I'm going to Littlehaven.
No hotels in Littlehaven, ma'am. I'm to drive you to a hotel in Omegapolis. All laid on for you by NPC.
Where the hell is Omegapolis?
It's a little north of Syracuse?
Never heard of it.
And yet there it is anyhow. Should be a four and a half hour run. Settle in, ma'am.
I don't need the ma'am. My name's Diana.
Protocols, ma'am. Mr Dax designs, enjoys and obeys protocols.
"Protocolization" is a thing we do at NPC.

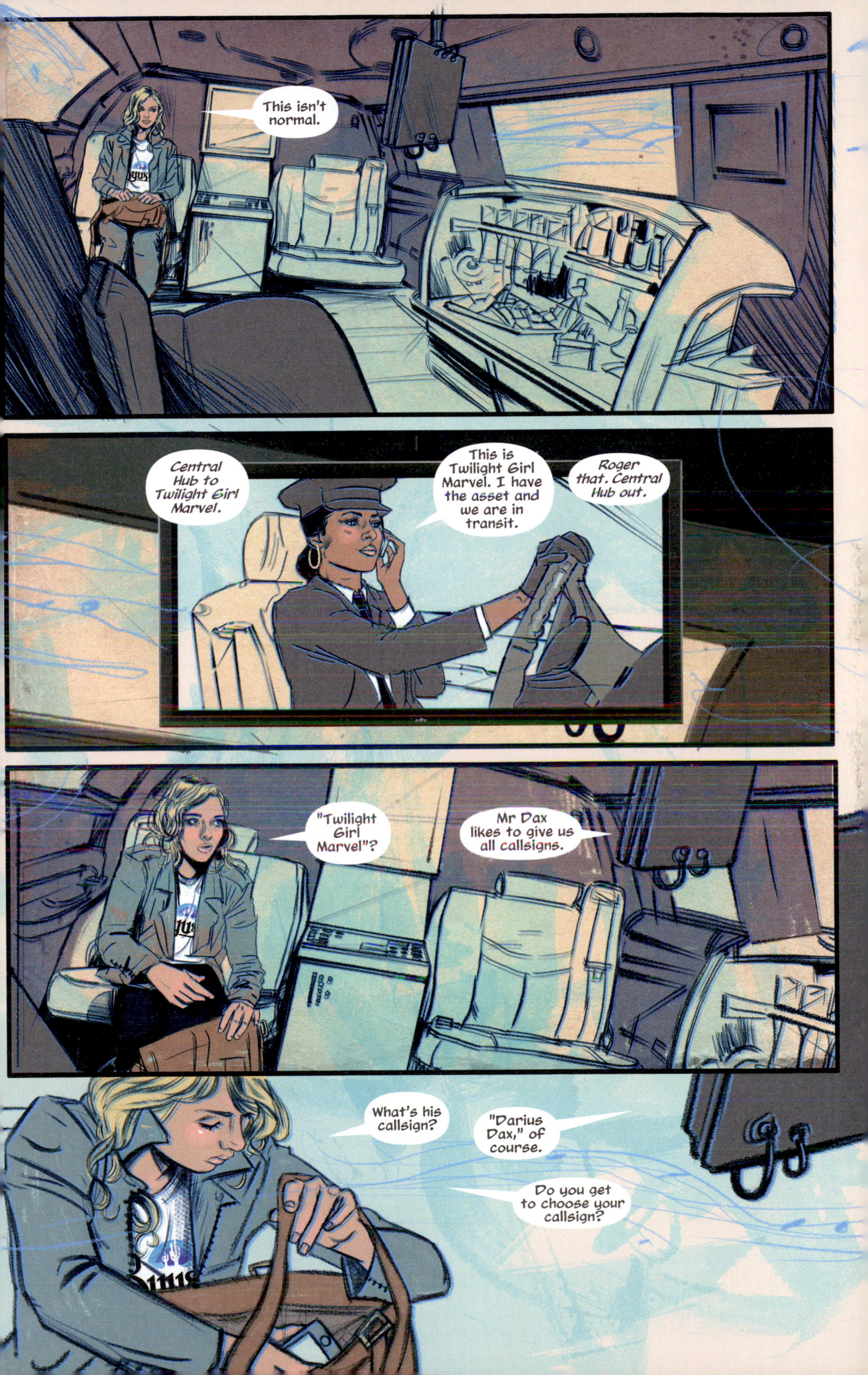
This isn't normal.
Central Hub to Twilight Girl Marvel.
This is Twilight Girl Marvel. I have the asset and we are in transit.
Roger that. Central Hub out.
"Twilight Girl Marvel"?
Mr Dax likes to give us all callsigns.
What's his callsign?
"Darius Dax," of course.
Do you get to choose your callsign?

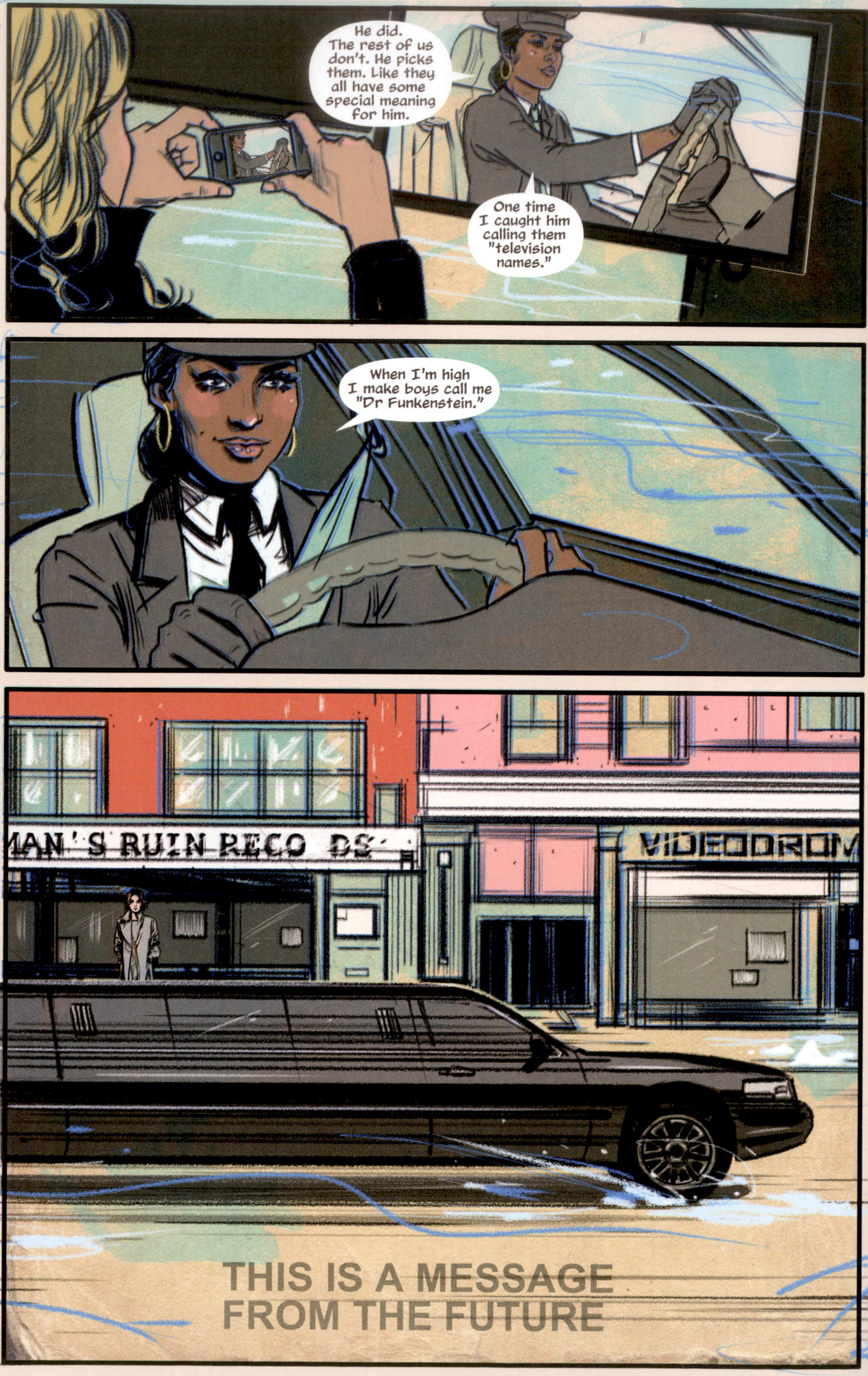
He did. The rest of us don't. He picks them. Like they all have some special meaning for him.
One time I caught him calling them "television names."
When I'm high I make boys call me "Dr Funkenstein."
MAN'S RUIN RECO DS
VIDEODROM
THIS IS A MESSAGE FROM THE FUTURE

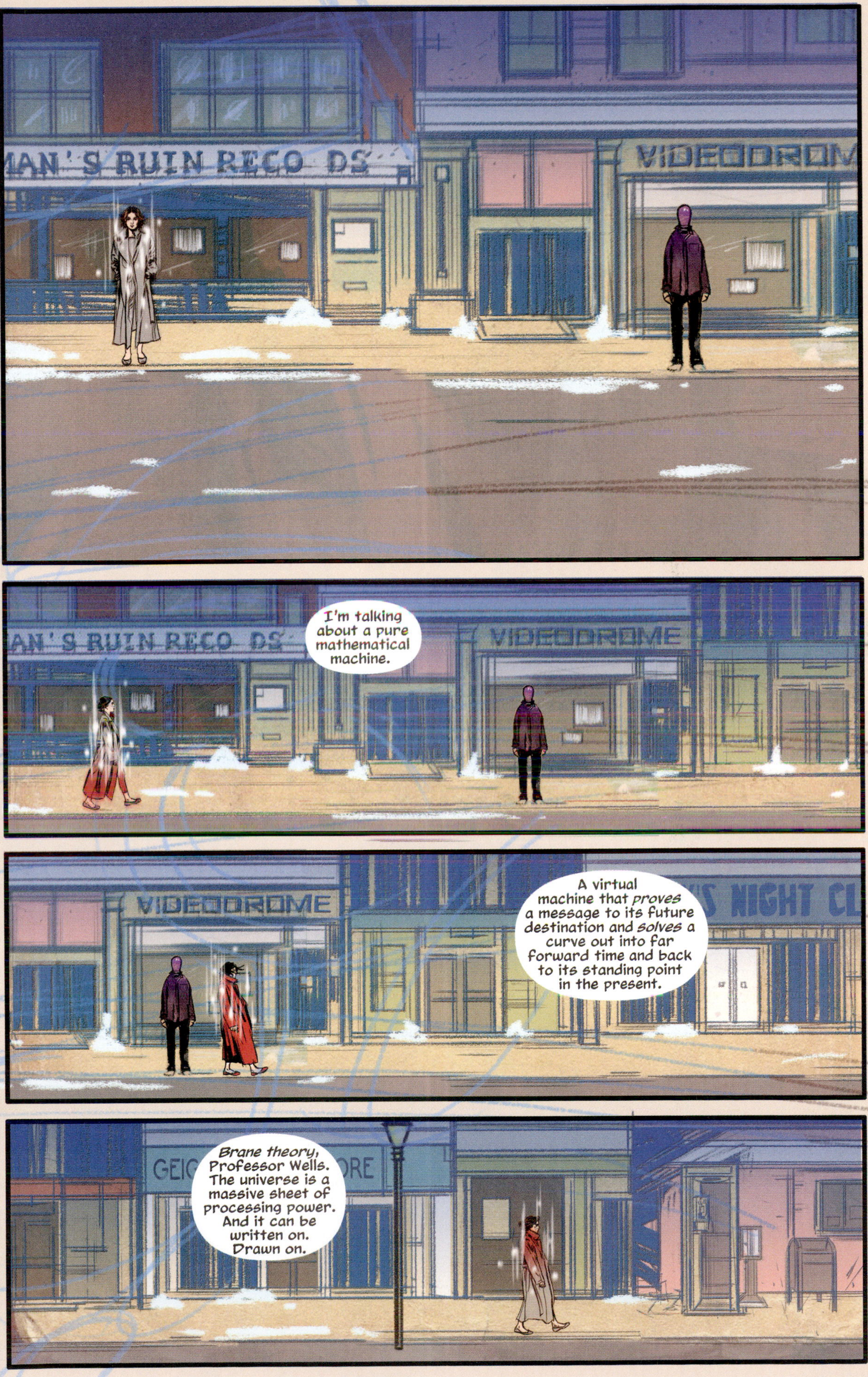

AN'S RUIN RECO DS
VIDEODROM
I'm talking about a pure mathematical machine.
A virtual machine that *proves* a message to its future destination and *solves* a curve out into far forward time and back to its standing point in the present.
Brane theory, Professor Wells. The universe is a massive sheet of processing power. And it can be written on. Drawn on.

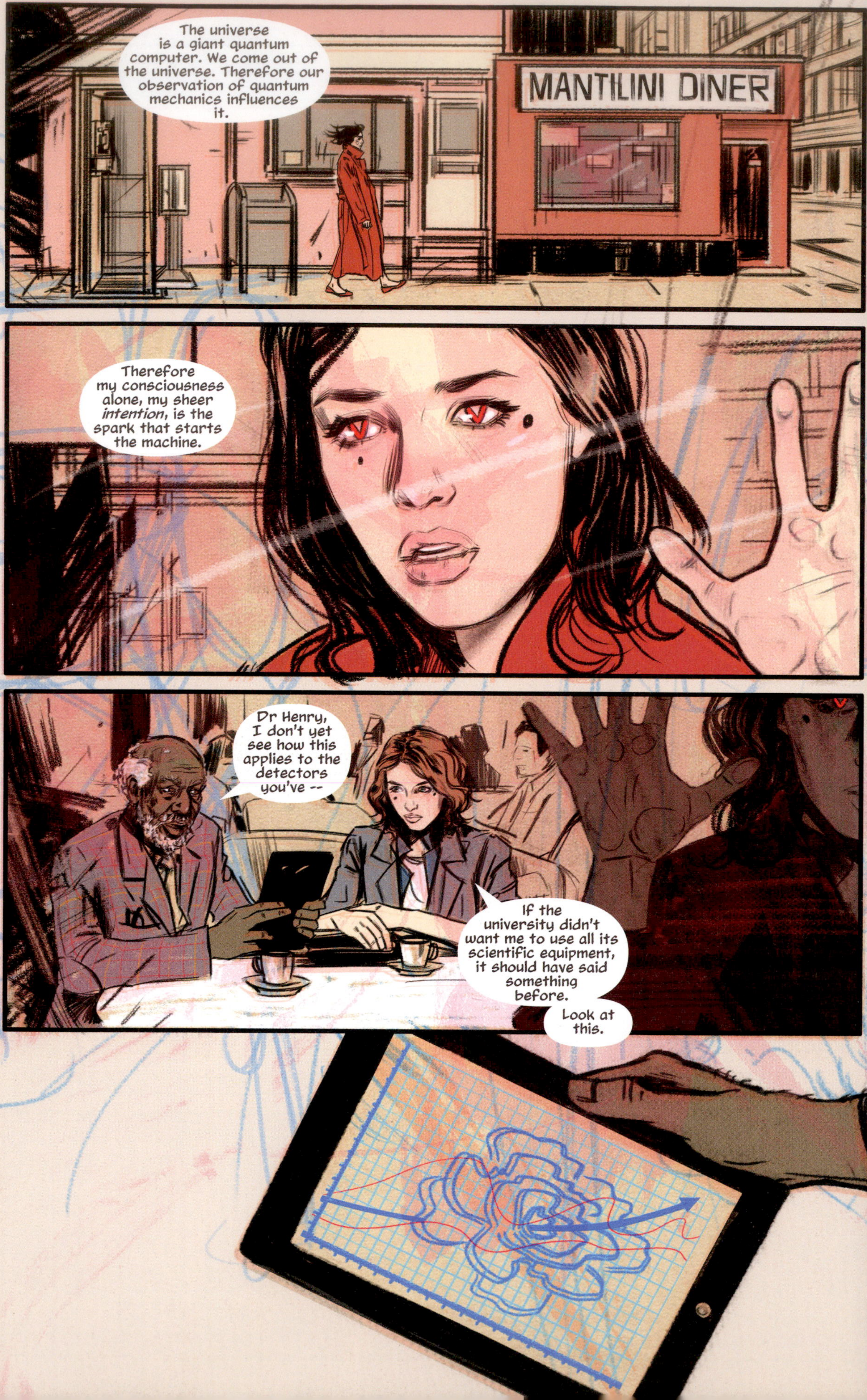
The universe is a giant quantum computer. We come out of the universe. Therefore our observation of quantum mechanics influences it.
MANTILINI DINER
Therefore my consciousness alone, my sheer *intention*, is the spark that starts the machine.
Dr Henry, I don't yet see how this applies to the detectors you've --
If the university didn't want me to use all its scientific equipment, it should have said something before.
Look at this.

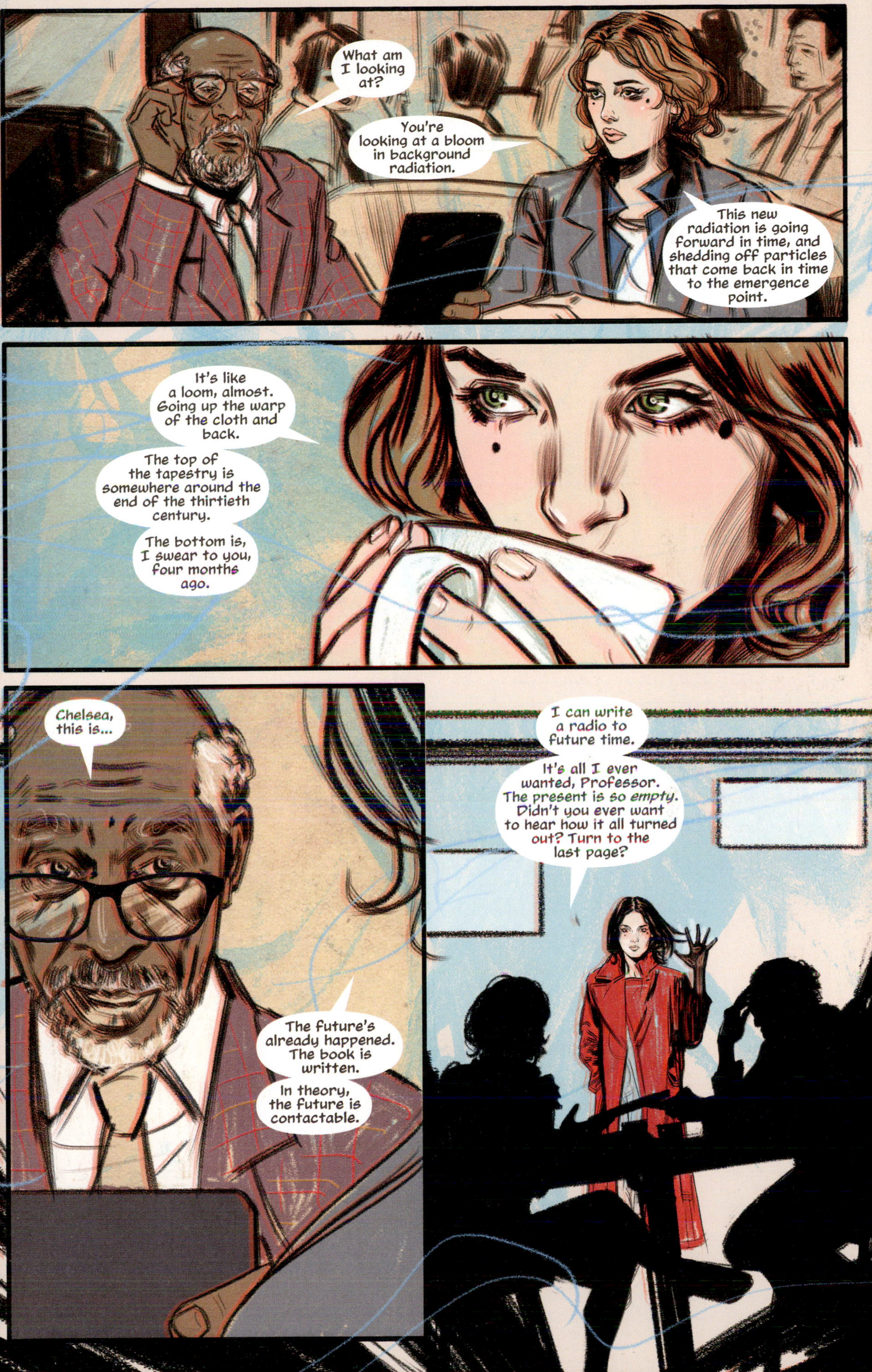
What am I looking at?
You're looking at a bloom in background radiation.
This new radiation is going forward in time, and shedding off particles that come back in time to the emergence point.
It's like a loom, almost. Going up the warp of the cloth and back.
The top of the tapestry is somewhere around the end of the thirtieth century.
The bottom is, I swear to you, four months ago.
Chelsea, this is...
The future's already happened. The book is written.
In theory, the future is contactable.
I can write a radio to future time.
It's all I ever wanted, Professor. The present is so empty. Didn't you ever want to hear how it all turned out? Turn to the last page?

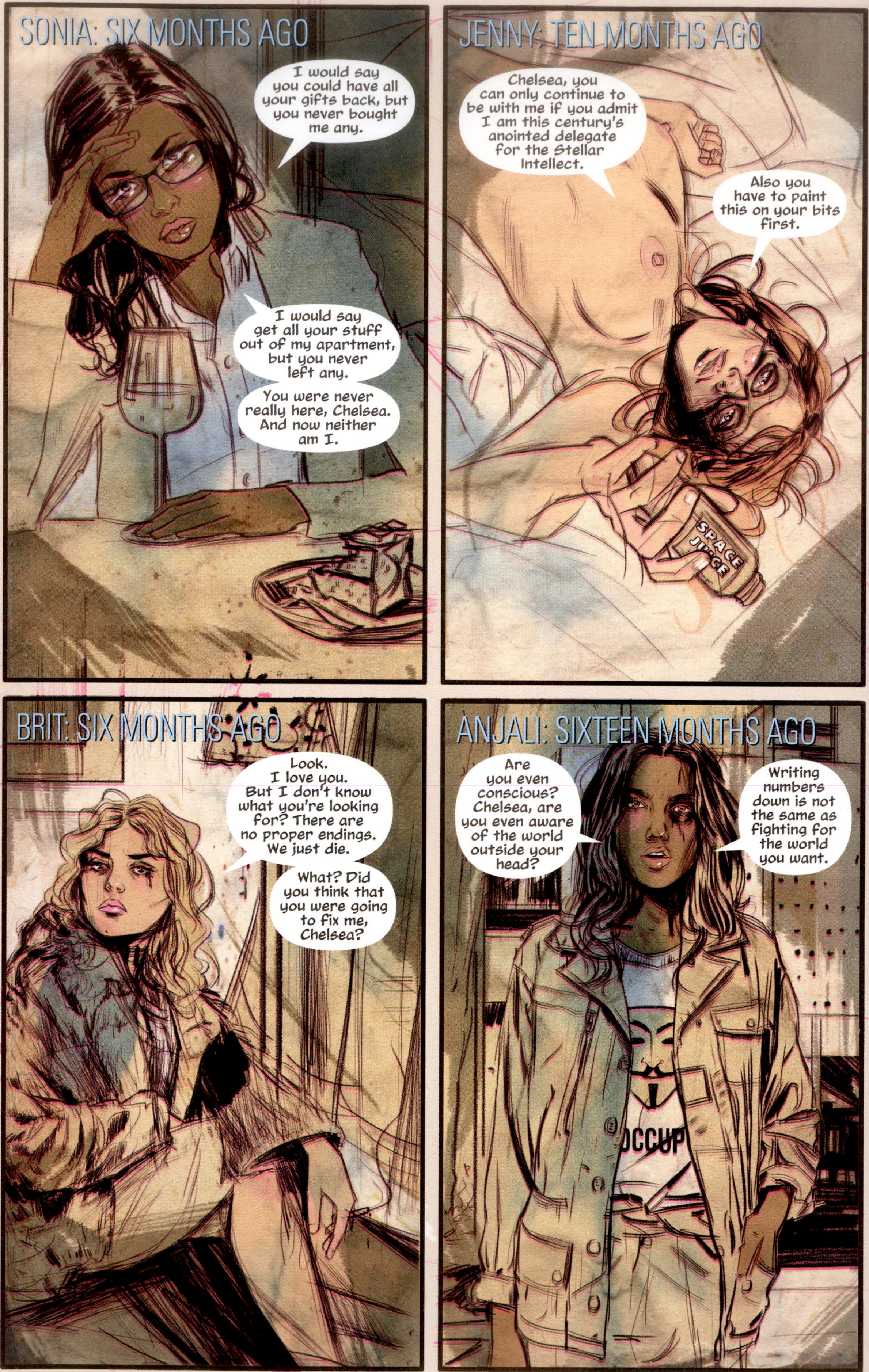
SONIA: SIX MONTHS AGO
I would say you could have all your gifts back, but you never bought me any.
I would say get all your stuff out of my apartment, but you never left any.
You were never really here, Chelsea. And now neither am I.
JENNY: TEN MONTHS AGO
Chelsea, you can only continue to be with me if you admit I am this century's anointed delegate for the Stellar Intellect.
Also you have to paint this on your bits first.
SPACE JUICE
BRIT: SIX MONTHS AGO
Look. I love you. But I don't know what you're looking for? There are no proper endings. We just die.
What? Did you think that you were going to fix me, Chelsea?
ANJALI: SIXTEEN MONTHS AGO
Are you even conscious? Chelsea, are you even aware of the world outside your head?
Writing numbers down is not the same as fighting for the world you want.
OCCUP

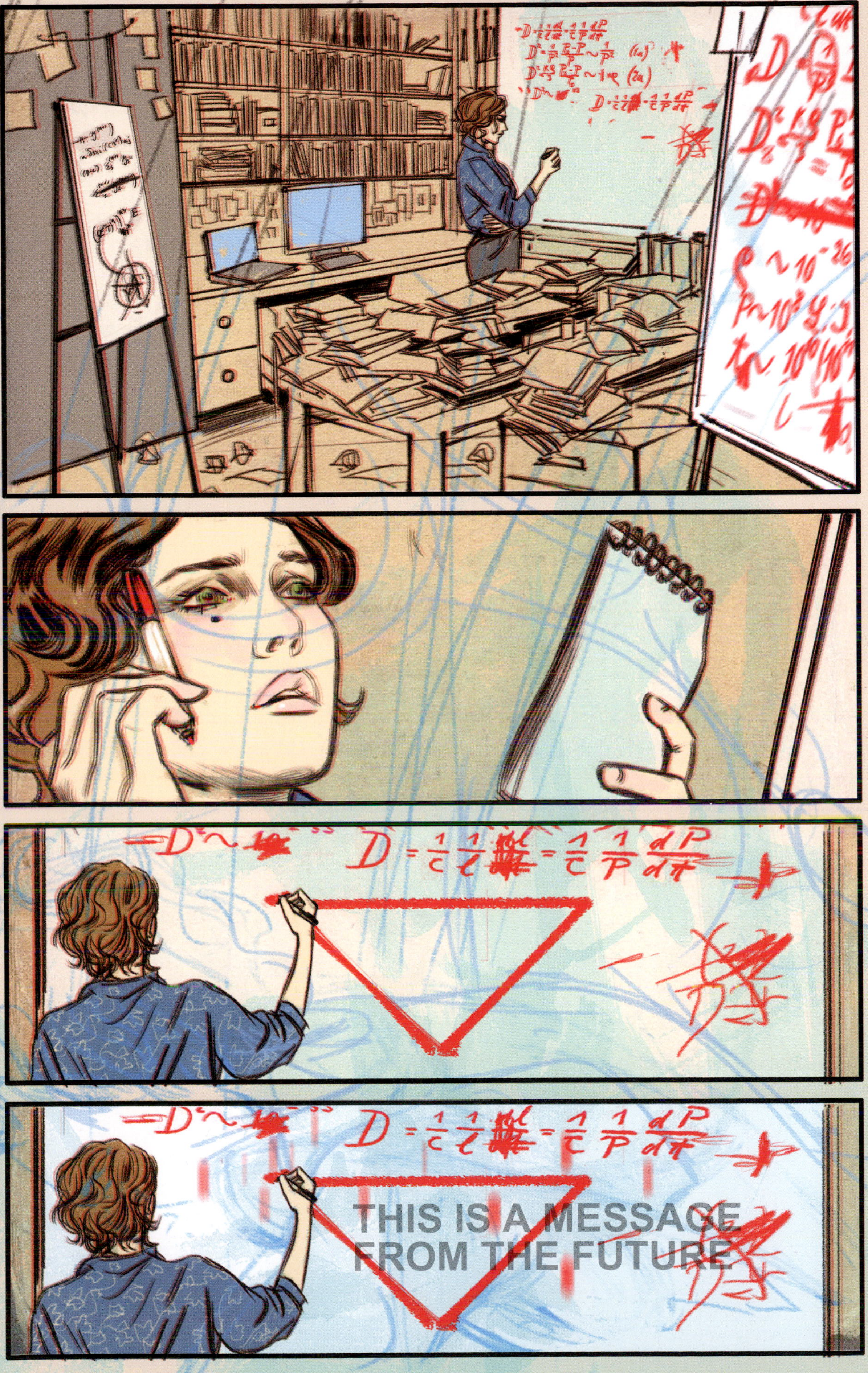
THIS IS A MESSAGE FROM THE FUTURE

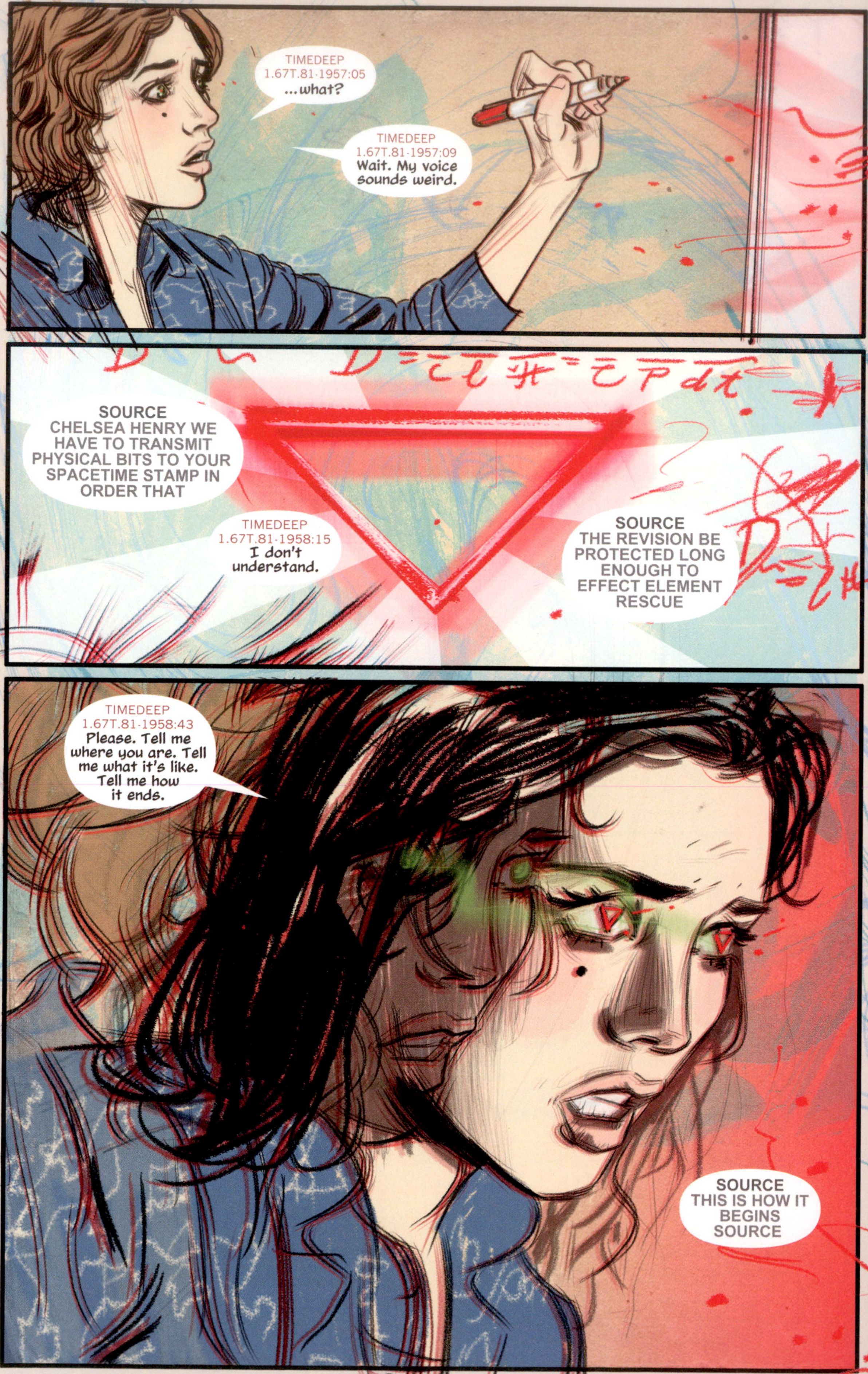
TIMEDEEP 1.67T.81-1957:05 ...what?
TIMEDEEP 1.67T.81-1957:09 Wait. My voice sounds weird.
SOURCE CHELSEA HENRY WE HAVE TO TRANSMIT PHYSICAL BITS TO YOUR SPACETIME STAMP IN ORDER THAT
TIMEDEEP 1.67T.81-1958:15 I don't understand.
SOURCE THE REVISION BE PROTECTED LONG ENOUGH TO EFFECT ELEMENT RESCUE
TIMEDEEP 1.67T.81-1958:43 Please. Tell me where you are. Tell me what it's like. Tell me how it ends.
SOURCE THIS IS HOW IT BEGINS SOURCE

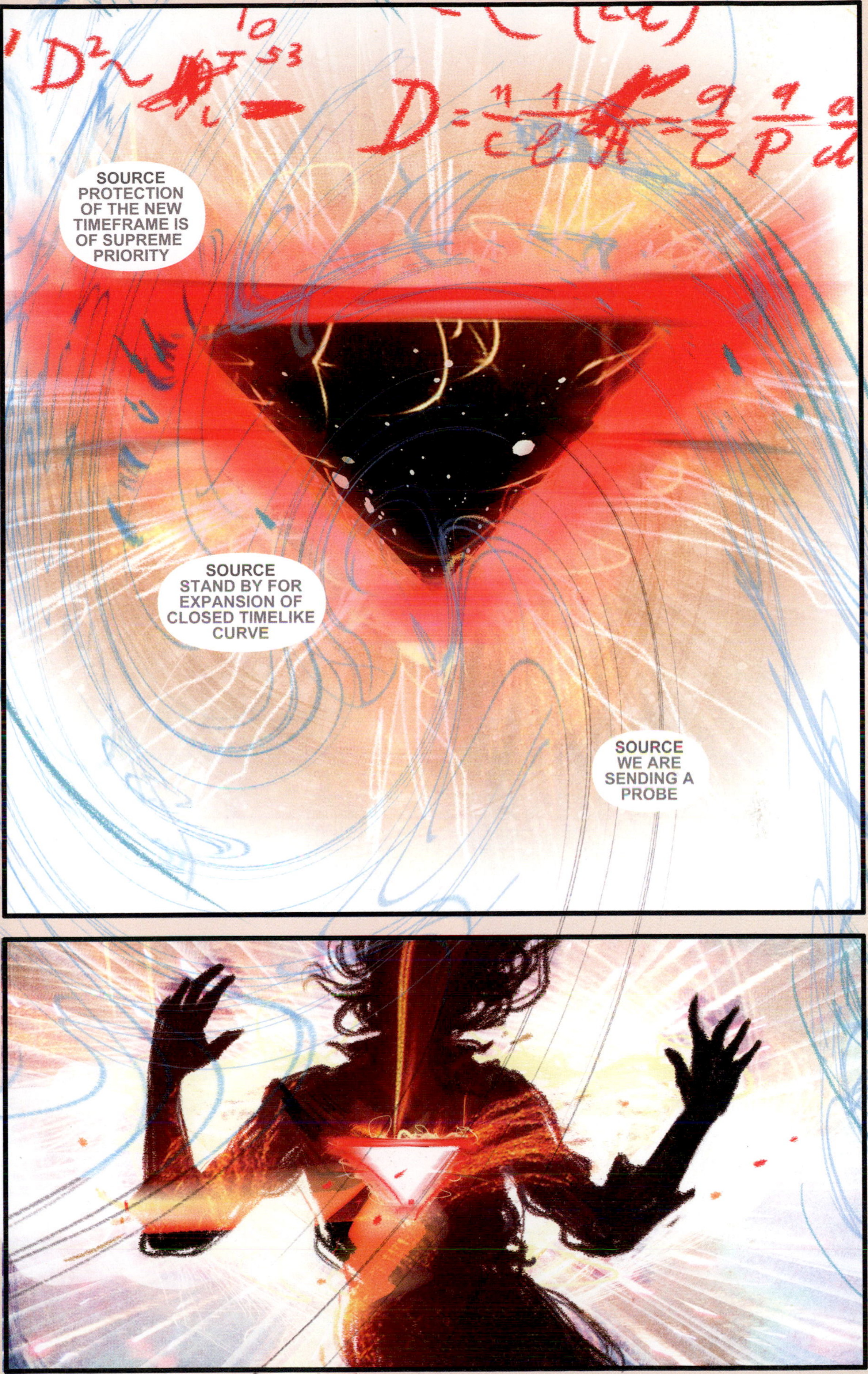
SOURCE PROTECTION OF THE NEW TIMEFRAME IS OF SUPREME PRIORITY
SOURCE STAND BY FOR EXPANSION OF CLOSED TIMELIKE CURVE
SOURCE WE ARE SENDING A PROBE

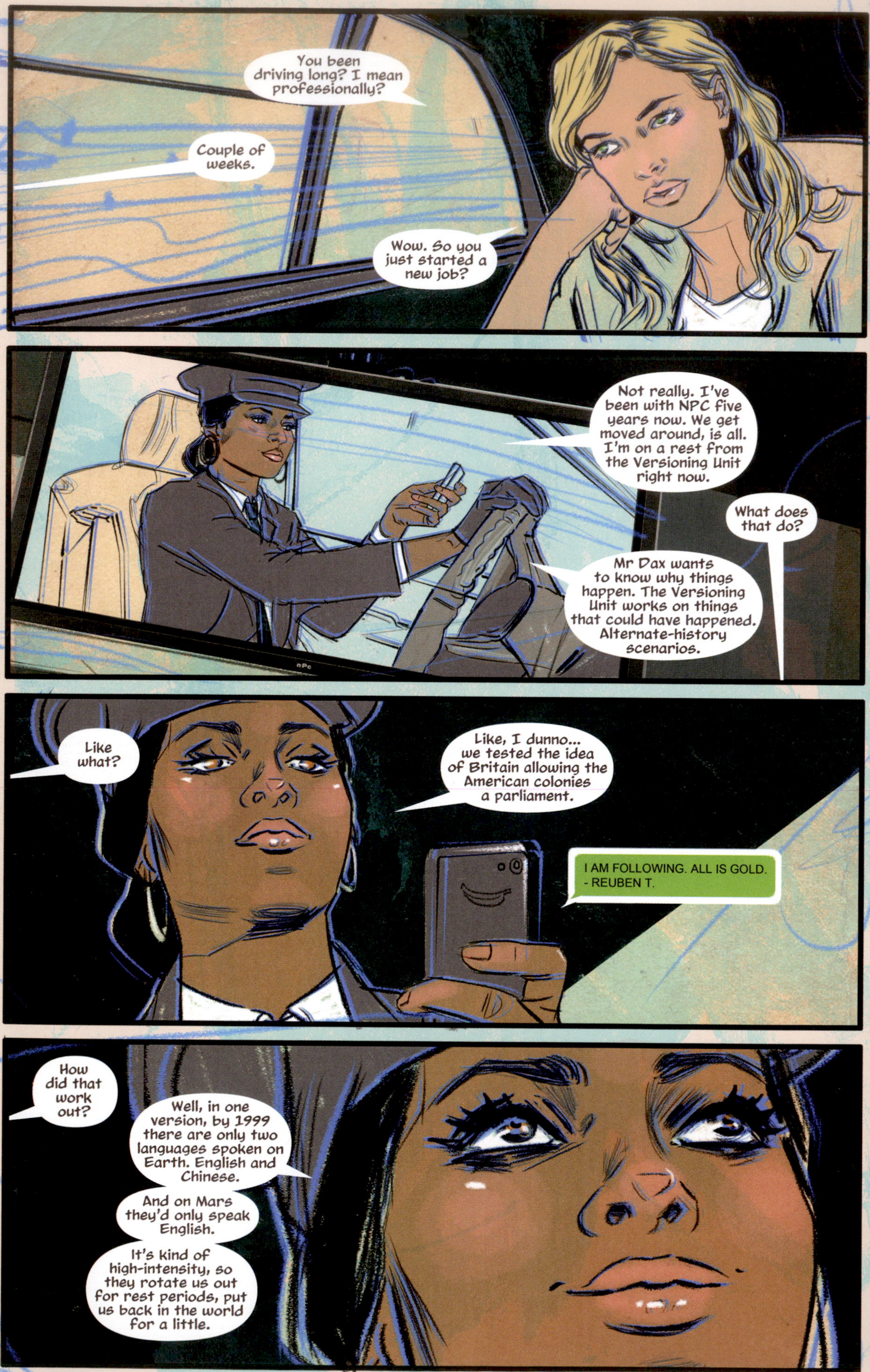
You been driving long? I mean professionally?
Couple of weeks.
Wow. So you just started a new job?
Not really. I've been with NPC five years now. We get moved around, is all. I'm on a rest from the Versioning Unit right now.
What does that do?
Mr Dax wants to know why things happen. The Versioning Unit works on things that could have happened. Alternate-history scenarios.
Like what?
Like, I dunno... we tested the idea of Britain allowing the American colonies a parliament.
I AM FOLLOWING. ALL IS GOLD.
- REUBEN T.
How did that work out?
Well, in one version, by 1999 there are only two languages spoken on Earth. English and Chinese.
And on Mars they'd only speak English.
It's kind of high-intensity, so they rotate us out for rest periods, put us back in the world for a little.

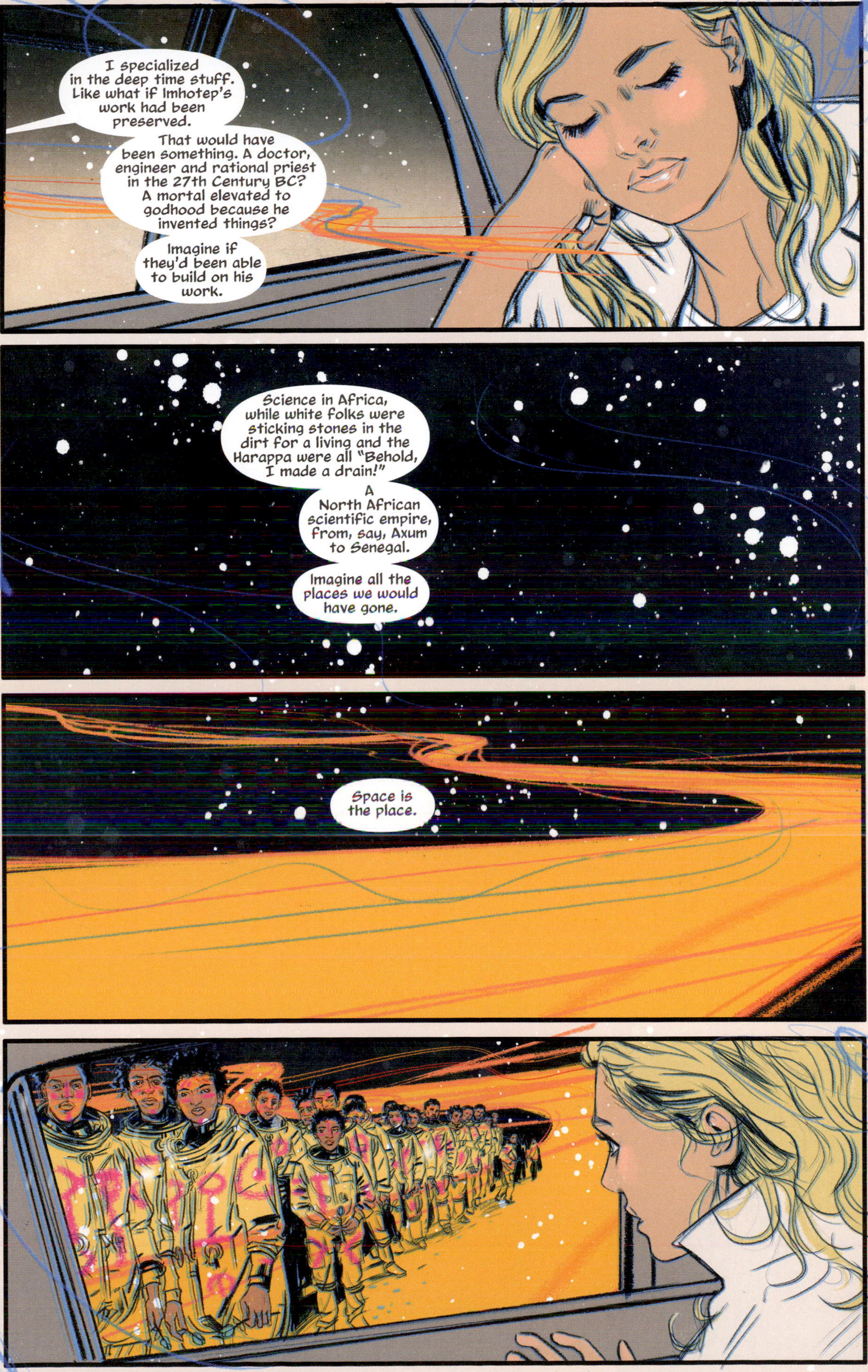
I specialized in the deep time stuff. Like what if Imhotep's work had been preserved.
That would have been something. A doctor, engineer and rational priest in the 27th Century BC? A mortal elevated to godhood because he invented things?
Imagine if they'd been able to build on his work.
Science in Africa, while white folks were sticking stones in the dirt for a living and the Harappa were all "Behold, I made a drain!"
A North African scientific empire, from, say, Axum to Senegal.
Imagine all the places we would have gone.
Space is the place.

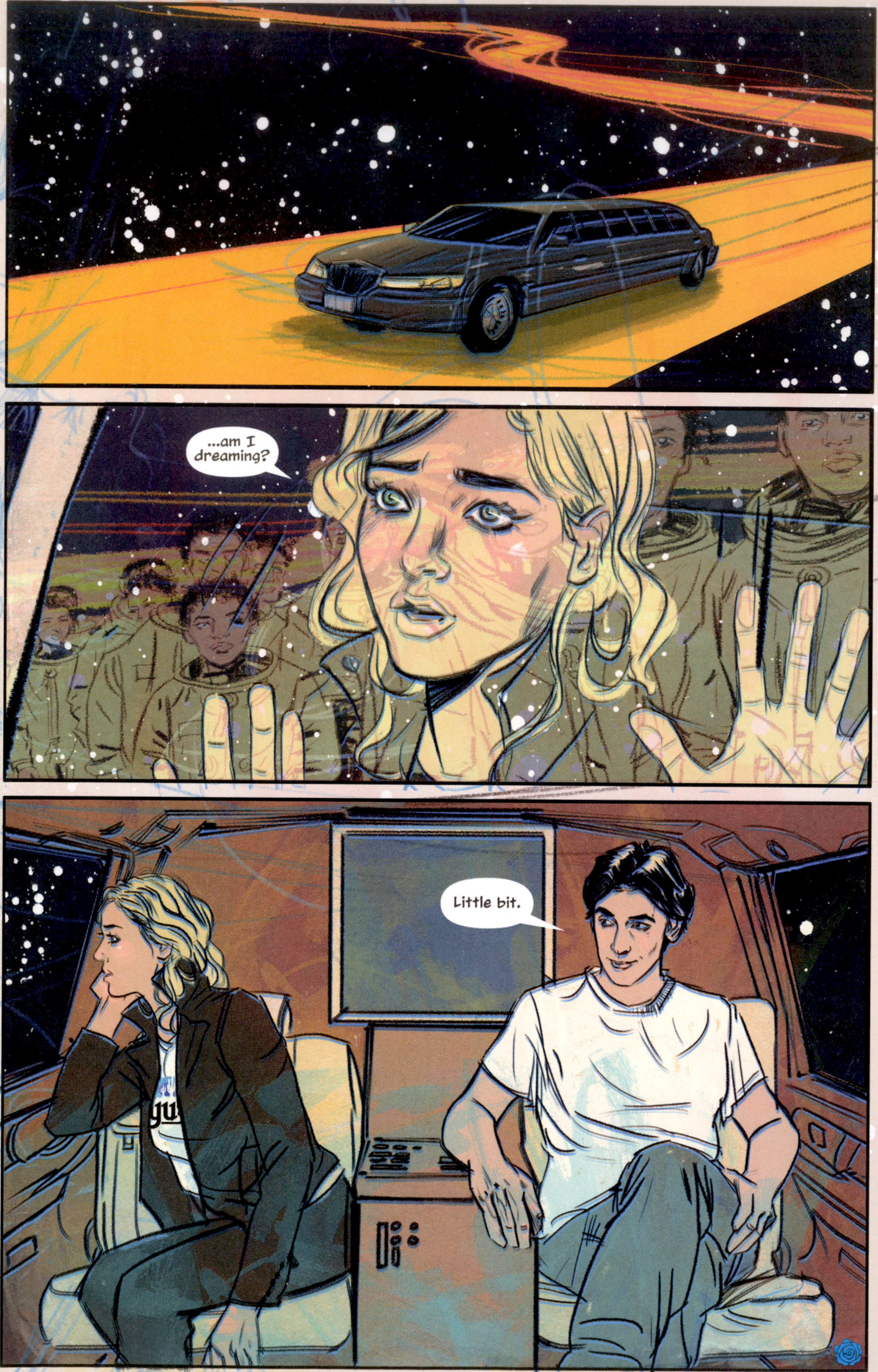
...am I dreaming?
Little bit.

"Twelve thousand years to see
the other side of the road."

THREE

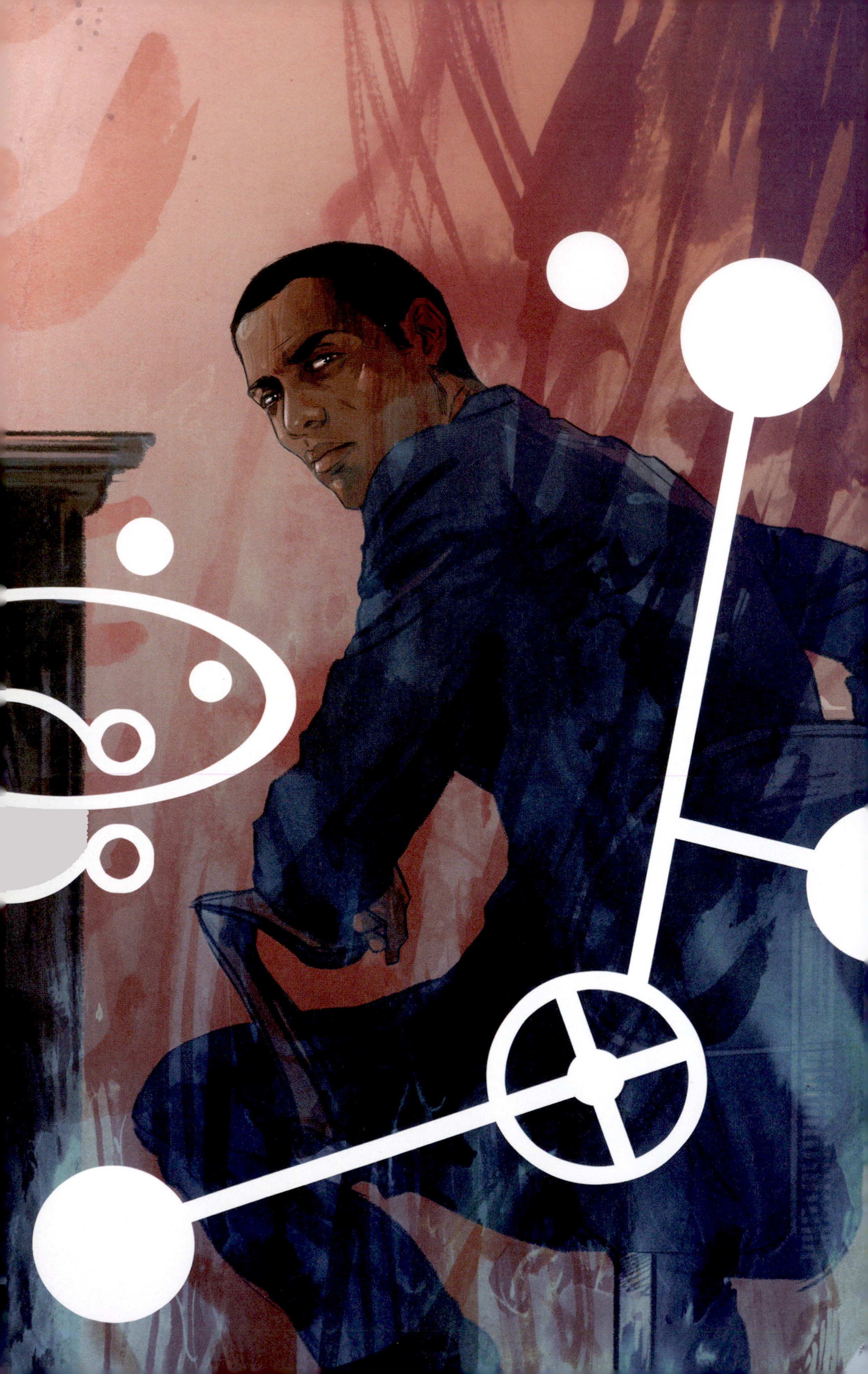

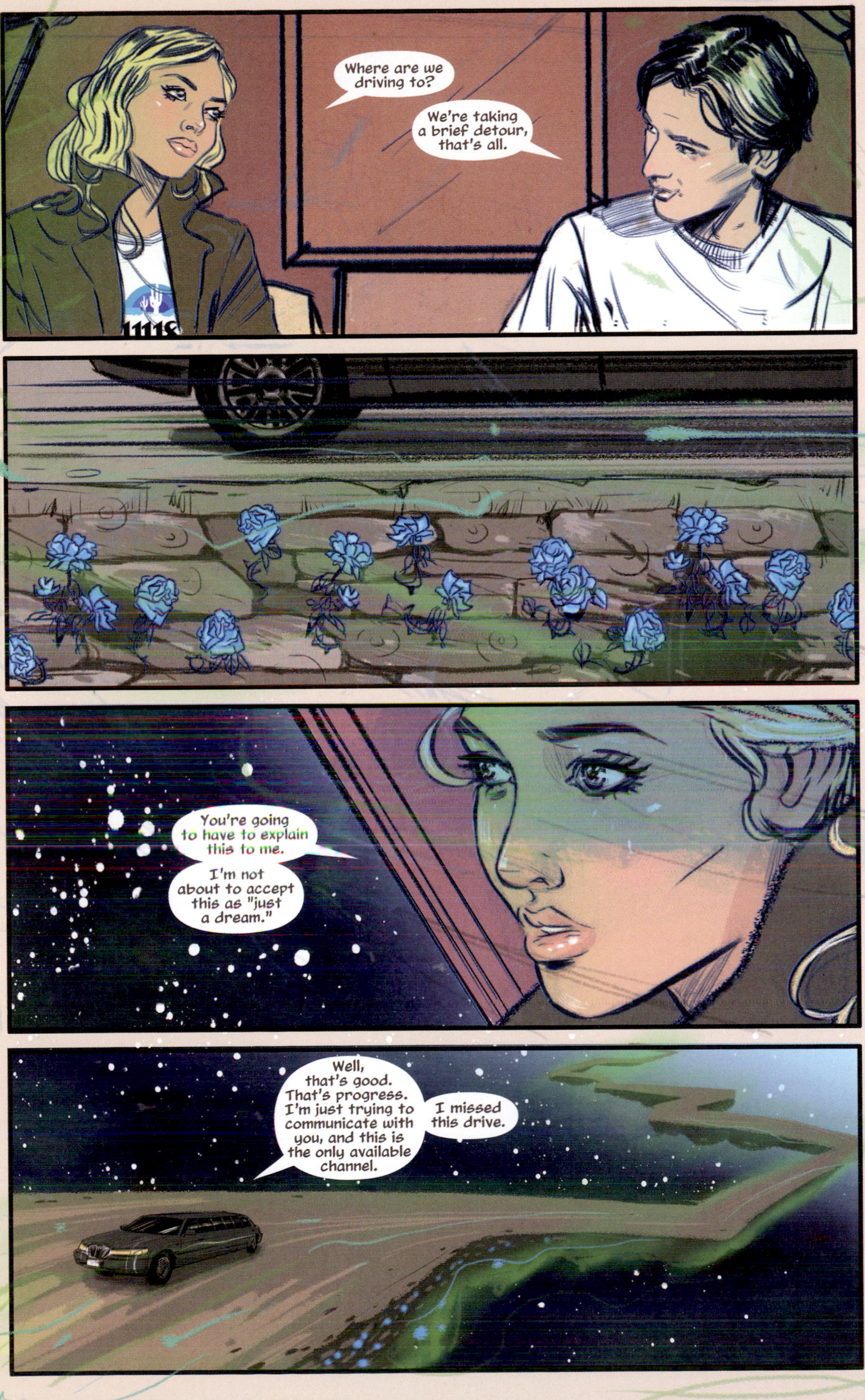
Where are we driving to?
We're taking a brief detour, that's all.
You're going to have to explain this to me.
I'm not about to accept this as "just a dream."
Well, that's good. That's progress. I'm just trying to communicate with you, and this is the only available channel.
I missed this drive.

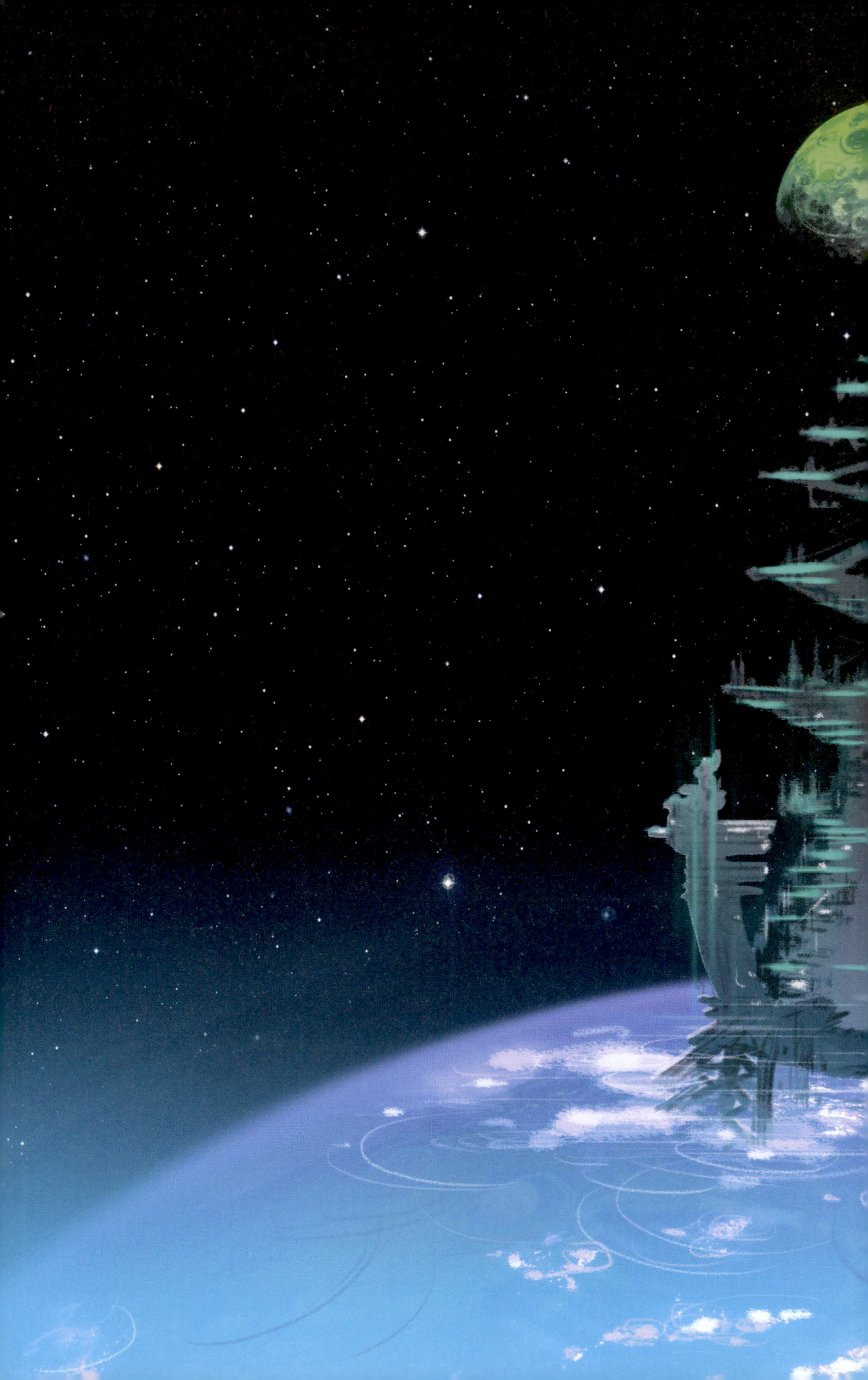

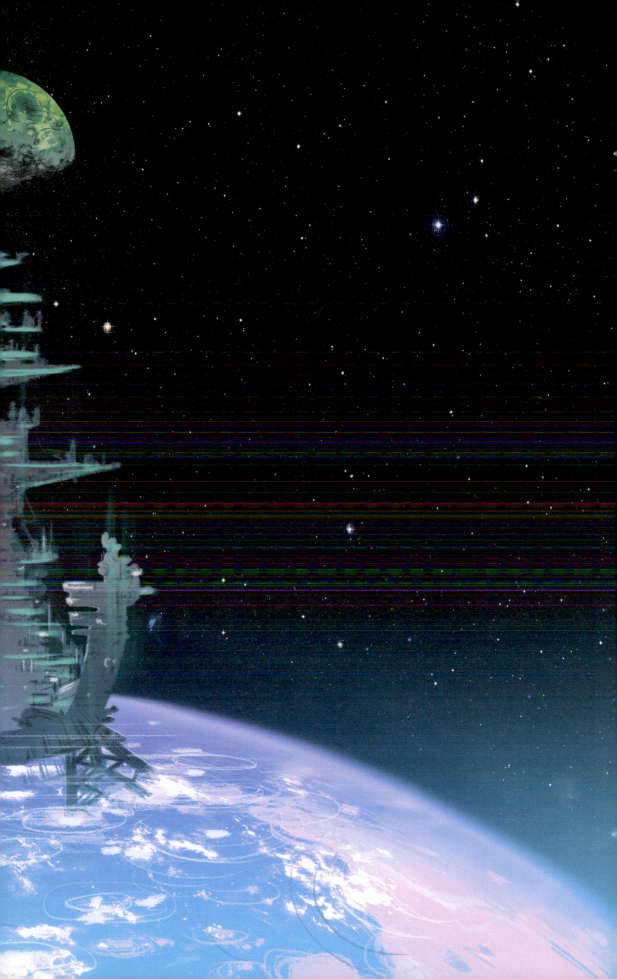

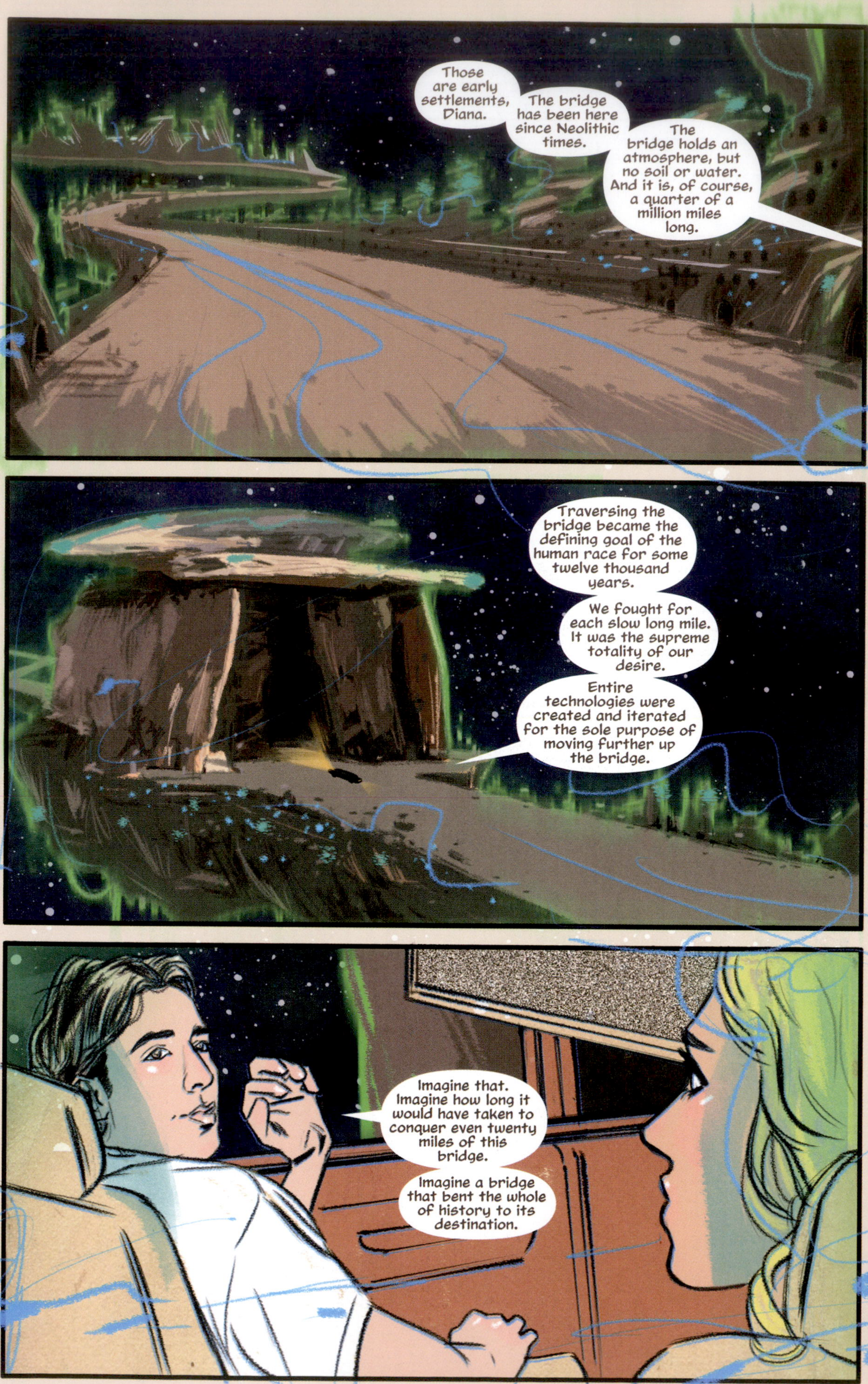
Those are early settlements, Diana.
The bridge has been here since Neolithic times.
The bridge holds an atmosphere, but no soil or water. And it is, of course, a quarter of a million miles long.
Traversing the bridge became the defining goal of the human race for some twelve thousand years.
We fought for each slow long mile. It was the supreme totality of our desire.
Entire technologies were created and iterated for the sole purpose of moving further up the bridge.
Imagine that. Imagine how long it would have taken to conquer even twenty miles of this bridge.
Imagine a bridge that bent the whole of history to its destination.

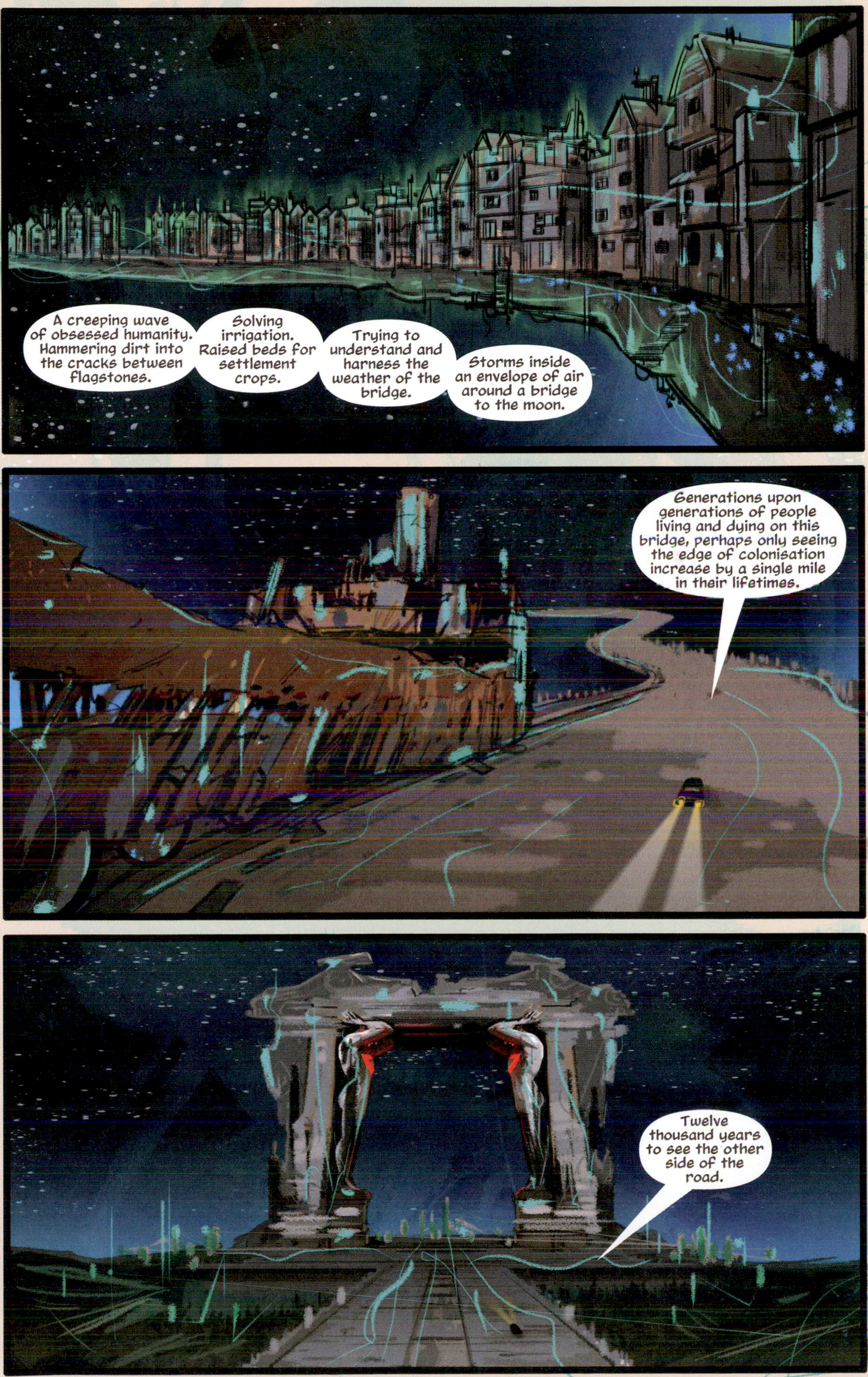
A creeping wave of obsessed humanity. Hammering dirt into the cracks between flagstones.
Solving irrigation. Raised beds for settlement crops.
Trying to understand and harness the weather of the bridge.
Storms inside an envelope of air around a bridge to the moon.
Generations upon generations of people living and dying on this bridge, perhaps only seeing the edge of colonisation increase by a single mile in their lifetimes.
Twelve thousand years to see the other side of the road.

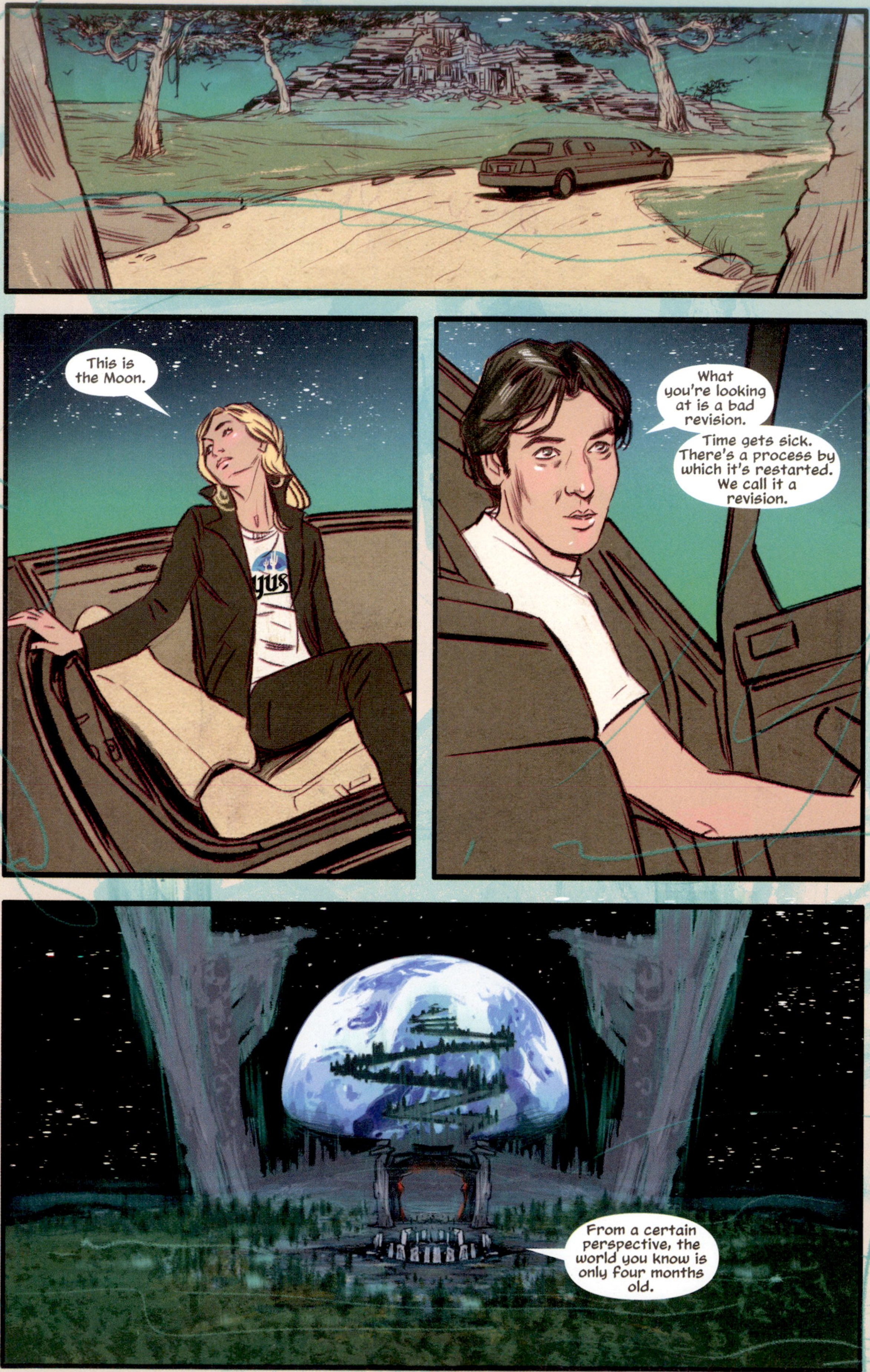
This is the Moon.
What you're looking at is a bad revision.
Time gets sick. There's a process by which it's restarted. We call it a revision.
From a certain perspective, the world you know is only four months old.

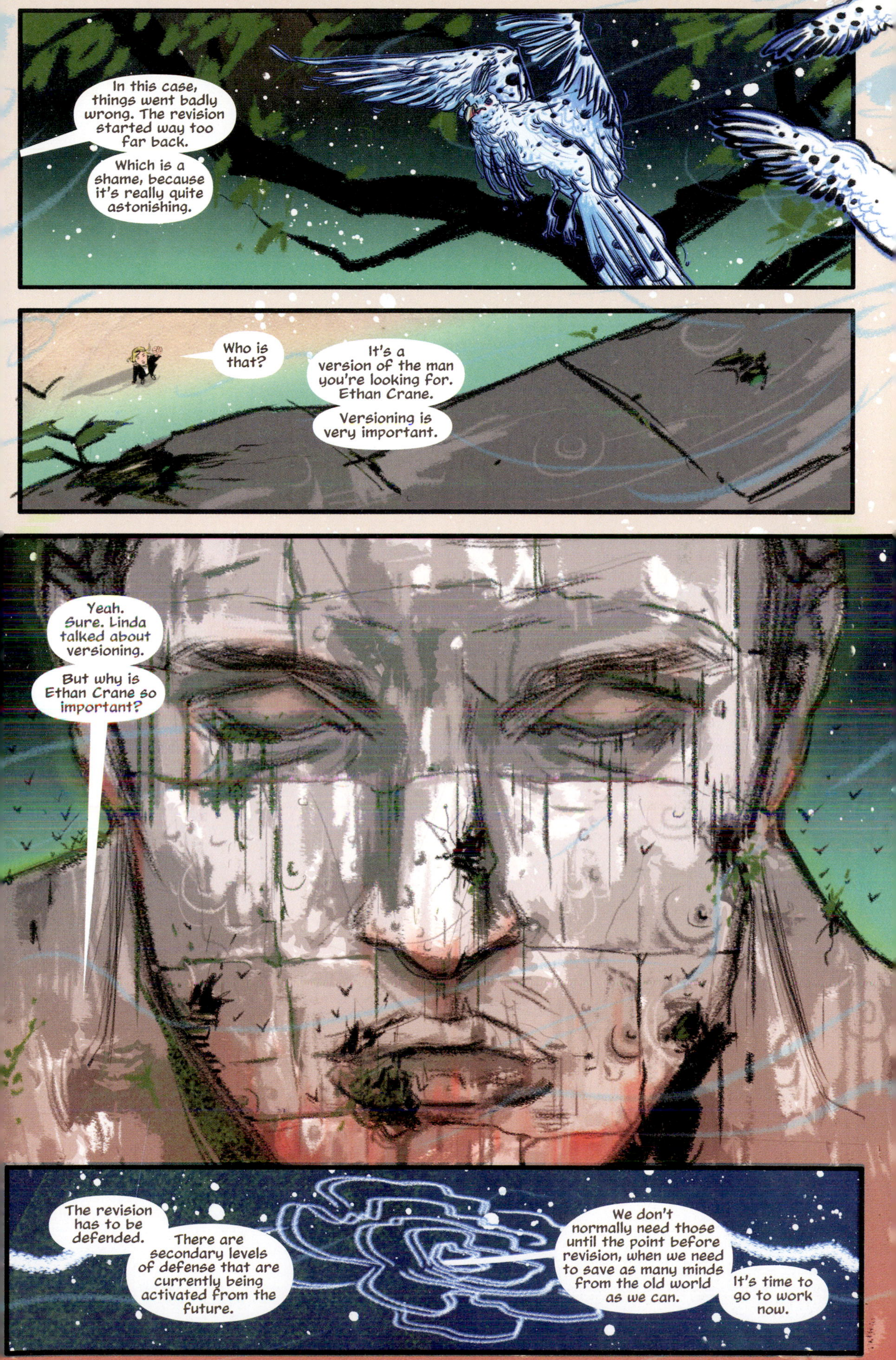
In this case, things went badly wrong. The revision started way too far back.
Which is a shame, because it's really quite astonishing.
Who is that?
It's a version of the man you're looking for. Ethan Crane.
Versioning is very important.
Yeah. Sure. Linda talked about versioning.
But why is Ethan Crane so important?
The revision has to be defended.
There are secondary levels of defense that are currently being activated from the future.
We don't normally need those until the point before revision, when we need to save as many minds from the old world as we can.
It's time to go to work now.

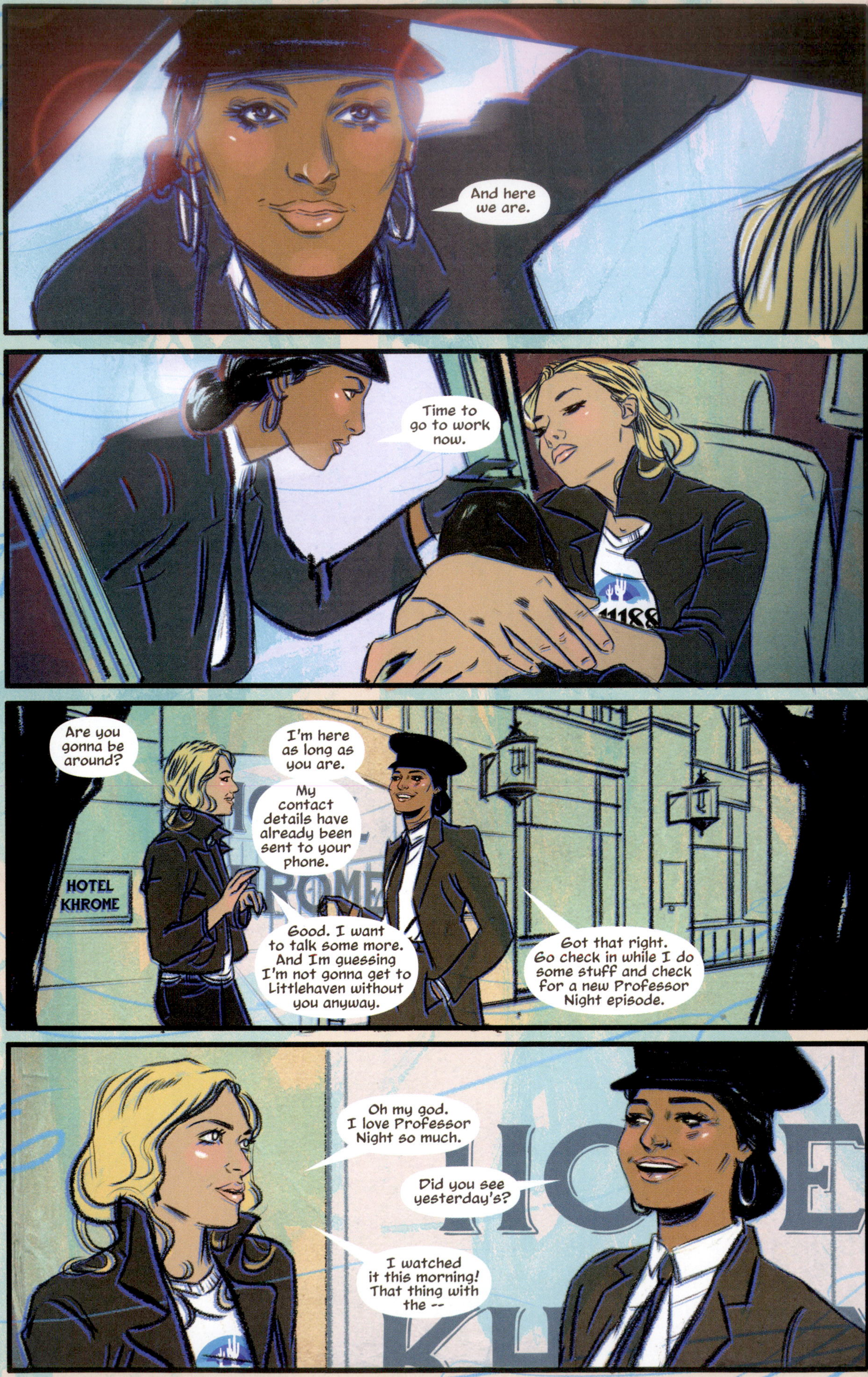
And here we are.
Time to go to work now.
Are you gonna be around?
I'm here as long as you are.
My contact details have already been sent to your phone.
HOTEL KHROME
Good. I want to talk some more. And Im guessing I'm not gonna get to Littlehaven without you anyway.
Got that right. Go check in while I do some stuff and check for a new Professor Night episode.
Oh my god. I love Professor Night so much.
Did you see yesterday's?
I watched it this morning! That thing with the --

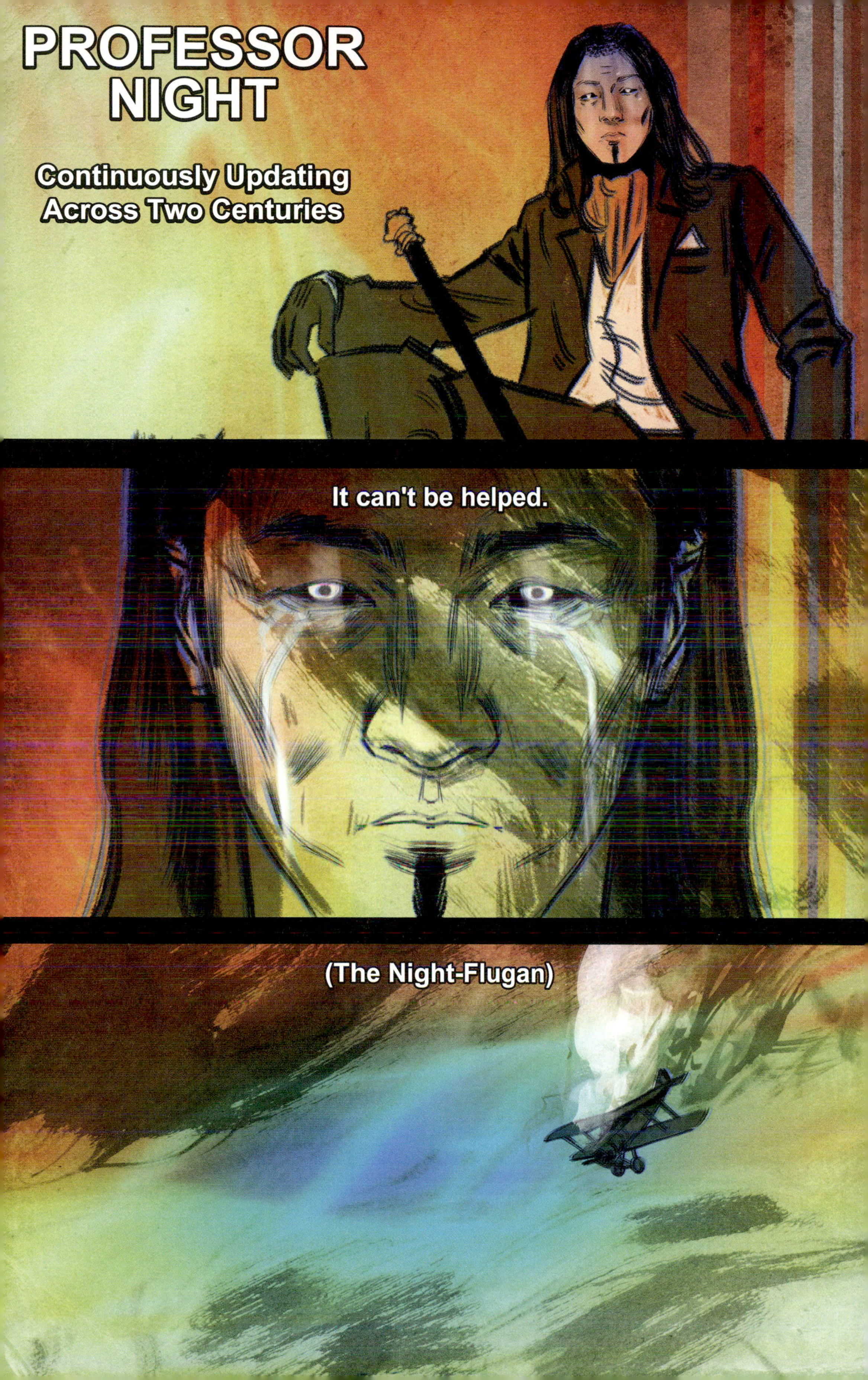
PROFESSOR NIGHT
Continuously Updating Across Two Centuries
It can't be helped.
(The Night-Flugan)

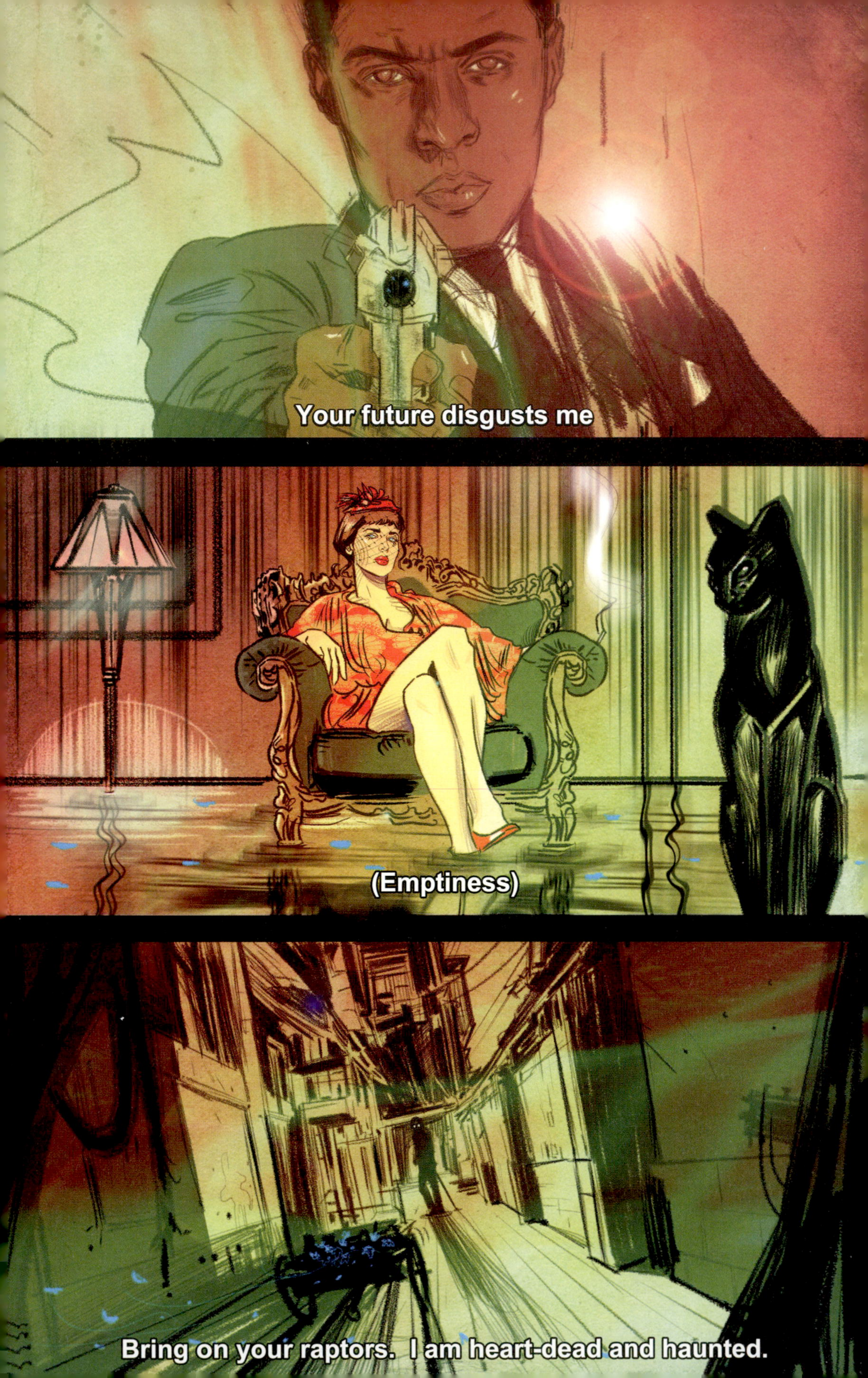
Your future disgusts me
(Emptiness)
Bring on your raptors. I am heart-dead and haunted.

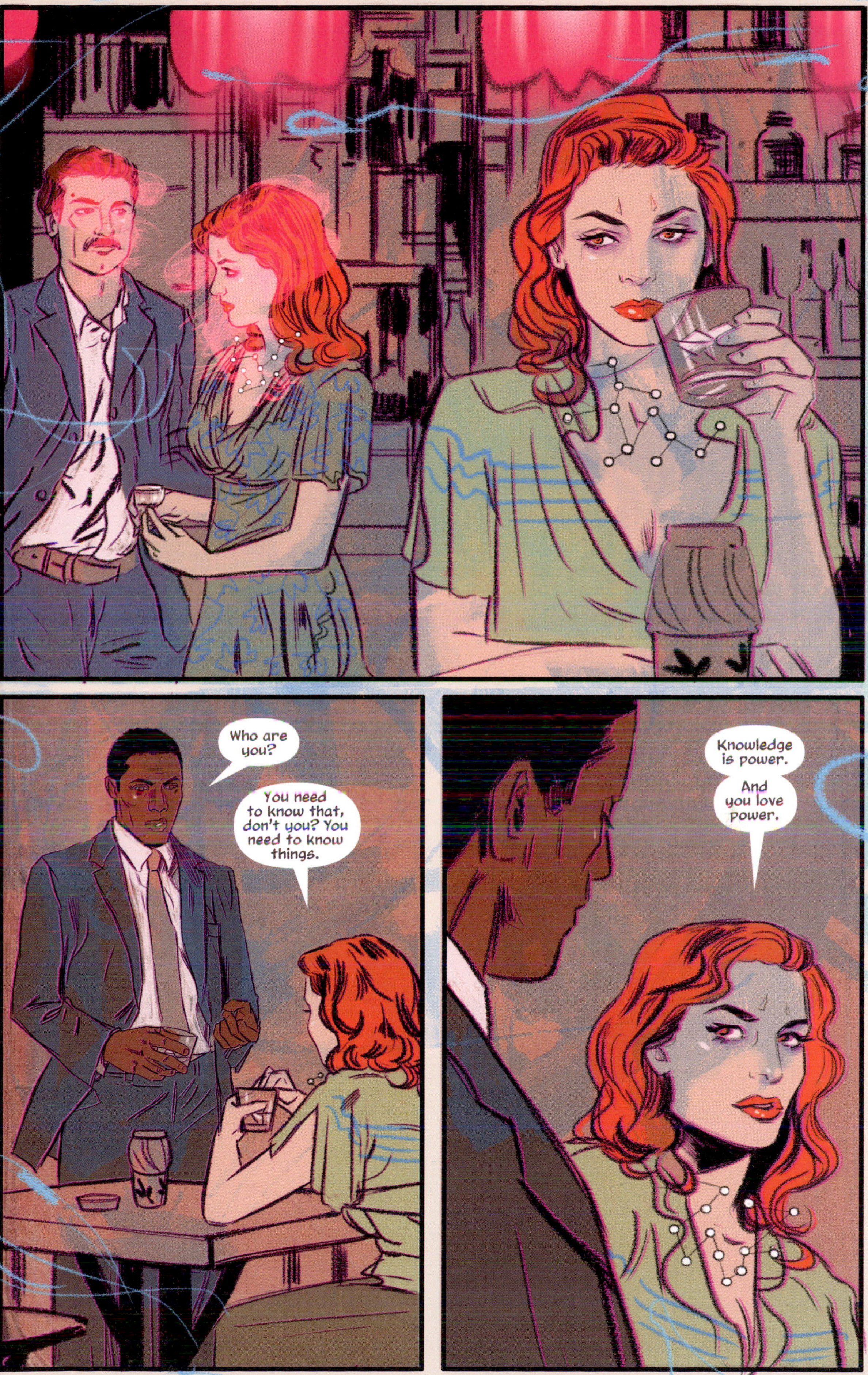
Who are you?
You need to know that, don't you? You need to know things.
Knowledge is power.
And you love power.

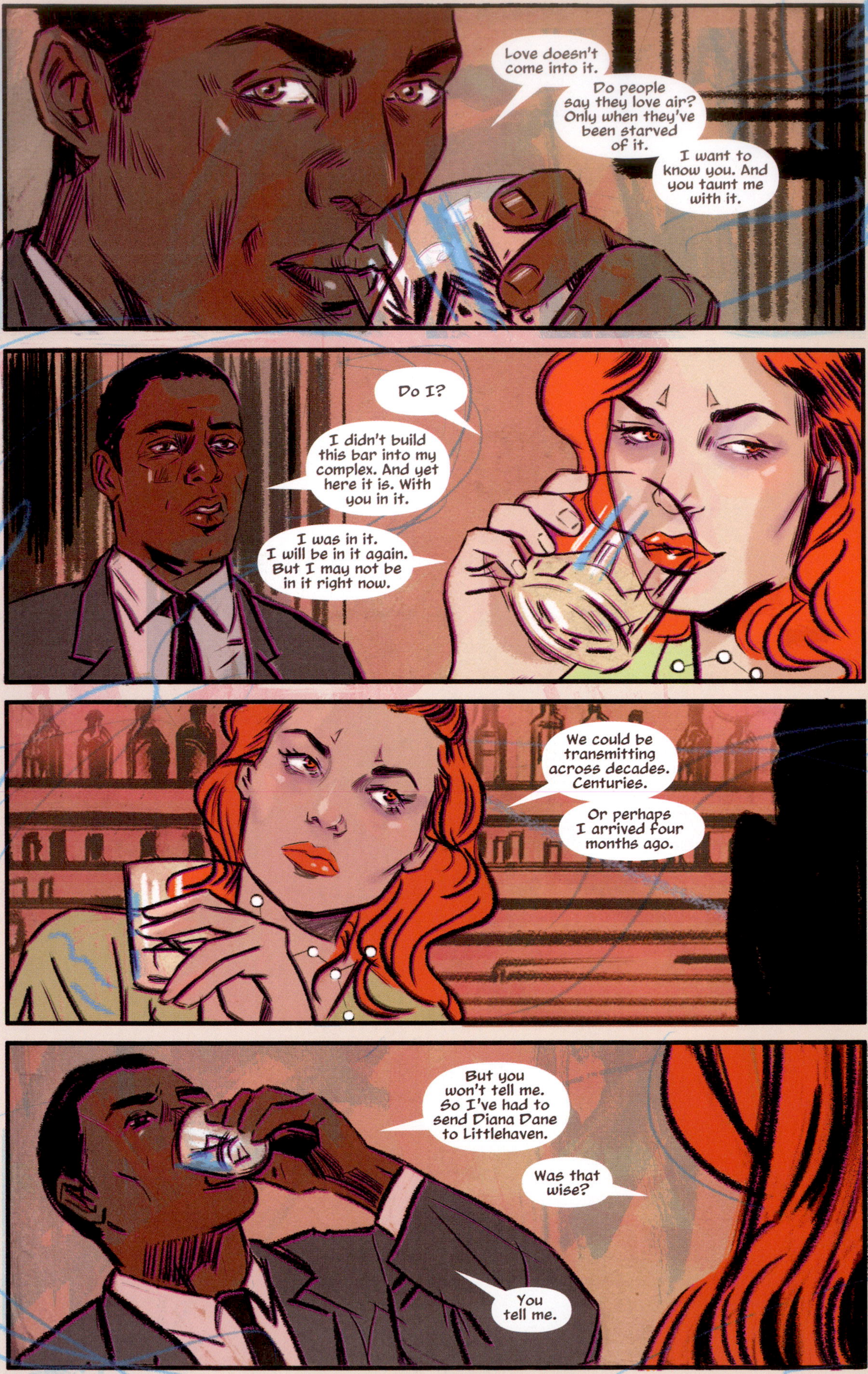
Love doesn't come into it.
Do people say they love air? Only when they've been starved of it.
I want to know you. And you taunt me with it.
Do I?
I didn't build this bar into my complex. And yet here it is. With you in it.
I was in it. I will be in it again. But I may not be in it right now.
We could be transmitting across decades. Centuries.
Or perhaps I arrived four months ago.
But you won't tell me. So I've had to send Diana Dane to Littlehaven.
Was that wise?
You tell me.

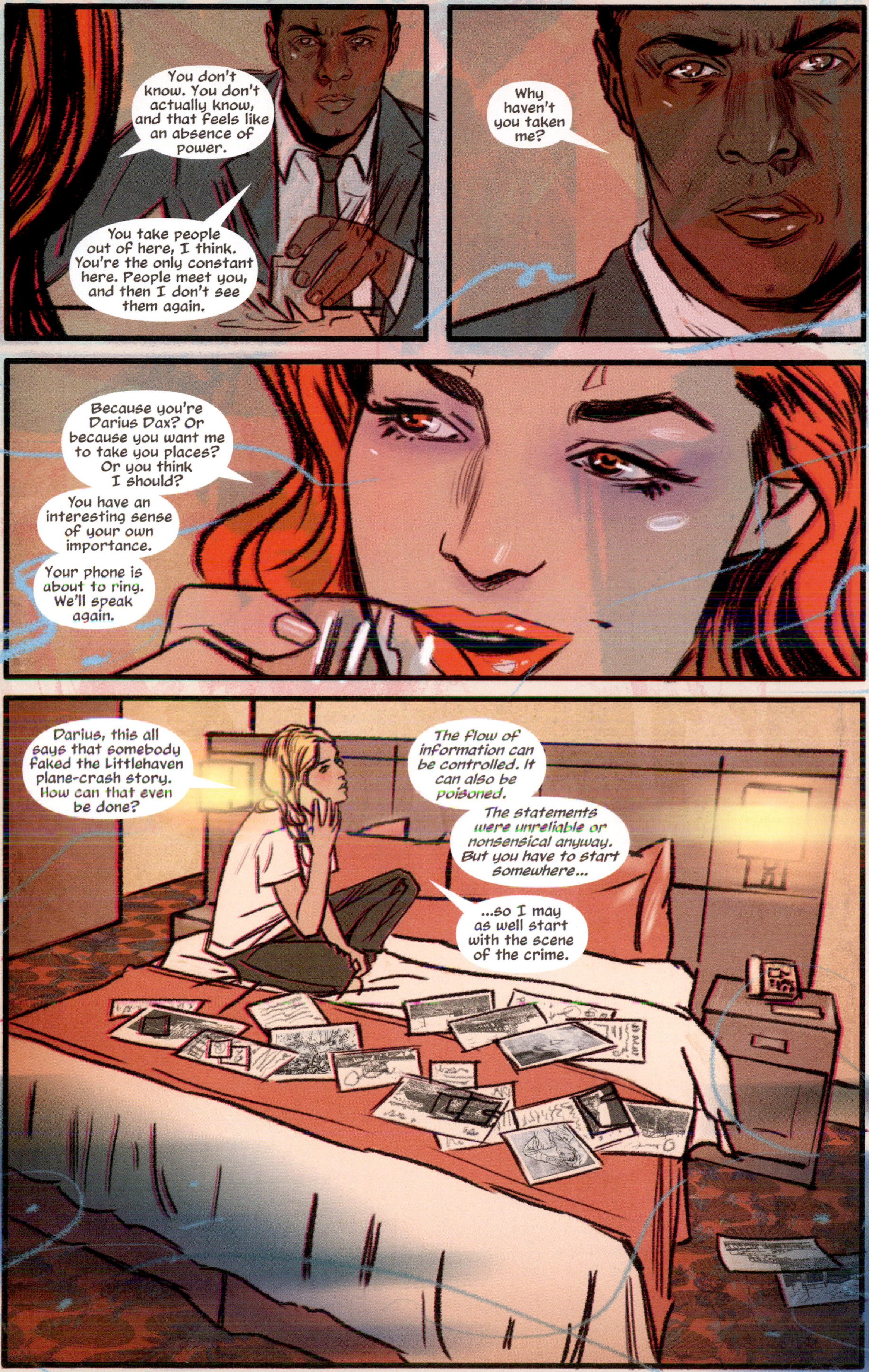
You don't know. You don't actually know, and that feels like an absence of power.
You take people out of here, I think. You're the only constant here. People meet you, and then I don't see them again.
Why haven't you taken me?
Because you're Darius Dax? Or because you want me to take you places? Or you think I should?
You have an interesting sense of your own importance.
Your phone is about to ring. We'll speak again.
Darius, this all says that somebody faked the Littlehaven plane-crash story. How can that even be done?
The flow of information can be controlled. It can also be poisoned.
The statements were unreliable or nonsensical anyway. But you have to start somewhere...
...so I may as well start with the scene of the crime.

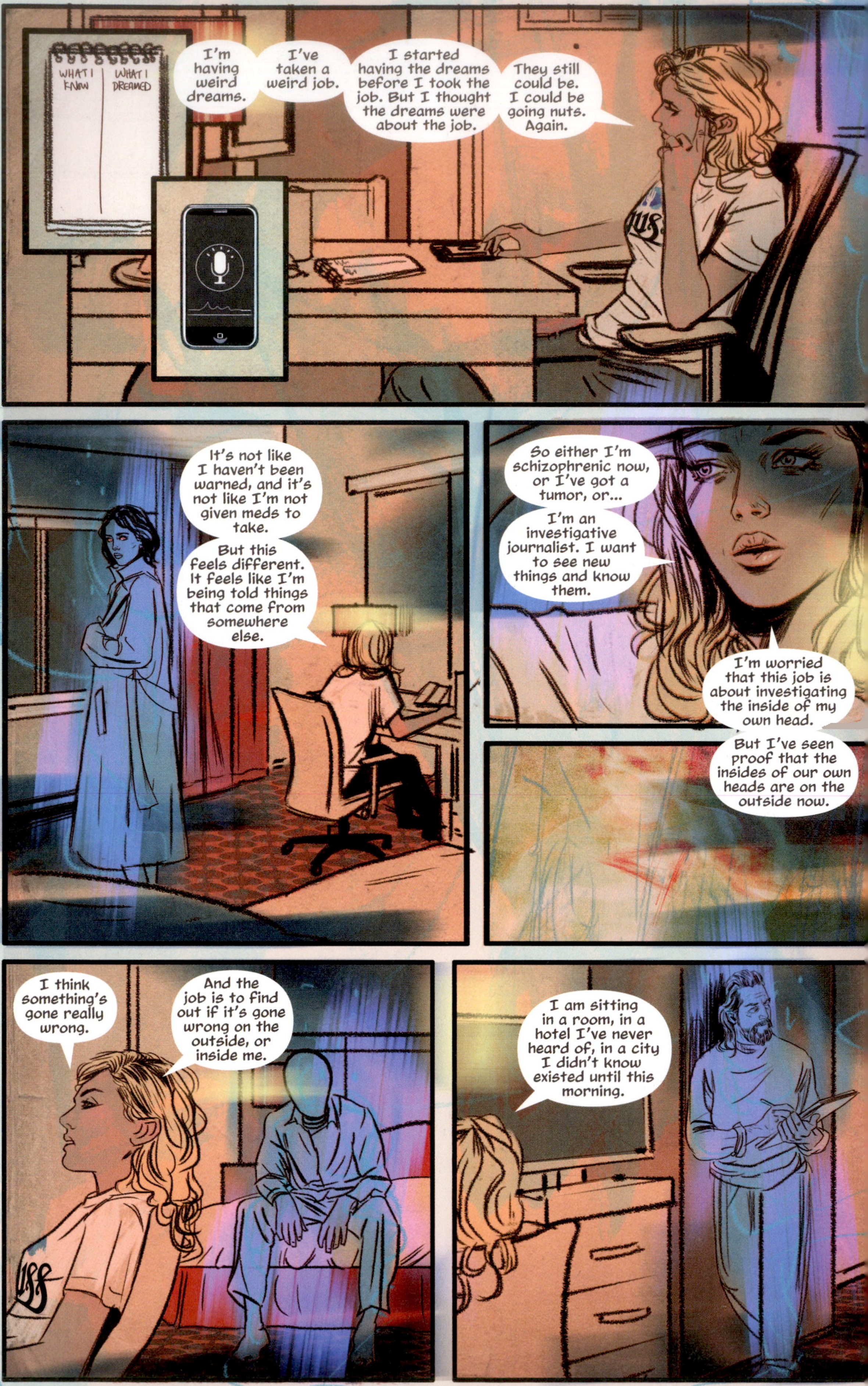
WHAT I KNOW
WHAT I DREAMED
I'm having weird dreams.
I've taken a weird job.
I started having the dreams before I took the job. But I thought the dreams were about the job.
They still could be. I could be going nuts. Again.
It's not like I haven't been warned, and it's not like I'm not given meds to take.
But this feels different. It feels like I'm being told things that come from somewhere else.
So either I'm schizophrenic now, or I've got a tumor, or...
I'm an investigative journalist. I want to see new things and know them.
I'm worried that this job is about investigating the inside of my own head.
But I've seen proof that the insides of our own heads are on the outside now.
I think something's gone really wrong.
And the job is to find out if it's gone wrong on the outside, or inside me.
I am sitting in a room, in a hotel I've never heard of, in a city I didn't know existed until this morning.

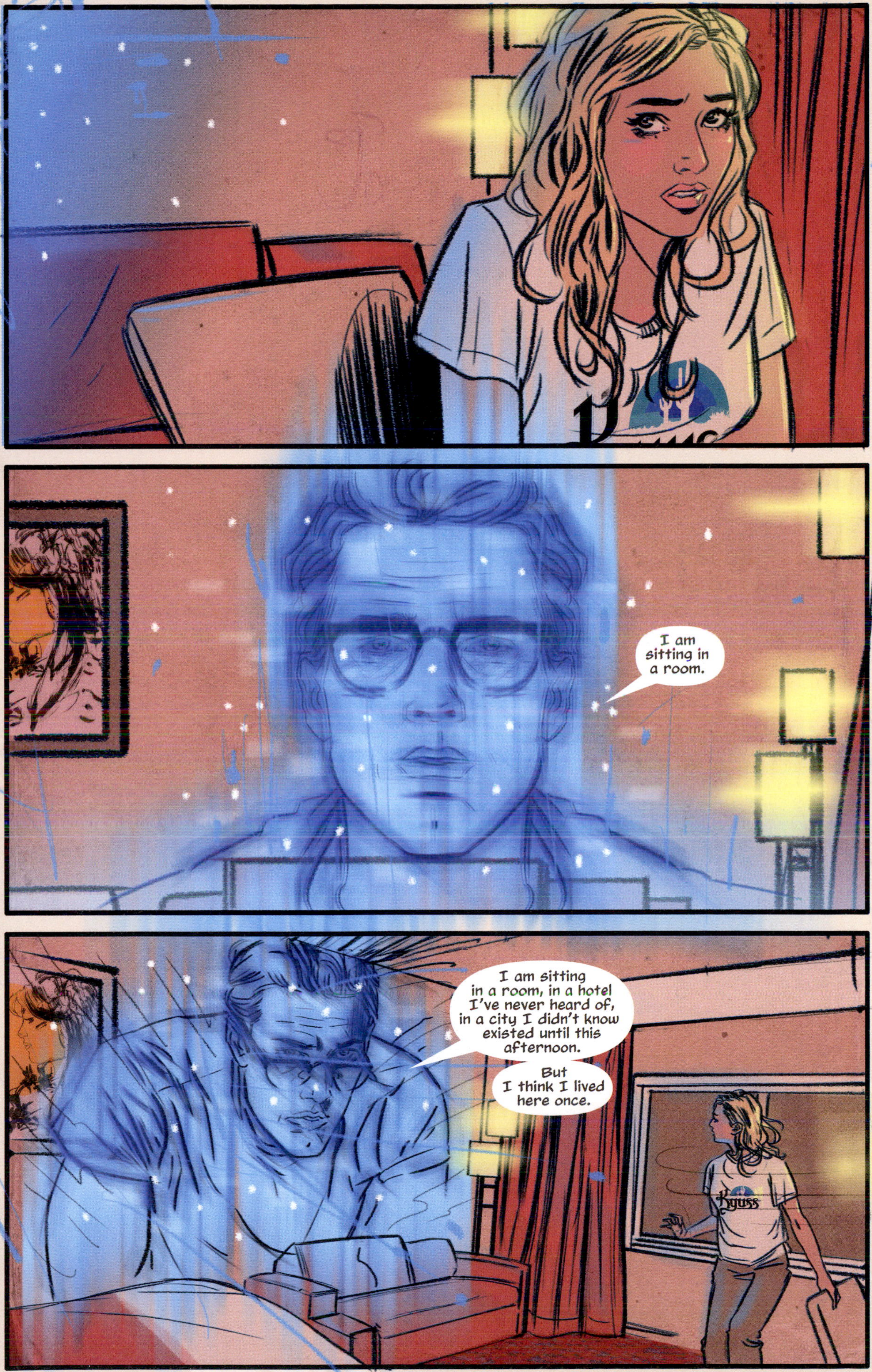
I am sitting in a room.
I am sitting in a room, in a hotel I've never heard of, in a city I didn't know existed until this afternoon.
But I think I lived here once.
Kyuss

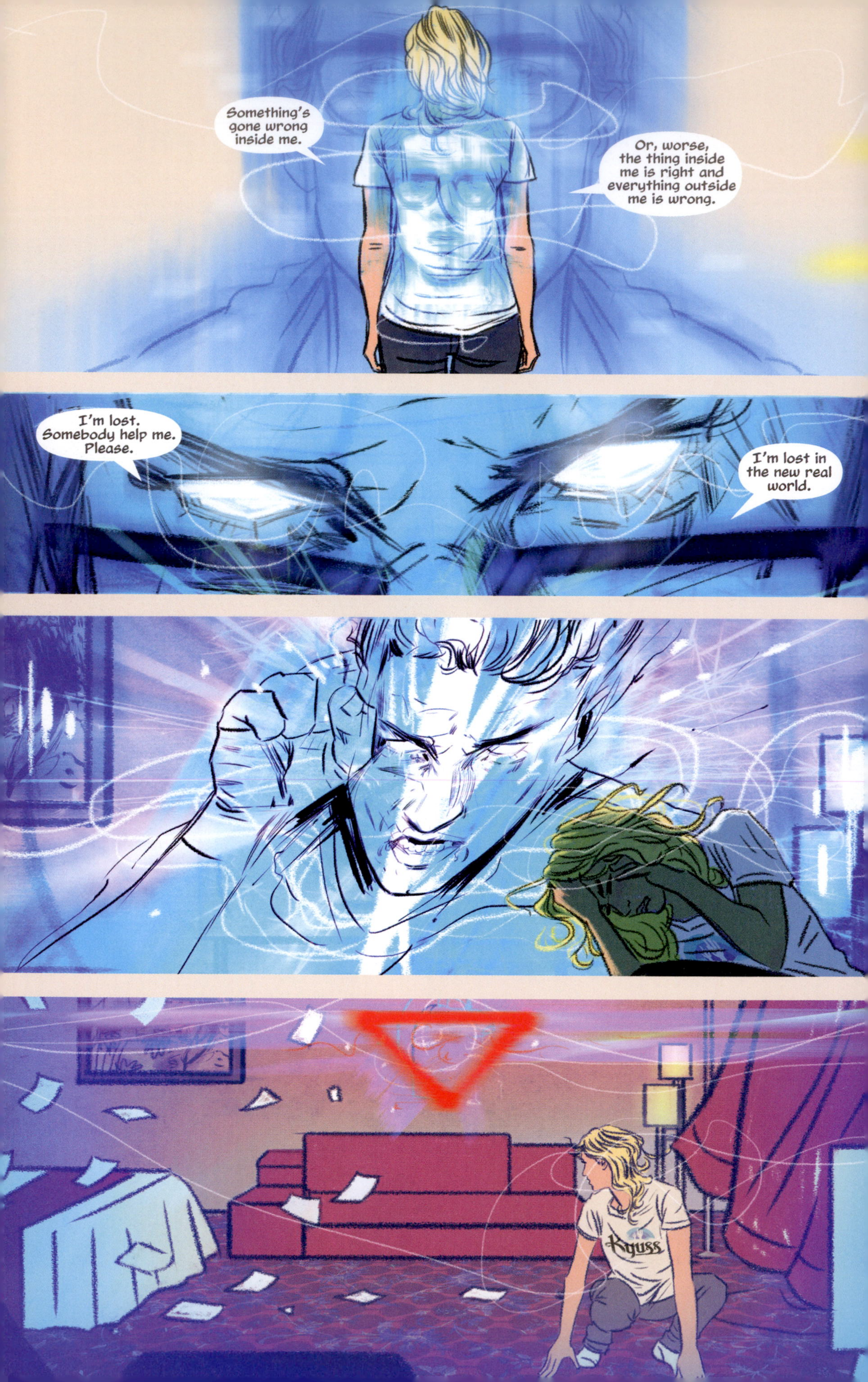
Something's gone wrong inside me.
Or, worse, the thing inside me is right and everything outside me is wrong.
I'm lost. Somebody help me. Please.
I'm lost in the new real world.
Kyuss

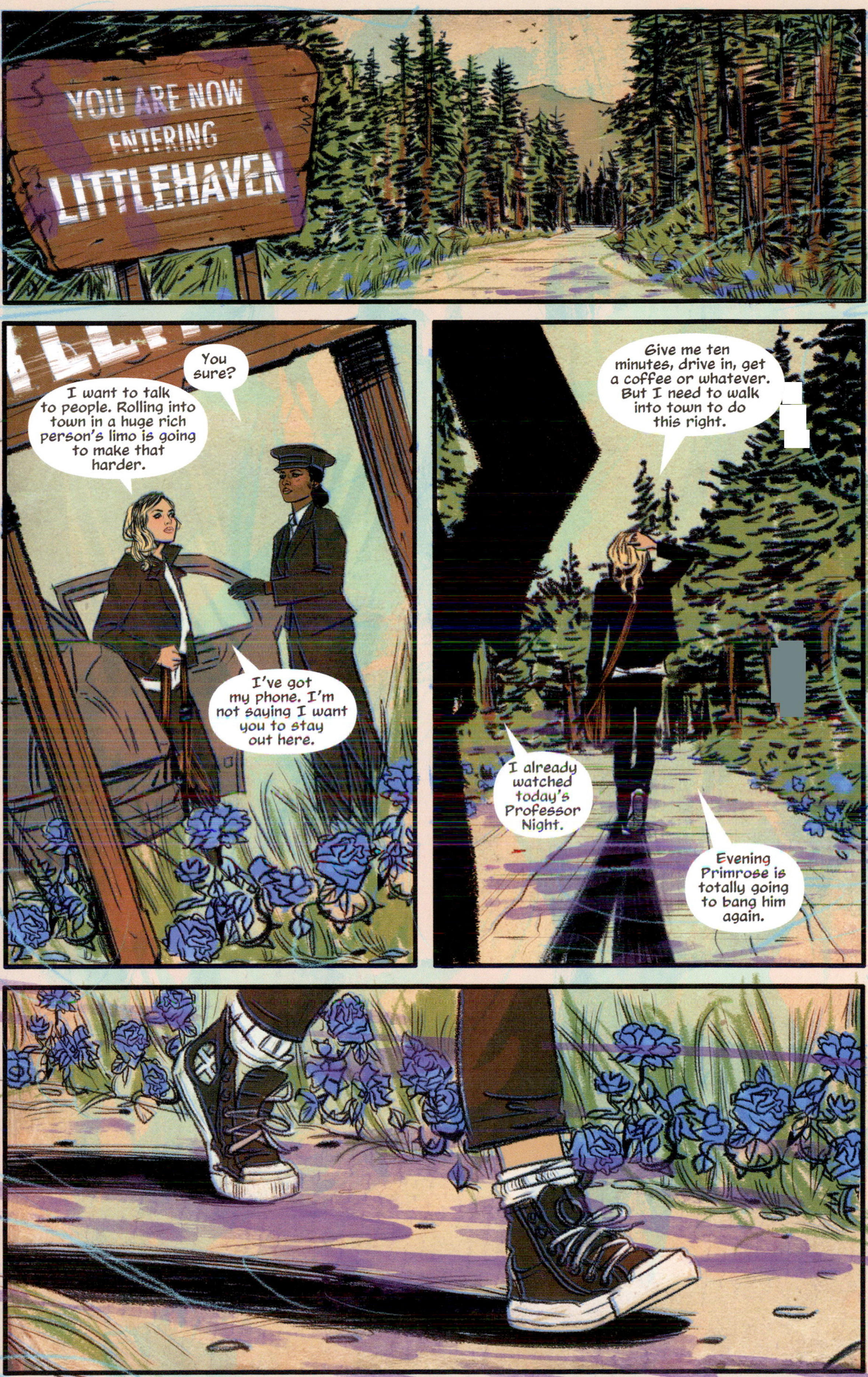
YOU ARE NOW ENTERING LITTLEHAVEN
I want to talk to people. Rolling into town in a huge rich person's limo is going to make that harder.
You sure?
I've got my phone. I'm not saying I want you to stay out here.
Give me ten minutes, drive in, get a coffee or whatever. But I need to walk into town to do this right.
I already watched today's Professor Night.
Evening Primrose is totally going to bang him again.

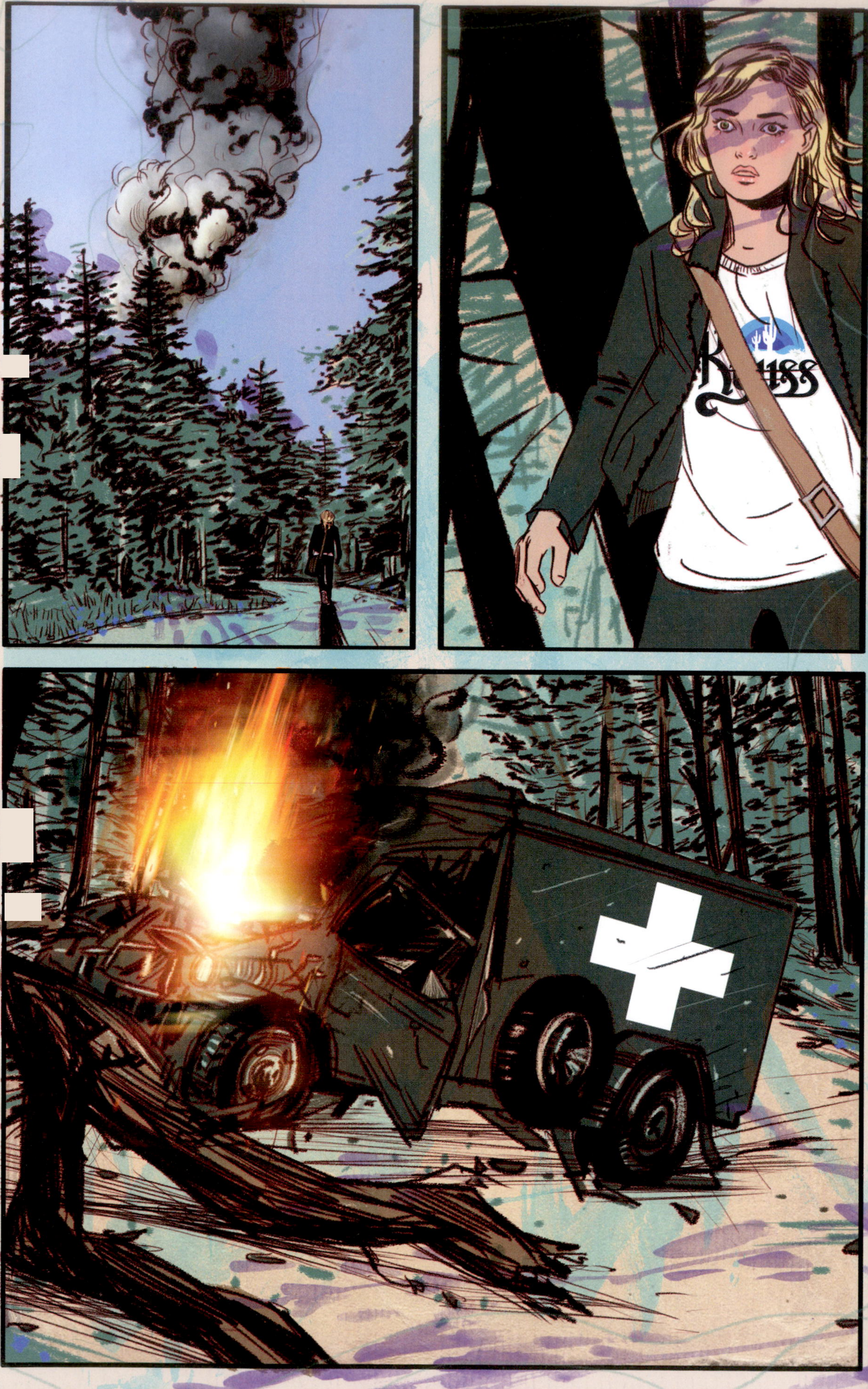

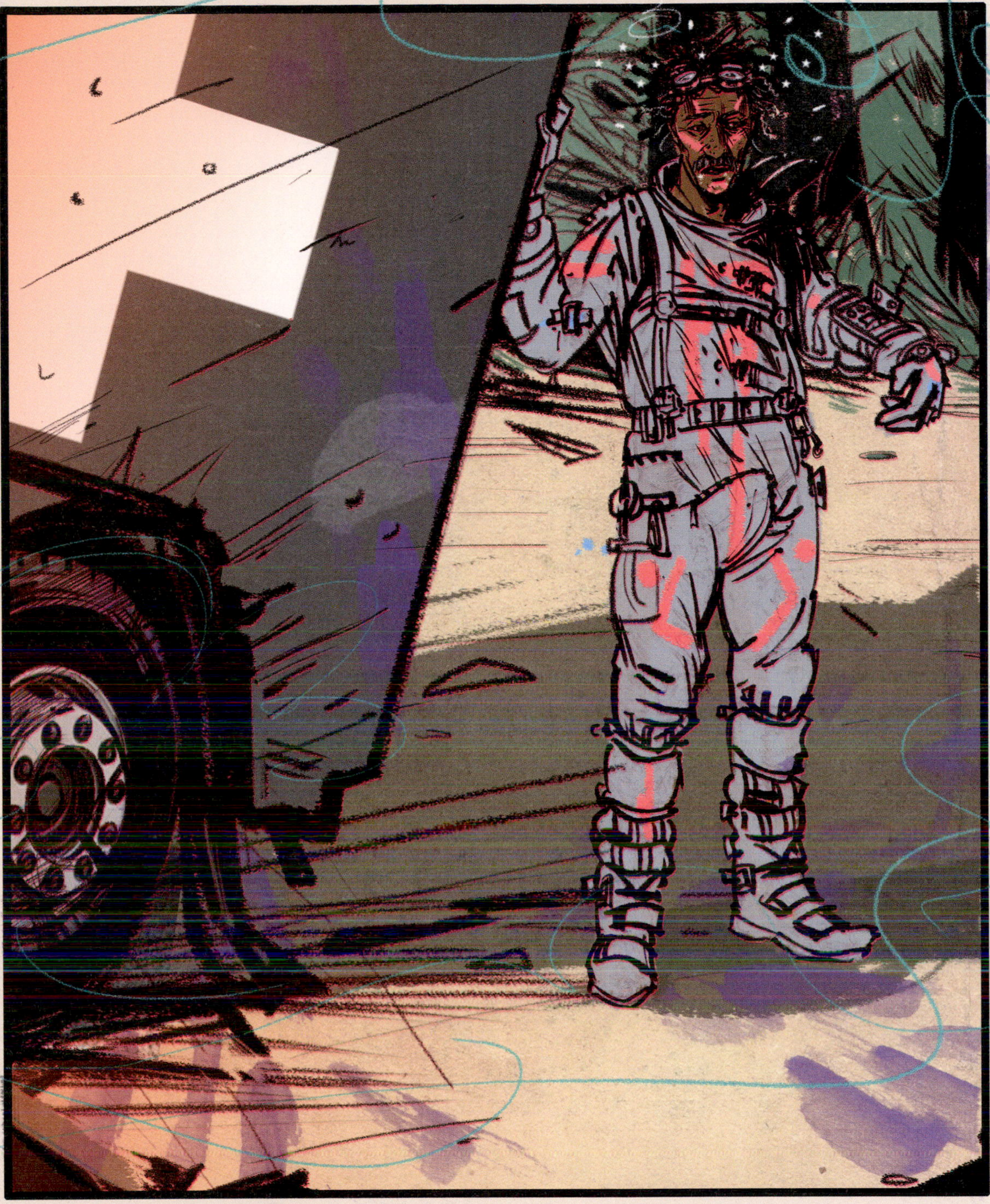
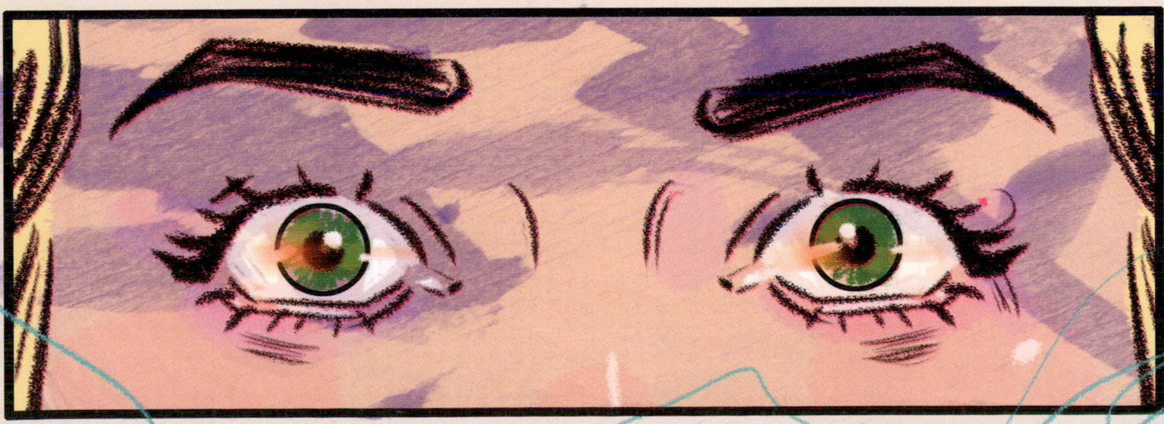

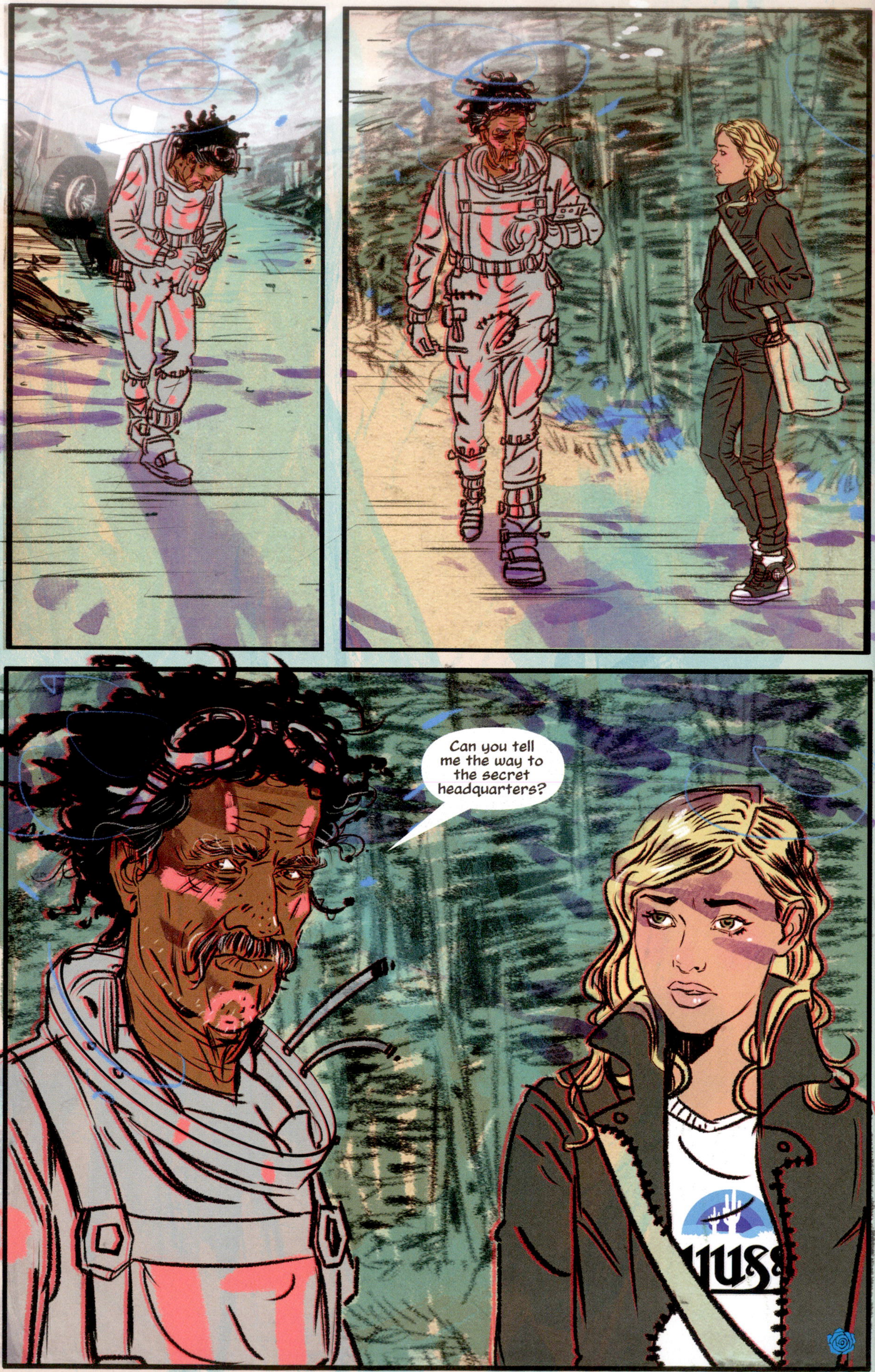
Can you tell me the way to the secret headquarters?

FOUR

"Time itself dies screaming."

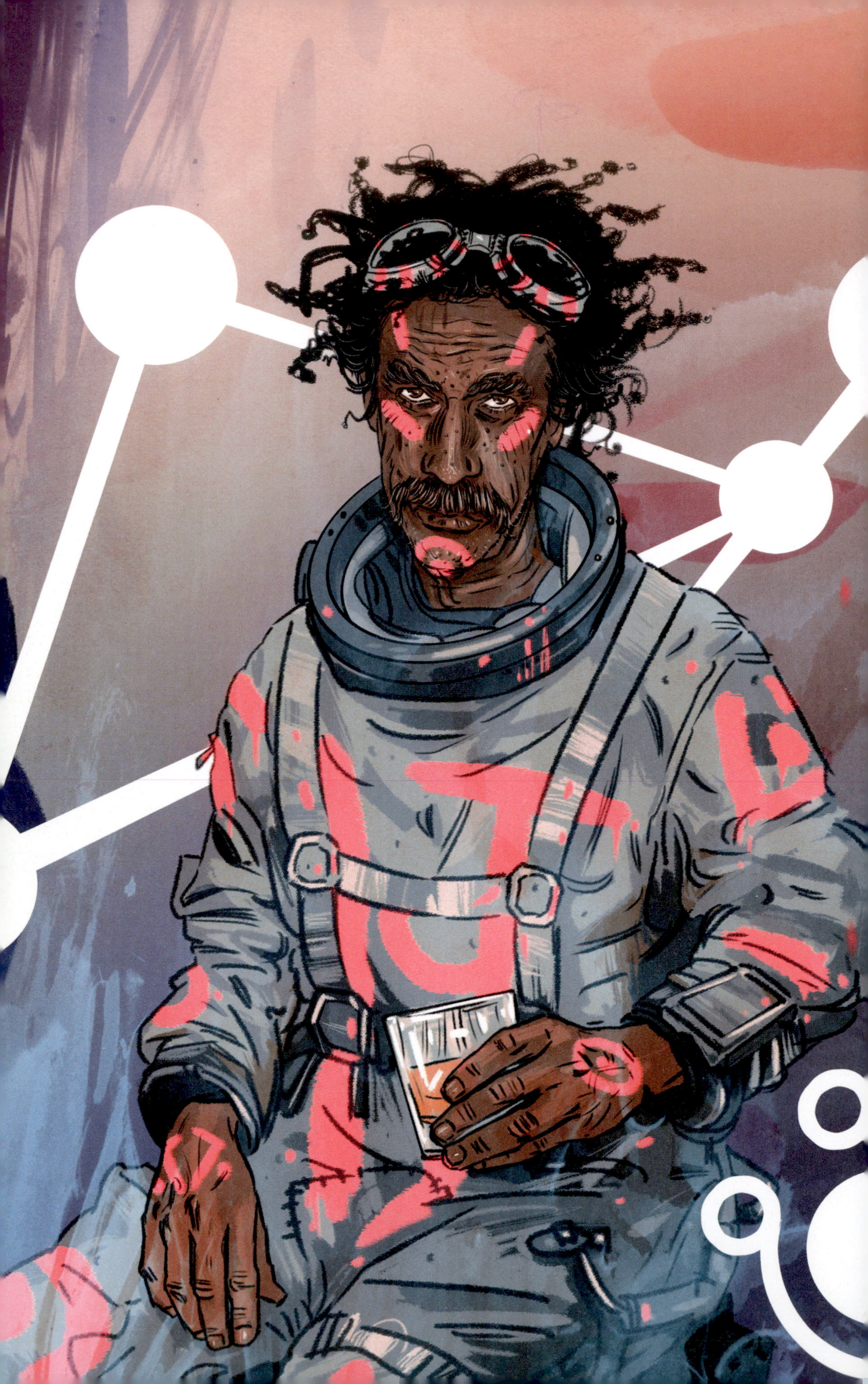

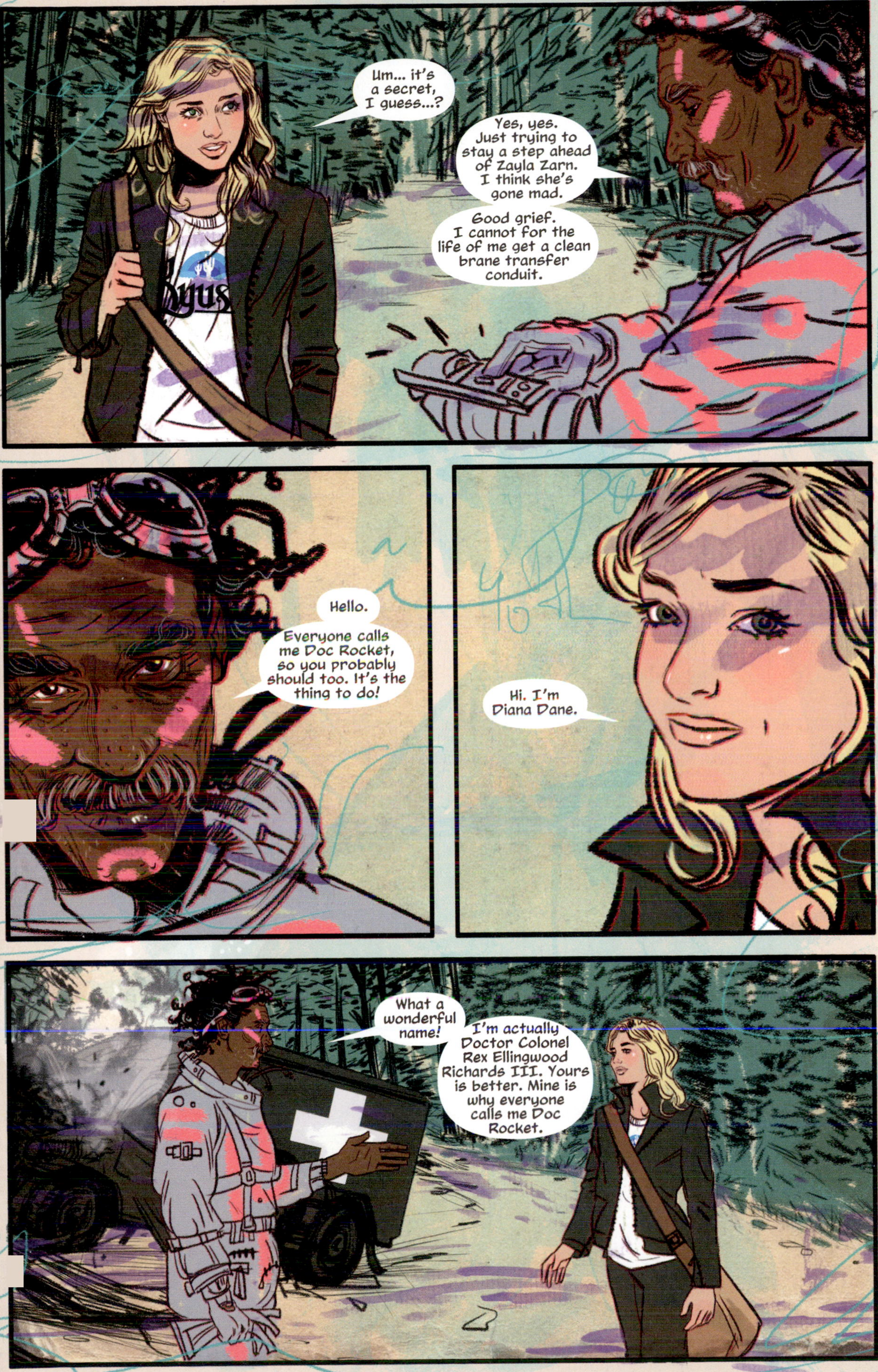

Um... it's a secret, I guess...?
Yes, yes. Just trying to stay a step ahead of Zayla Zarn. I think she's gone mad.
Good grief. I cannot for the life of me get a clean brane transfer conduit.
Hello.
Everyone calls me Doc Rocket, so you probably should too. It's the thing to do!
Hi. I'm Diana Dane.
What a wonderful name!
I'm actually Doctor Colonel Rex Ellingwood Richards III. Yours is better. Mine is why everyone calls me Doc Rocket.

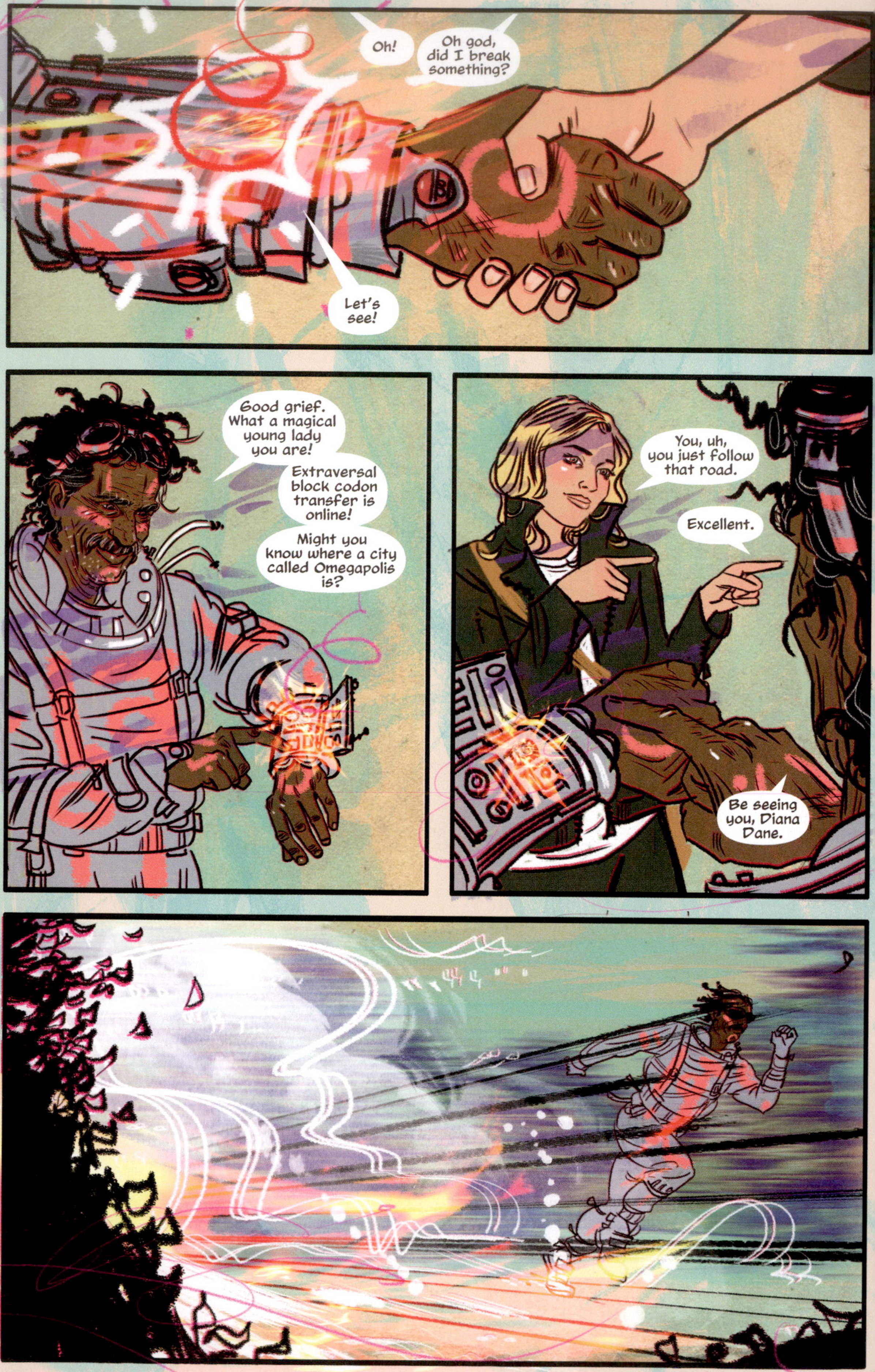
Oh!
Oh god, did I break something?
Let's see!
Good grief. What a magical young lady you are!
Extraversal block codon transfer is online!
Might you know where a city called Omegapolis is?
You, uh, you just follow that road.
Excellent.
Be seeing you, Diana Dane.

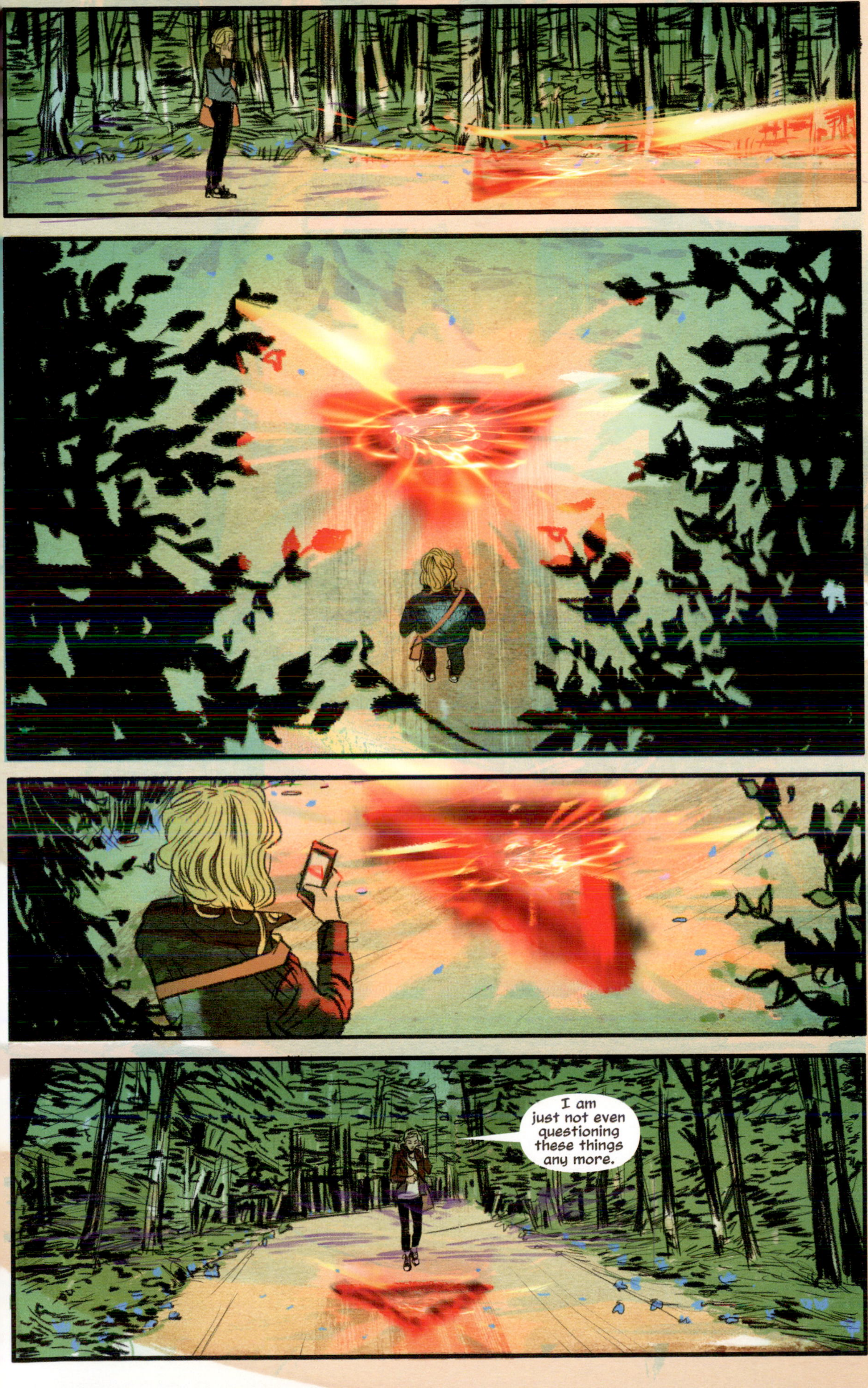
I am just not even questioning these things any more.

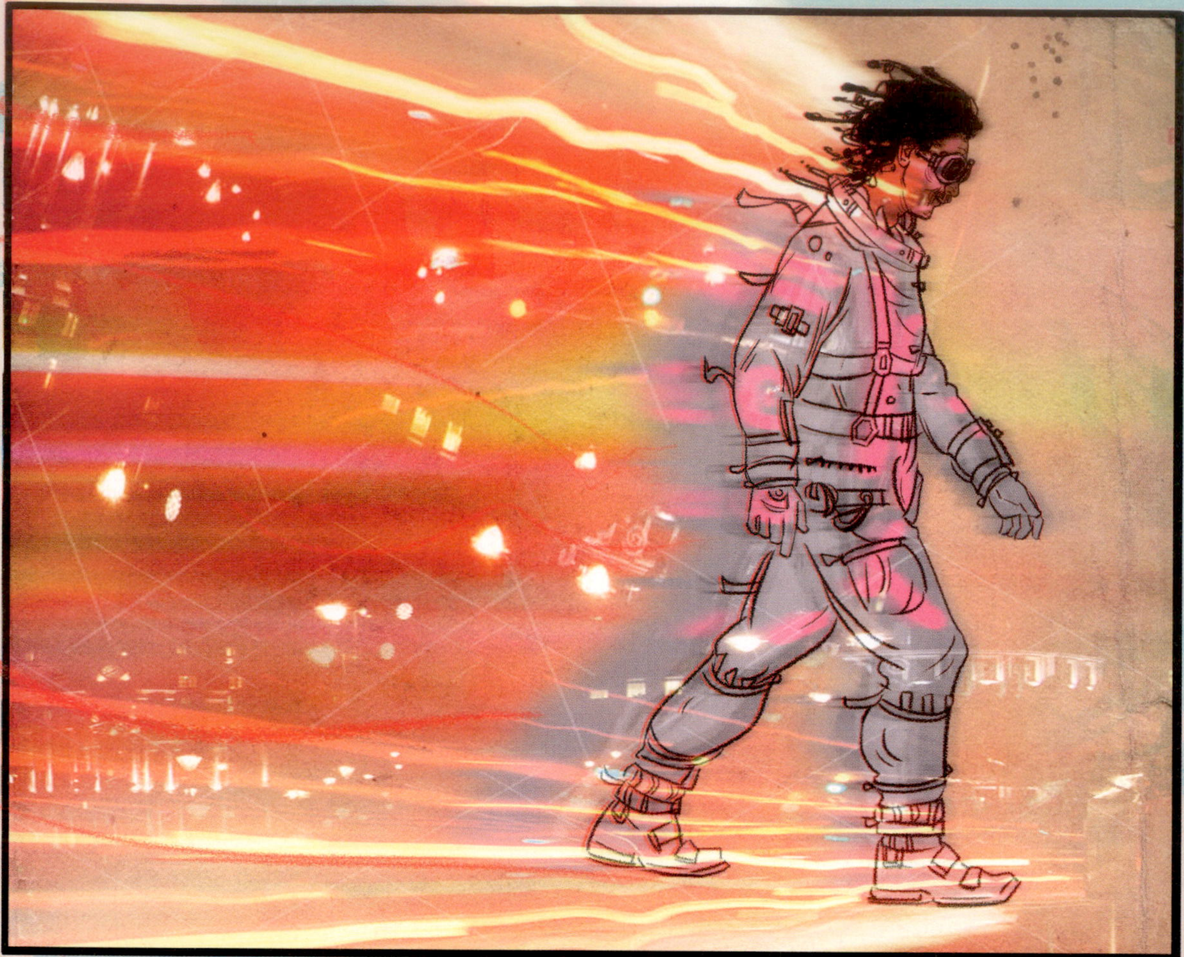

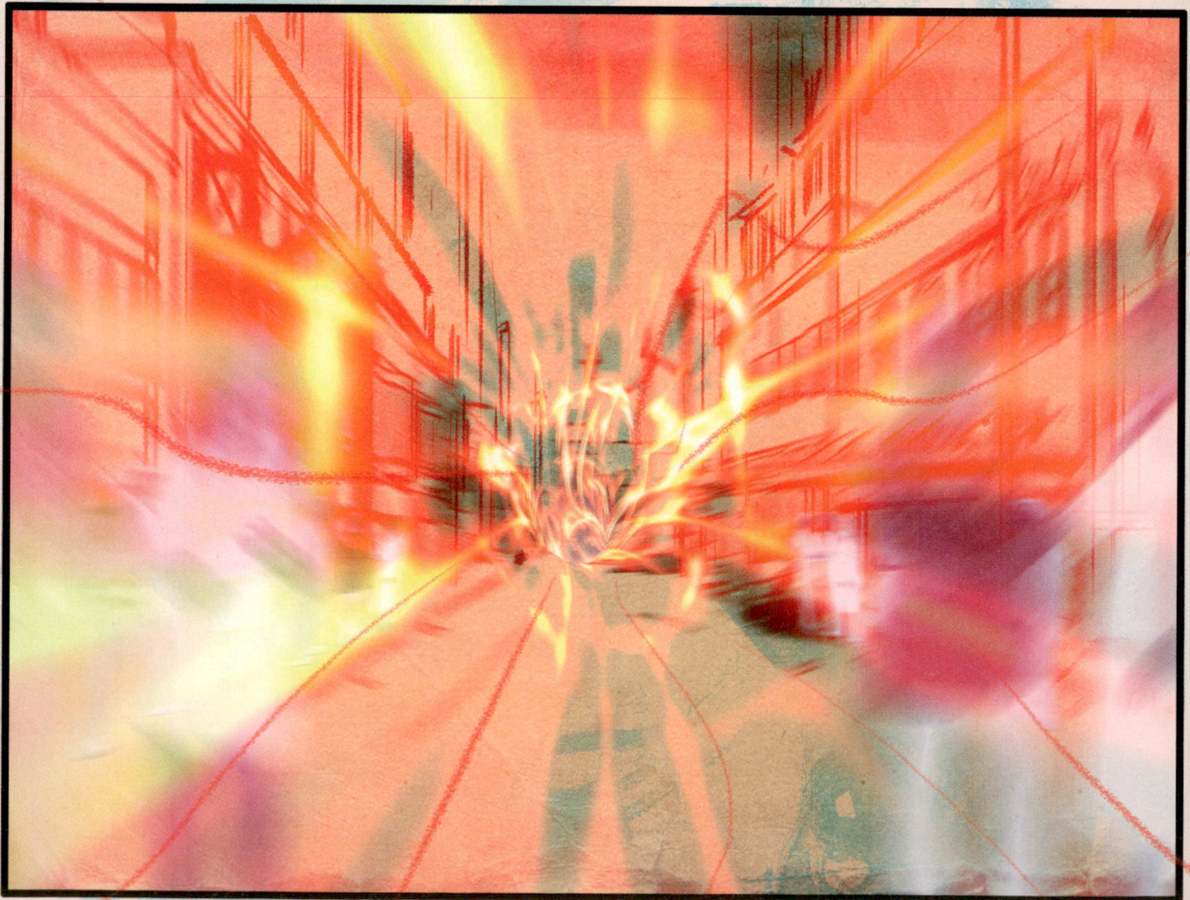

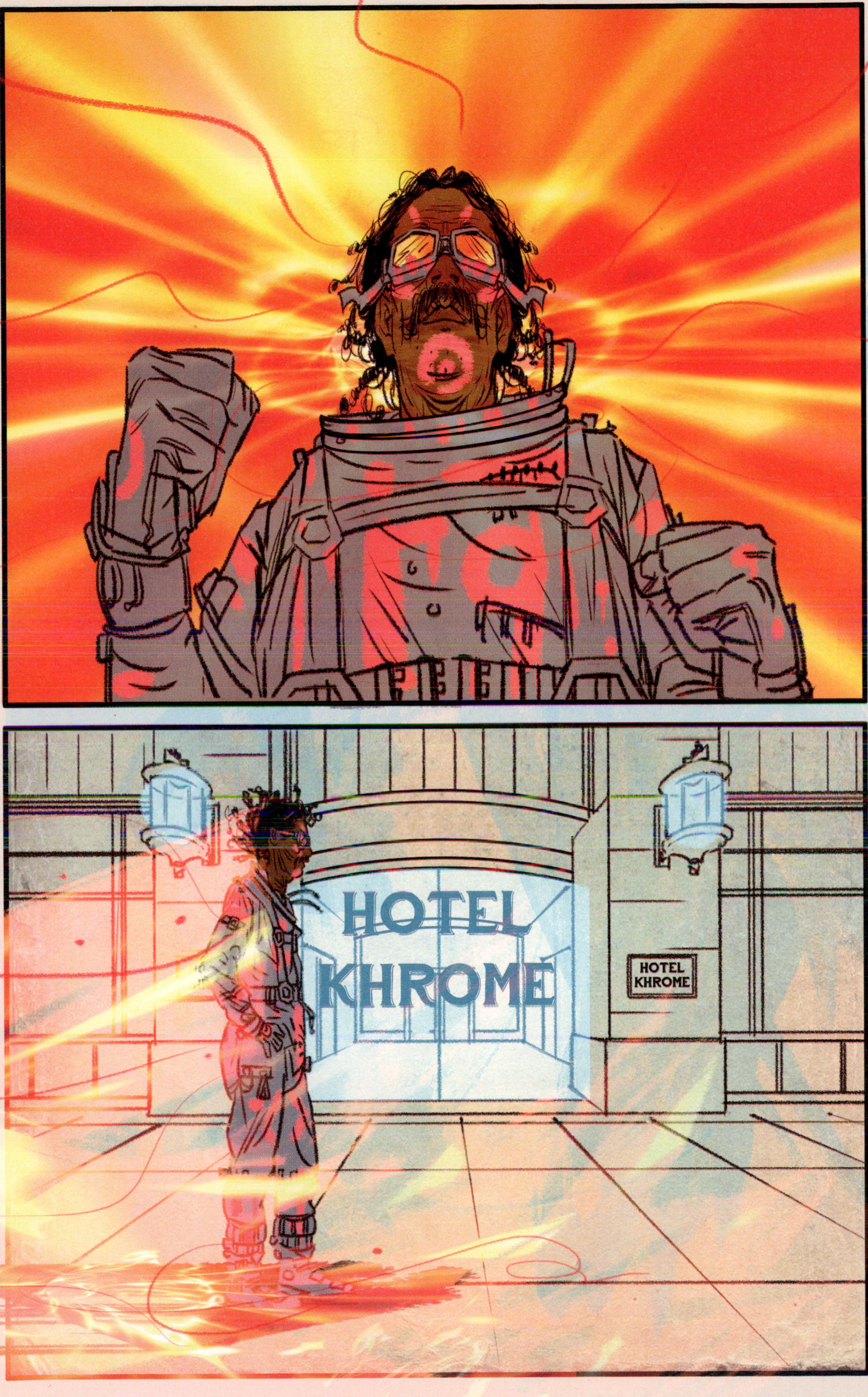
HOTEL
KHROME
HOTEL
KHROME

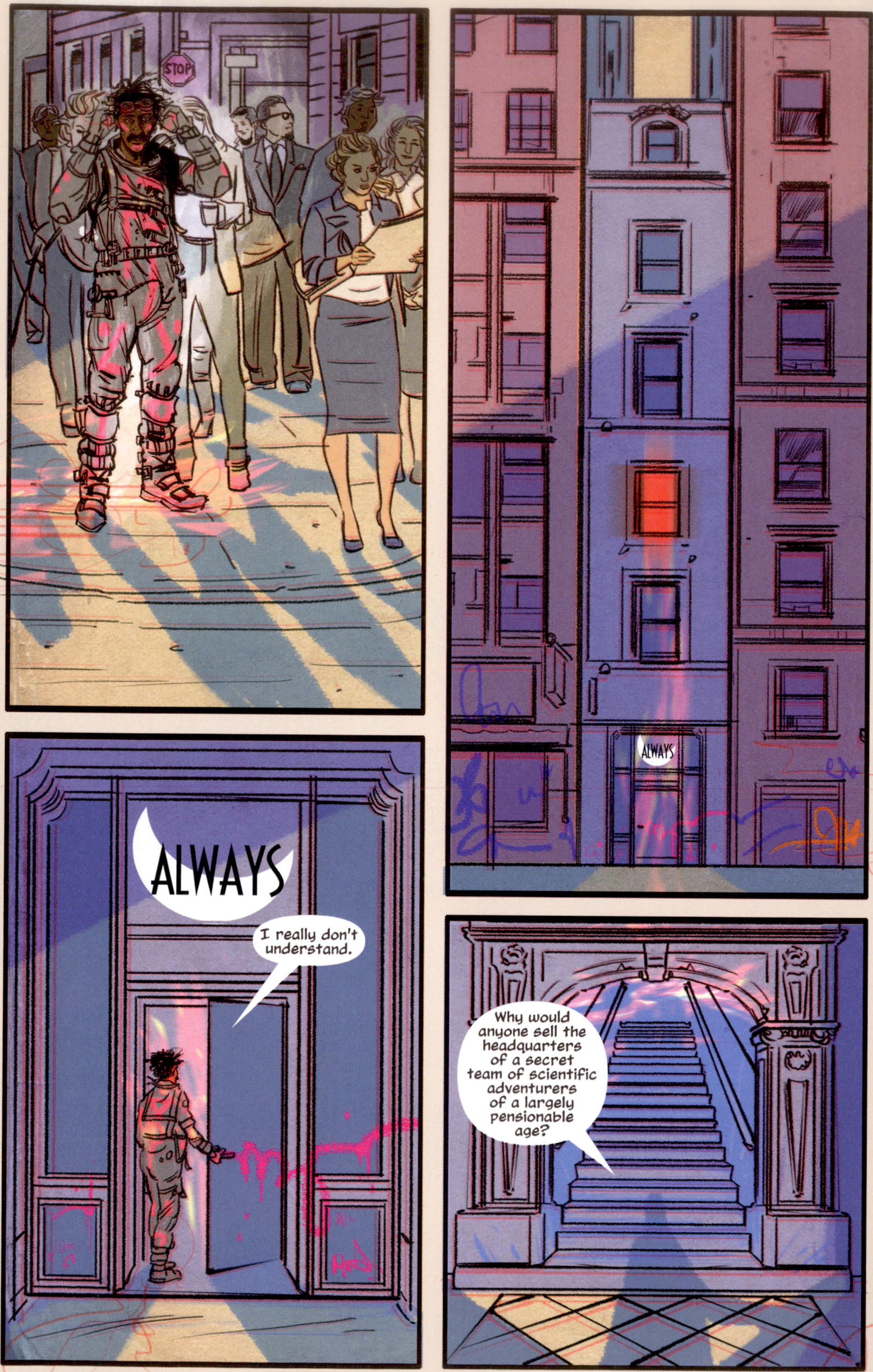

STOP
ALWAYS
ALWAYS
I really don't understand.
Why would anyone sell the headquarters of a secret team of scientific adventurers of a largely pensionable age?

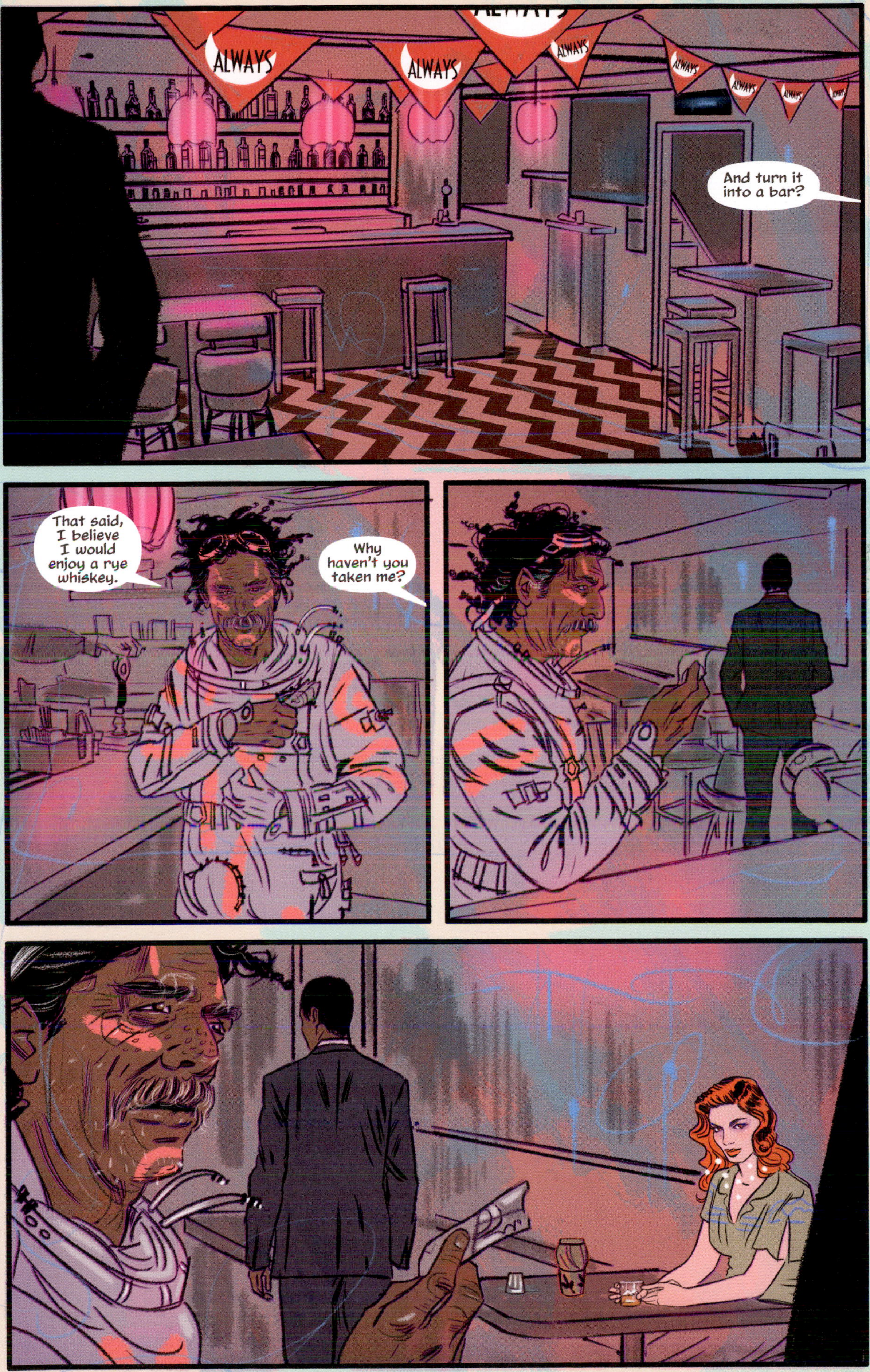
ALWAYS
ALWAYS
ALWAYS
ALWAYS
And turn it into a bar?
That said, I believe I would enjoy a rye whiskey.
Why haven't you taken me?

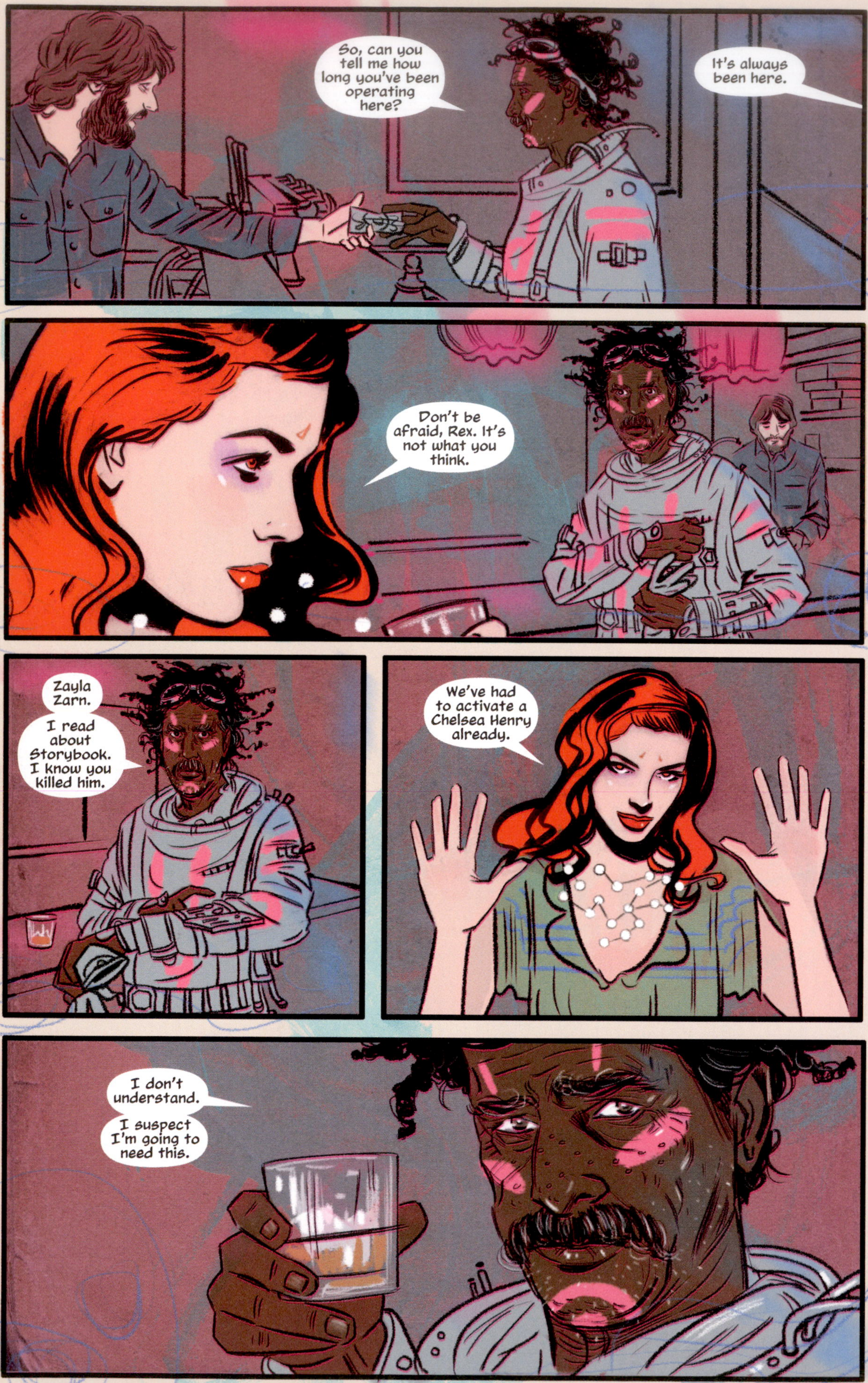

So, can you tell me how long you've been operating here?
It's always been here.
Don't be afraid, Rex. It's not what you think.
Zayla Zarn.
I read about Storybook. I know you killed him.
We've had to activate a Chelsea Henry already.
I don't understand.
I suspect I'm going to need this.

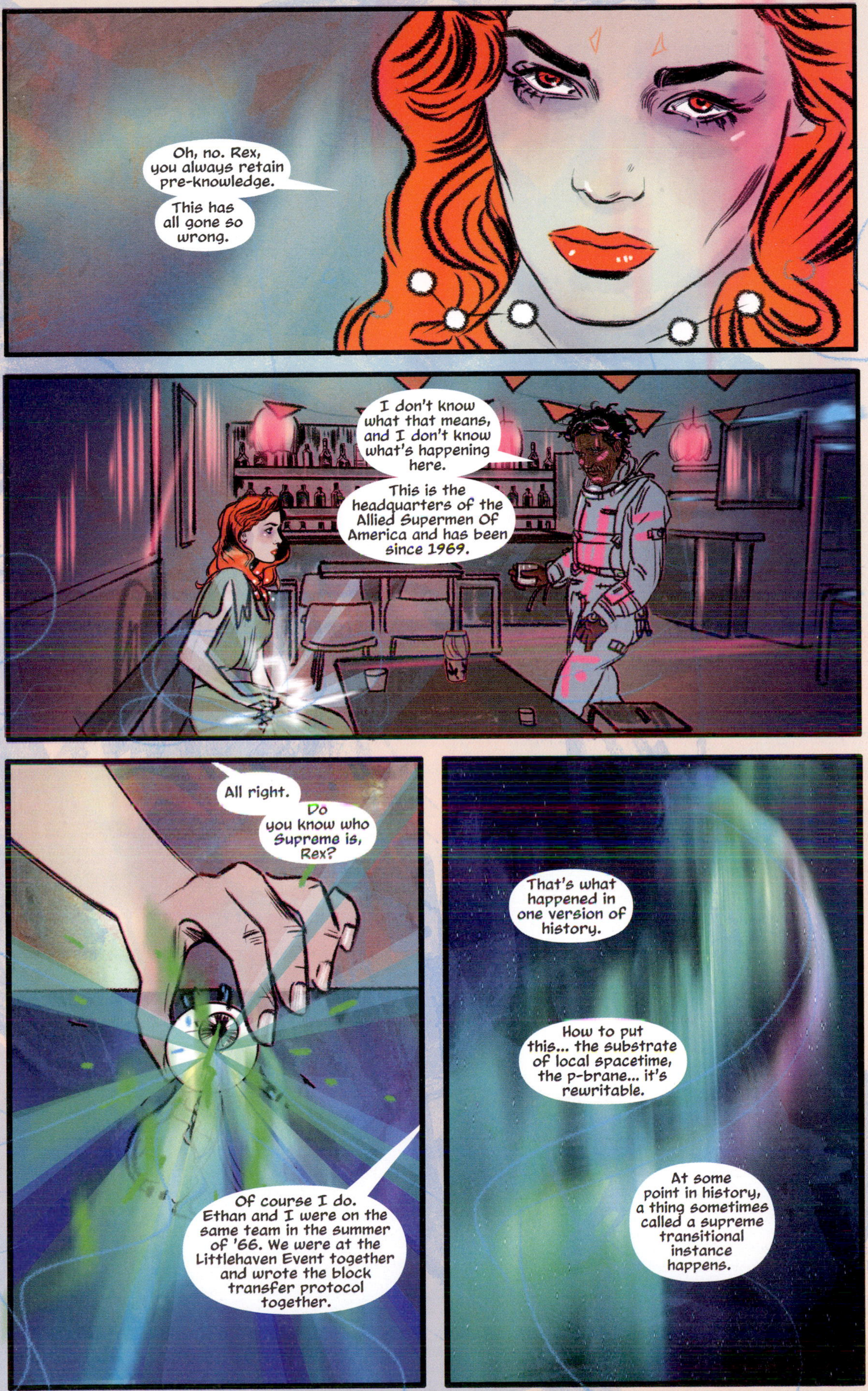

Oh, no. Rex, you always retain pre-knowledge.
This has all gone so wrong.
I don't know what that means, and I don't know what's happening here.
This is the headquarters of the Allied Supermen Of America and has been since 1969.
All right.
Do you know who Supreme is, Rex?
Of course I do. Ethan and I were on the same team in the summer of '66. We were at the Littlehaven Event together and wrote the block transfer protocol together.
That's what happened in one version of history.
How to put this... the substrate of local spacetime, the p-brane... it's rewritable.
At some point in history, a thing sometimes called a supreme transitional instance happens.

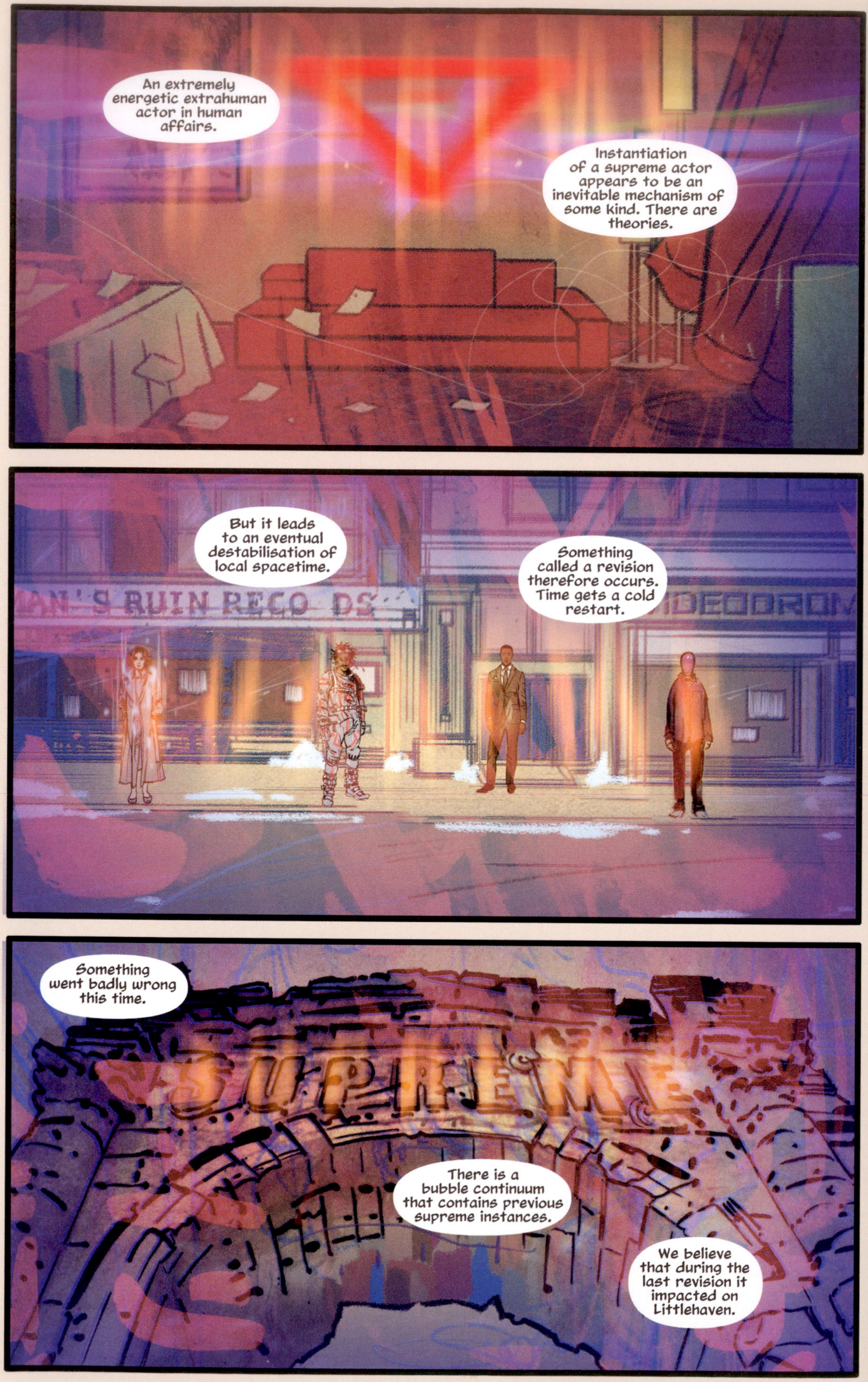

An extremely energetic extrahuman actor in human affairs.
Instantiation of a supreme actor appears to be an inevitable mechanism of some kind. There are theories.
But it leads to an eventual destabilisation of local spacetime.
Something called a revision therefore occurs. Time gets a cold restart.
Something went badly wrong this time.
SUPREME
There is a bubble continuum that contains previous supreme instances.
We believe that during the last revision it impacted on Littlehaven.

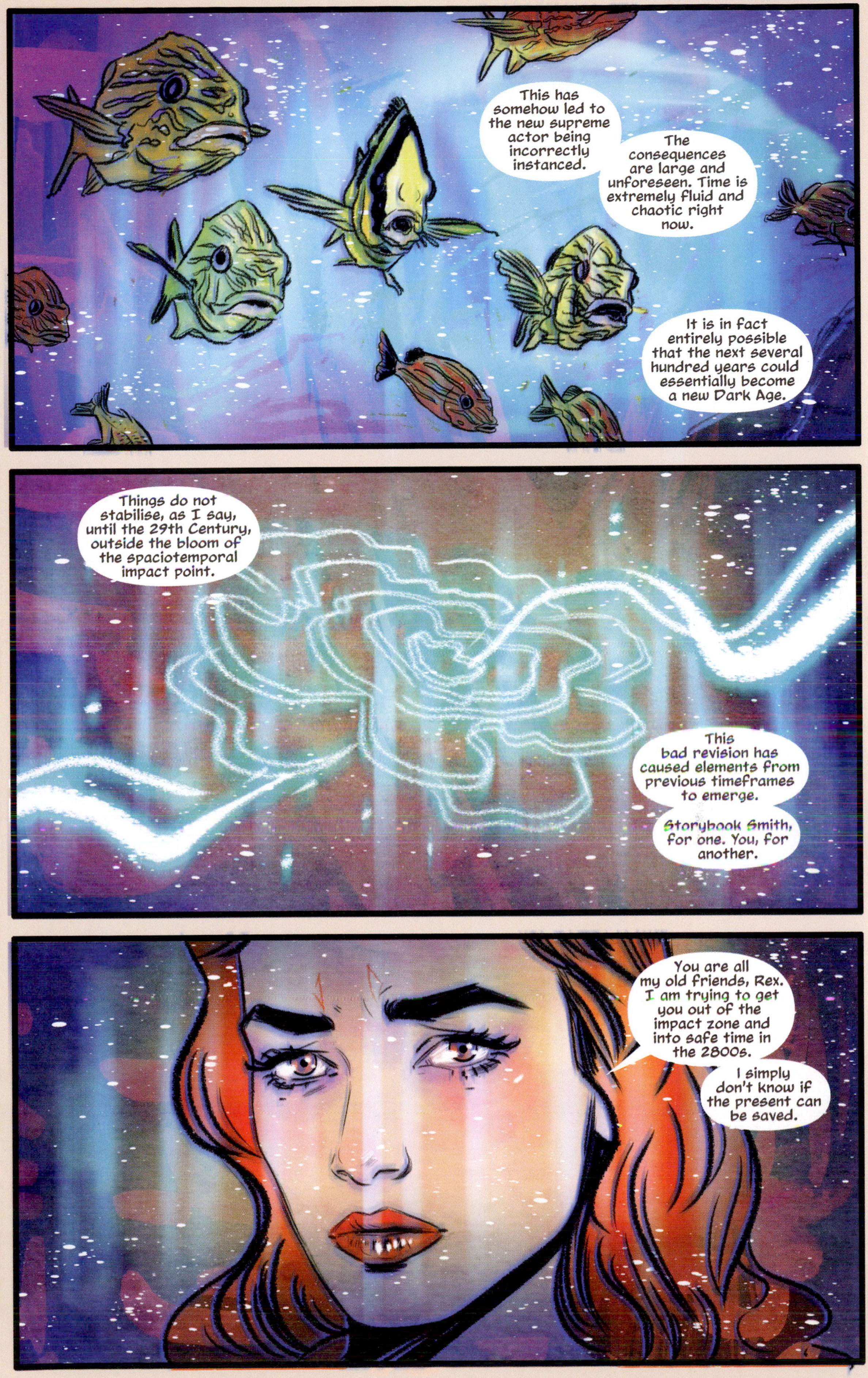
This has somehow led to the new supreme actor being incorrectly instanced.
The consequences are large and unforeseen. Time is extremely fluid and chaotic right now.
It is in fact entirely possible that the next several hundred years could essentially become a new Dark Age.
Things do not stabilise, as I say, until the 29th Century, outside the bloom of the spaciotemporal impact point.
This bad revision has caused elements from previous timeframes to emerge.
Storybook Smith, for one. You, for another.
You are all my old friends, Rex. I am trying to get you out of the impact zone and into safe time in the 2800s.
I simply don't know if the present can be saved.

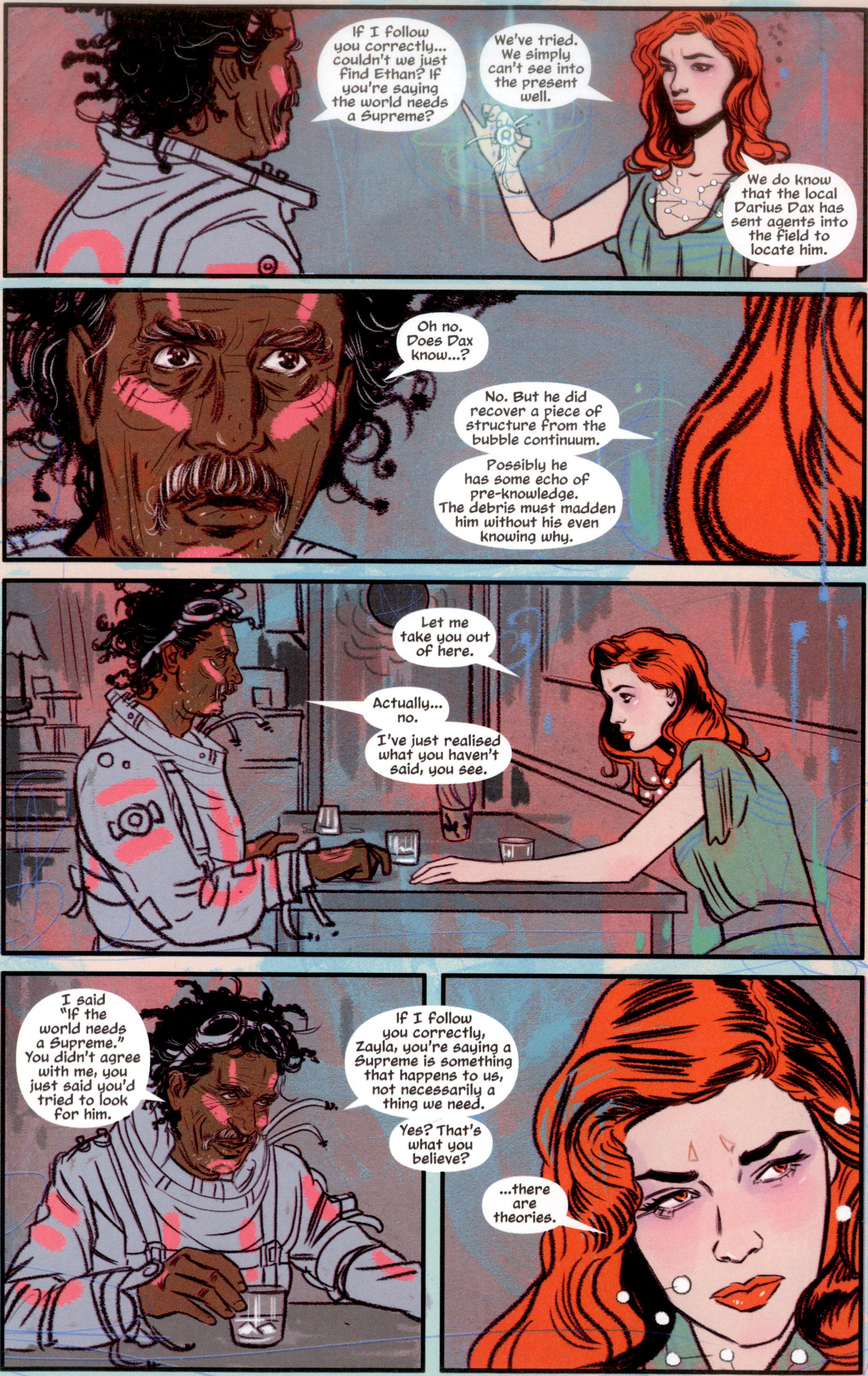
If I follow you correctly... couldn't we just find Ethan? If you're saying the world needs a Supreme?
We've tried. We simply can't see into the present well.
We do know that the local Darius Dax has sent agents into the field to locate him.
Oh no. Does Dax know...?
No. But he did recover a piece of structure from the bubble continuum.
Possibly he has some echo of pre-knowledge. The debris must madden him without his even knowing why.
Let me take you out of here.
Actually... no.
I've just realised what you haven't said, you see.
I said "If the world needs a Supreme." You didn't agree with me, you just said you'd tried to look for him.
If I follow you correctly, Zayla, you're saying a Supreme is something that happens to us, not necessarily a thing we need.
Yes? That's what you believe?
...there are theories.

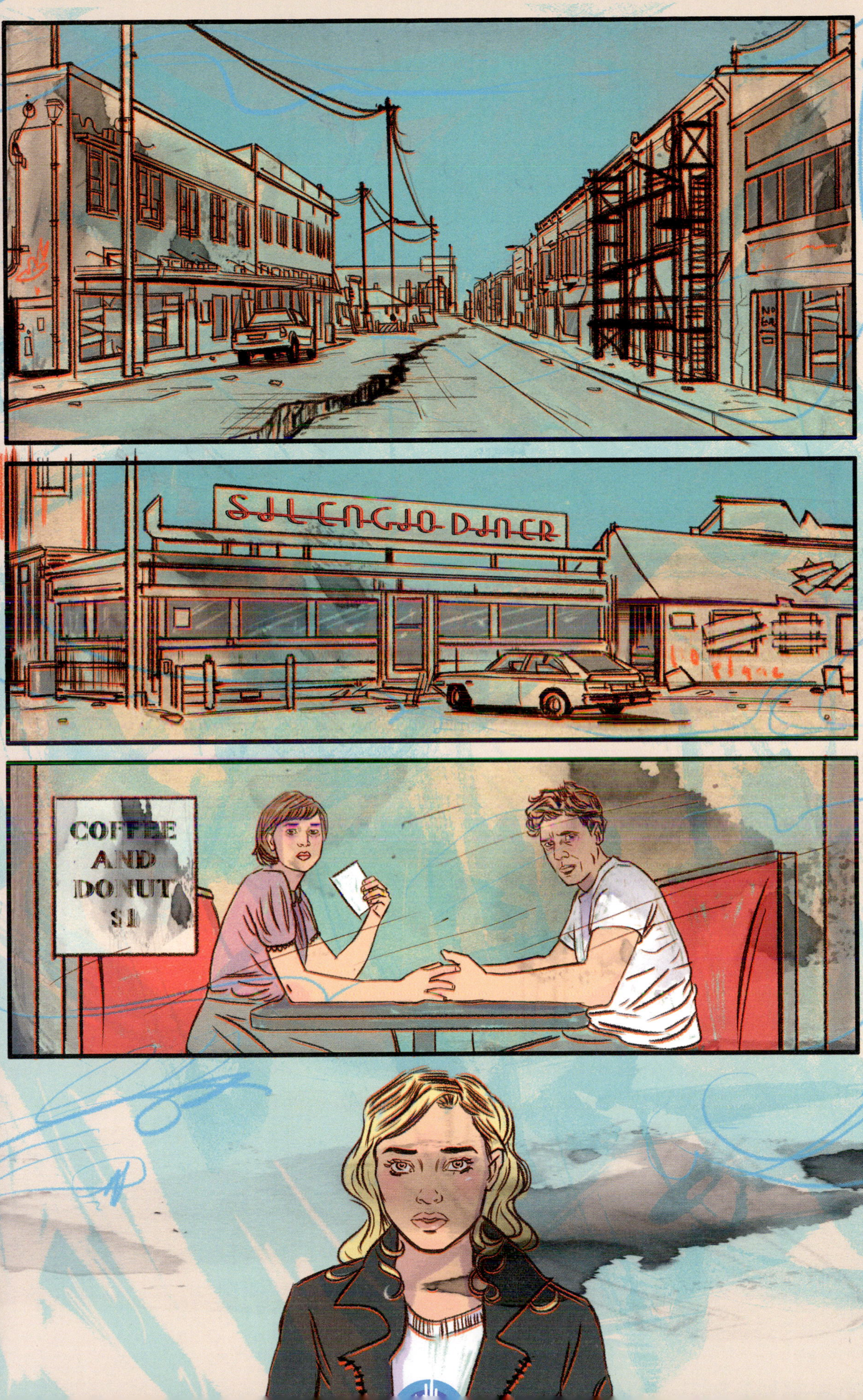
SILENCIO DINER
COFFEE AND DONUT $1

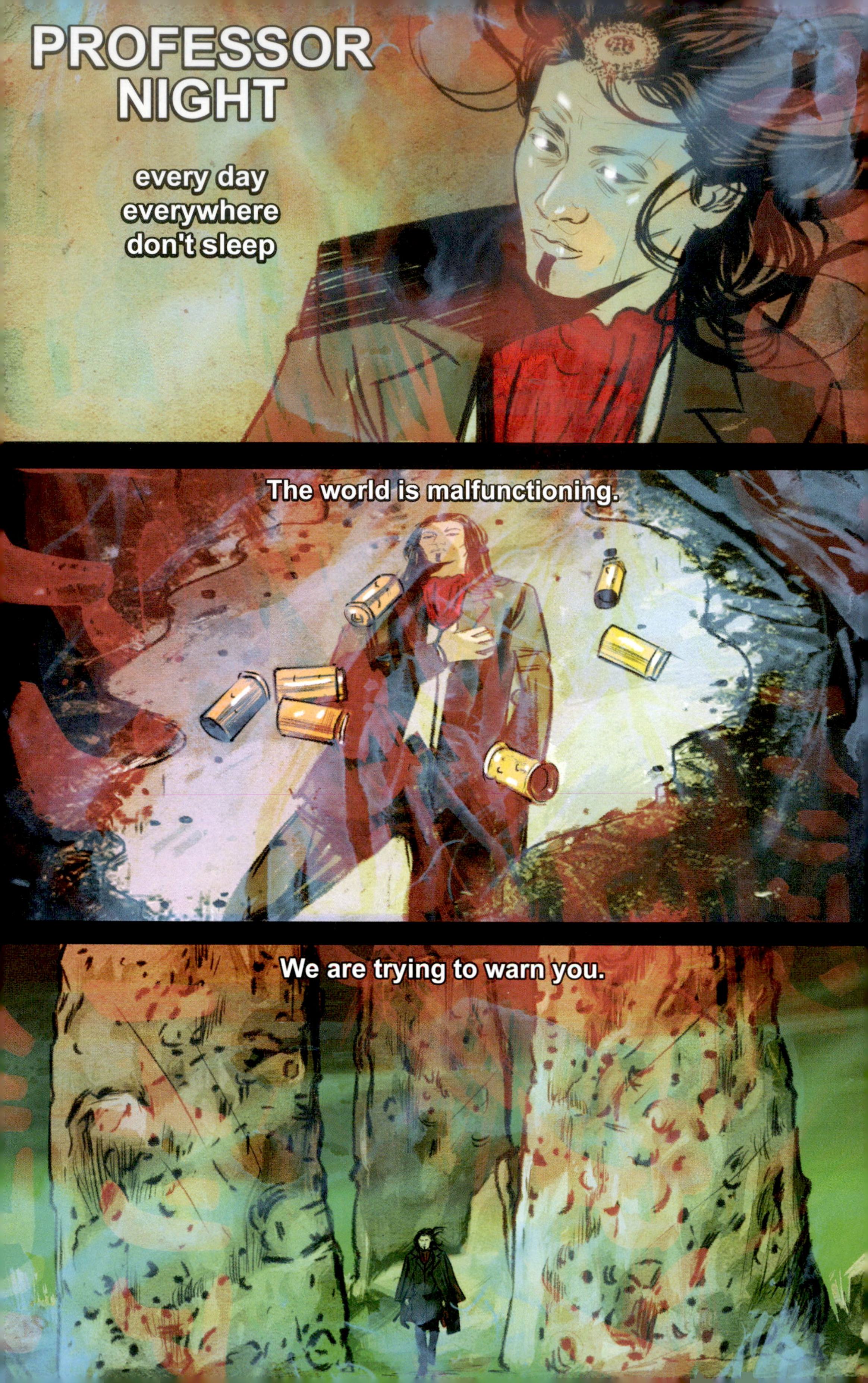
PROFESSOR NIGHT
every day
everywhere
don't sleep
The world is malfunctioning.
We are trying to warn you.

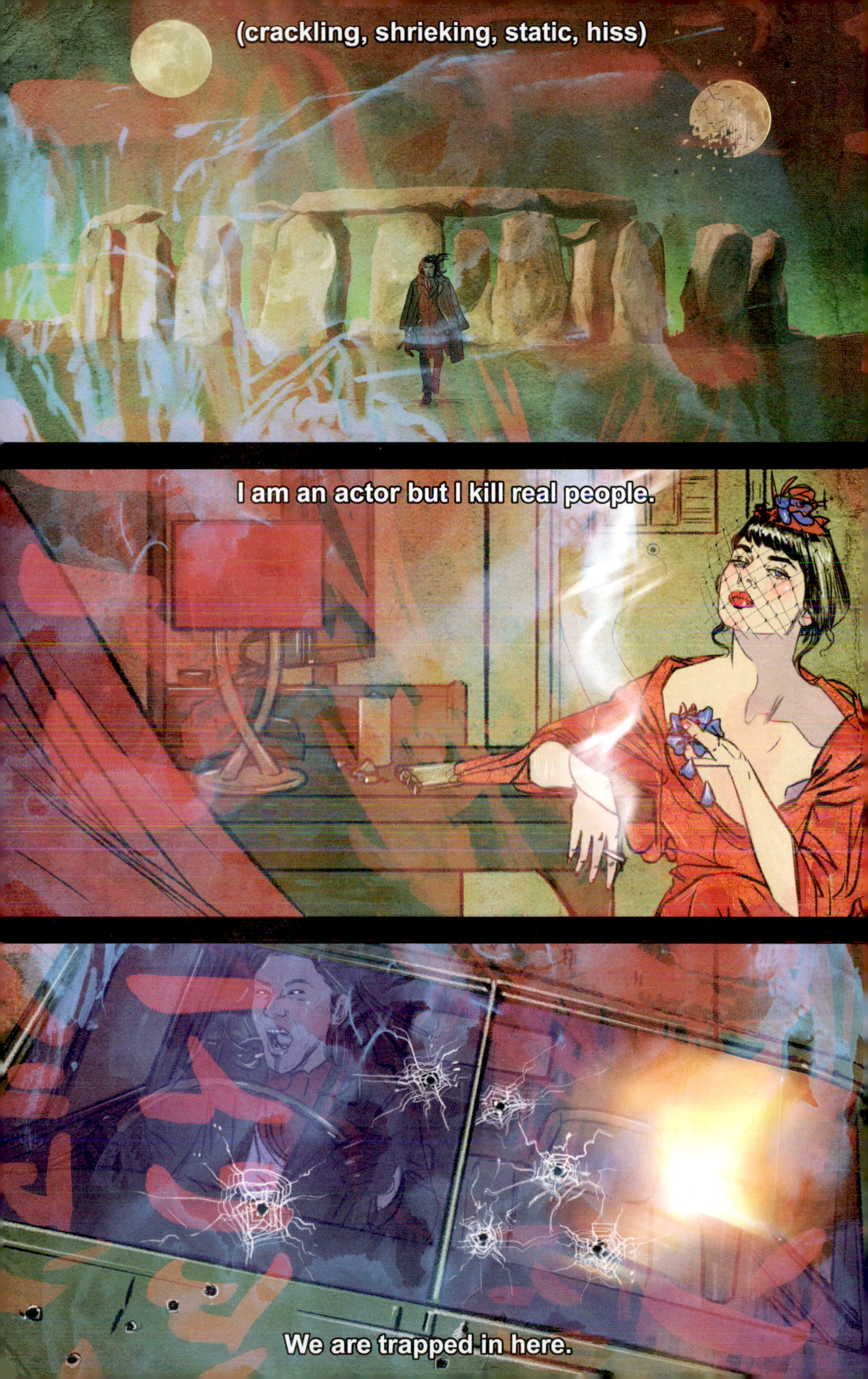
(crackling, shrieking, static, hiss)
I am an actor but I kill real people.
We are trapped in here.

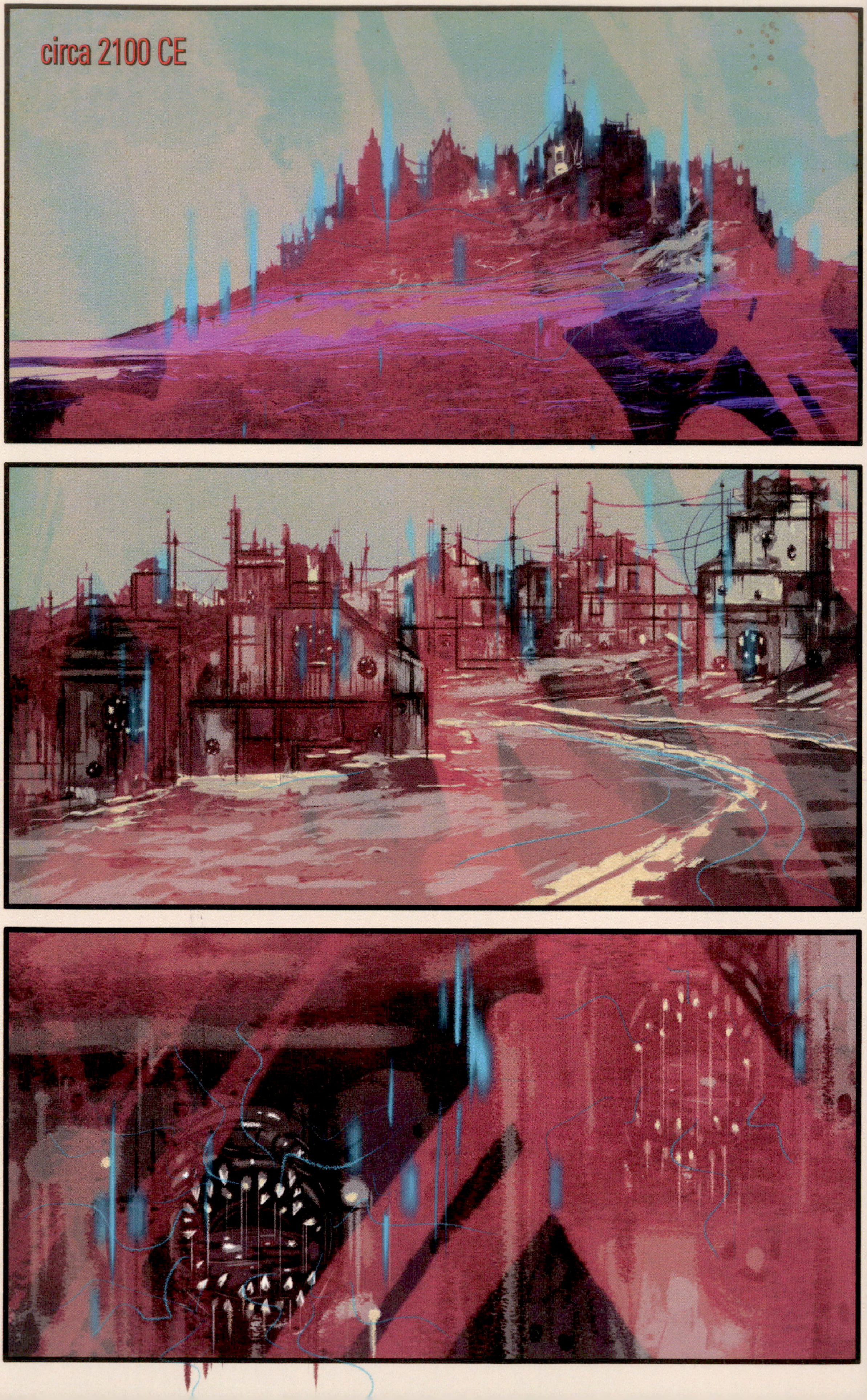
circa 2100 CE

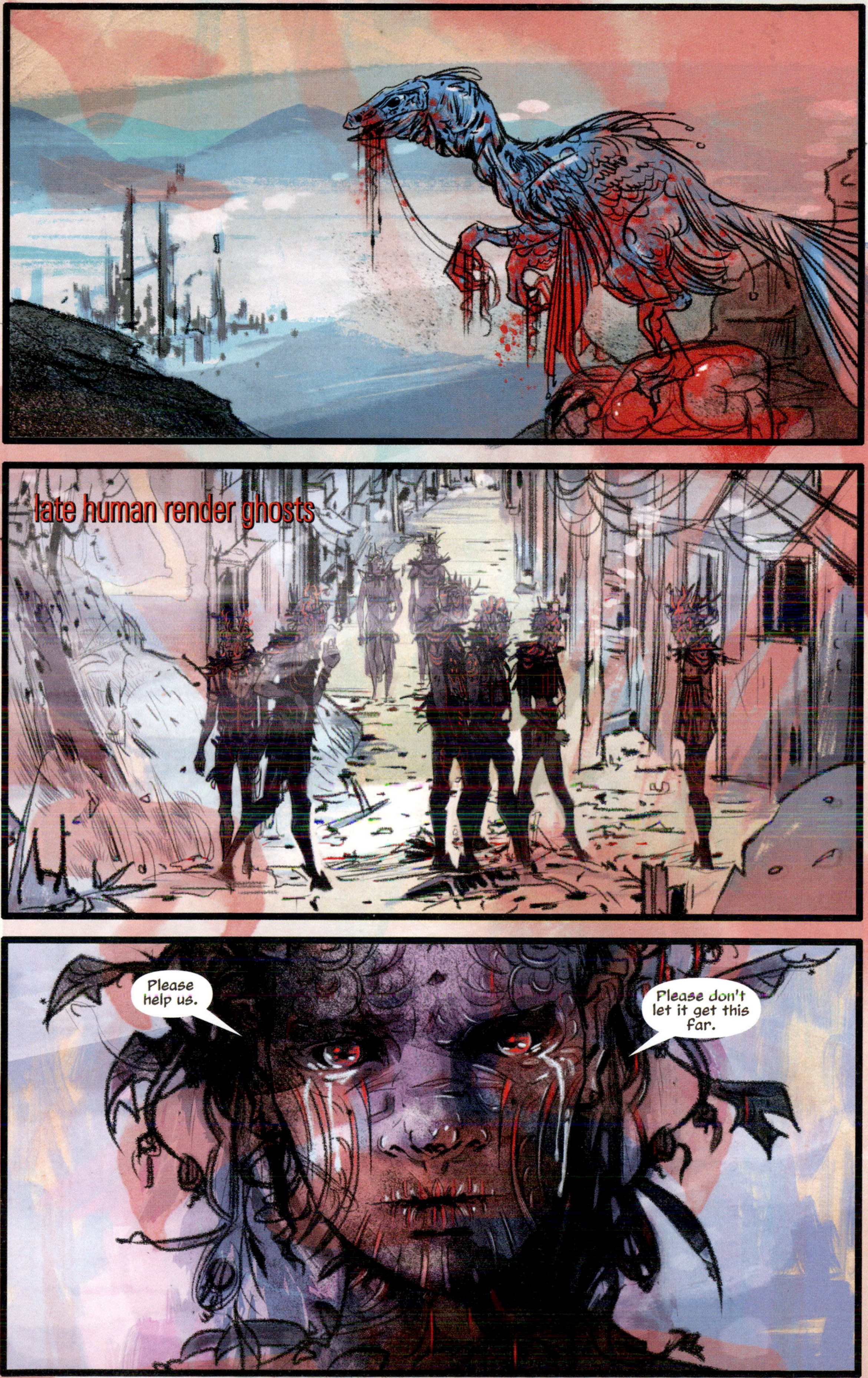
late human render ghosts
Please help us.
Please don't let it get this far.

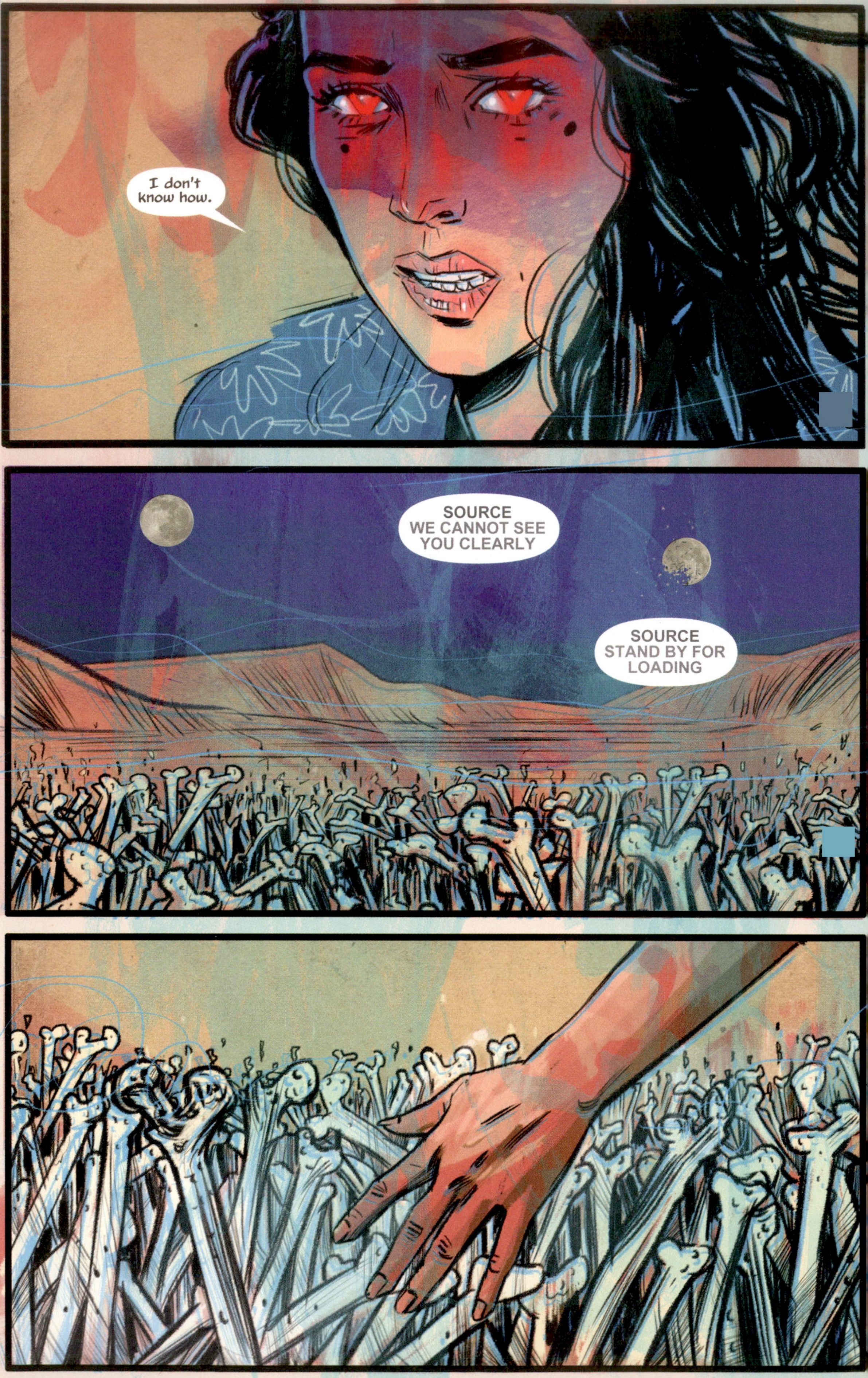
I don't know how.
SOURCE WE CANNOT SEE YOU CLEARLY
SOURCE STAND BY FOR LOADING

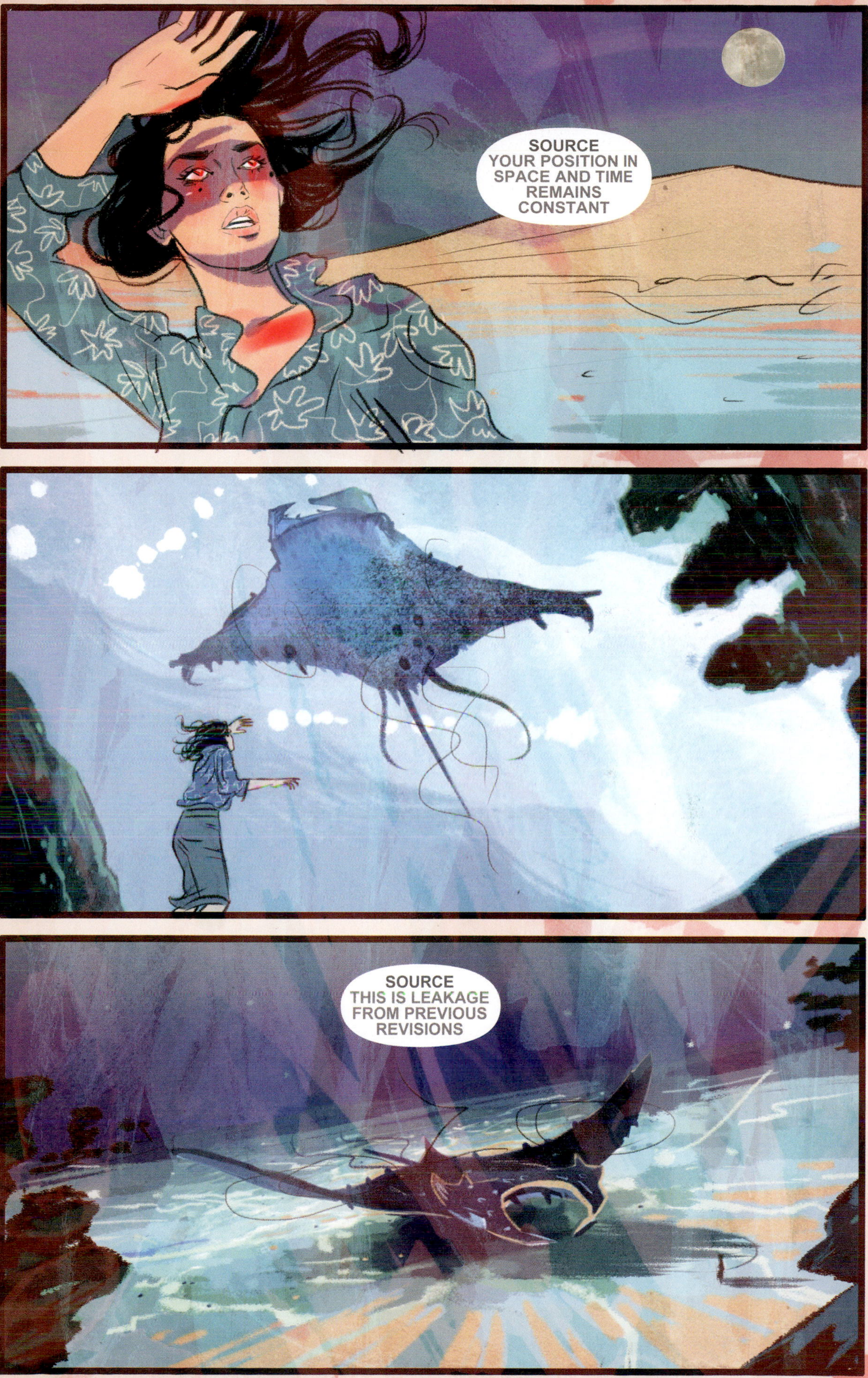
SOURCE
YOUR POSITION IN SPACE AND TIME REMAINS CONSTANT
SOURCE
THIS IS LEAKAGE FROM PREVIOUS REVISIONS

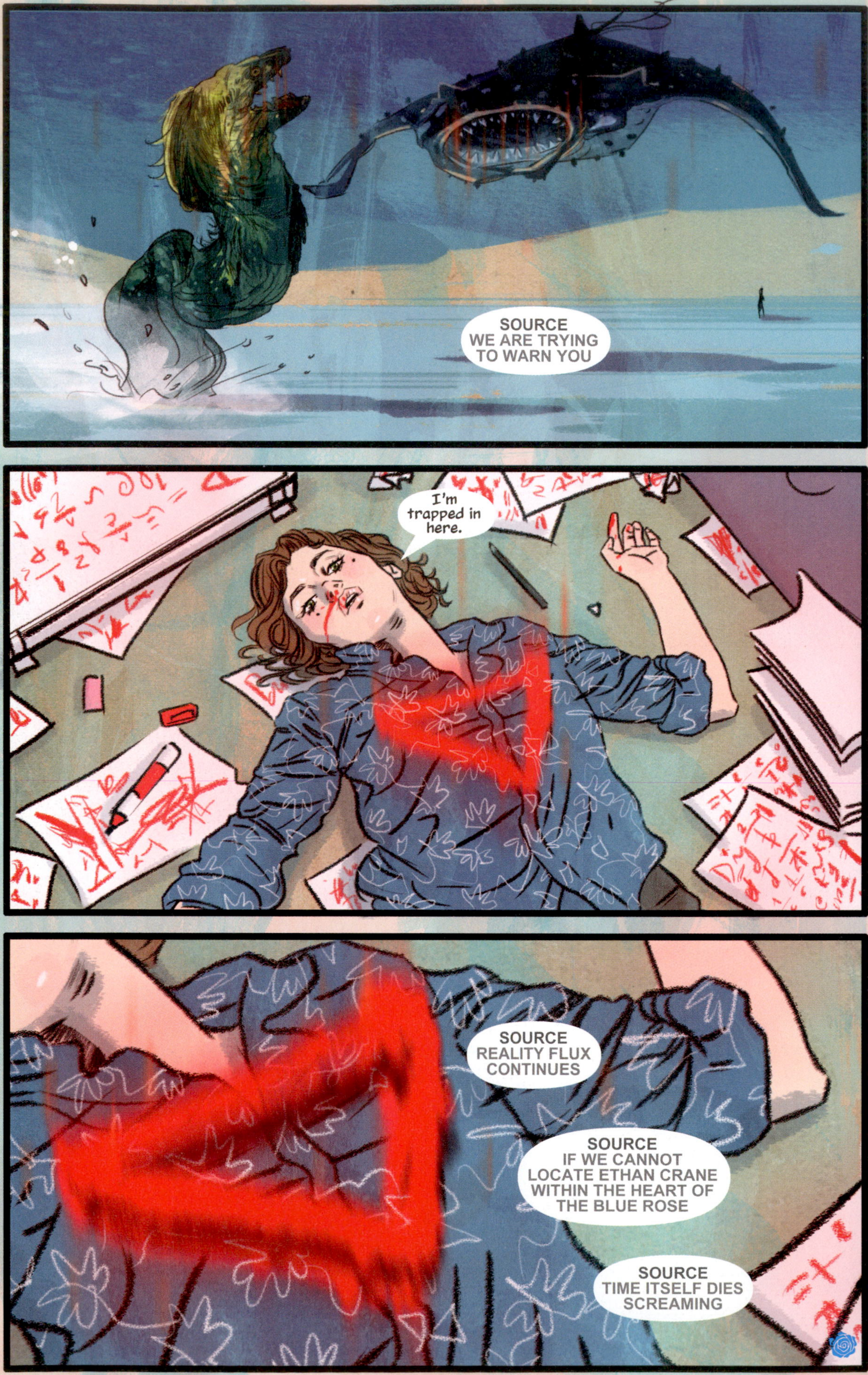
SOURCE WE ARE TRYING TO WARN YOU
I'm trapped in here.
SOURCE REALITY FLUX CONTINUES
SOURCE IF WE CANNOT LOCATE ETHAN CRANE WITHIN THE HEART OF THE BLUE ROSE
SOURCE TIME ITSELF DIES SCREAMING

"Recursive human pupa."

FIVE

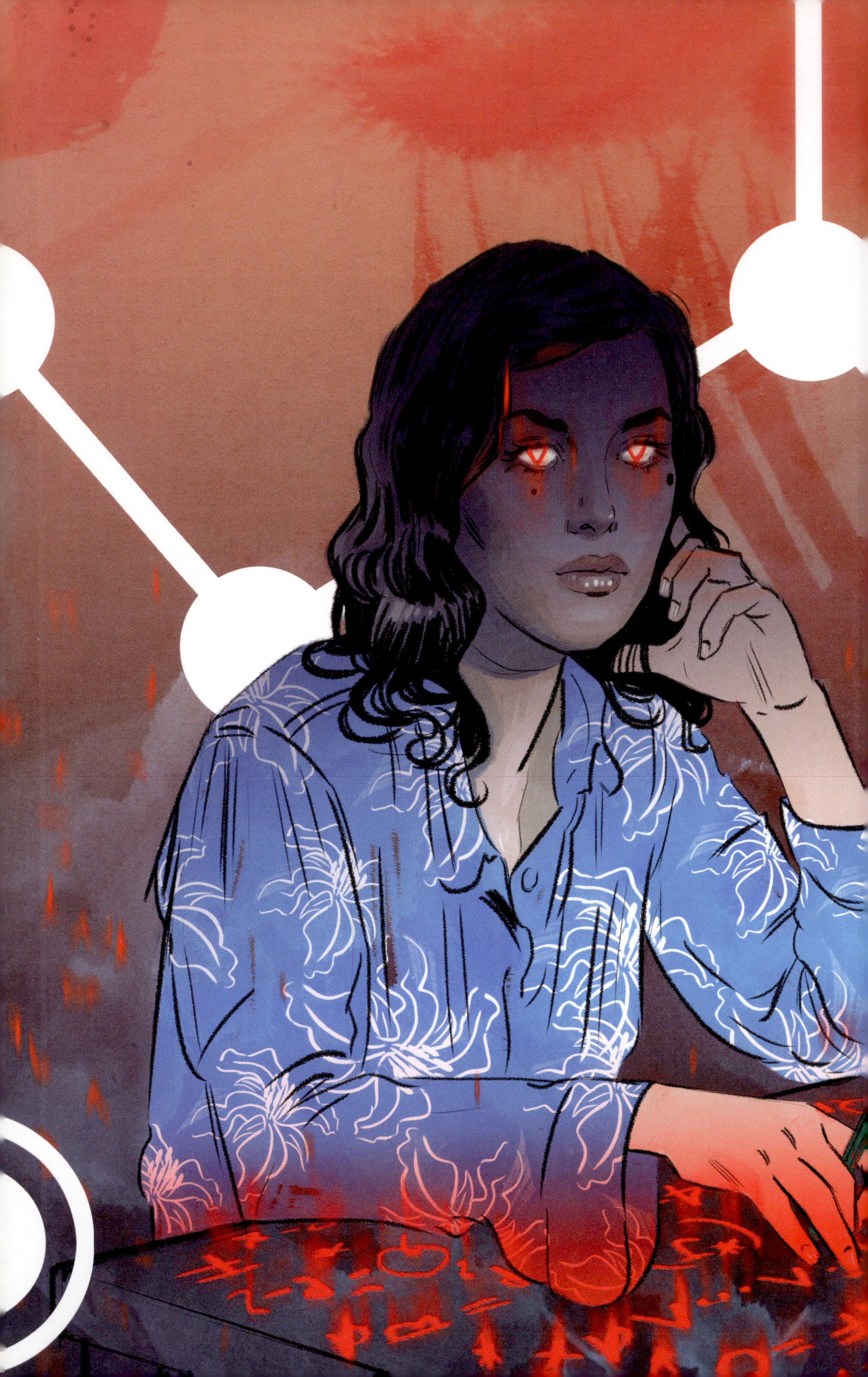

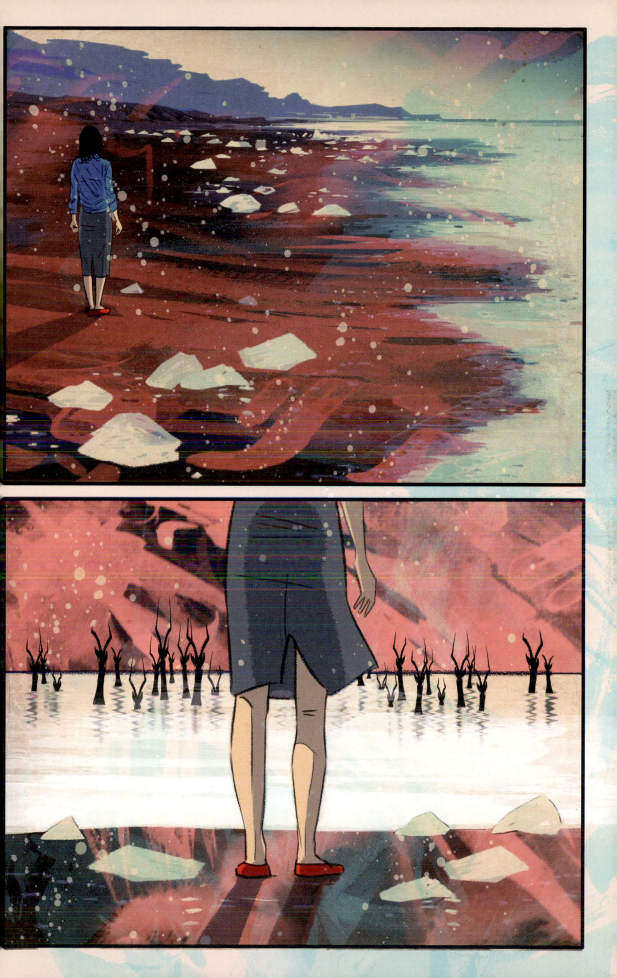

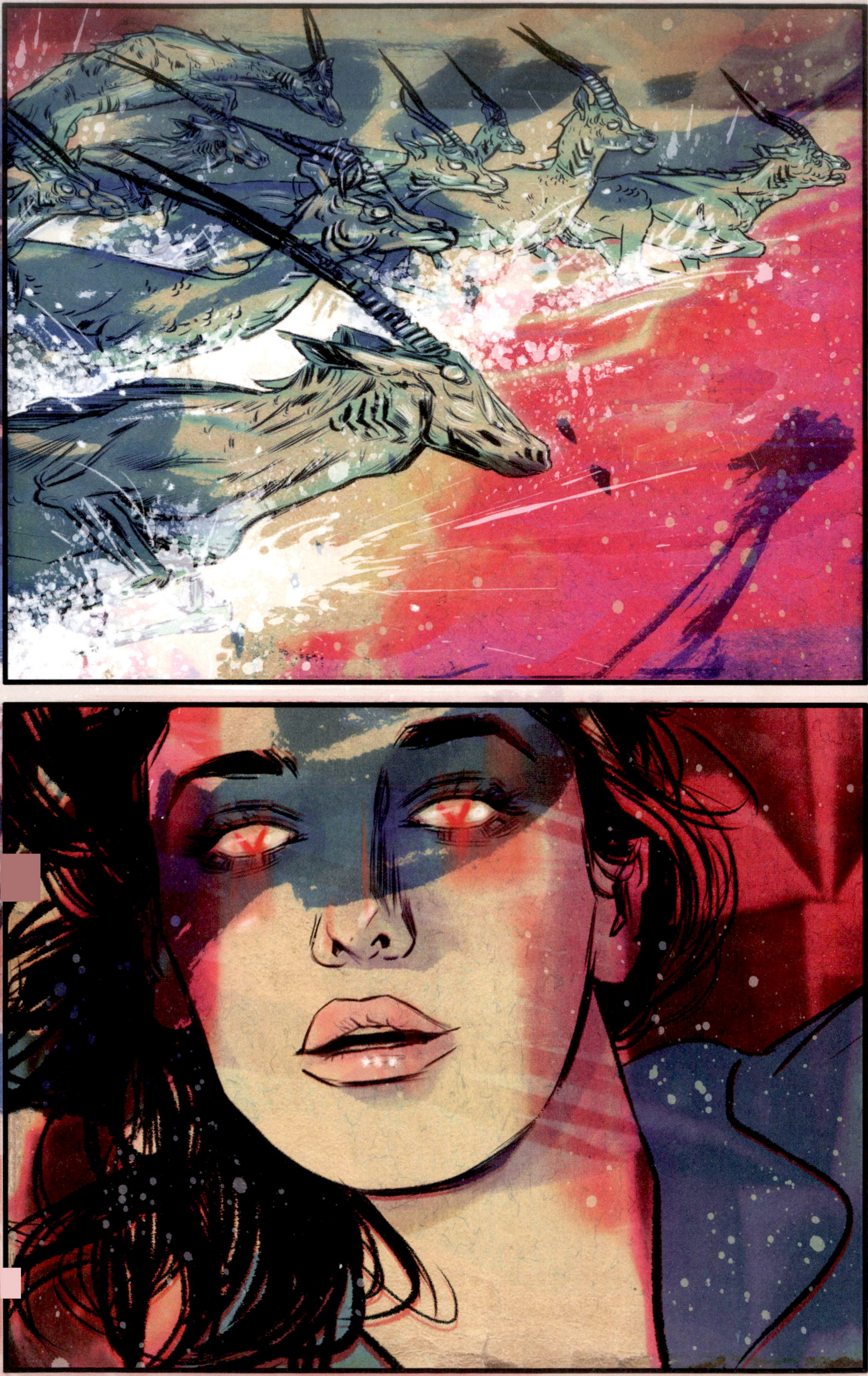

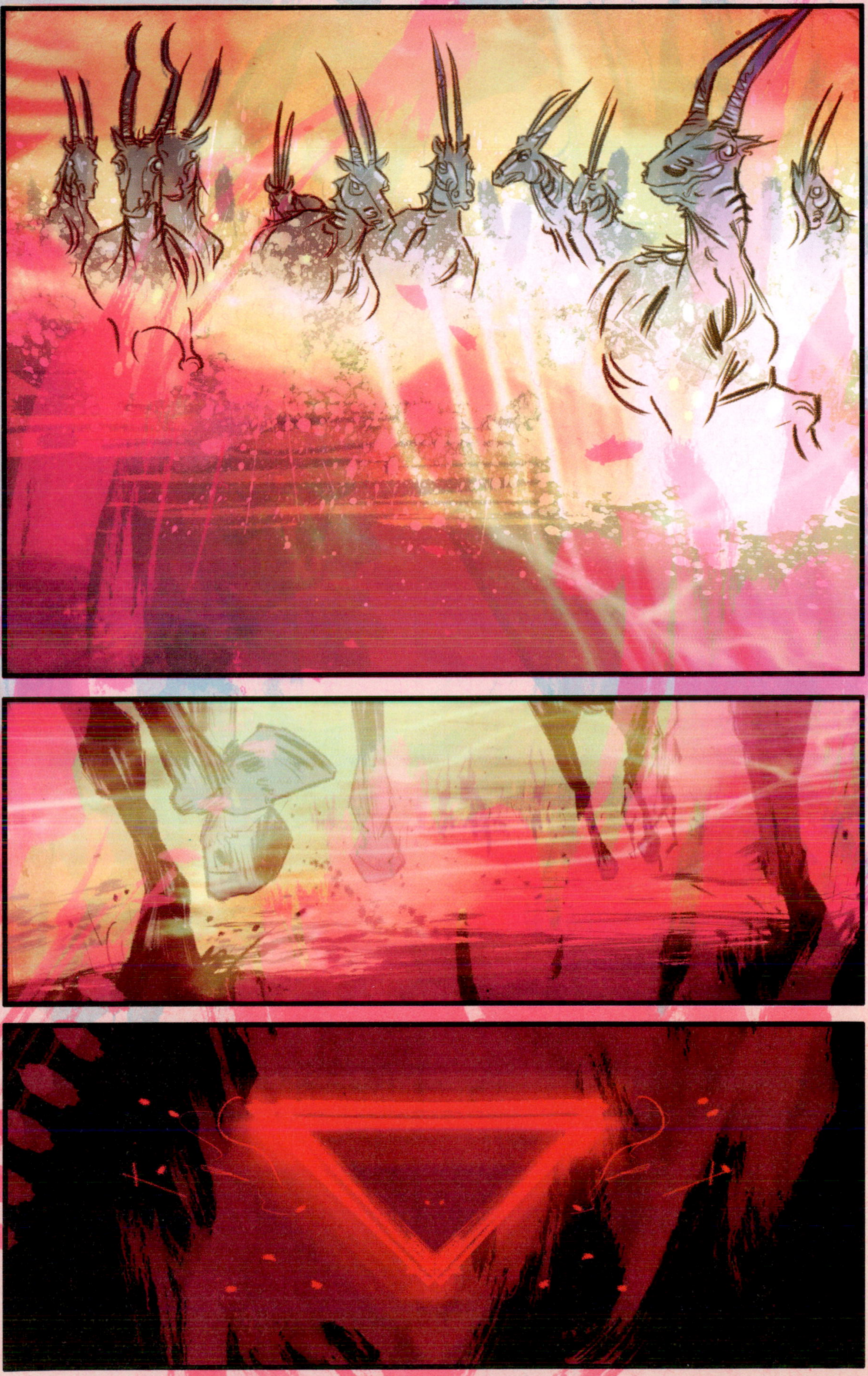

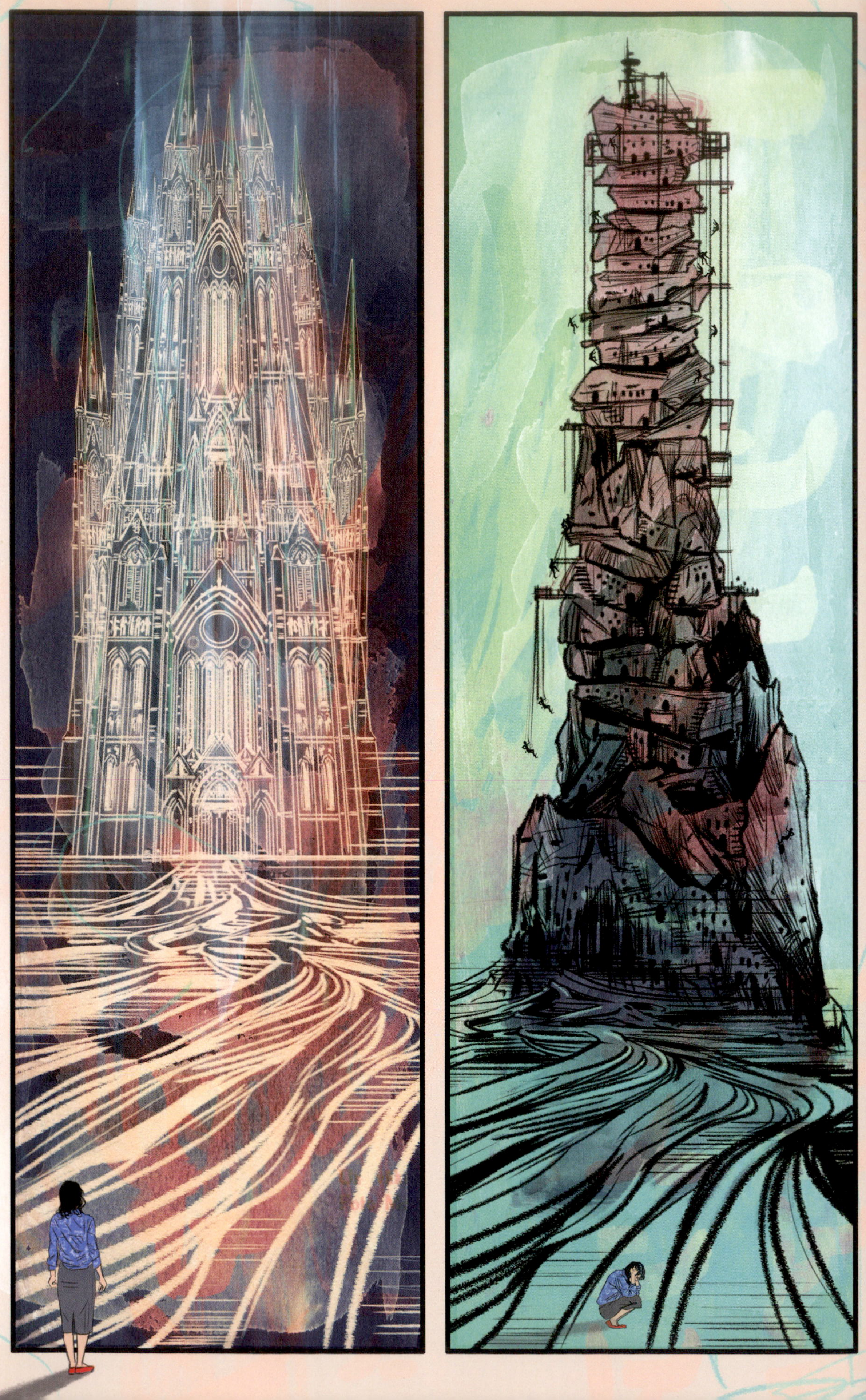

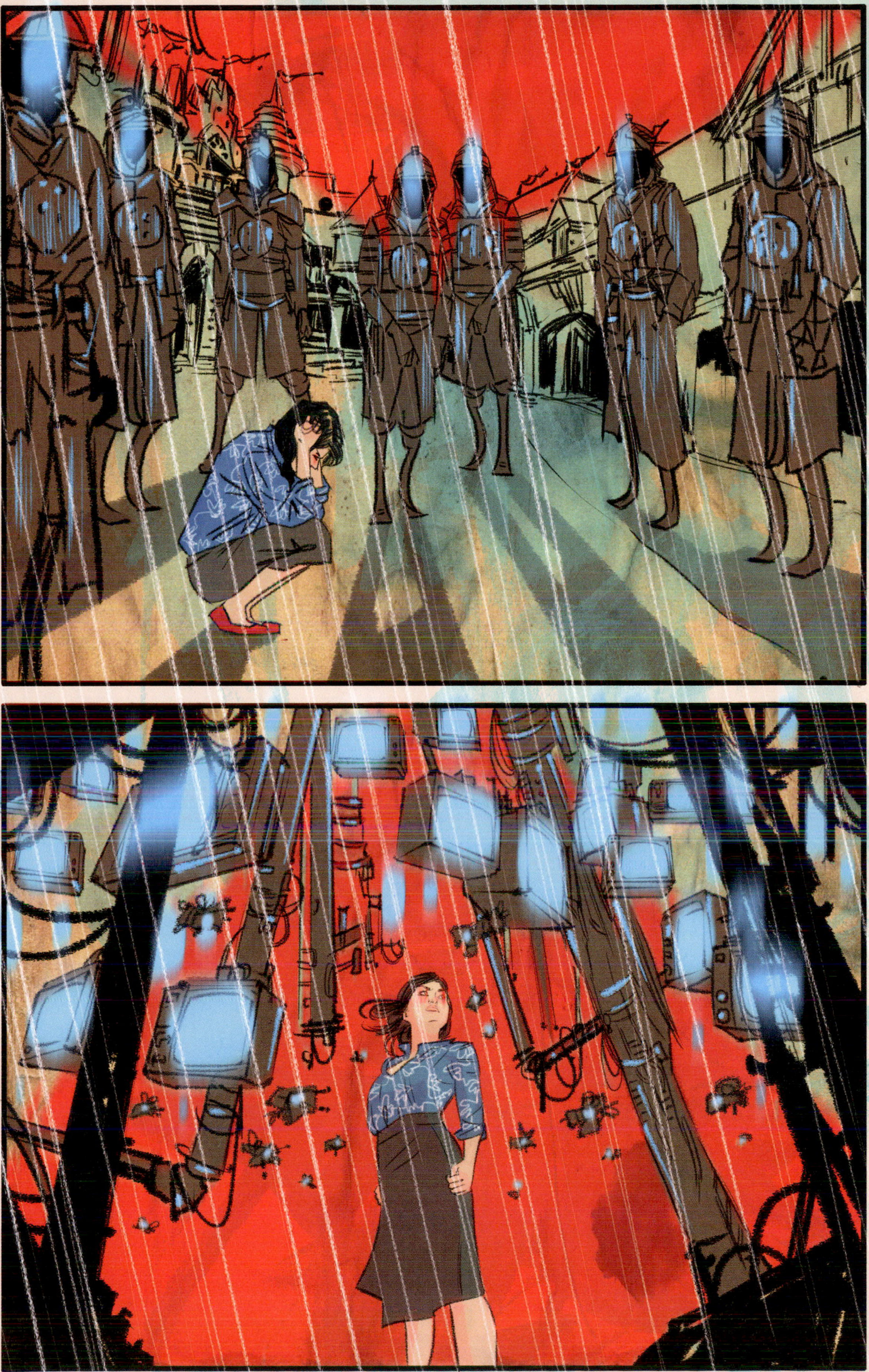

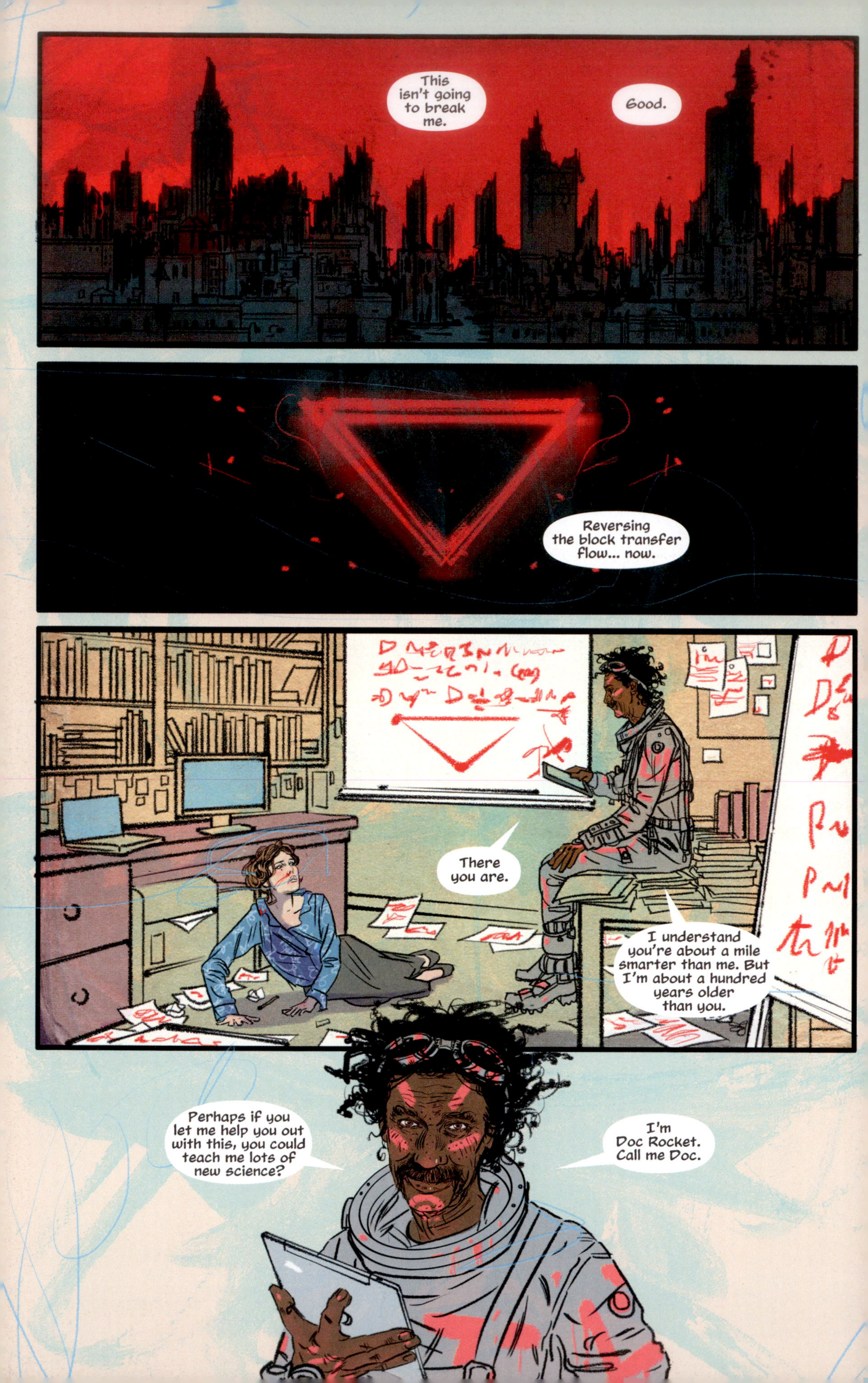
This isn't going to break me.
Good.
Reversing the block transfer flow... now.
There you are.
I understand you're about a mile smarter than me. But I'm about a hundred years older than you.
Perhaps if you let me help you out with this, you could teach me lots of new science?
I'm Doc Rocket. Call me Doc.

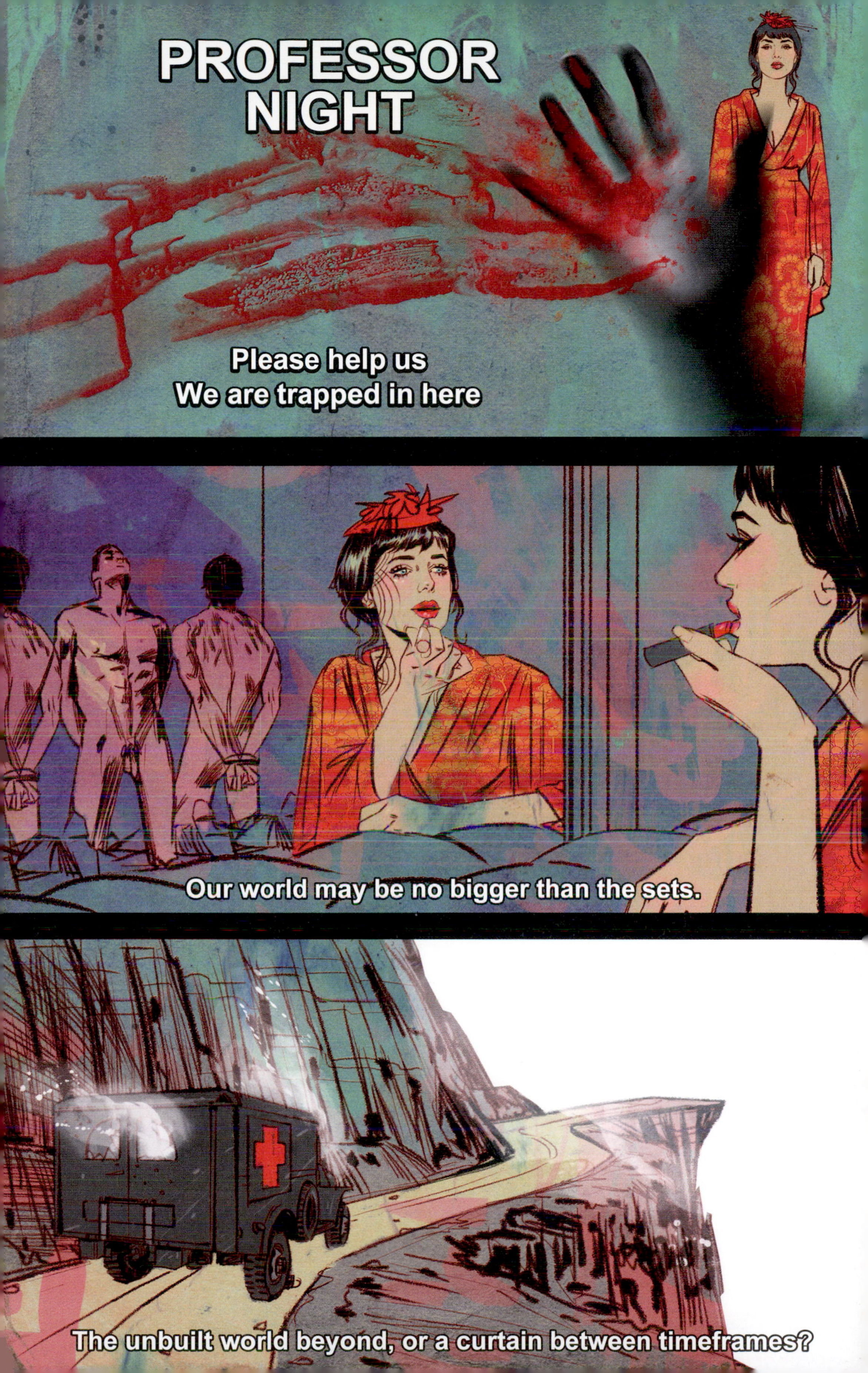
PROFESSOR NIGHT
Please help us
We are trapped in here
Our world may be no bigger than the sets.
The unbuilt world beyond, or a curtain between timeframes?

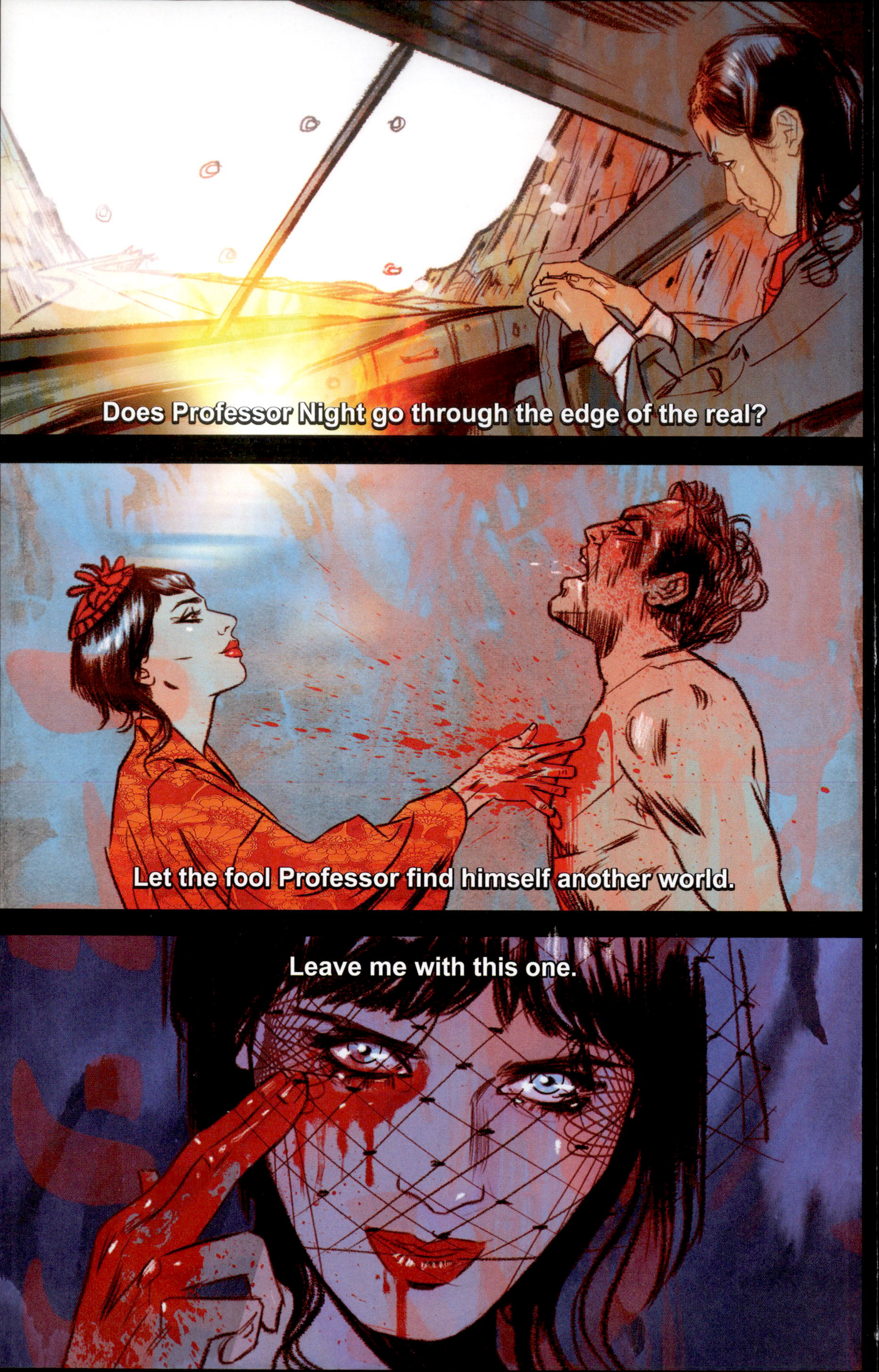
Does Professor Night go through the edge of the real?
Let the fool Professor find himself another world.
Leave me with this one.

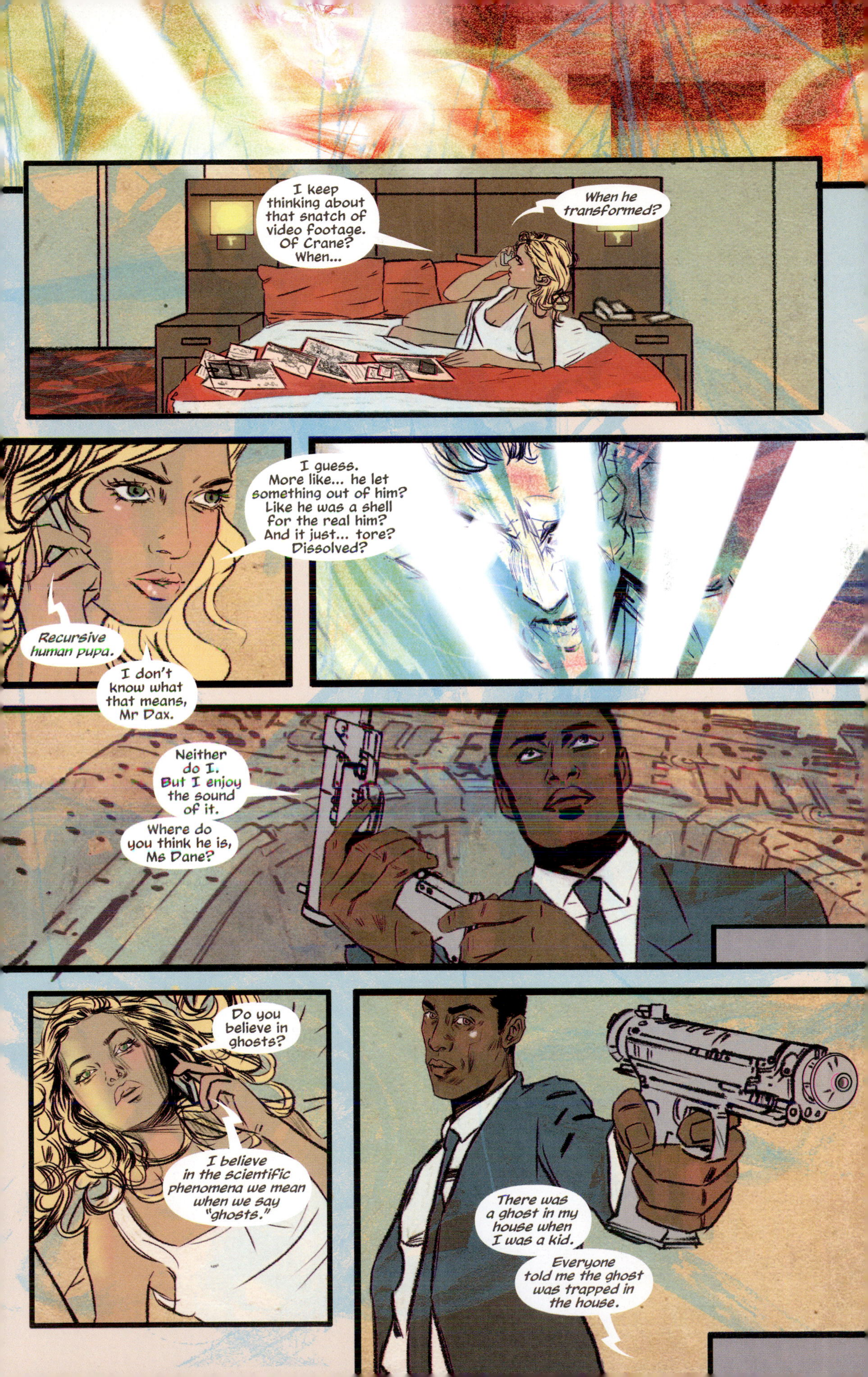

I keep thinking about that snatch of video footage. Of Crane? When...
When he transformed?
I guess. More like... he let something out of him? Like he was a shell for the real him? And it just... tore? Dissolved?
Recursive human pupa.
I don't know what that means, Mr Dax.
Neither do I. But I enjoy the sound of it.
Where do you think he is, Ms Dane?
Do you believe in ghosts?
I believe in the scientific phenomena we mean when we say "ghosts."
There was a ghost in my house when I was a kid.
Everyone told me the ghost was trapped in the house.

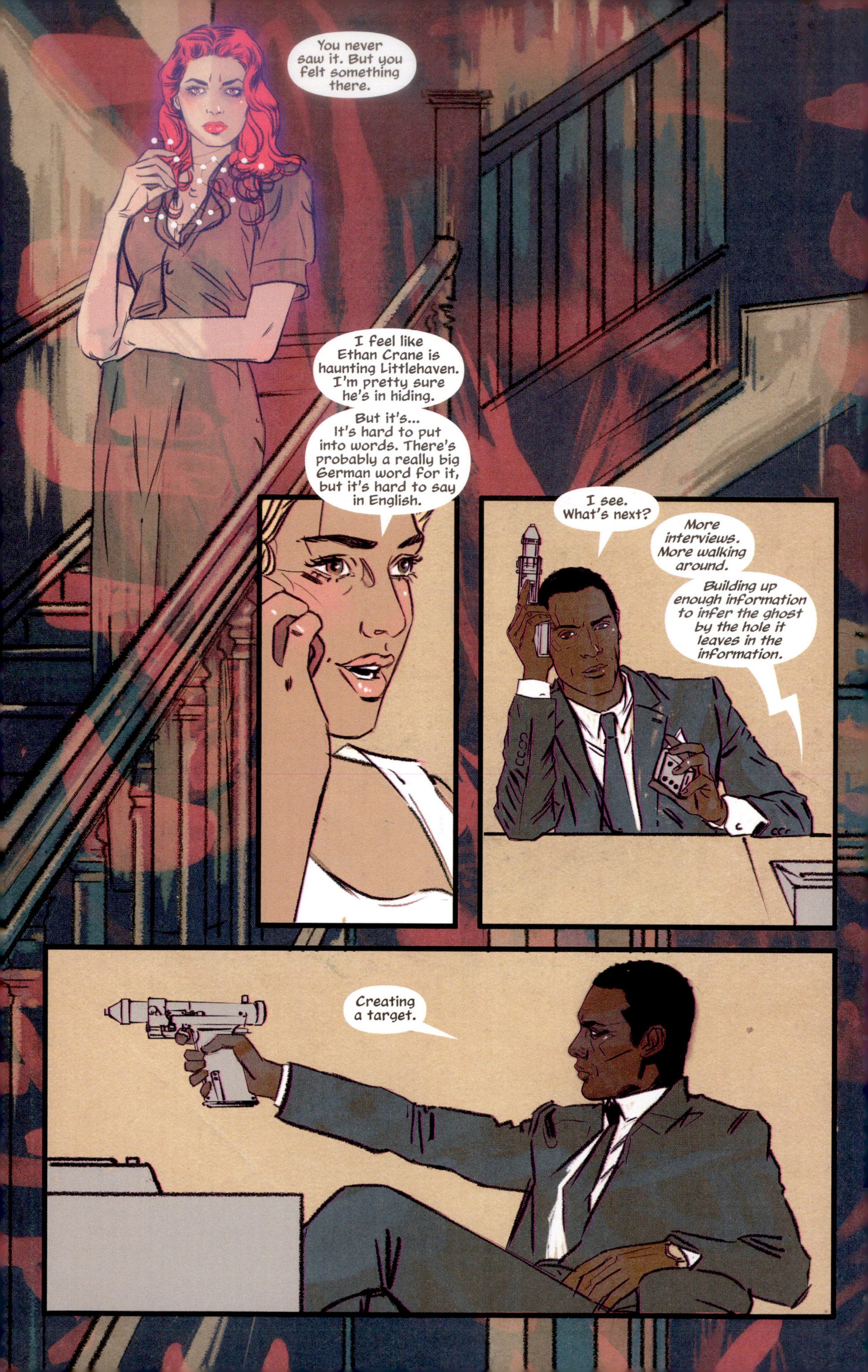
You never saw it. But you felt something there.
I feel like Ethan Crane is haunting Littlehaven. I'm pretty sure he's in hiding.
But it's... It's hard to put into words. There's probably a really big German word for it, but it's hard to say in English.
I see. What's next?
More interviews. More walking around.
Building up enough information to infer the ghost by the hole it leaves in the information.
Creating a target.

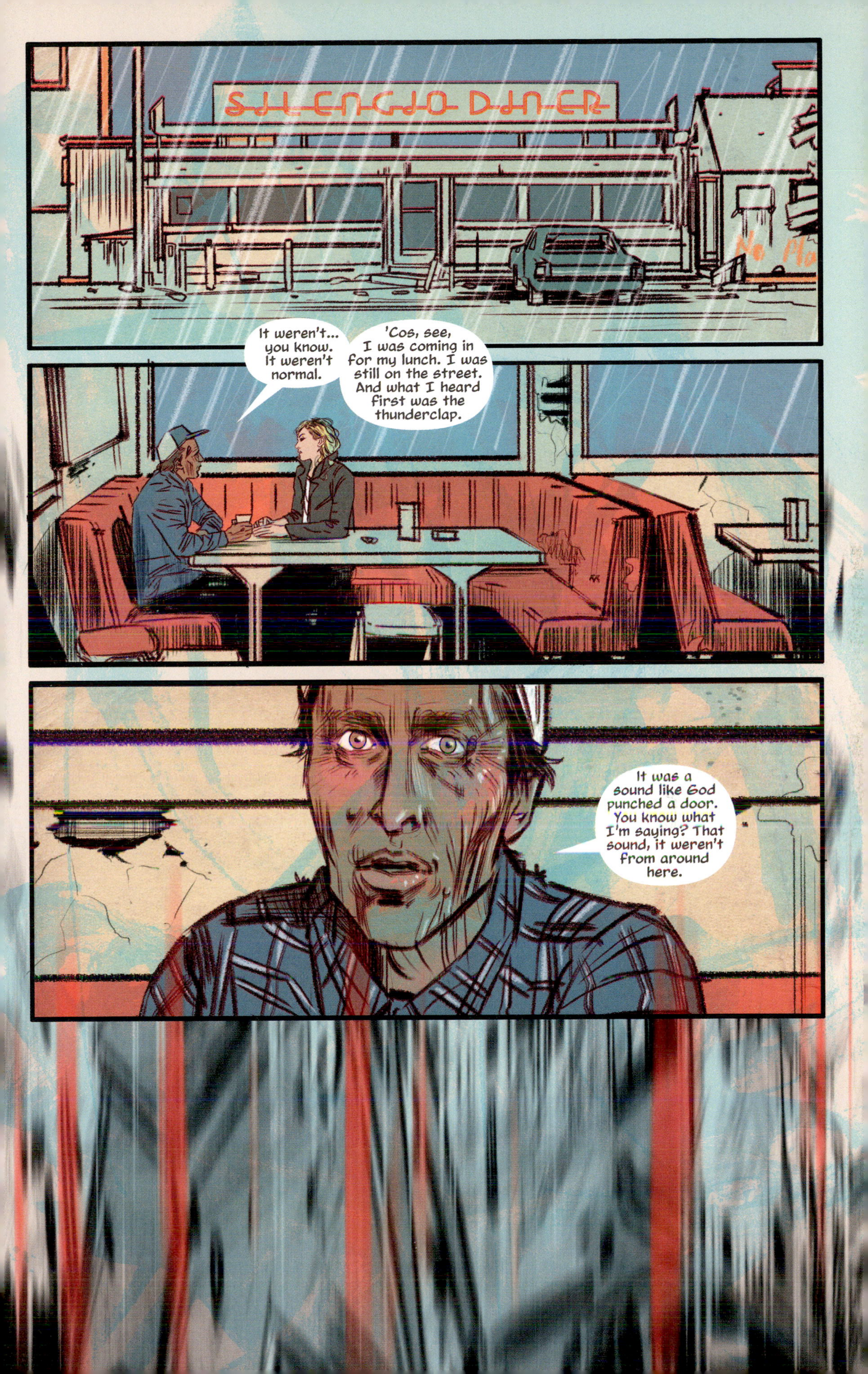
SILENCIO DINER
It weren't... you know. It weren't normal.
'Cos, see, I was coming in for my lunch. I was still on the street. And what I heard first was the thunderclap.
It was a sound like God punched a door. You know what I'm saying? That sound, it weren't from around here.

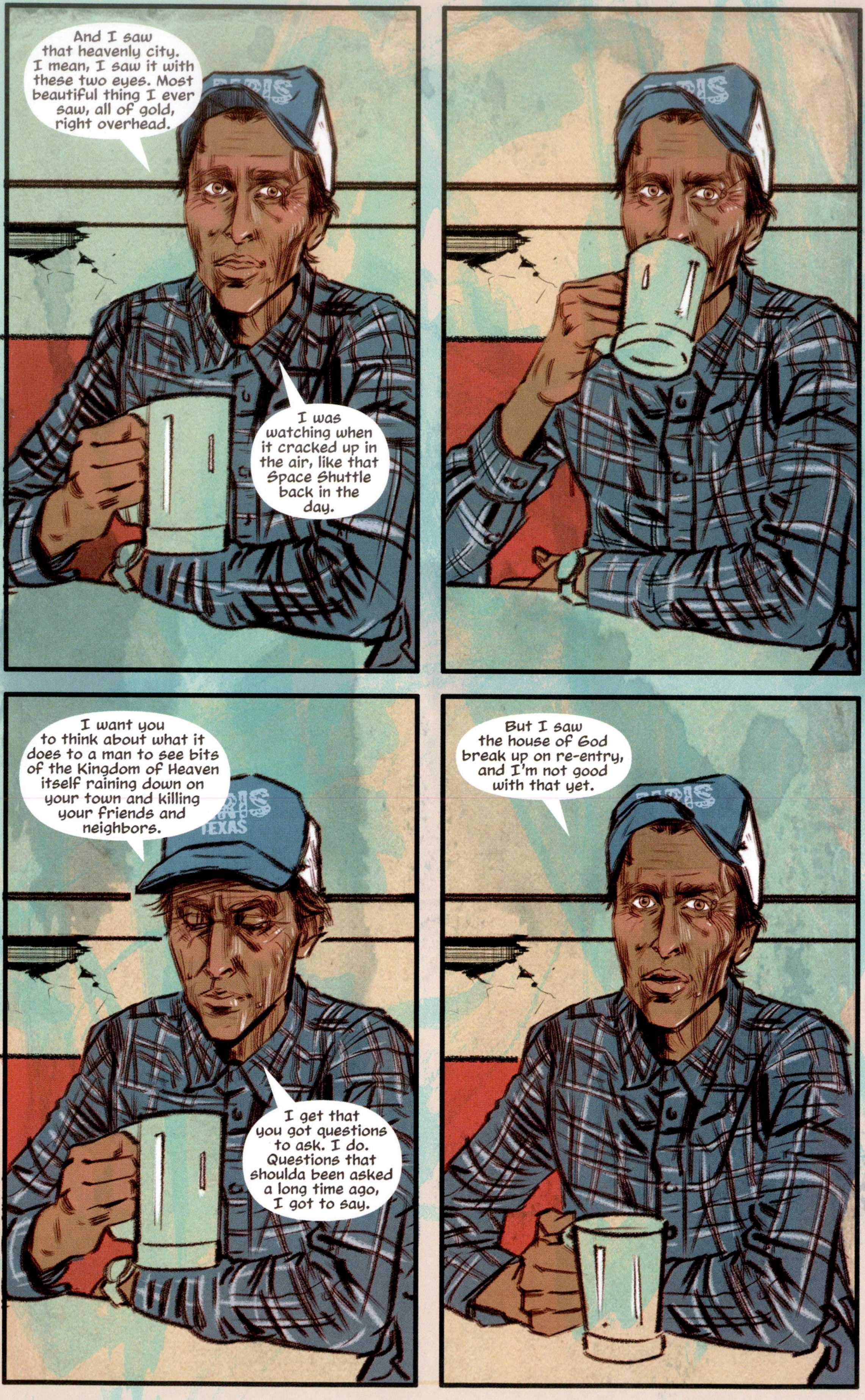
And I saw that heavenly city. I mean, I saw it with these two eyes. Most beautiful thing I ever saw, all of gold, right overhead.
I was watching when it cracked up in the air, like that Space Shuttle back in the day.
I want you to think about what it does to a man to see bits of the Kingdom of Heaven itself raining down on your town and killing your friends and neighbors.
I get that you got questions to ask. I do. Questions that shoulda been asked a long time ago, I got to say.
But I saw the house of God break up on re-entry, and I'm not good with that yet.

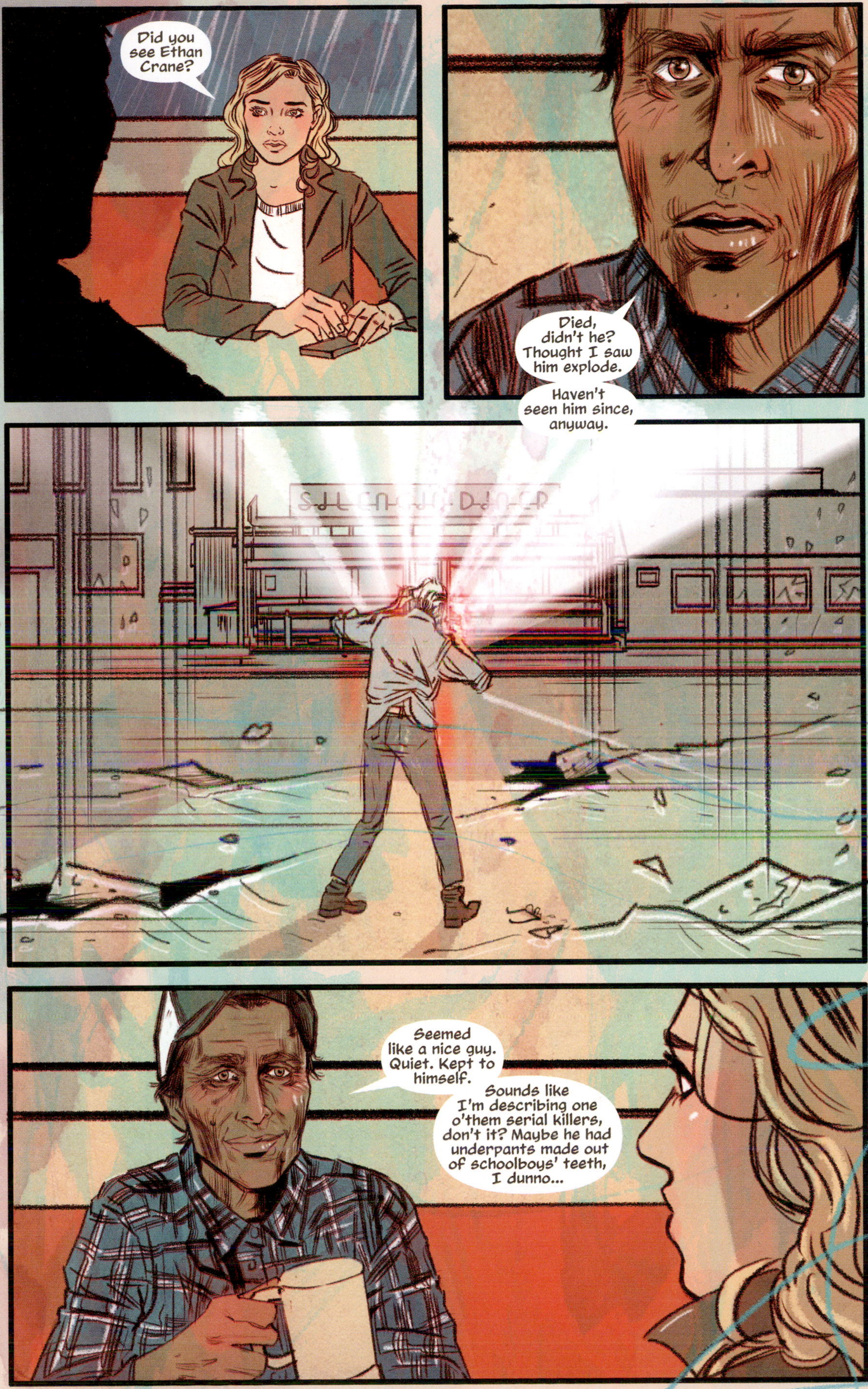
Did you see Ethan Crane?
Died, didn't he? Thought I saw him explode.
Haven't seen him since, anyway.
Seemed like a nice guy. Quiet. Kept to himself.
Sounds like I'm describing one o'them serial killers, don't it? Maybe he had underpants made out of schoolboys' teeth, I dunno...

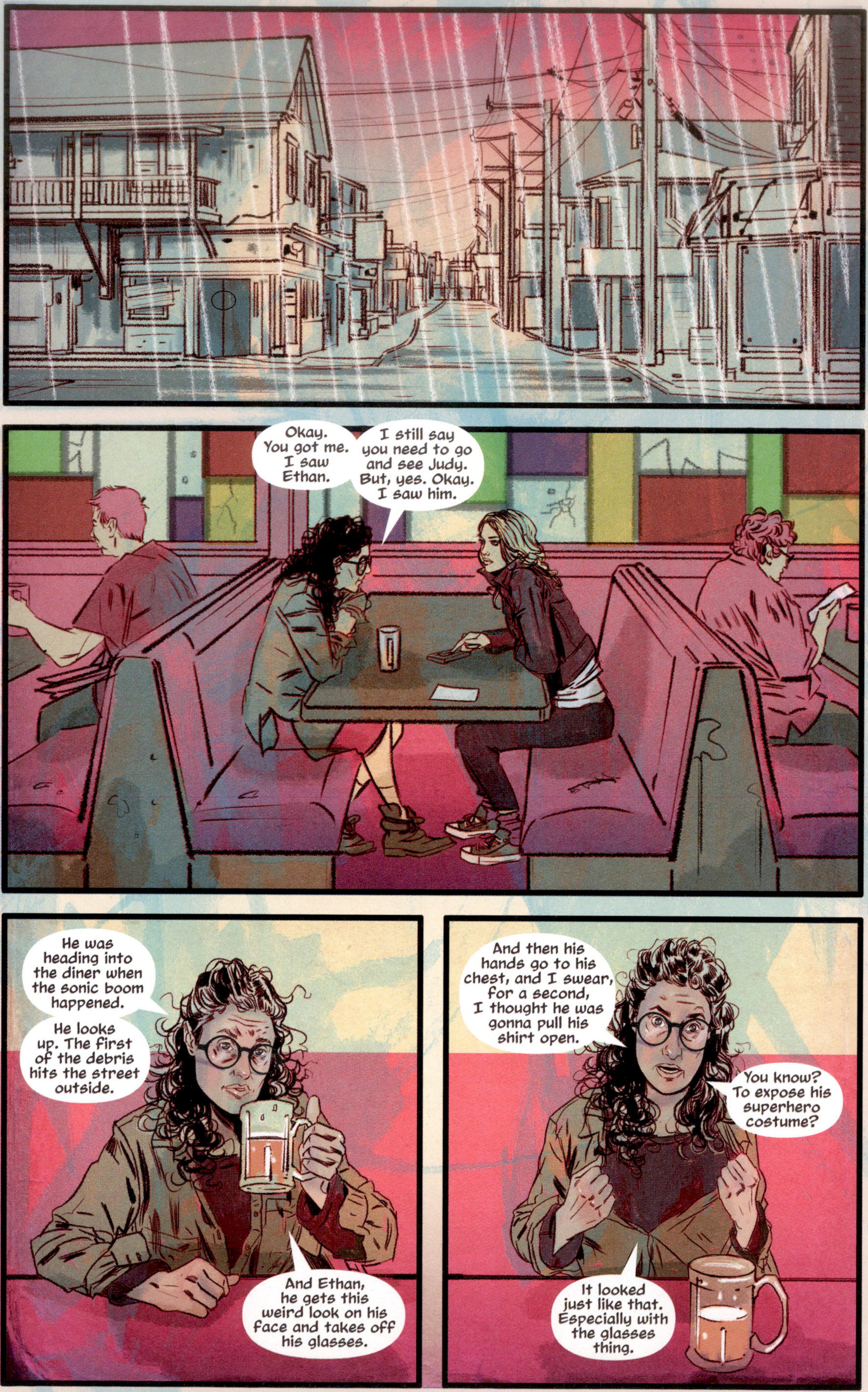
Okay. You got me. I saw Ethan.
I still say you need to go and see Judy. But, yes. Okay. I saw him.
He was heading into the diner when the sonic boom happened.
He looks up. The first of the debris hits the street outside.
And Ethan, he gets this weird look on his face and takes off his glasses.
And then his hands go to his chest, and I swear, for a second, I thought he was gonna pull his shirt open.
You know? To expose his superhero costume?
It looked just like that. Especially with the glasses thing.

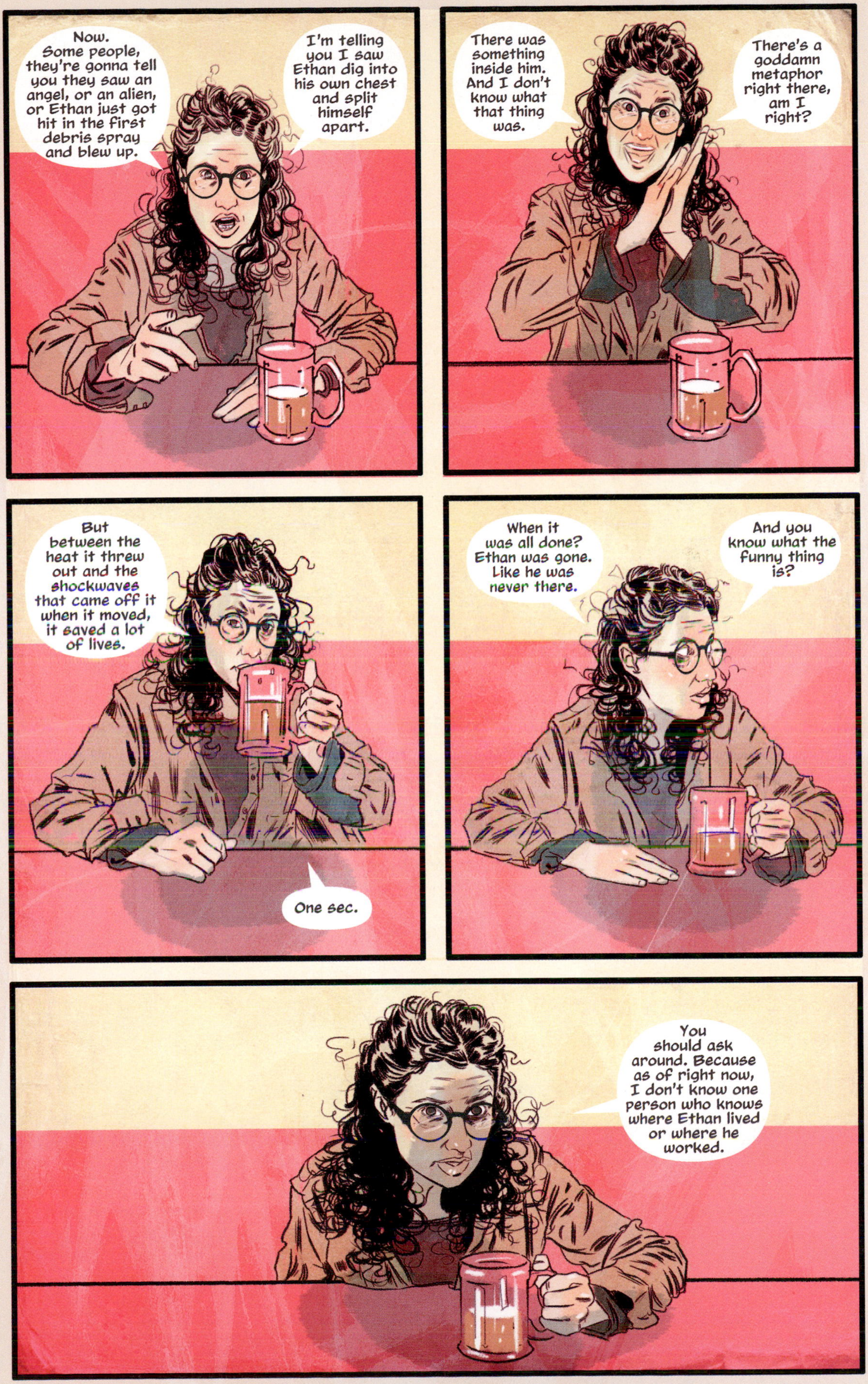
Now. Some people, they're gonna tell you they saw an angel, or an alien, or Ethan just got hit in the first debris spray and blew up.
I'm telling you I saw Ethan dig into his own chest and split himself apart.
There was something inside him. And I don't know what that thing was.
There's a goddamn metaphor right there, am I right?
But between the heat it threw out and the shockwaves that came off it when it moved, it saved a lot of lives.
One sec.
When it was all done? Ethan was gone. Like he was never there.
And you know what the funny thing is?
You should ask around. Because as of right now, I don't know one person who knows where Ethan lived or where he worked.

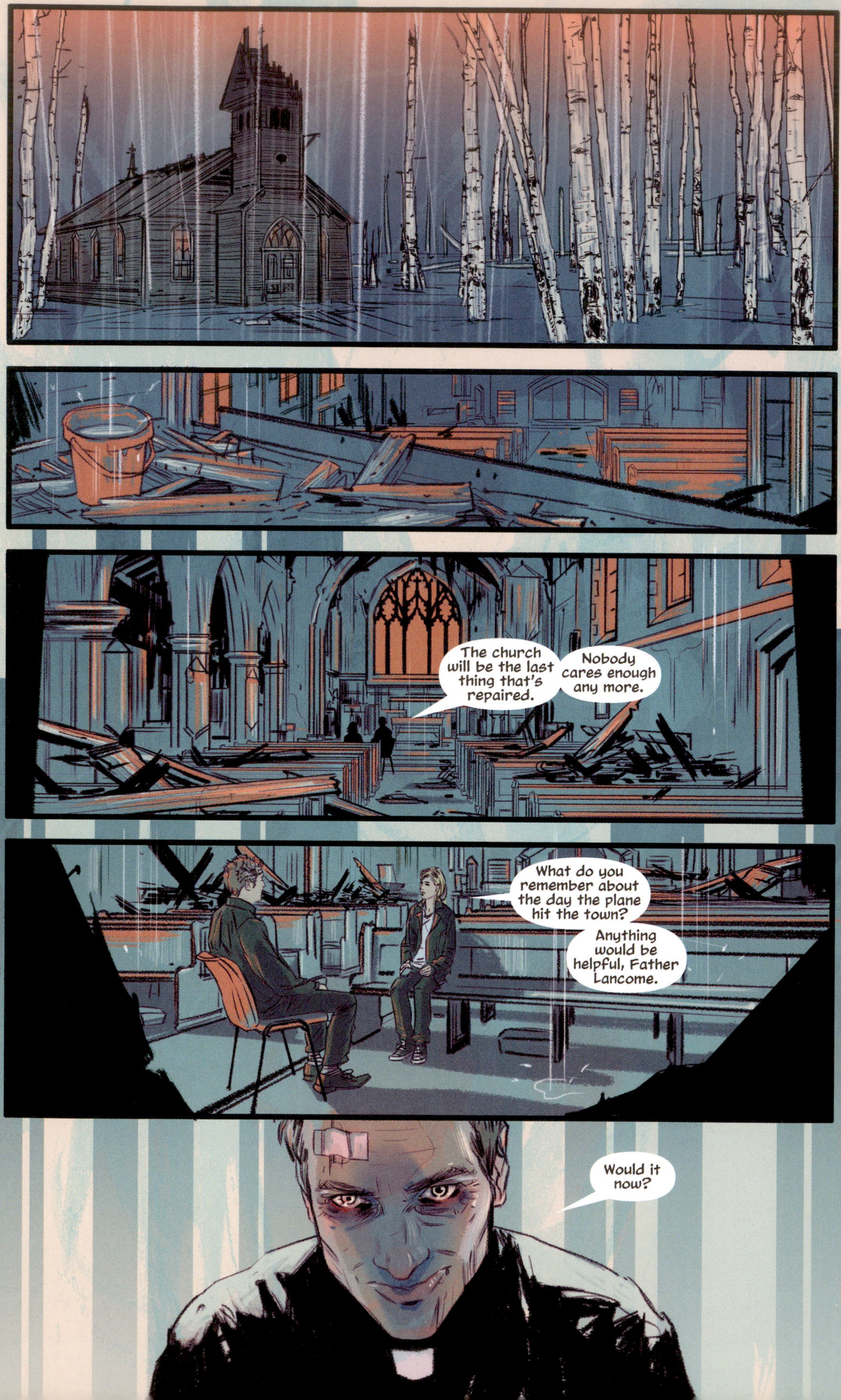
The church will be the last thing that's repaired.
Nobody cares enough any more.
What do you remember about the day the plane hit the town?
Anything would be helpful, Father Lancome.
Would it now?

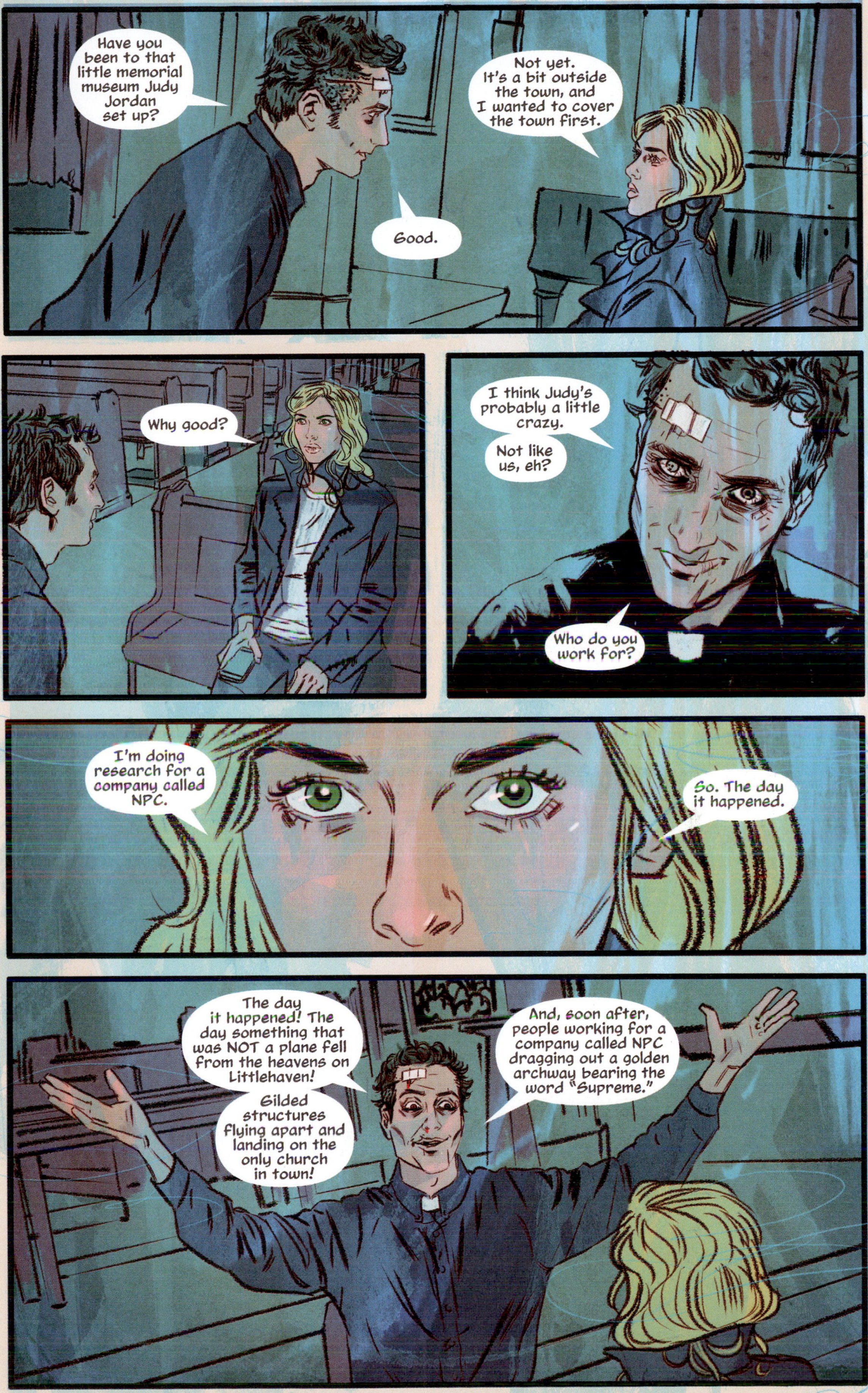
Have you been to that little memorial museum Judy Jordan set up?
Not yet. It's a bit outside the town, and I wanted to cover the town first.
Good.
Why good?
I think Judy's probably a little crazy.
Not like us, eh?
Who do you work for?
I'm doing research for a company called NPC.
So. The day it happened.
The day it happened! The day something that was NOT a plane fell from the heavens on Littlehaven!
Gilded structures flying apart and landing on the only church in town!
And, soon after, people working for a company called NPC dragging out a golden archway bearing the word "Supreme."

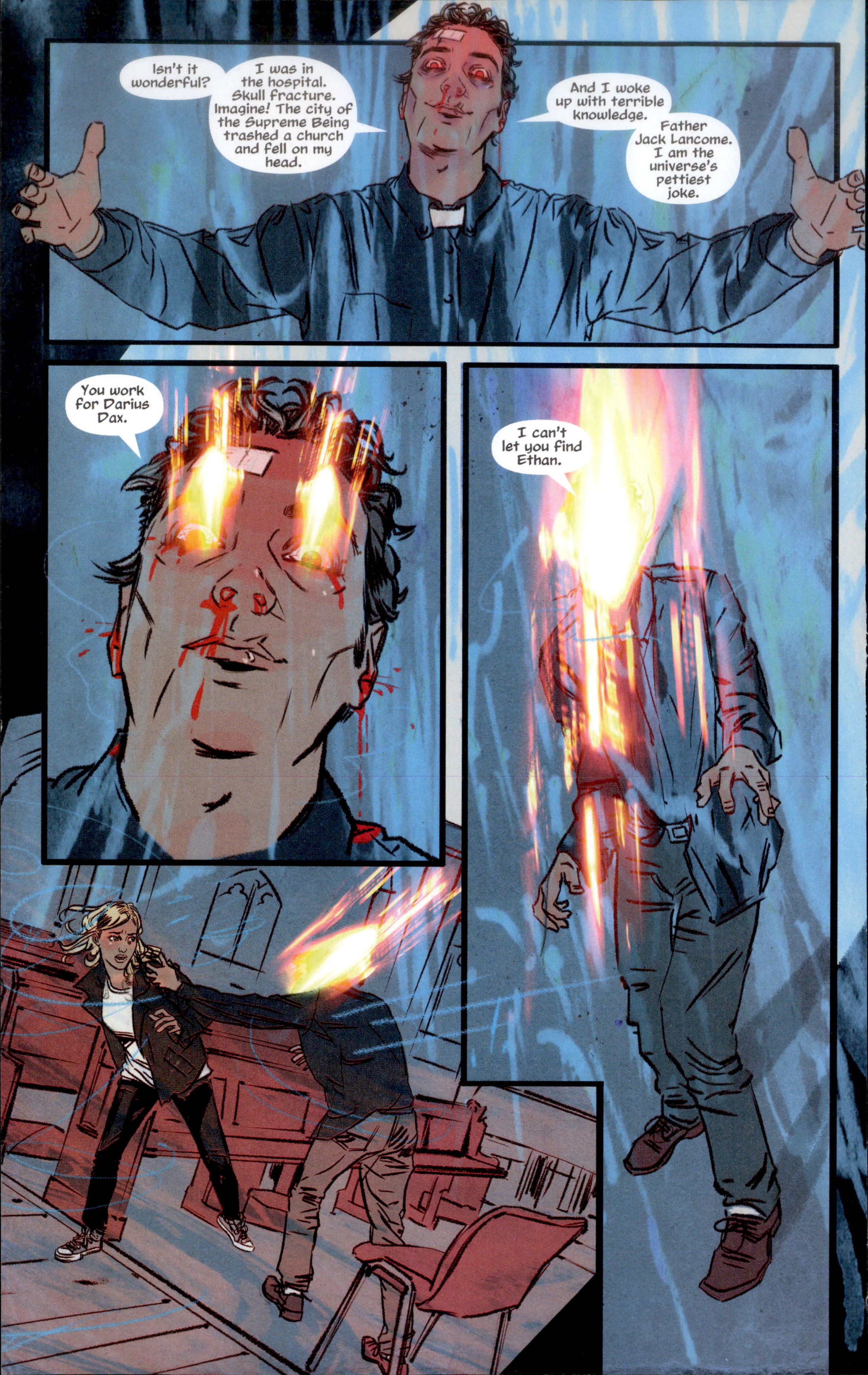
Isn't it wonderful?
I was in the hospital. Skull fracture. Imagine! The city of the Supreme Being trashed a church and fell on my head.
And I woke up with terrible knowledge.
Father Jack Lancome. I am the universe's pettiest joke.
You work for Darius Dax.
I can't let you find Ethan.

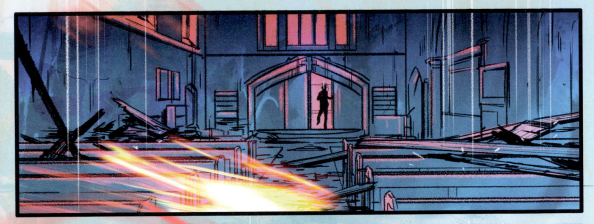

Down.

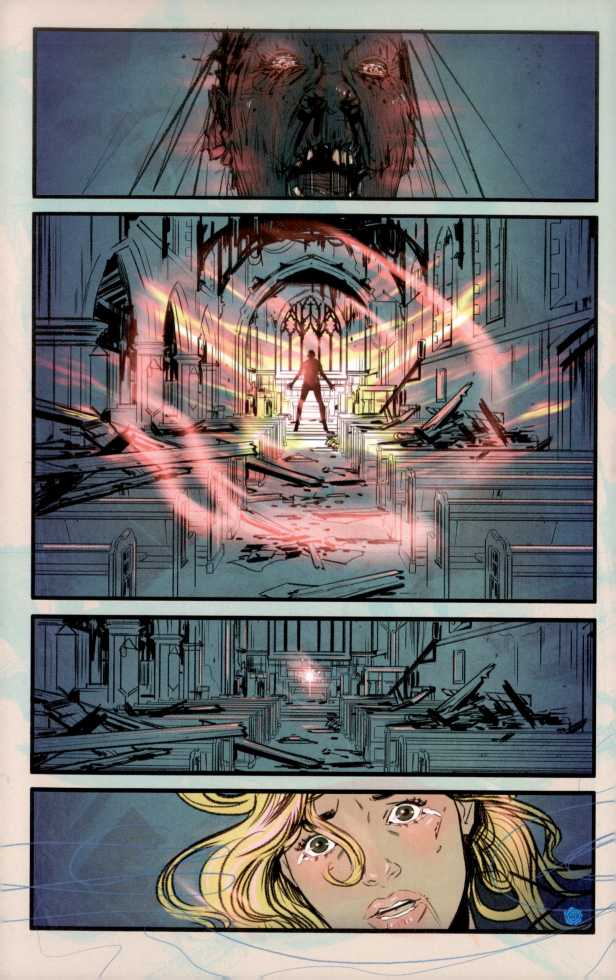

SIX

"It is time to act upon the world."

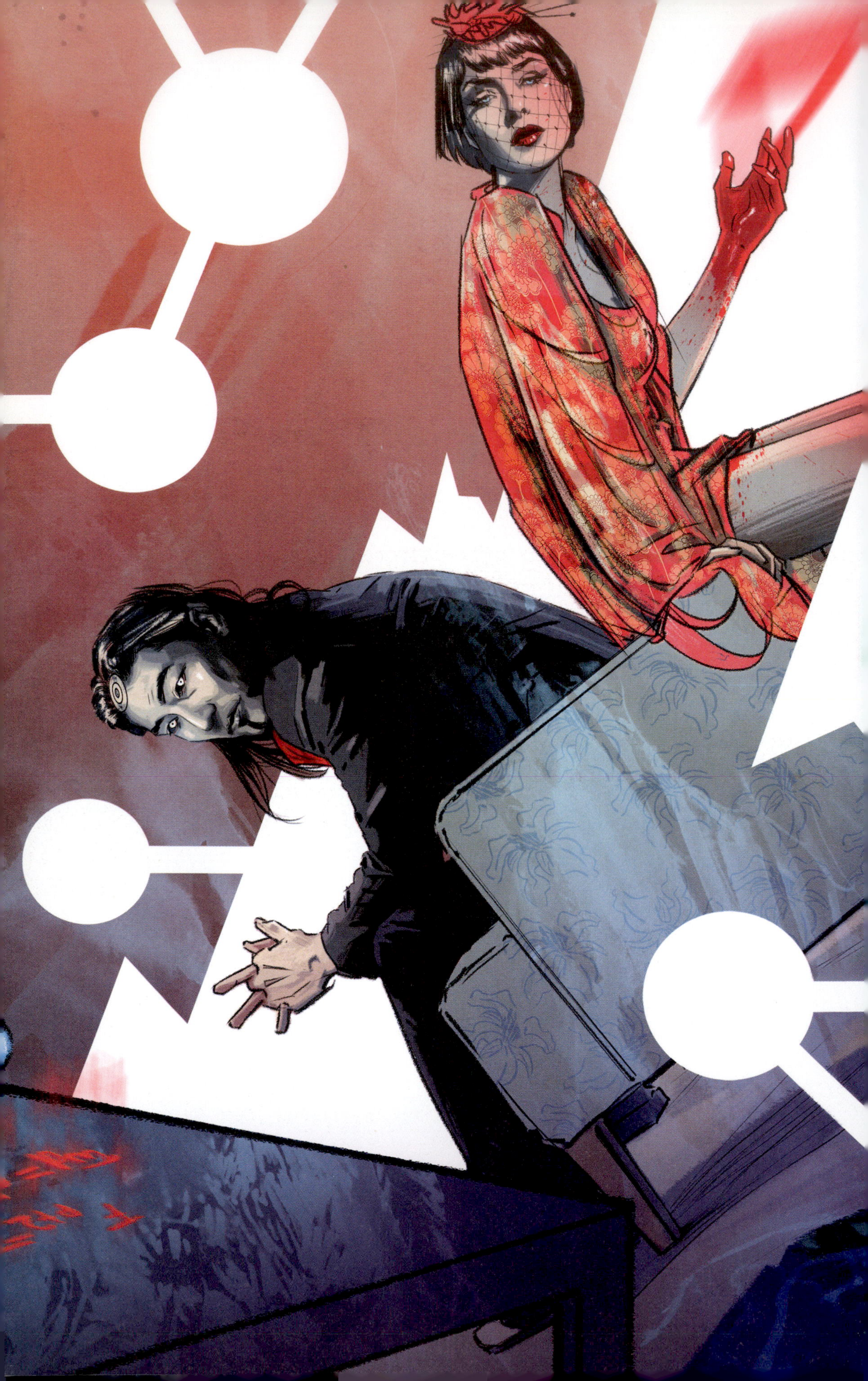

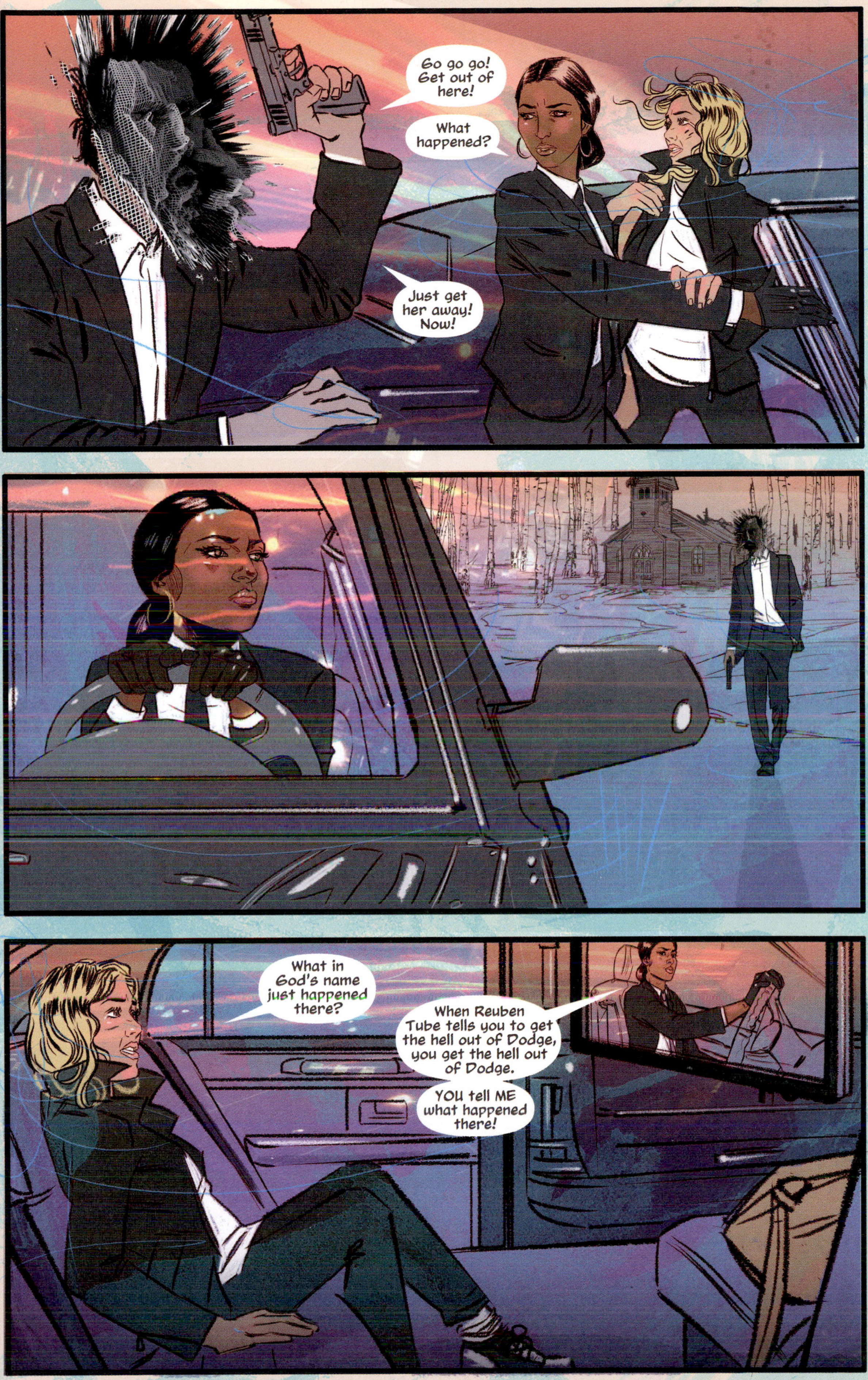
Go go go! Get out of here!
What happened?
Just get her away! Now!
What in God's name just happened there?
When Reuben Tube tells you to get the hell out of Dodge, you get the hell out of Dodge.
YOU tell ME what happened there!

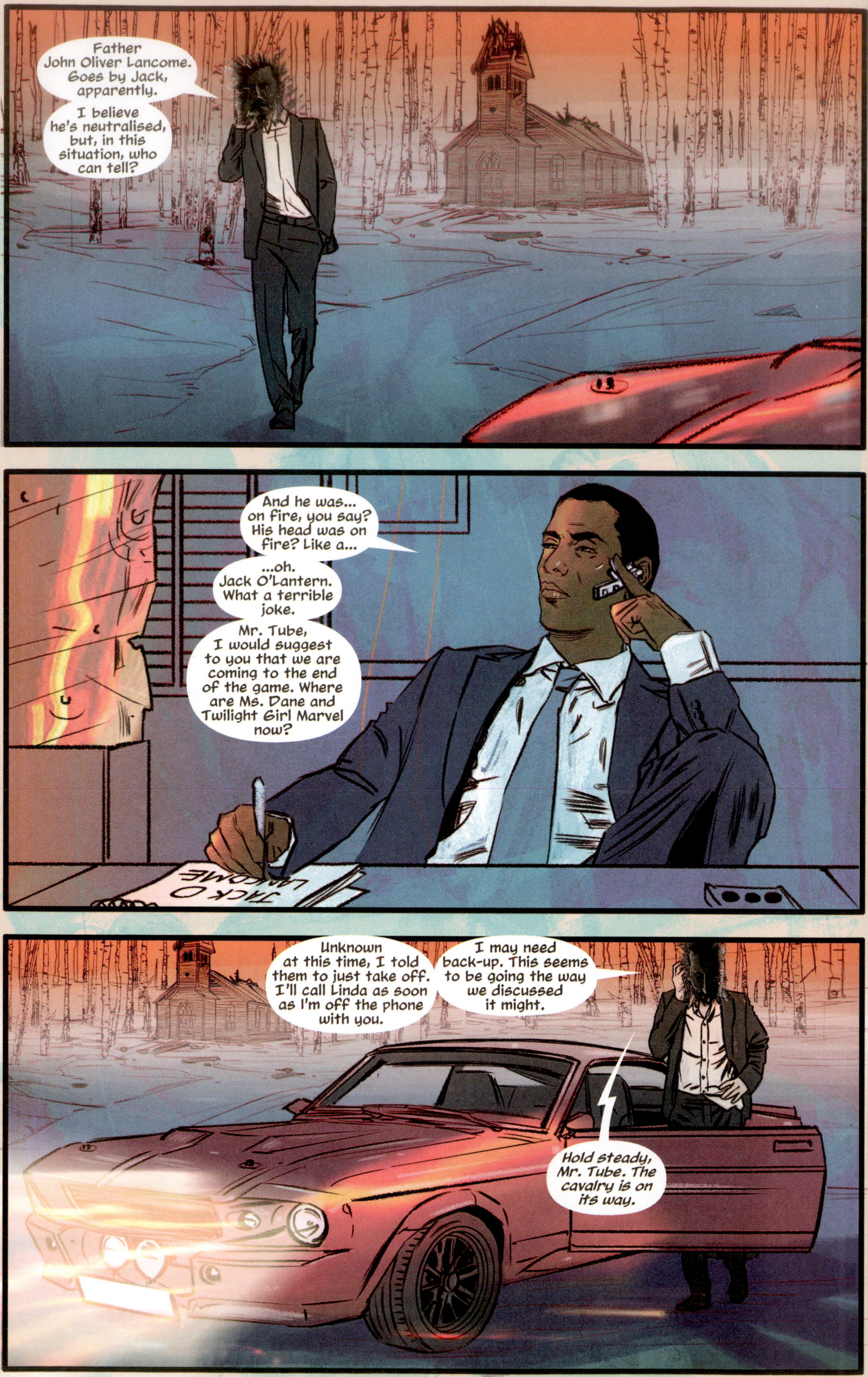
Father John Oliver Lancome. Goes by Jack, apparently.
I believe he's neutralised, but, in this situation, who can tell?
And he was... on fire, you say? His head was on fire? Like a...
...oh. Jack O'Lantern. What a terrible joke.
Mr. Tube, I would suggest to you that we are coming to the end of the game. Where are Ms. Dane and Twilight Girl Marvel now?
JACK O LANCOME
Unknown at this time, I told them to just take off. I'll call Linda as soon as I'm off the phone with you.
I may need back-up. This seems to be going the way we discussed it might.
Hold steady, Mr. Tube. The cavalry is on its way.

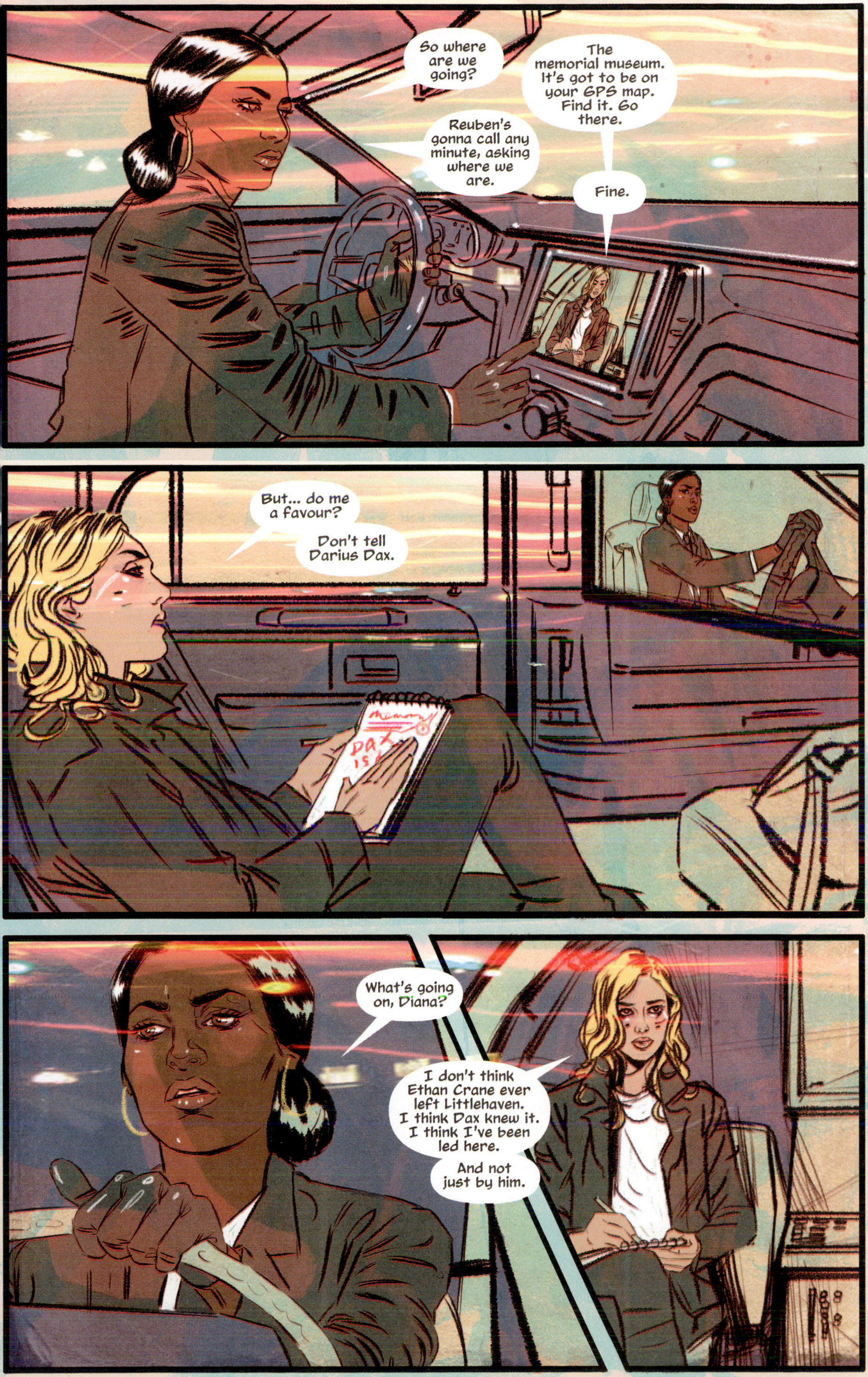
So where are we going?
Reuben's gonna call any minute, asking where we are.
The memorial museum. It's got to be on your GPS map. Find it. Go there.
Fine.
But... do me a favour?
Don't tell Darius Dax.
What's going on, Diana?
I don't think Ethan Crane ever left Littlehaven. I think Dax knew it. I think I've been led here.
And not just by him.

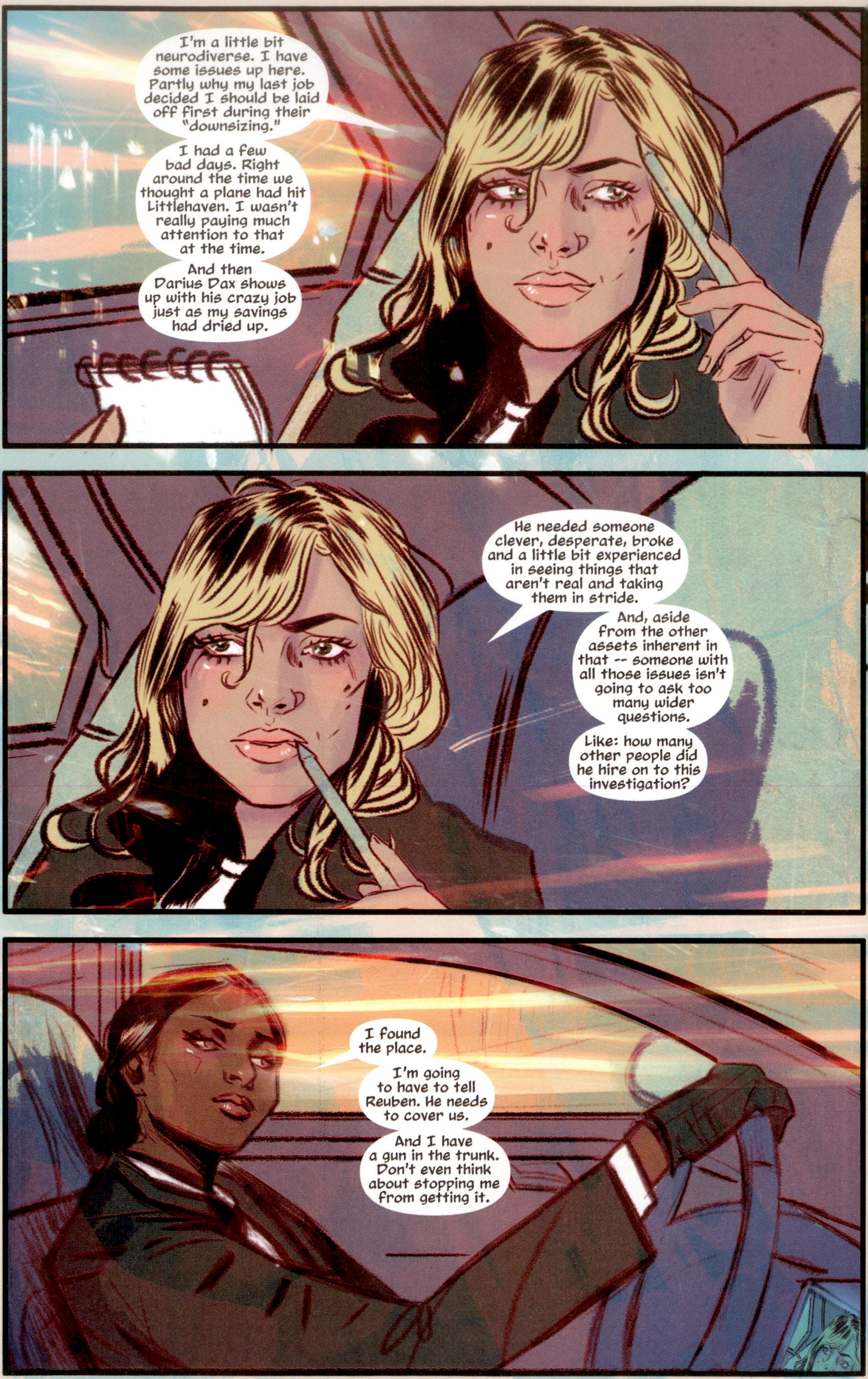
I'm a little bit neurodiverse. I have some issues up here. Partly why my last job decided I should be laid off first during their "downsizing."
I had a few bad days. Right around the time we thought a plane had hit Littlehaven. I wasn't really paying much attention to that at the time.
And then Darius Dax shows up with his crazy job just as my savings had dried up.
He needed someone clever, desperate, broke and a little bit experienced in seeing things that aren't real and taking them in stride.
And, aside from the other assets inherent in that -- someone with all those issues isn't going to ask too many wider questions.
Like: how many other people did he hire on to this investigation?
I found the place.
I'm going to have to tell Reuben. He needs to cover us.
And I have a gun in the trunk. Don't even think about stopping me from getting it.

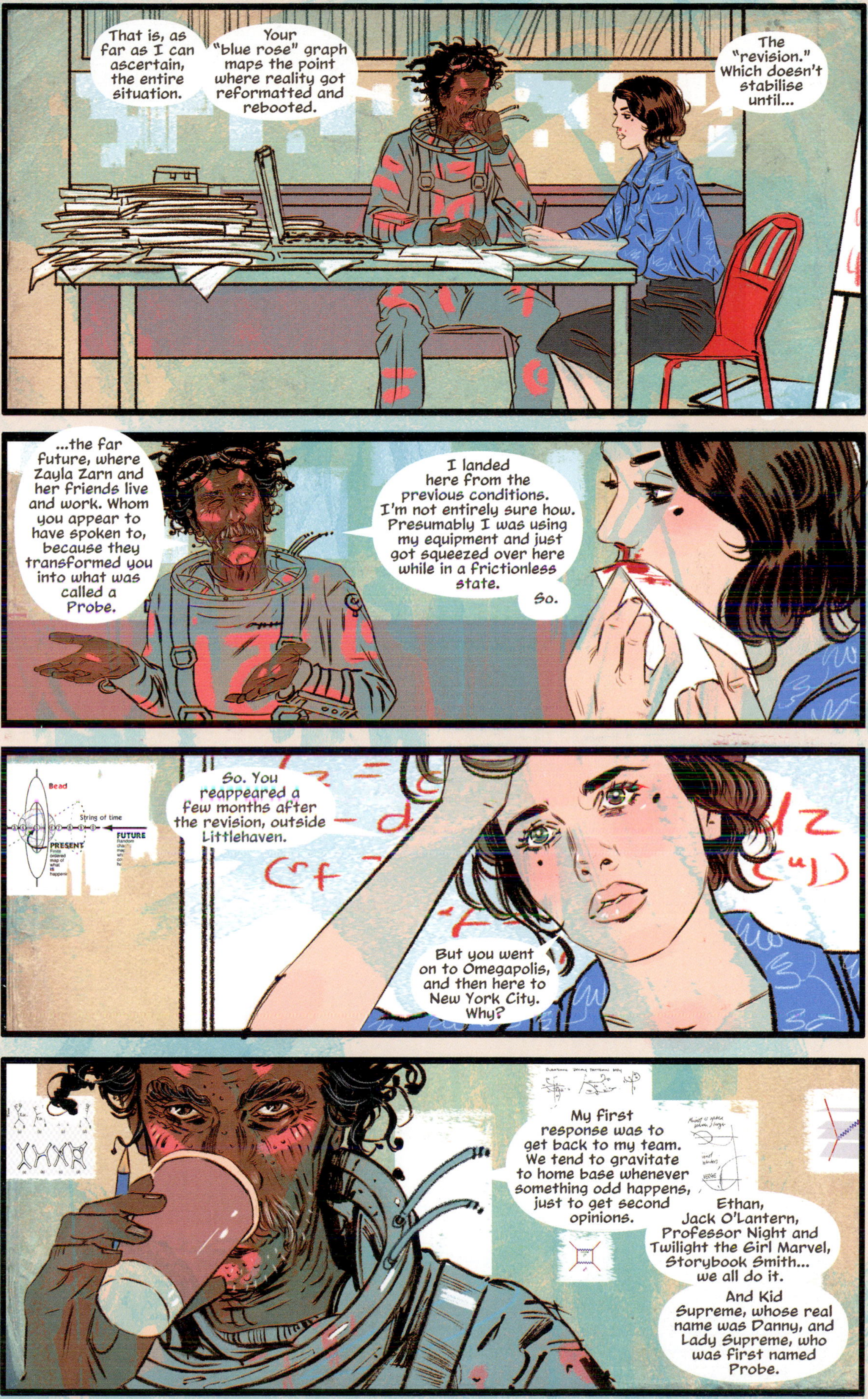
That is, as far as I can ascertain, the entire situation.
Your "blue rose" graph maps the point where reality got reformatted and rebooted.
The "revision." Which doesn't stabilise until...
...the far future, where Zayla Zarn and her friends live and work. Whom you appear to have spoken to, because they transformed you into what was called a Probe.
I landed here from the previous conditions. I'm not entirely sure how. Presumably I was using my equipment and just got squeezed over here while in a frictionless state.
So.
So. You reappeared a few months after the revision, outside Littlehaven.
But you went on to Omegapolis, and then here to New York City. Why?
My first response was to get back to my team. We tend to gravitate to home base whenever something odd happens, just to get second opinions.
Ethan, Jack O'Lantern, Professor Night and Twilight the Girl Marvel, Storybook Smith... we all do it.
And Kid Supreme, whose real name was Danny, and Lady Supreme, who was first named Probe.

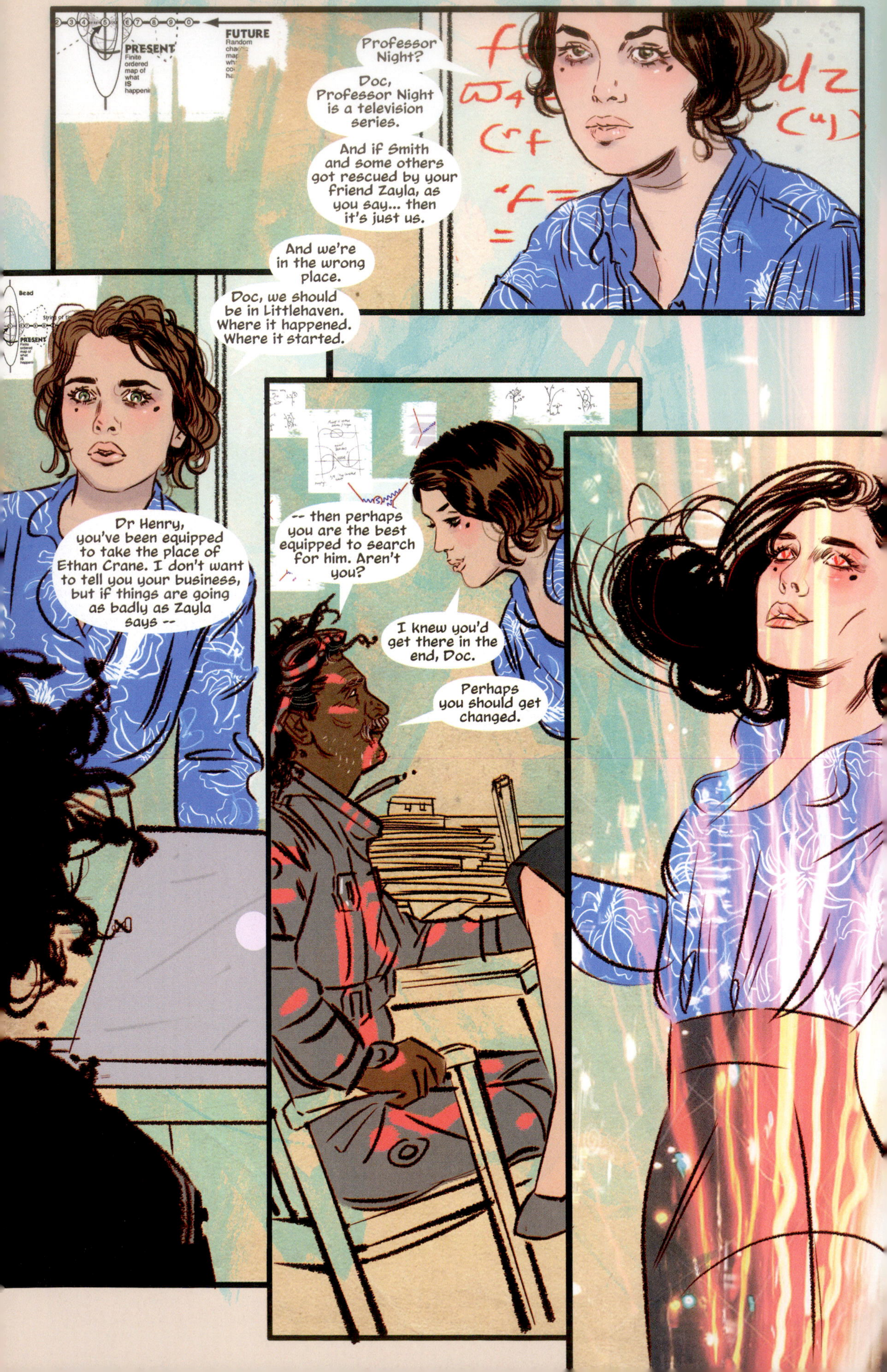
FUTURE
PRESENT
Professor Night?
Doc, Professor Night is a television series.
And if Smith and some others got rescued by your friend Zayla, as you say... then it's just us.
And we're in the wrong place.
Doc, we should be in Littlehaven. Where it happened. Where it started.
Dr Henry, you've been equipped to take the place of Ethan Crane. I don't want to tell you your business, but if things are going as badly as Zayla says --
-- then perhaps you are the best equipped to search for him. Aren't you?
I knew you'd get there in the end, Doc.
Perhaps you should get changed.

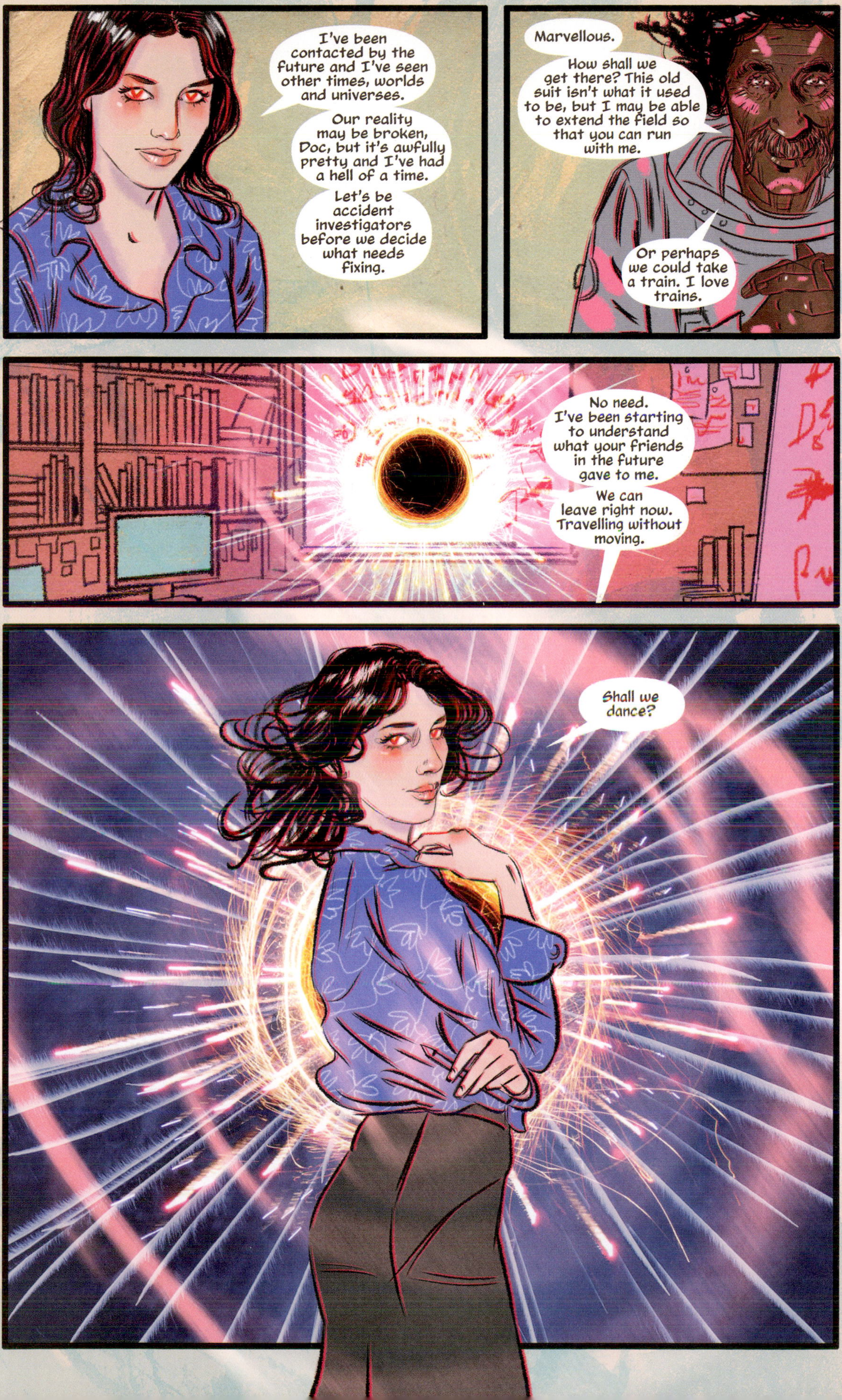
I've been contacted by the future and I've seen other times, worlds and universes.
Our reality may be broken, Doc, but it's awfully pretty and I've had a hell of a time.
Let's be accident investigators before we decide what needs fixing.
Marvellous.
How shall we get there? This old suit isn't what it used to be, but I may be able to extend the field so that you can run with me.
Or perhaps we could take a train. I love trains.
No need. I've been starting to understand what your friends in the future gave to me.
We can leave right now. Travelling without moving.
Shall we dance?

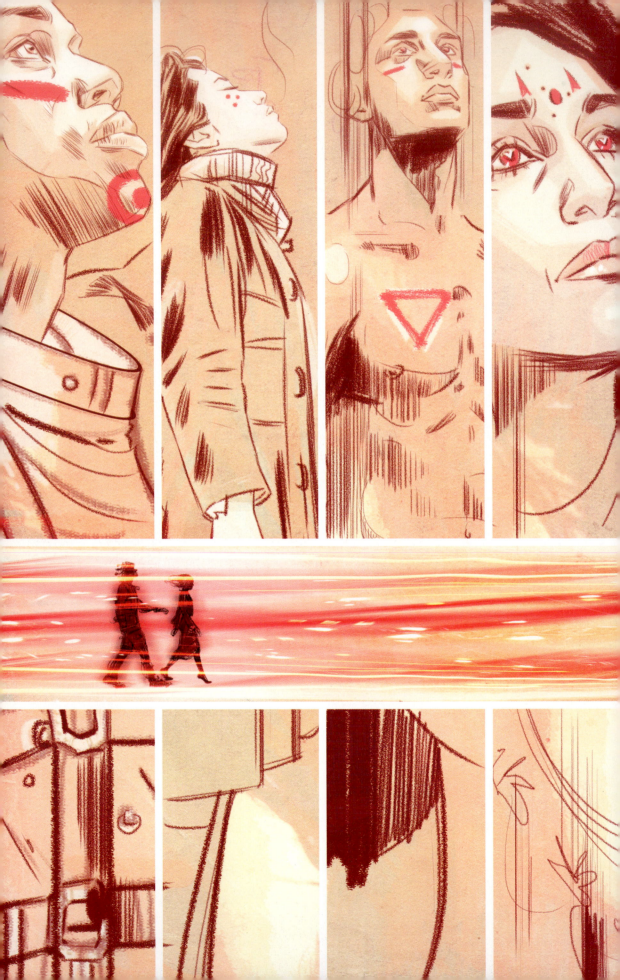

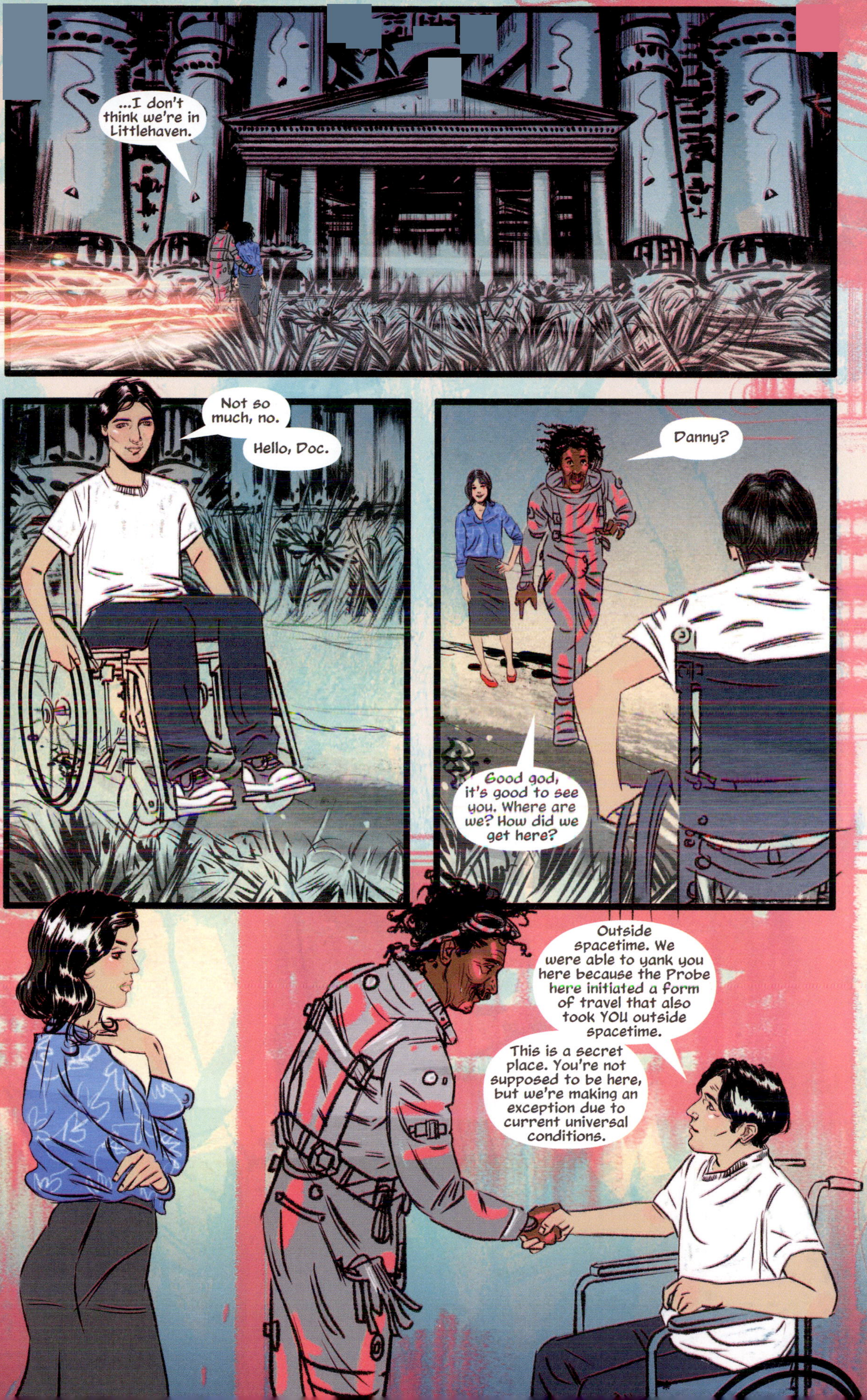
...I don't think we're in Littlehaven.
Not so much, no.
Hello, Doc.
Danny?
Good god, it's good to see you. Where are we? How did we get here?
Outside spacetime. We were able to yank you here because the Probe here initiated a form of travel that also took YOU outside spacetime.
This is a secret place. You're not supposed to be here, but we're making an exception due to current universal conditions.

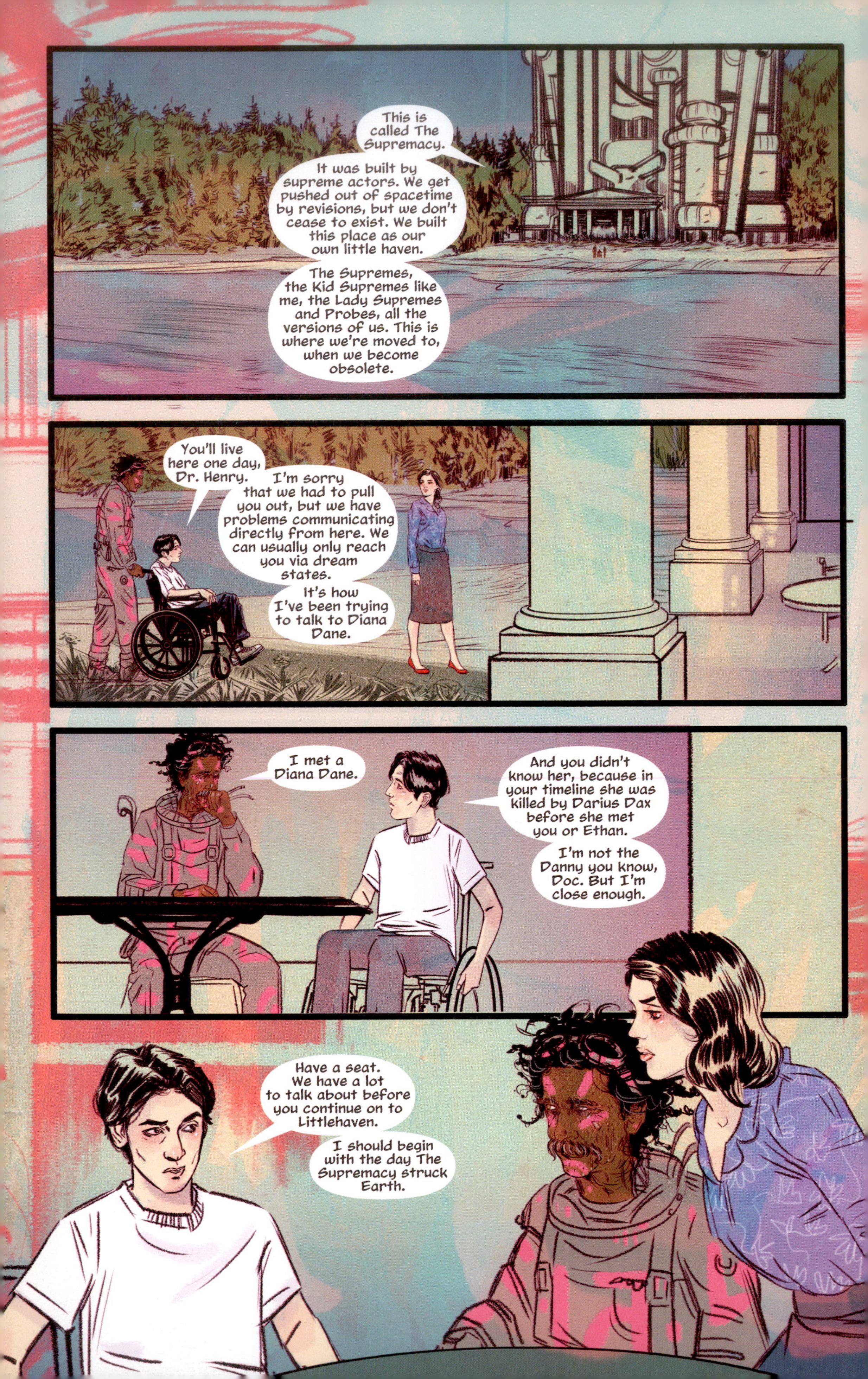
This is called The Supremacy.
It was built by supreme actors. We get pushed out of spacetime by revisions, but we don't cease to exist. We built this place as our own little haven.
The Supremes, the Kid Supremes like me, the Lady Supremes and Probes, all the versions of us. This is where we're moved to, when we become obsolete.
You'll live here one day, Dr. Henry.
I'm sorry that we had to pull you out, but we have problems communicating directly from here. We can usually only reach you via dream states.
It's how I've been trying to talk to Diana Dane.
I met a Diana Dane.
And you didn't know her, because in your timeline she was killed by Darius Dax before she met you or Ethan.
I'm not the Danny you know, Doc. But I'm close enough.
Have a seat. We have a lot to talk about before you continue on to Littlehaven.
I should begin with the day The Supremacy struck Earth.

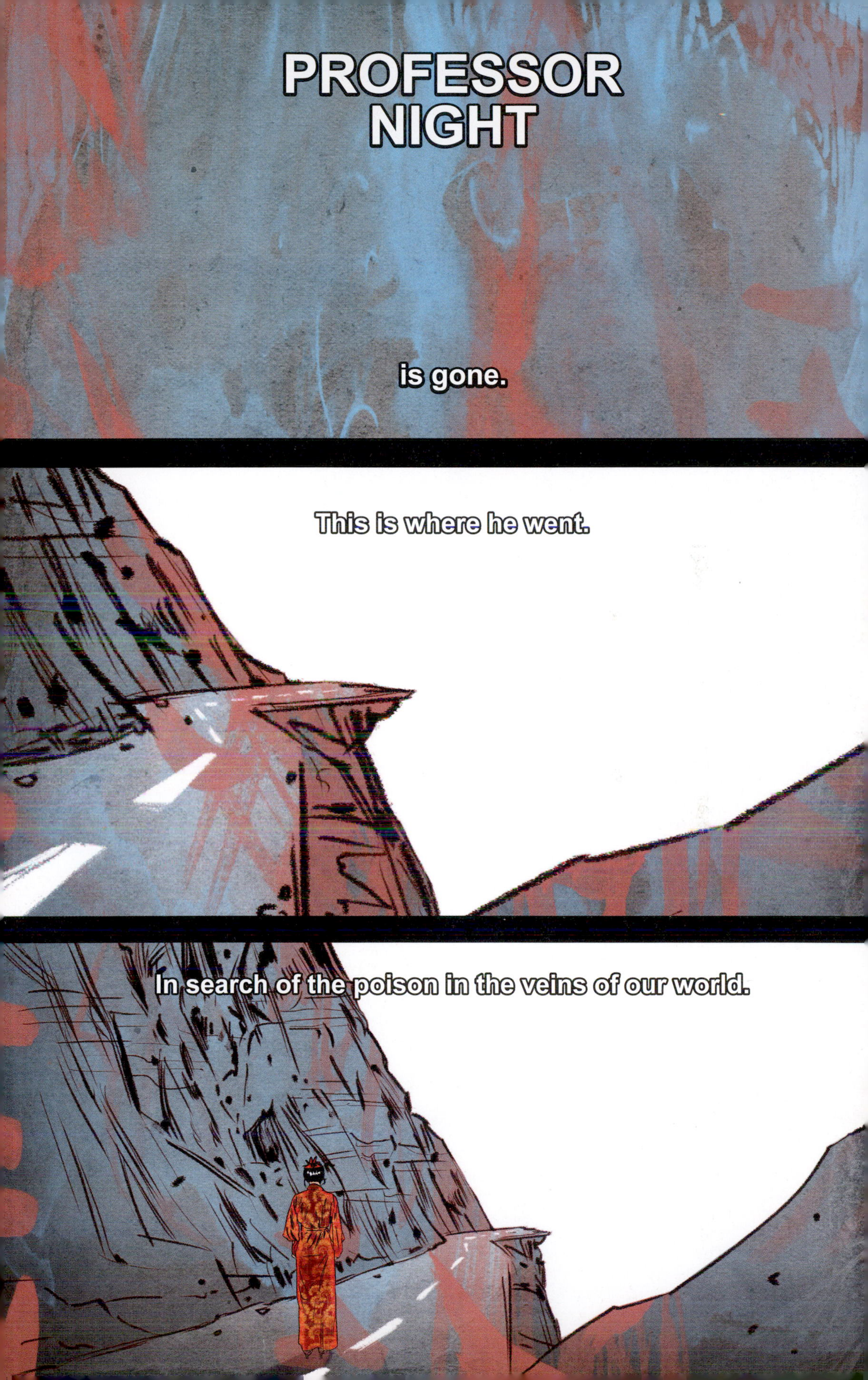
PROFESSOR NIGHT
is gone.
This is where he went.
In search of the poison in the veins of our world.

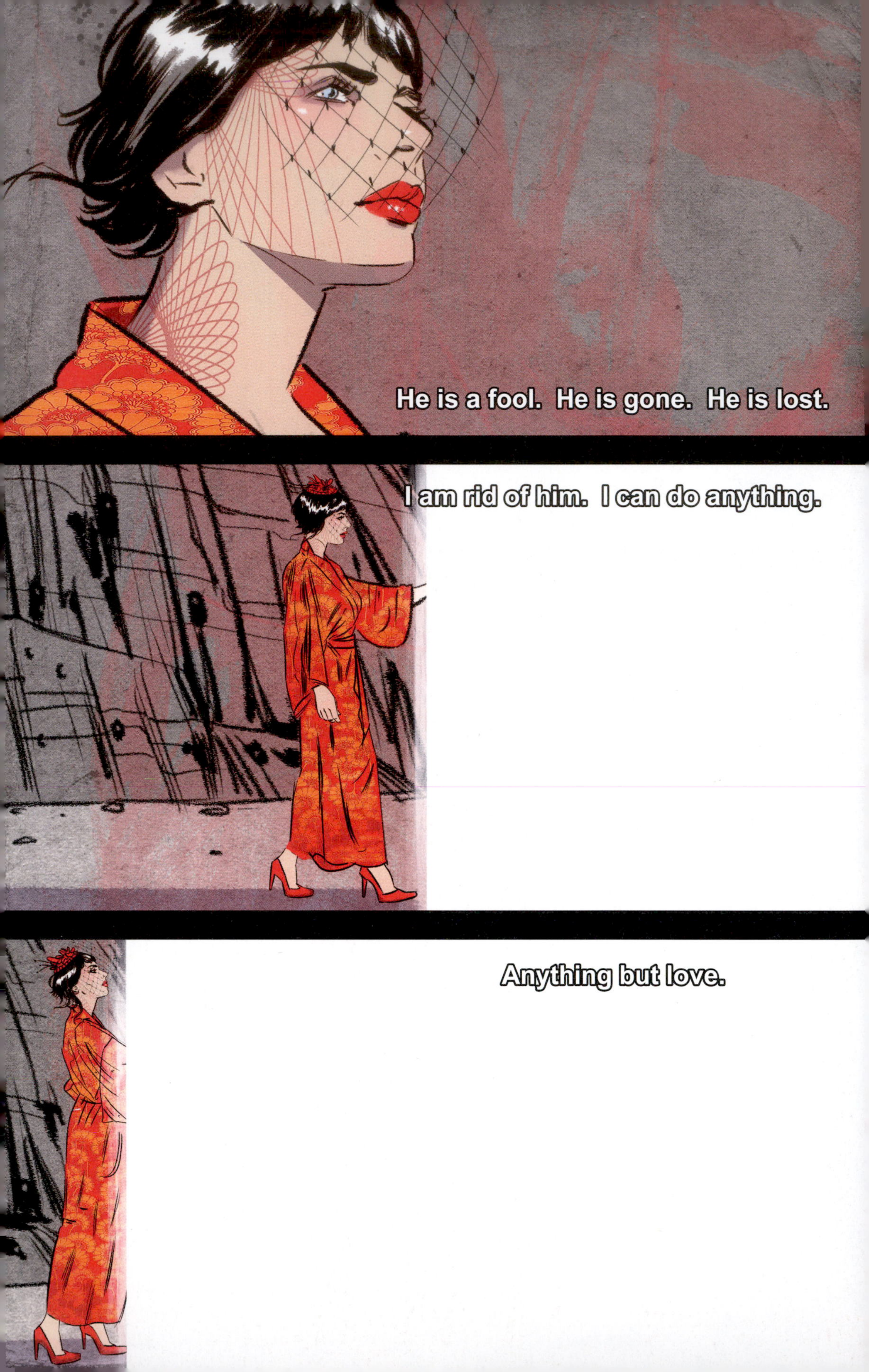
He is a fool. He is gone. He is lost.
I am rid of him. I can do anything.
Anything but love.

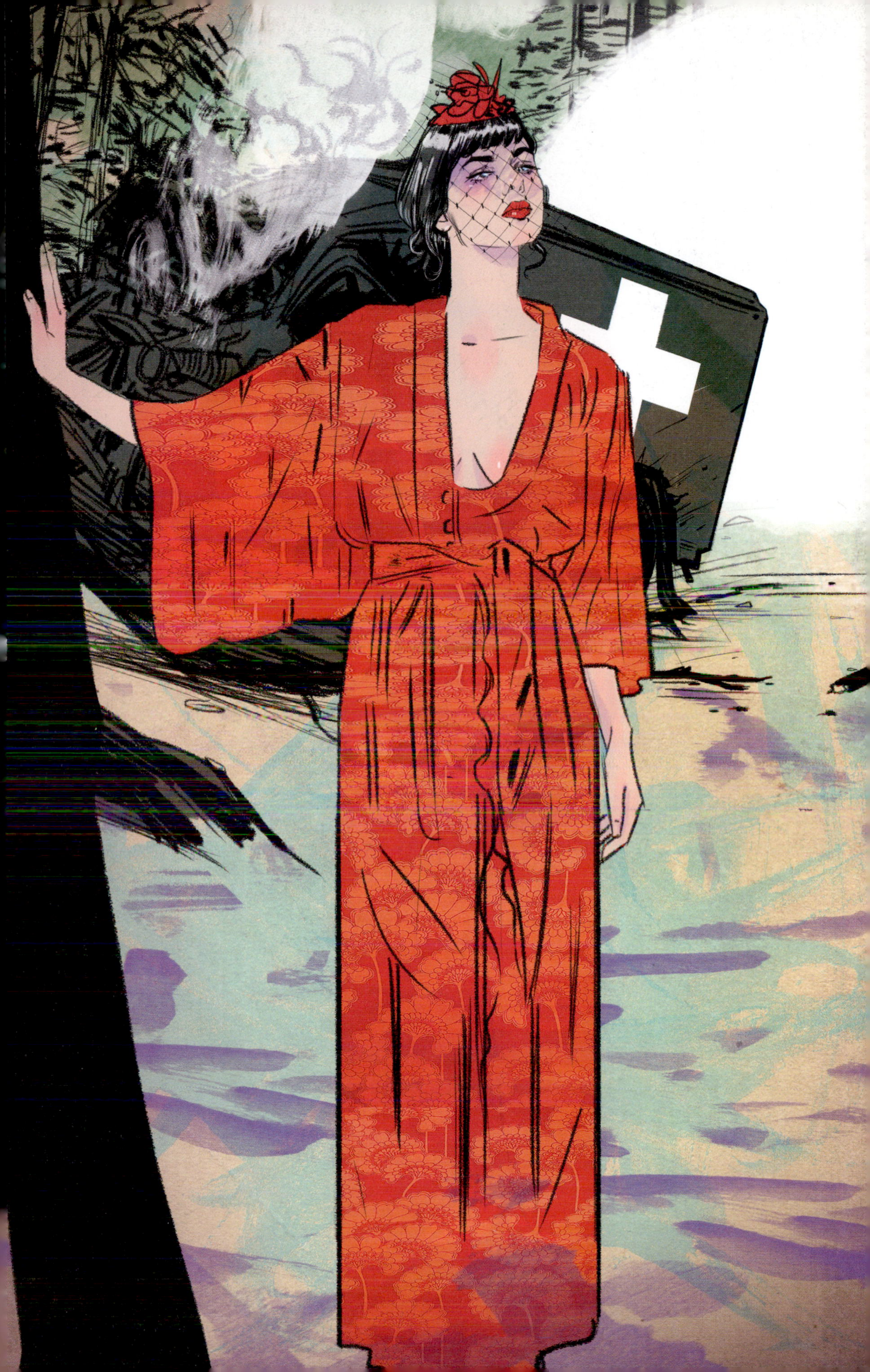

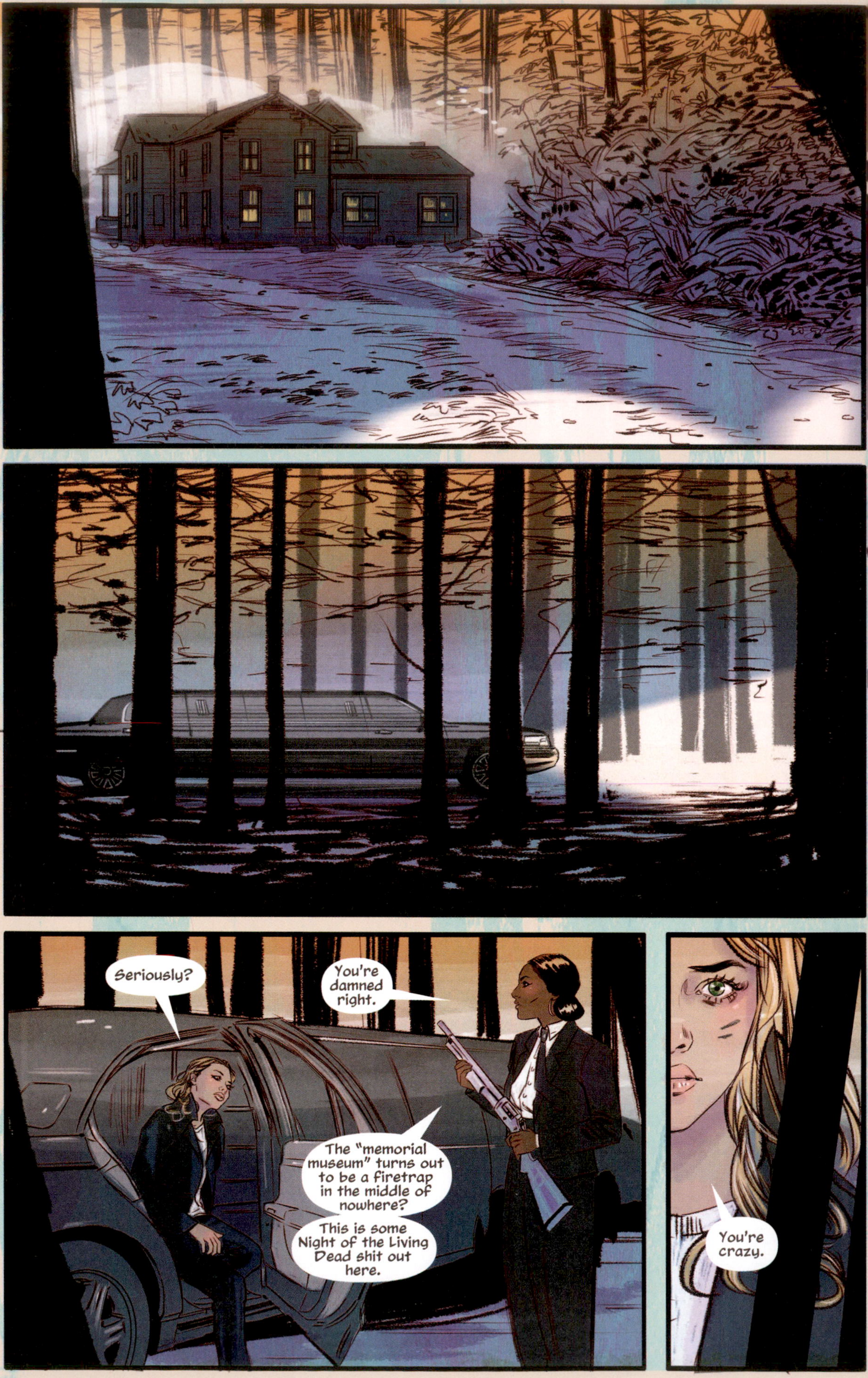
Seriously?
You're damned right.
The "memorial museum" turns out to be a firetrap in the middle of nowhere?
This is some Night of the Living Dead shit out here.
You're crazy.

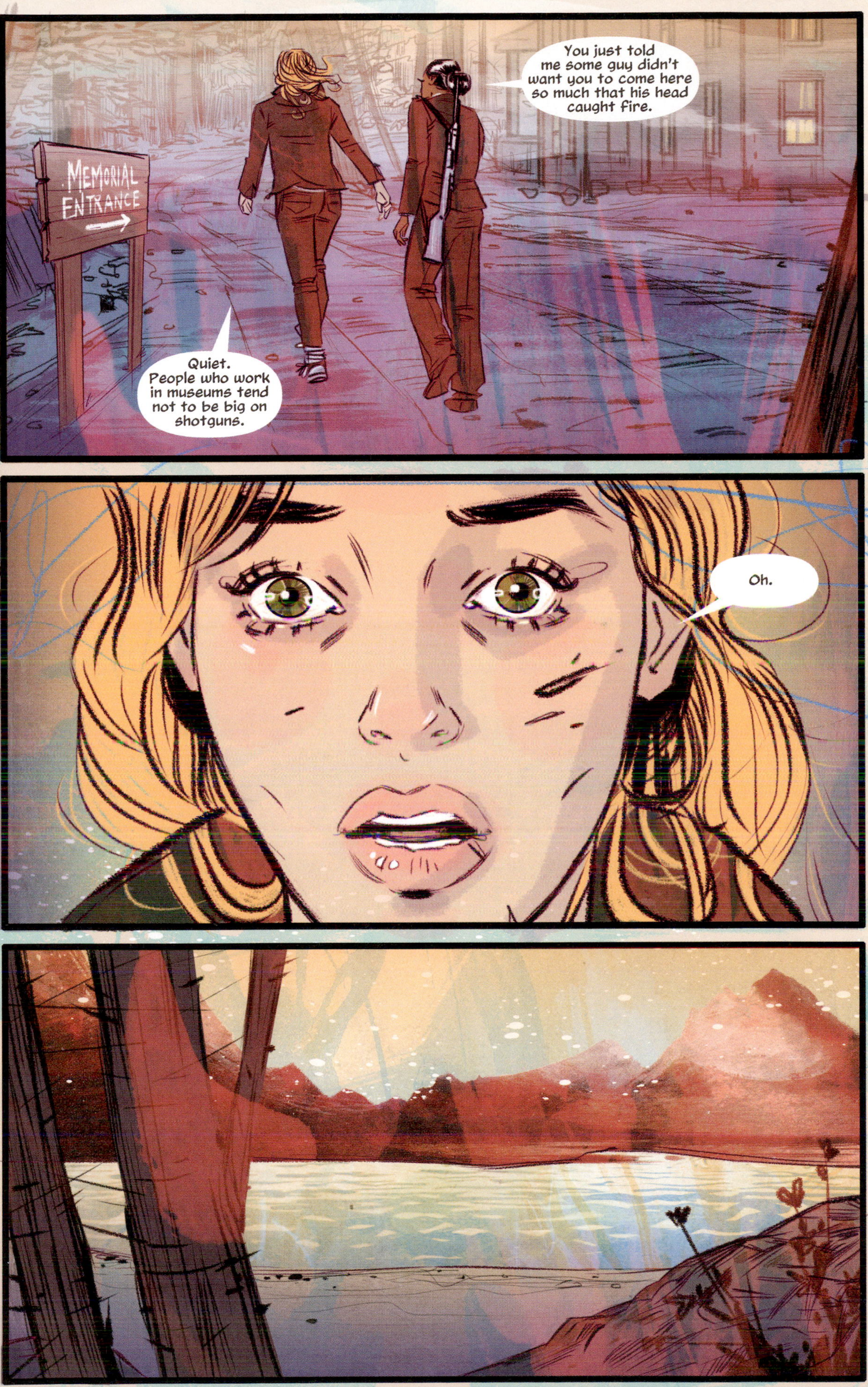
MEMORIAL ENTRANCE
You just told me some guy didn't want you to come here so much that his head caught fire.
Quiet. People who work in museums tend not to be big on shotguns.
Oh.

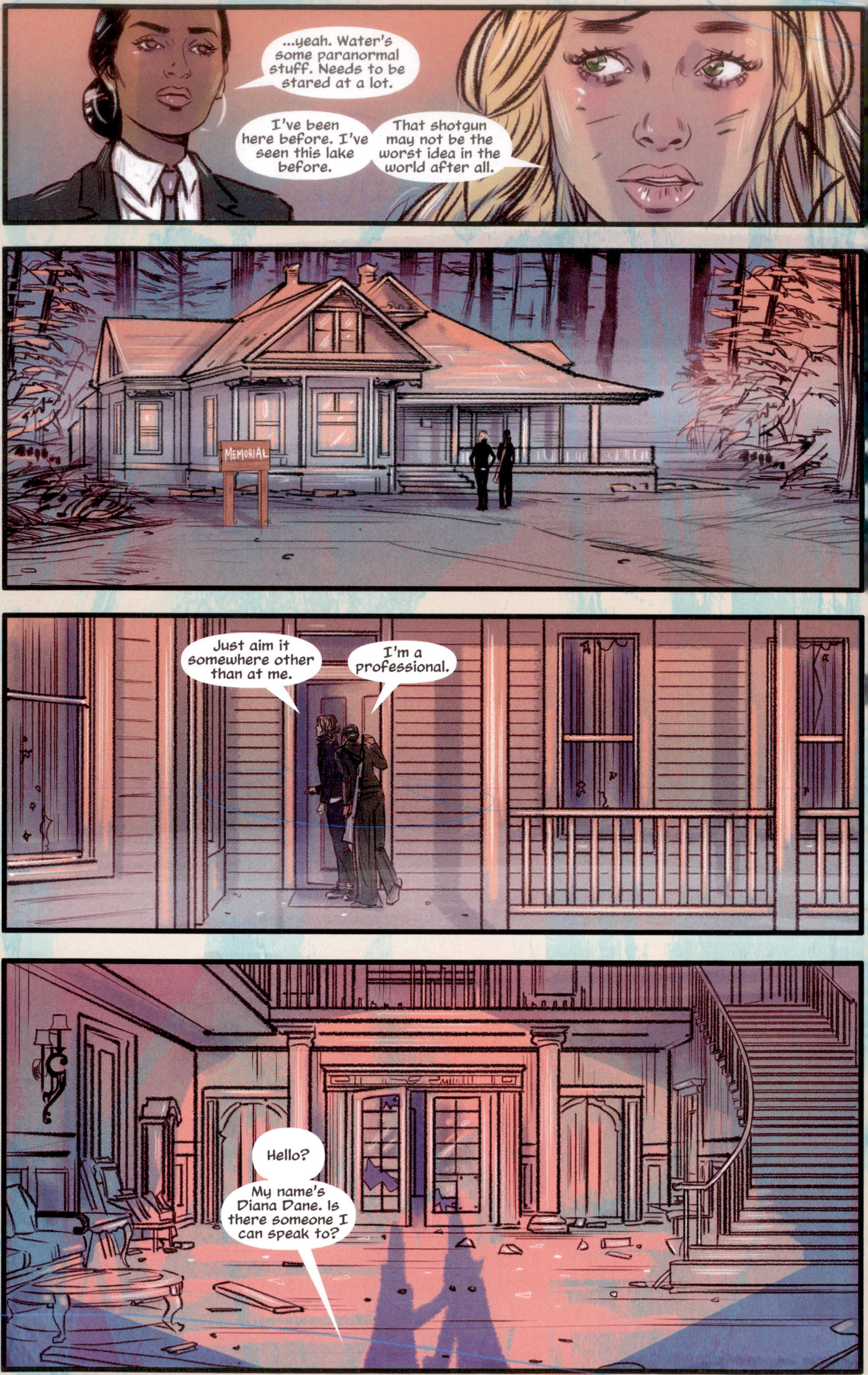
...yeah. Water's some paranormal stuff. Needs to be stared at a lot.
I've been here before. I've seen this lake before.
That shotgun may not be the worst idea in the world after all.
MEMORIAL
Just aim it somewhere other than at me.
I'm a professional.
Hello?
My name's Diana Dane. Is there someone I can speak to?

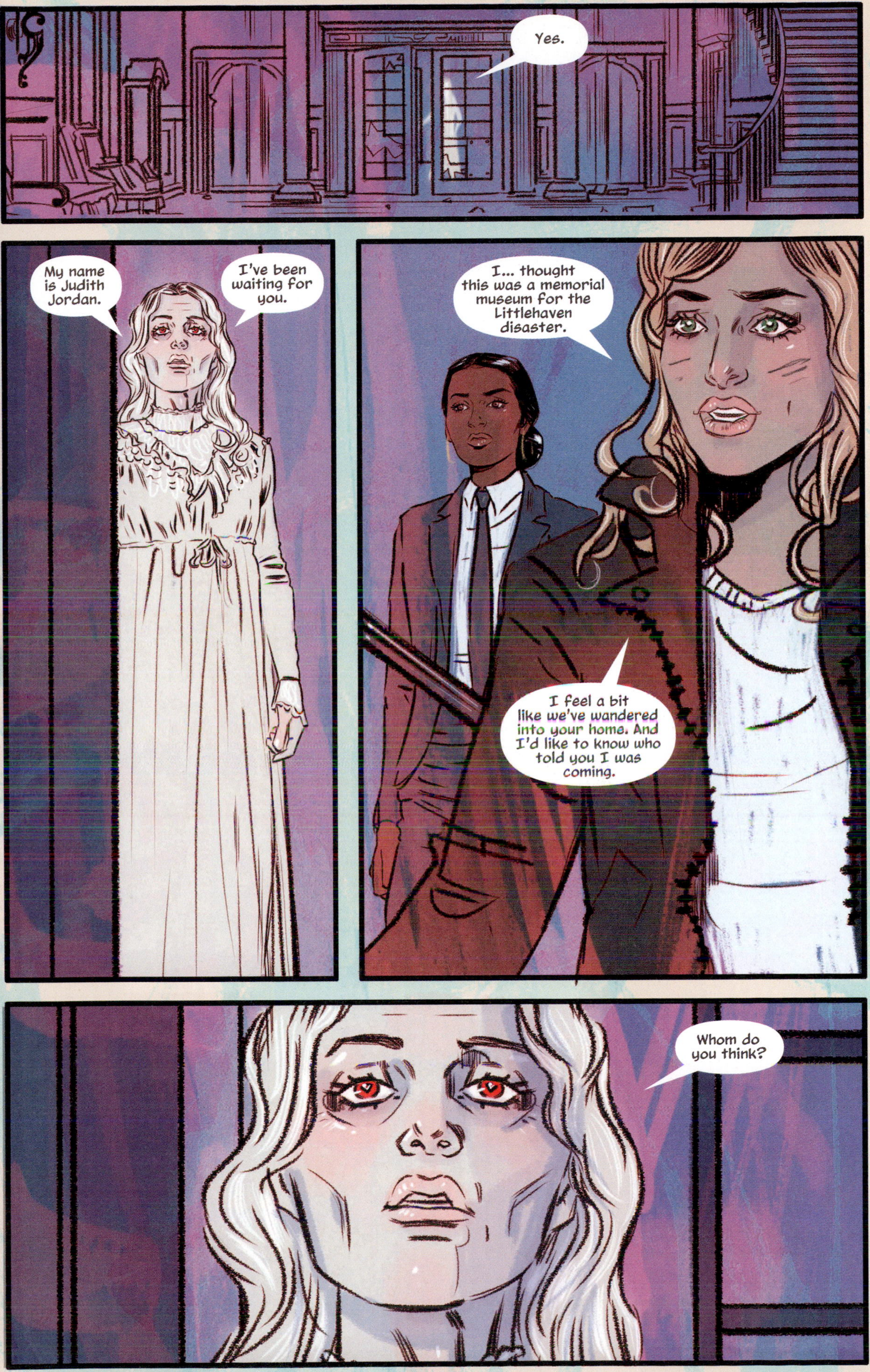
Yes.
My name is Judith Jordan.
I've been waiting for you.
I... thought this was a memorial museum for the Littlehaven disaster.
I feel a bit like we've wandered into your home. And I'd like to know who told you I was coming.
Whom do you think?

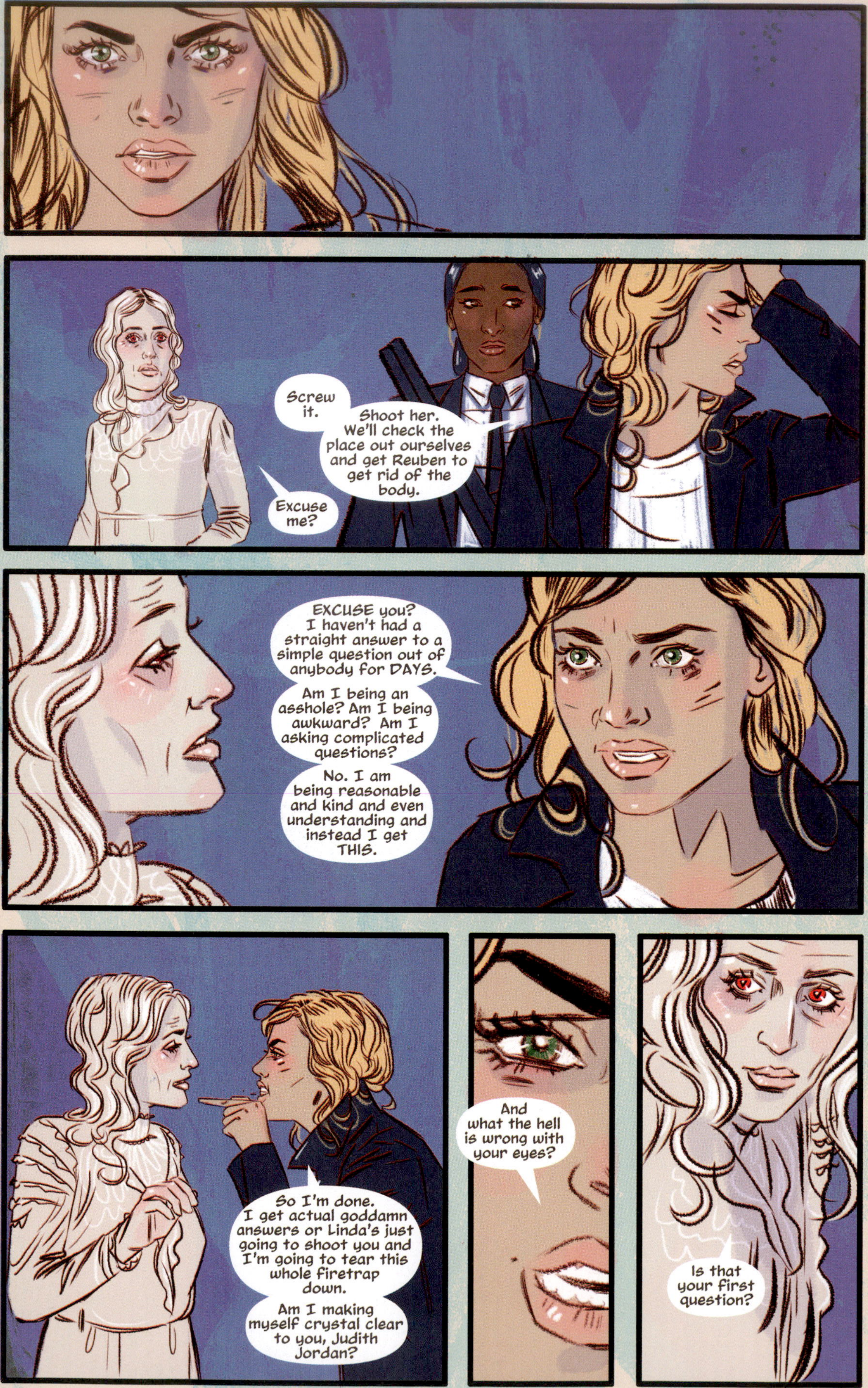
Screw it.
Shoot her. We'll check the place out ourselves and get Reuben to get rid of the body.
Excuse me?
EXCUSE you? I haven't had a straight answer to a simple question out of anybody for DAYS.
Am I being an asshole? Am I being awkward? Am I asking complicated questions?
No. I am being reasonable and kind and even understanding and instead I get THIS.
So I'm done. I get actual goddamn answers or Linda's just going to shoot you and I'm going to tear this whole firetrap down.
Am I making myself crystal clear to you, Judith Jordan?
And what the hell is wrong with your eyes?
Is that your first question?

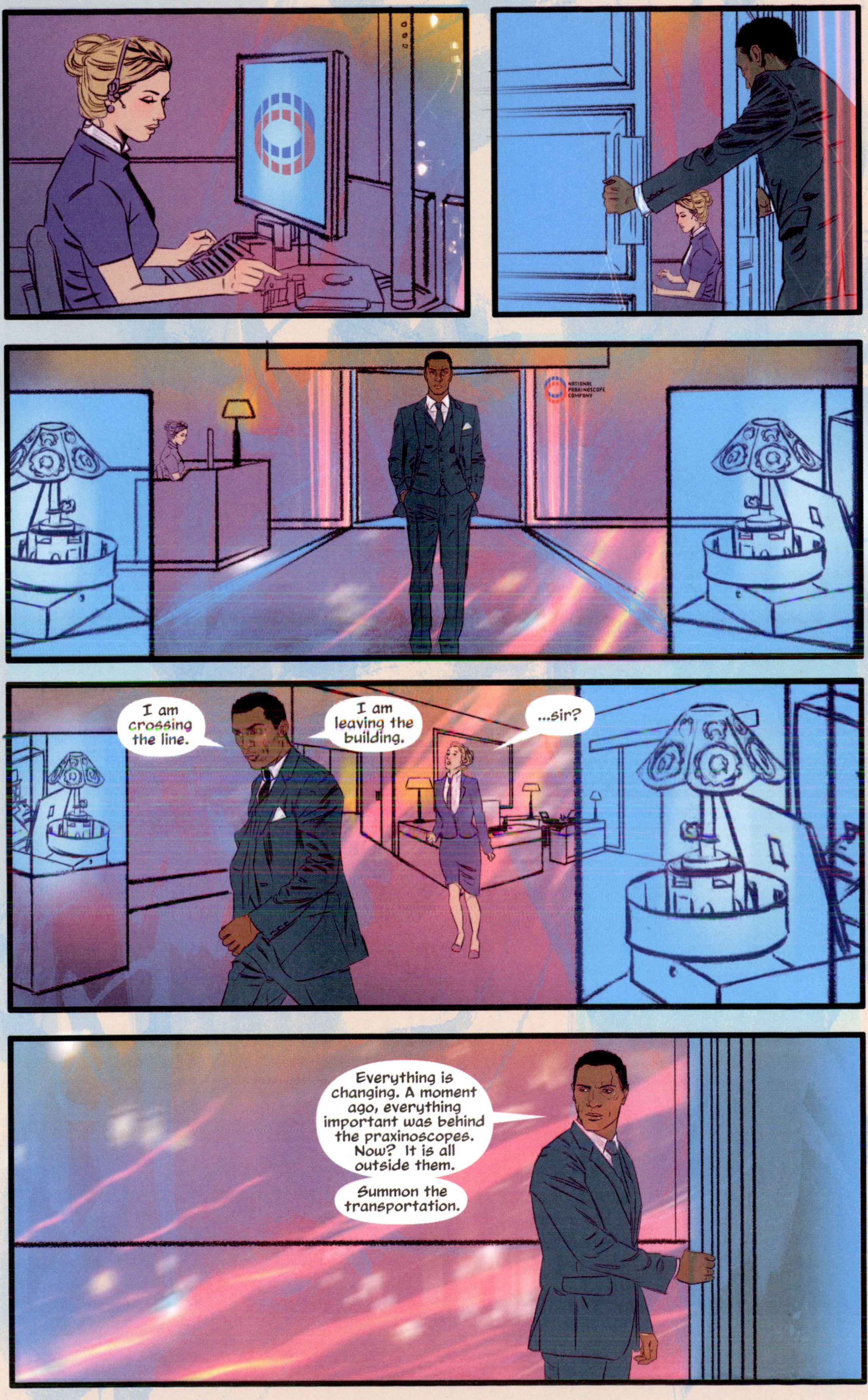
NATIONAL PRAXINOSCOPE COMPANY
I am crossing the line.
I am leaving the building.
...sir?
Everything is changing. A moment ago, everything important was behind the praxinoscopes. Now? It is all outside them.
Summon the transportation.

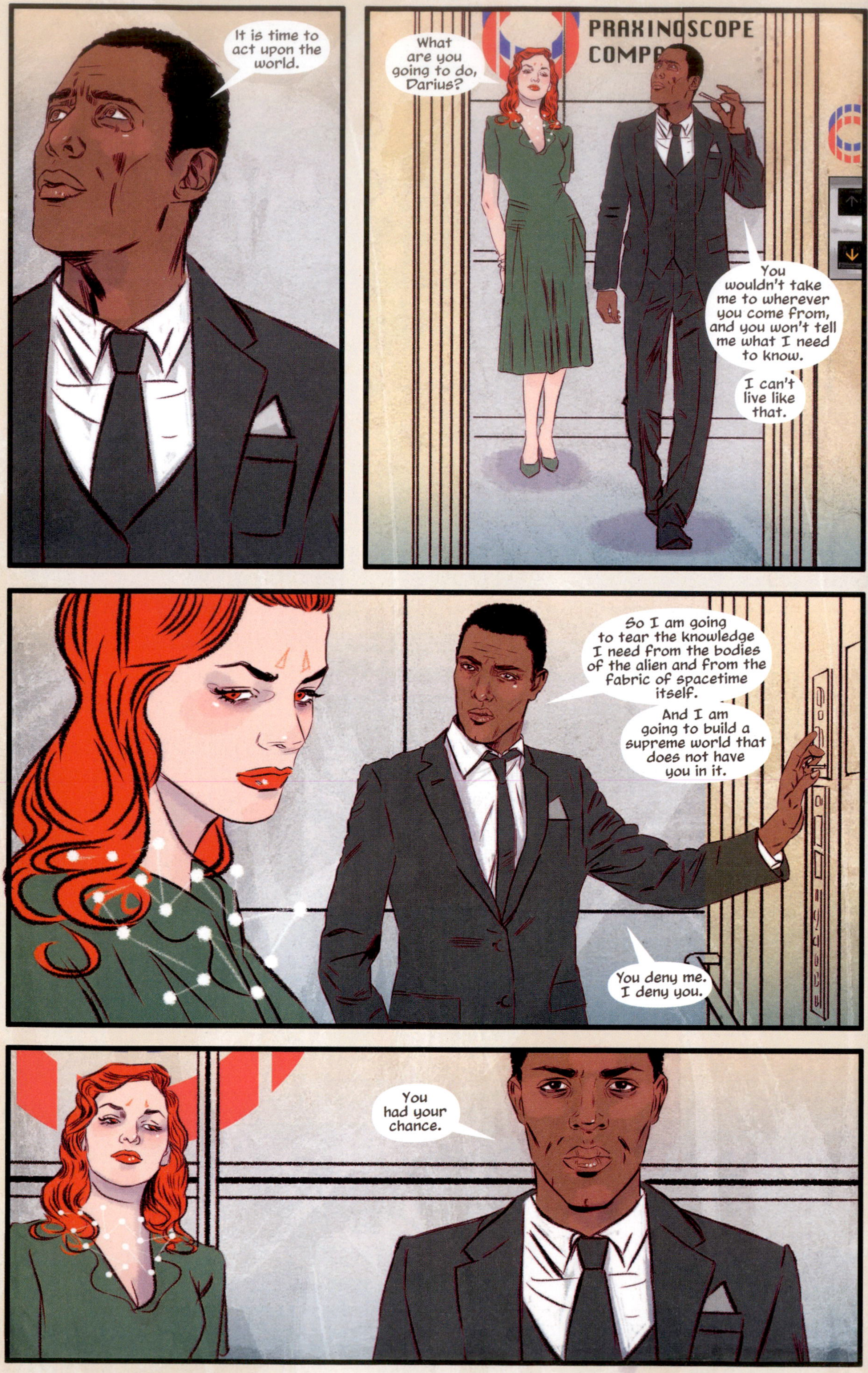
It is time to act upon the world.
What are you going to do, Darius?
PRAXINOSCOPE COMPA
You wouldn't take me to wherever you come from, and you won't tell me what I need to know.
I can't live like that.
So I am going to tear the knowledge I need from the bodies of the alien and from the fabric of spacetime itself.
And I am going to build a supreme world that does not have you in it.
You deny me. I deny you.
You had your chance.

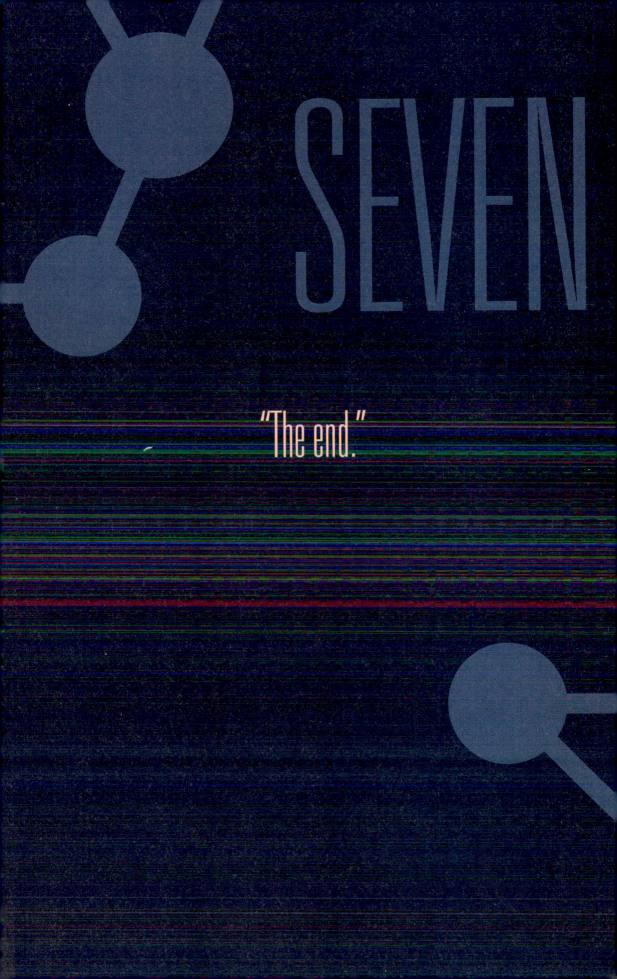

SEVEN

"The end."

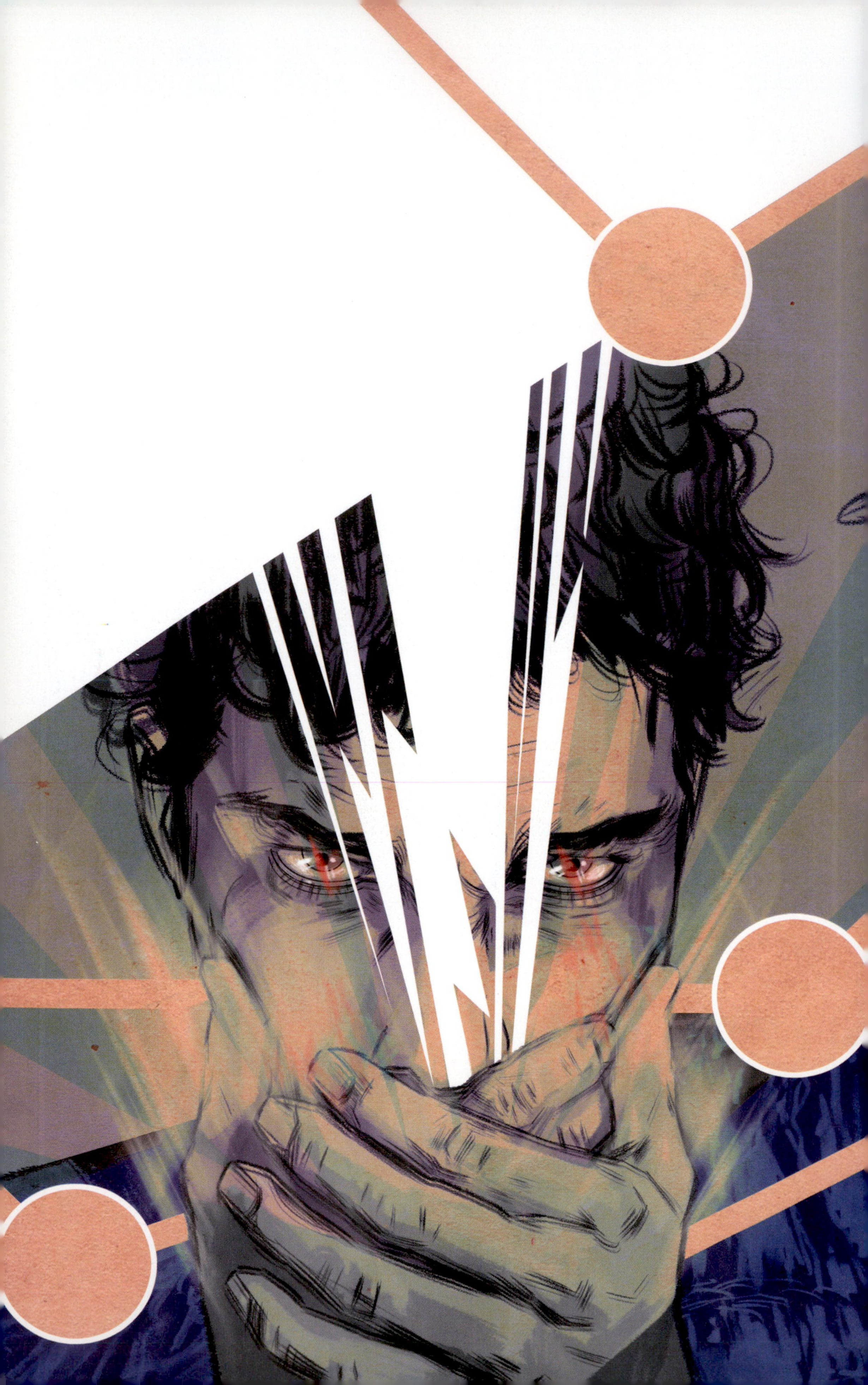

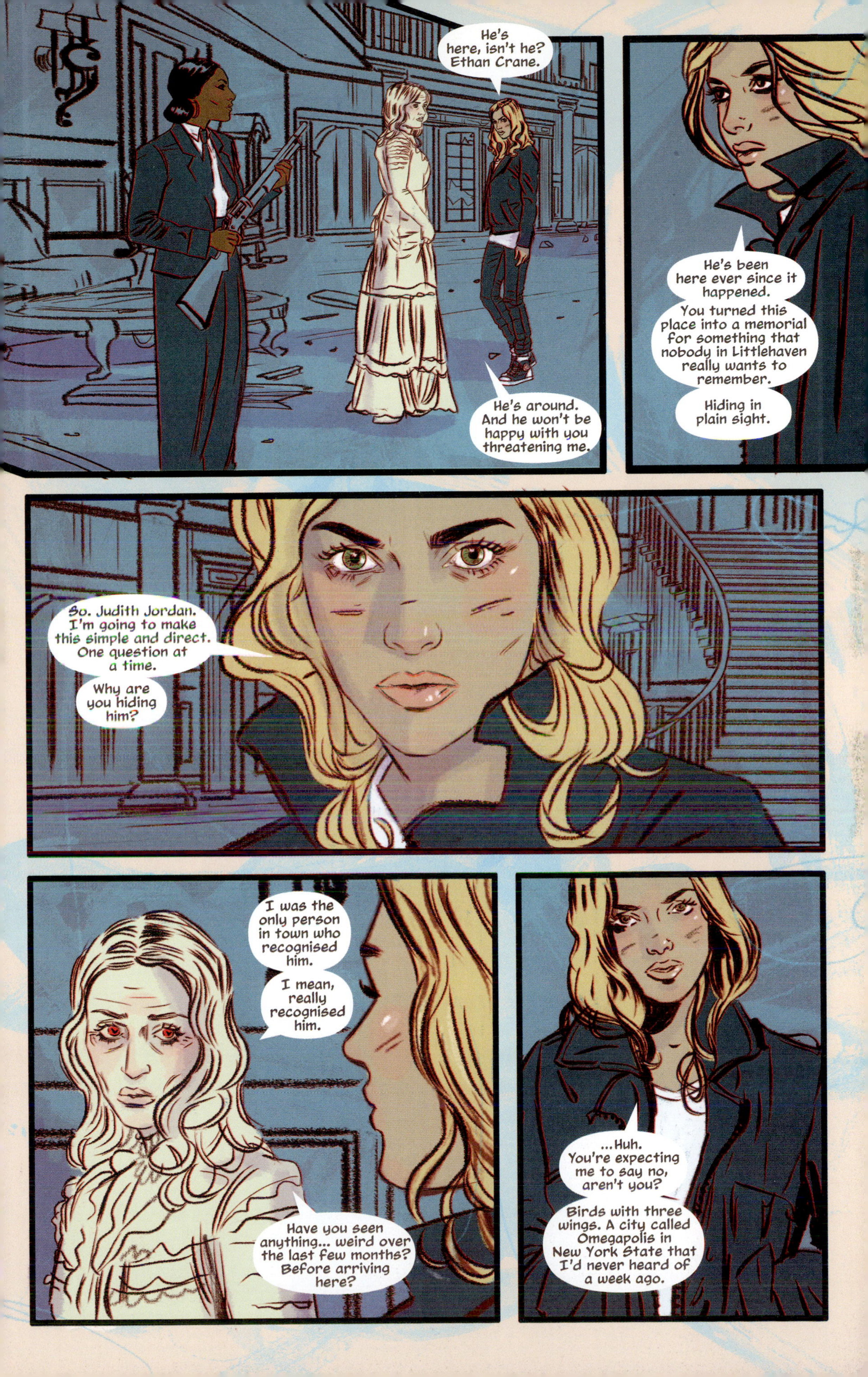
He's here, isn't he? Ethan Crane.
He's around. And he won't be happy with you threatening me.
He's been here ever since it happened.
You turned this place into a memorial for something that nobody in Littlehaven really wants to remember.
Hiding in plain sight.
So. Judith Jordan. I'm going to make this simple and direct. One question at a time.
Why are you hiding him?
I was the only person in town who recognised him.
I mean, really recognised him.
Have you seen anything... weird over the last few months? Before arriving here?
...Huh. You're expecting me to say no, aren't you?
Birds with three wings. A city called Omegapolis in New York State that I'd never heard of a week ago.

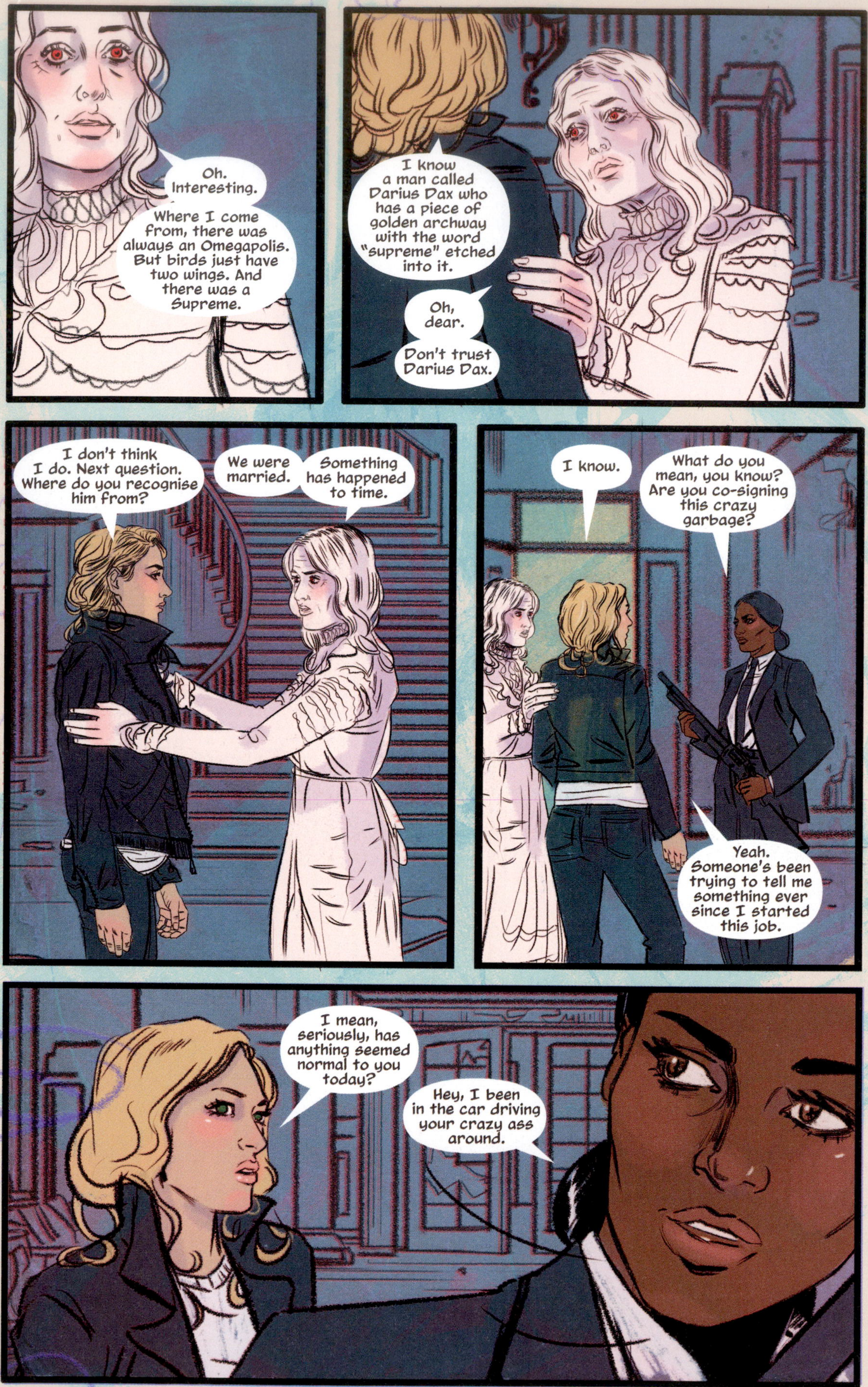
Oh. Interesting.
Where I come from, there was always an Omegapolis. But birds just have two wings. And there was a Supreme.
I know a man called Darius Dax who has a piece of golden archway with the word "supreme" etched into it.
Oh, dear.
Don't trust Darius Dax.
I don't think I do. Next question. Where do you recognise him from?
We were married.
Something has happened to time.
I know.
What do you mean, you know? Are you co-signing this crazy garbage?
Yeah. Someone's been trying to tell me something ever since I started this job.
I mean, seriously, has anything seemed normal to you today?
Hey, I been in the car driving your crazy ass around.

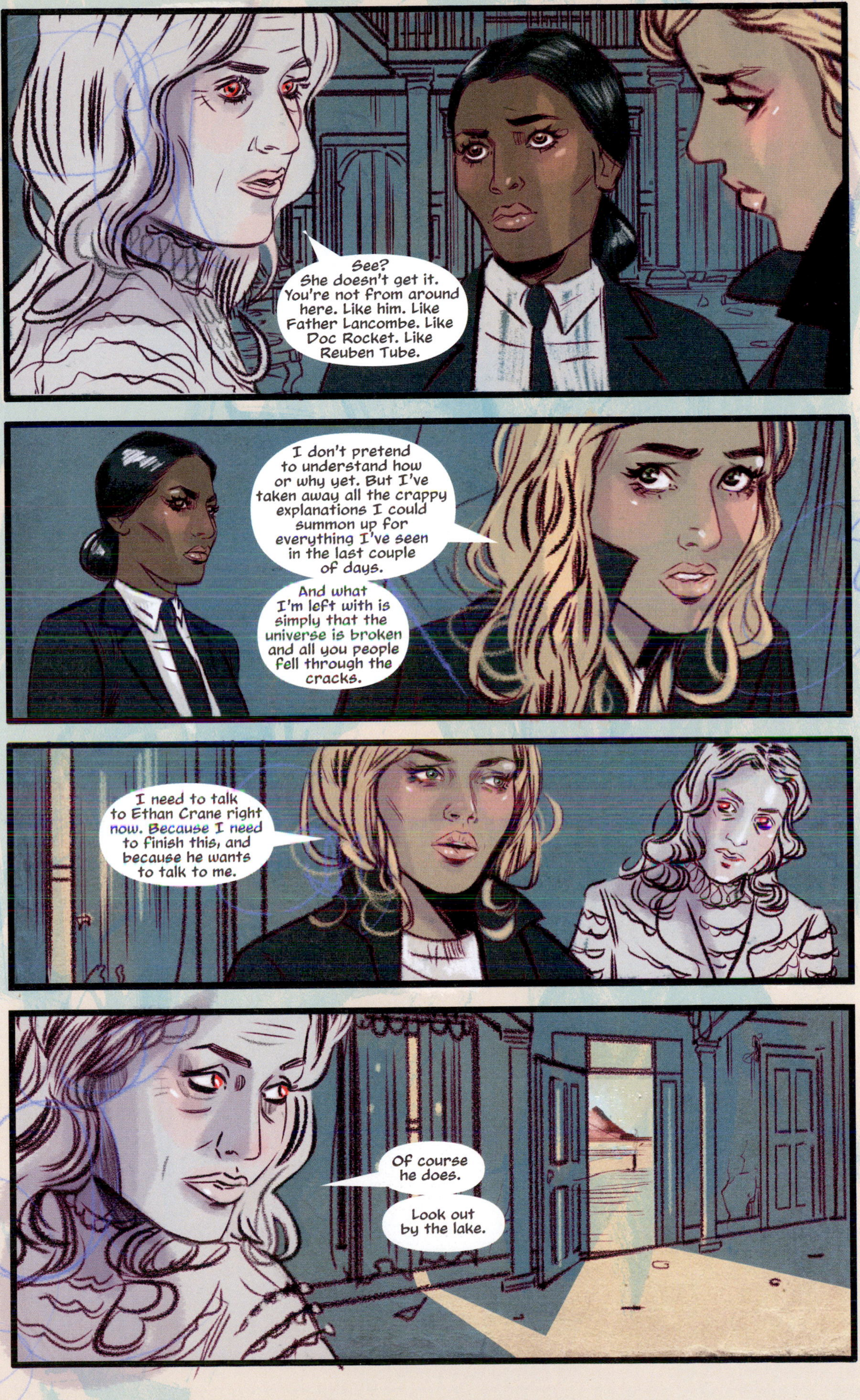
See? She doesn't get it. You're not from around here. Like him. Like Father Lancombe. Like Doc Rocket. Like Reuben Tube.
I don't pretend to understand how or why yet. But I've taken away all the crappy explanations I could summon up for everything I've seen in the last couple of days.
And what I'm left with is simply that the universe is broken and all you people fell through the cracks.
I need to talk to Ethan Crane right now. Because I need to finish this, and because he wants to talk to me.
Of course he does.
Look out by the lake.

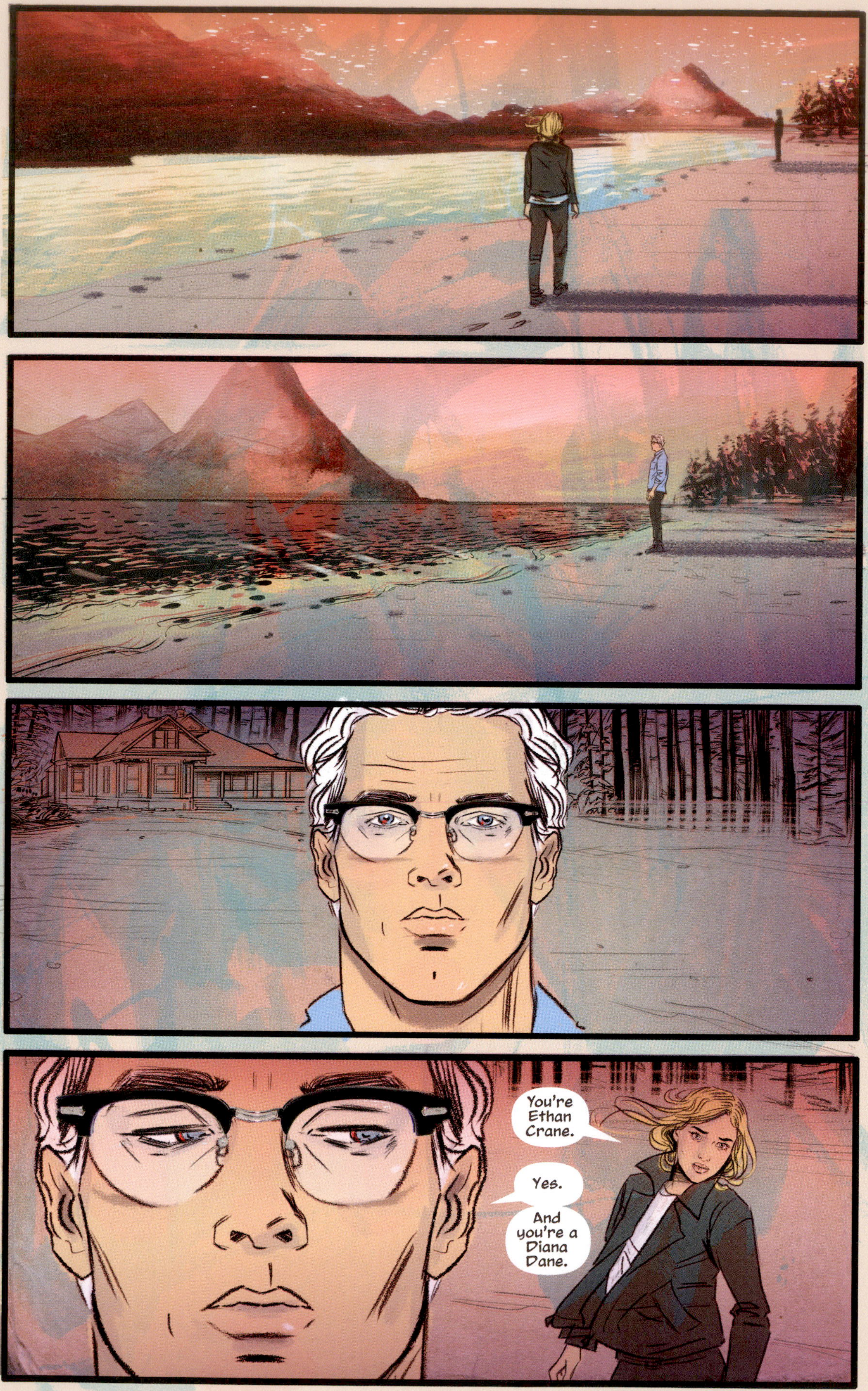
You're Ethan Crane.
Yes.
And you're a Diana Dane.

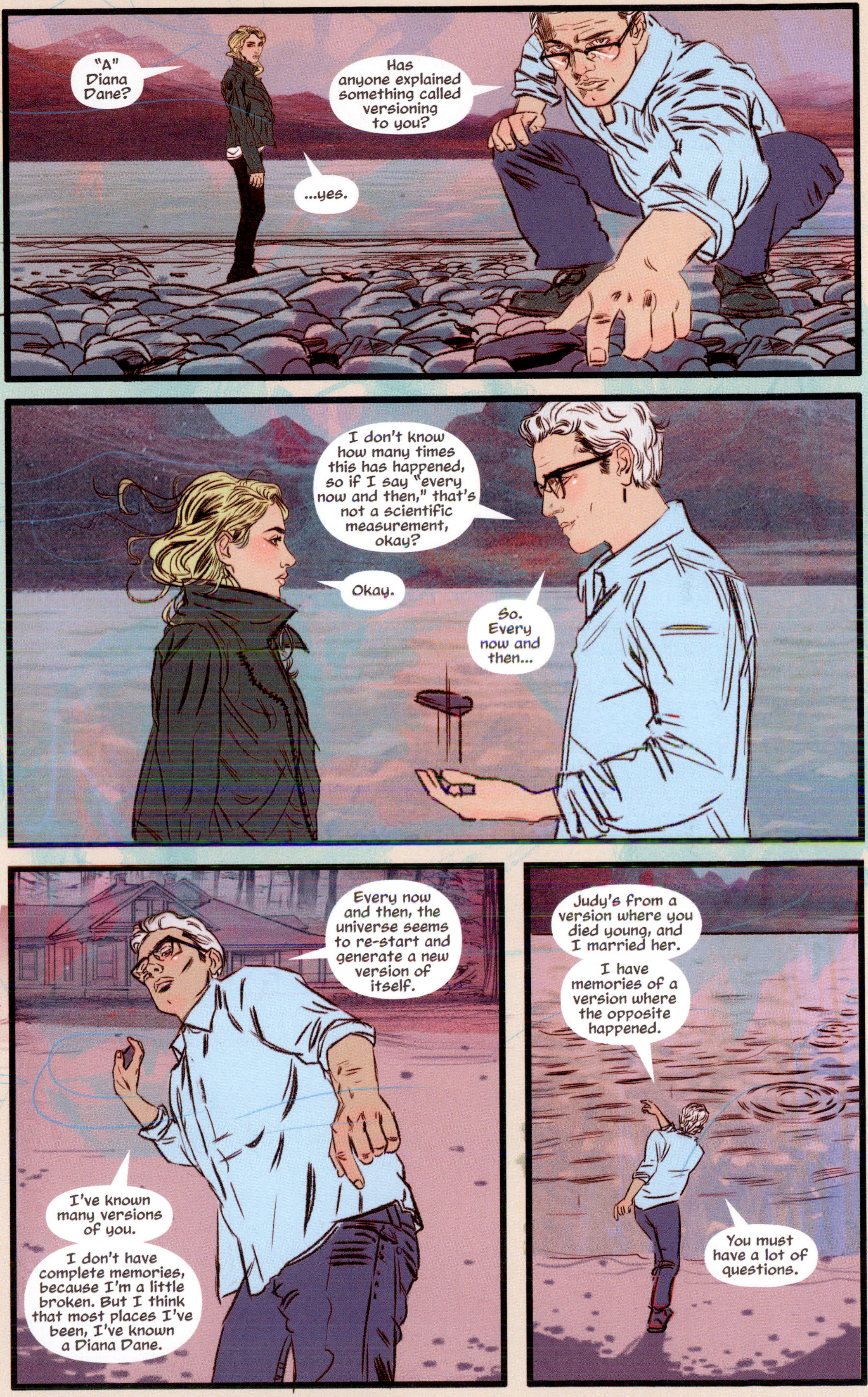
"A" Diana Dane?
Has anyone explained something called versioning to you?
...yes.
I don't know how many times this has happened, so if I say "every now and then," that's not a scientific measurement, okay?
Okay.
So. Every now and then...
Every now and then, the universe seems to re-start and generate a new version of itself.
I've known many versions of you.
I don't have complete memories, because I'm a little broken. But I think that most places I've been, I've known a Diana Dane.
Judy's from a version where you died young, and I married her.
I have memories of a version where the opposite happened.
You must have a lot of questions.

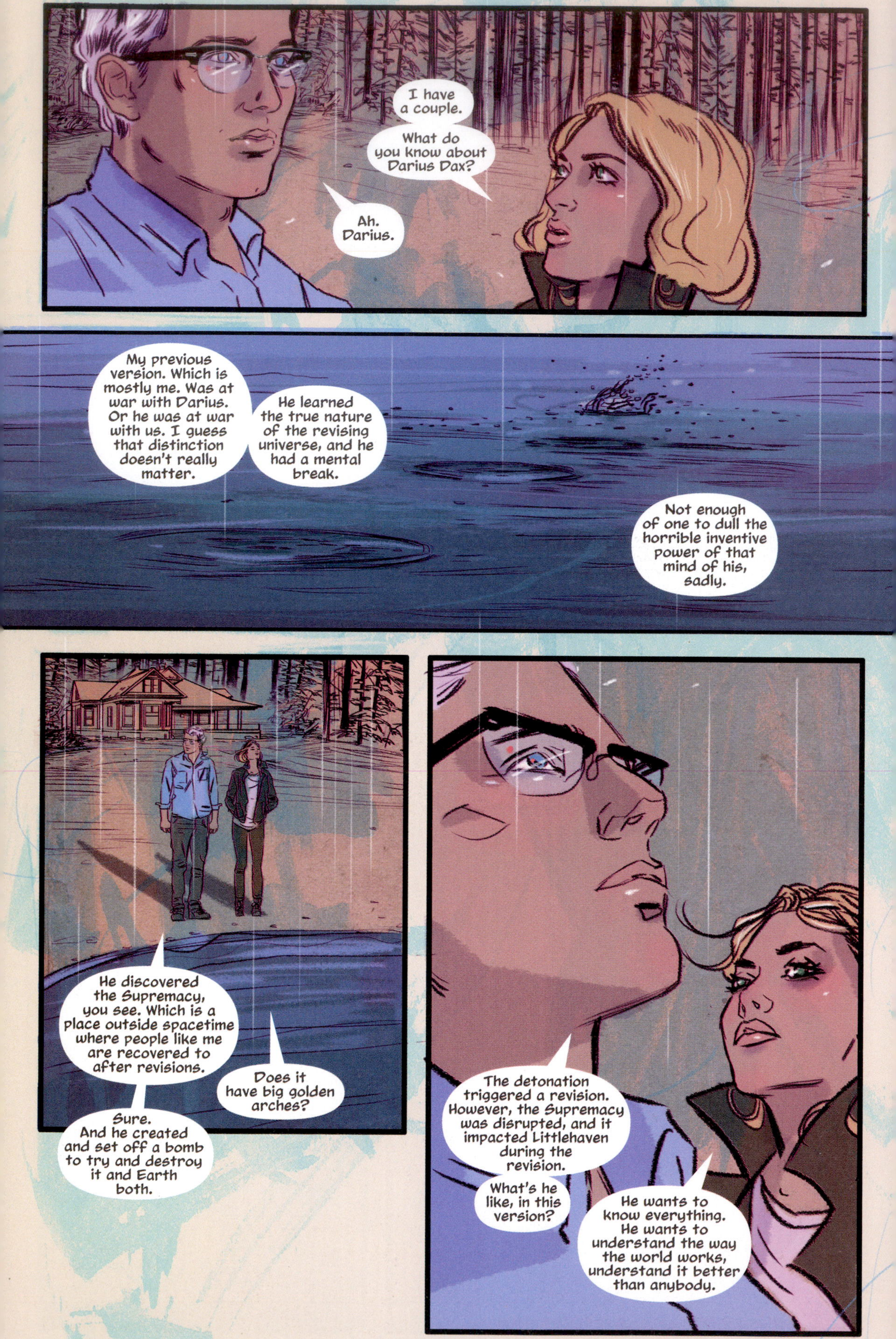
I have a couple.
What do you know about Darius Dax?
Ah. Darius.
My previous version. Which is mostly me. Was at war with Darius. Or he was at war with us. I guess that distinction doesn't really matter.
He learned the true nature of the revising universe, and he had a mental break.
Not enough of one to dull the horrible inventive power of that mind of his, sadly.
He discovered the Supremacy, you see. Which is a place outside spacetime where people like me are recovered to after revisions.
Does it have big golden arches?
Sure. And he created and set off a bomb to try and destroy it and Earth both.
The detonation triggered a revision. However, the Supremacy was disrupted, and it impacted Littlehaven during the revision.
What's he like, in this version?
He wants to know everything. He wants to understand the way the world works, understand it better than anybody.

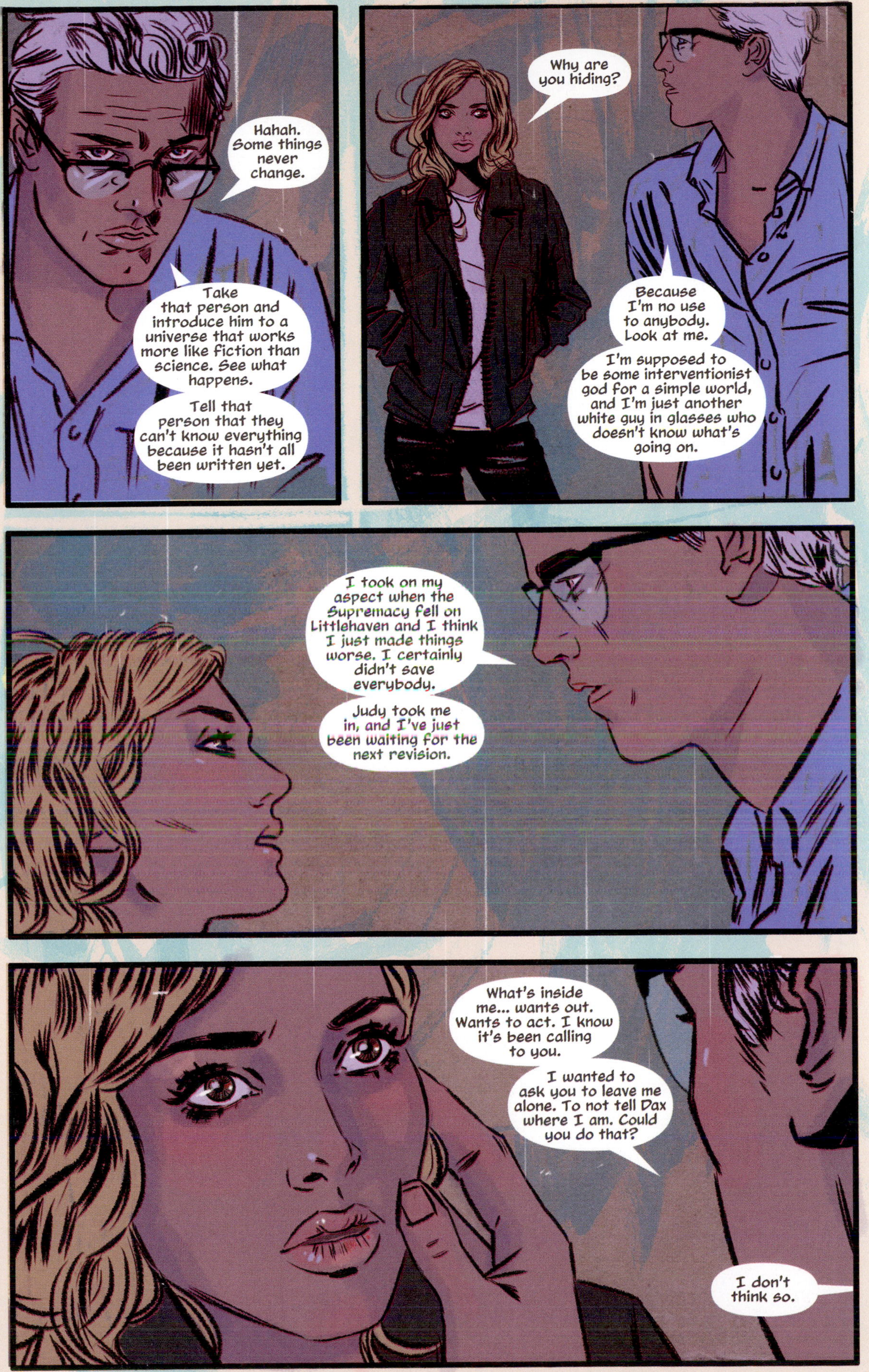
Hahah. Some things never change.
Take that person and introduce him to a universe that works more like fiction than science. See what happens.
Tell that person that they can't know everything because it hasn't all been written yet.
Why are you hiding?
Because I'm no use to anybody. Look at me.
I'm supposed to be some interventionist god for a simple world, and I'm just another white guy in glasses who doesn't know what's going on.
I took on my aspect when the Supremacy fell on Littlehaven and I think I just made things worse. I certainly didn't save everybody.
Judy took me in, and I've just been waiting for the next revision.
What's inside me... wants out. Wants to act. I know it's been calling to you.
I wanted to ask you to leave me alone. To not tell Dax where I am. Could you do that?
I don't think so.

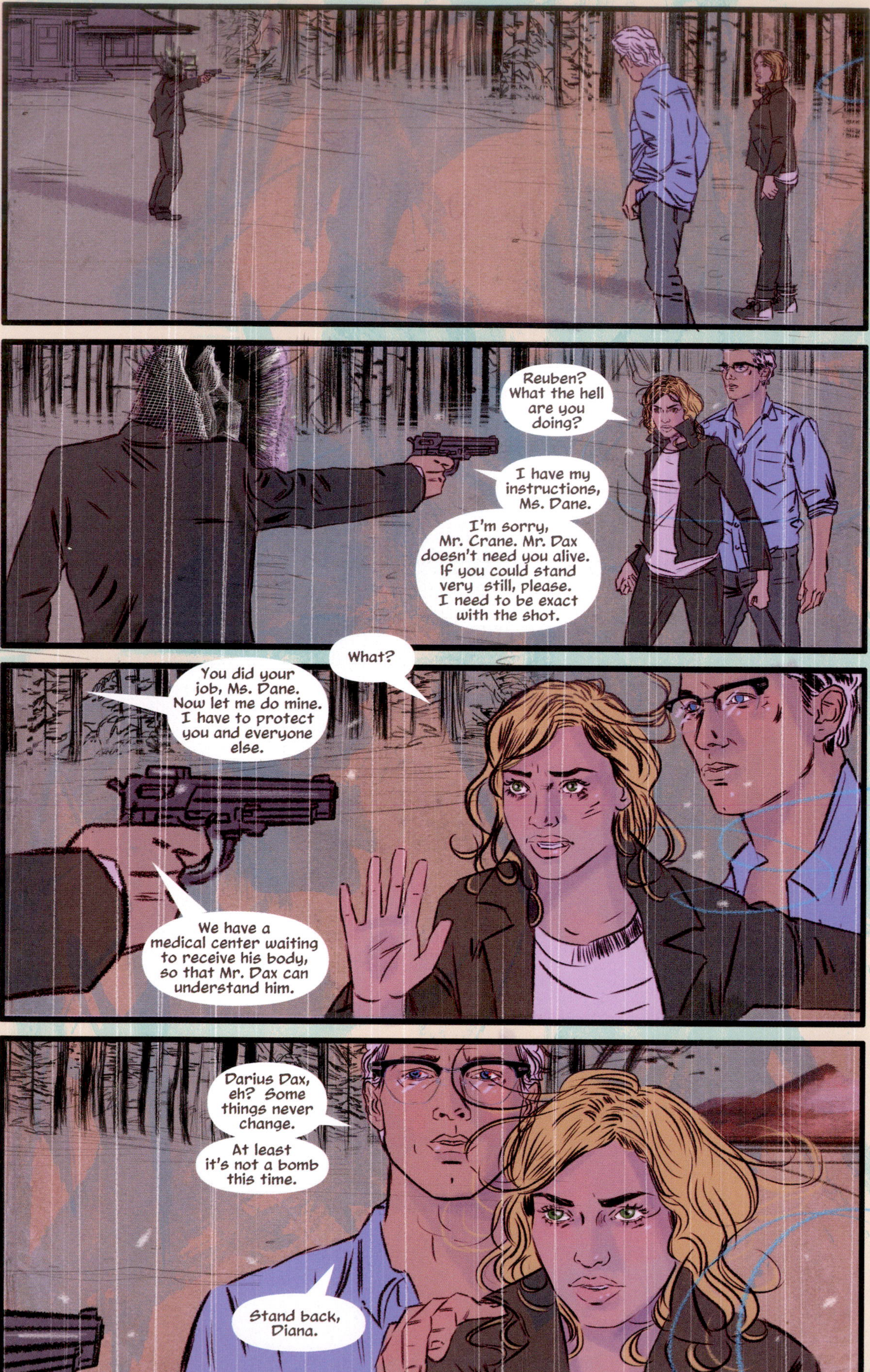
Reuben? What the hell are you doing?
I have my instructions, Ms. Dane.
I'm sorry, Mr. Crane. Mr. Dax doesn't need you alive. If you could stand very still, please. I need to be exact with the shot.
What?
You did your job, Ms. Dane. Now let me do mine. I have to protect you and everyone else.
We have a medical center waiting to receive his body, so that Mr. Dax can understand him.
Darius Dax, eh? Some things never change.
At least it's not a bomb this time.
Stand back, Diana.

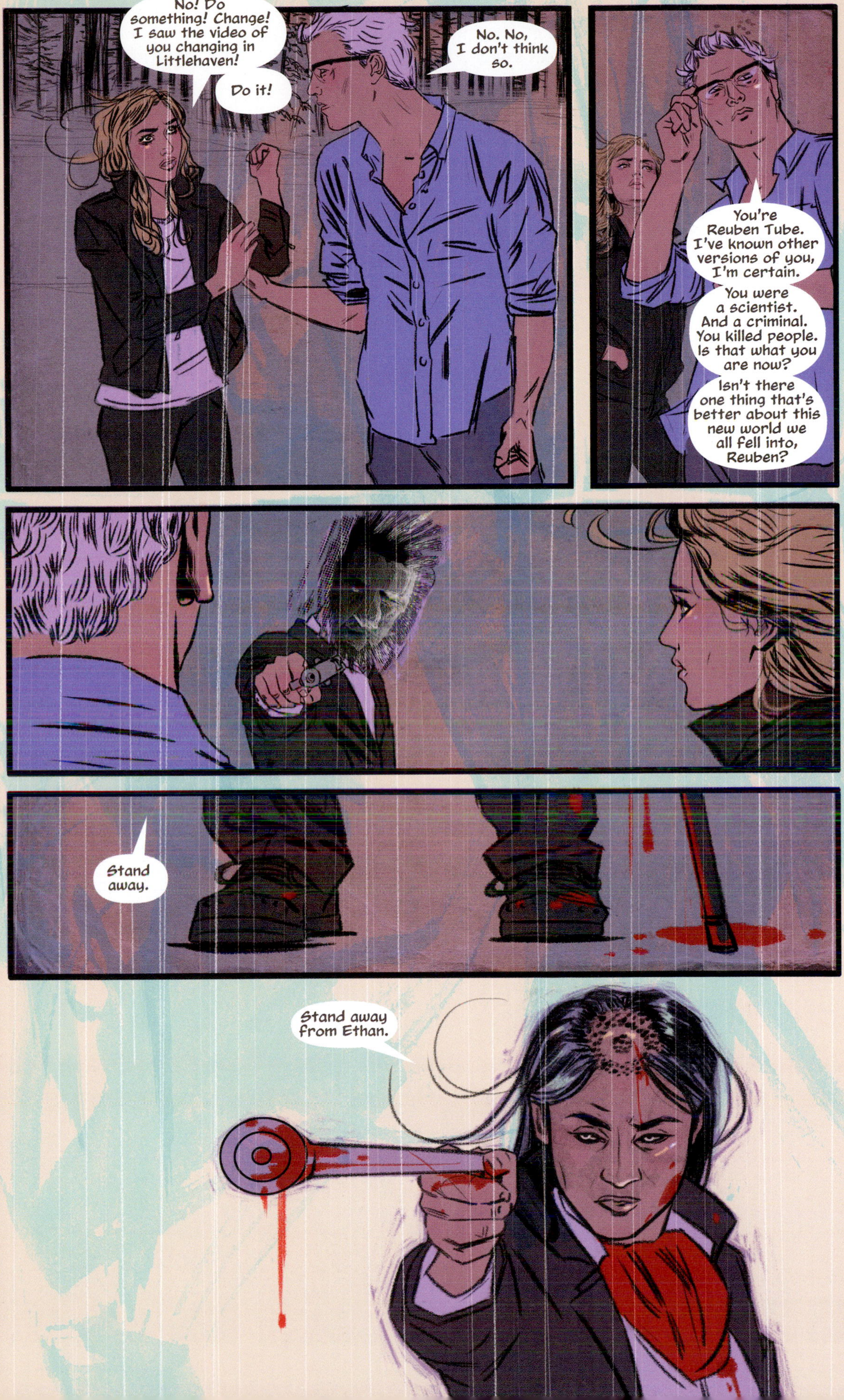
No! Do something! Change! I saw the video of you changing in Littlehaven!
Do it!
No. No, I don't think so.
You're Reuben Tube. I've known other versions of you, I'm certain.
You were a scientist. And a criminal. You killed people. Is that what you are now?
Isn't there one thing that's better about this new world we all fell into, Reuben?
Stand away.
Stand away from Ethan.

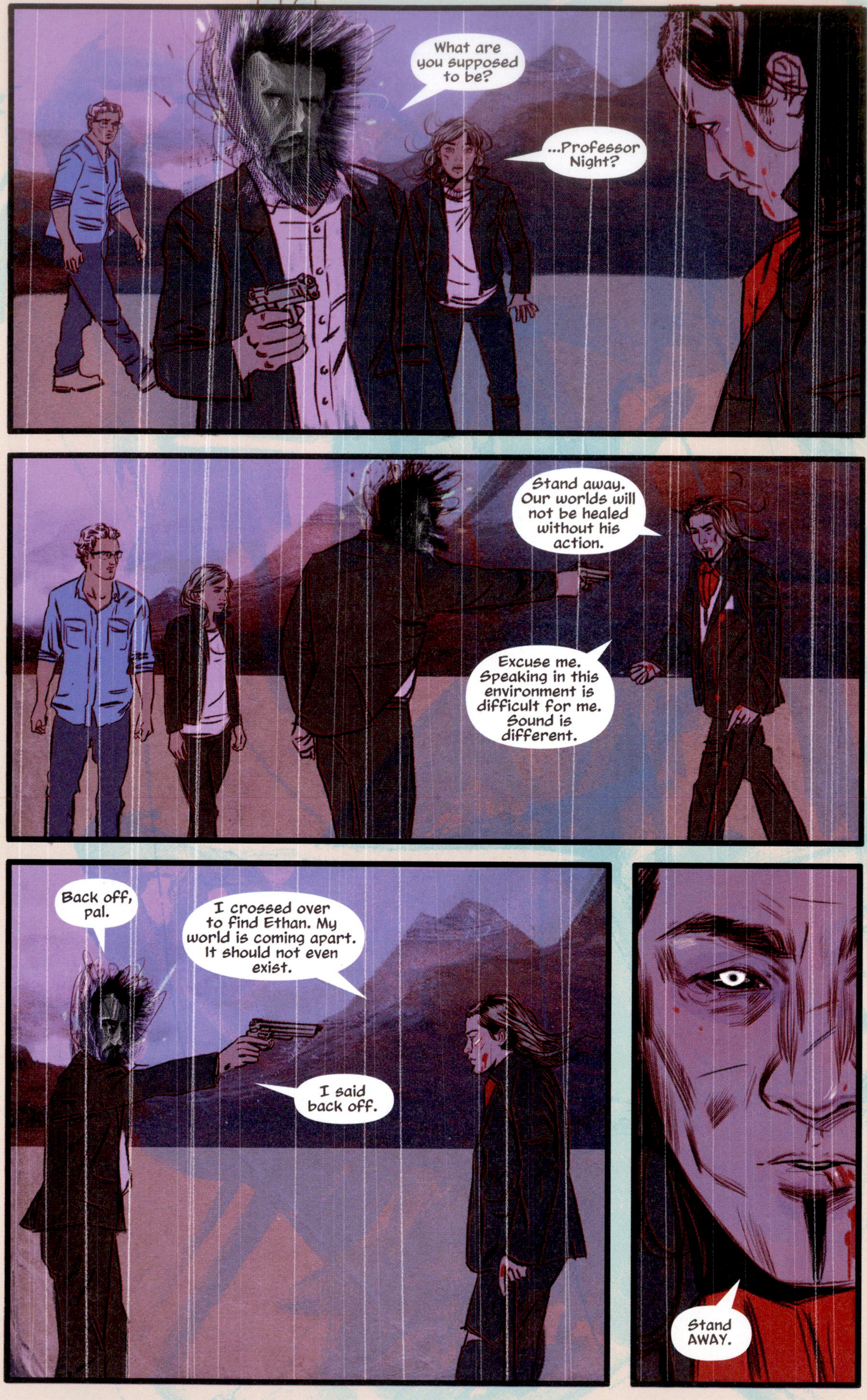
What are you supposed to be?
...Professor Night?
Stand away. Our worlds will not be healed without his action.
Excuse me. Speaking in this environment is difficult for me. Sound is different.
Back off, pal.
I crossed over to find Ethan. My world is coming apart. It should not even exist.
I said back off.
Stand AWAY.

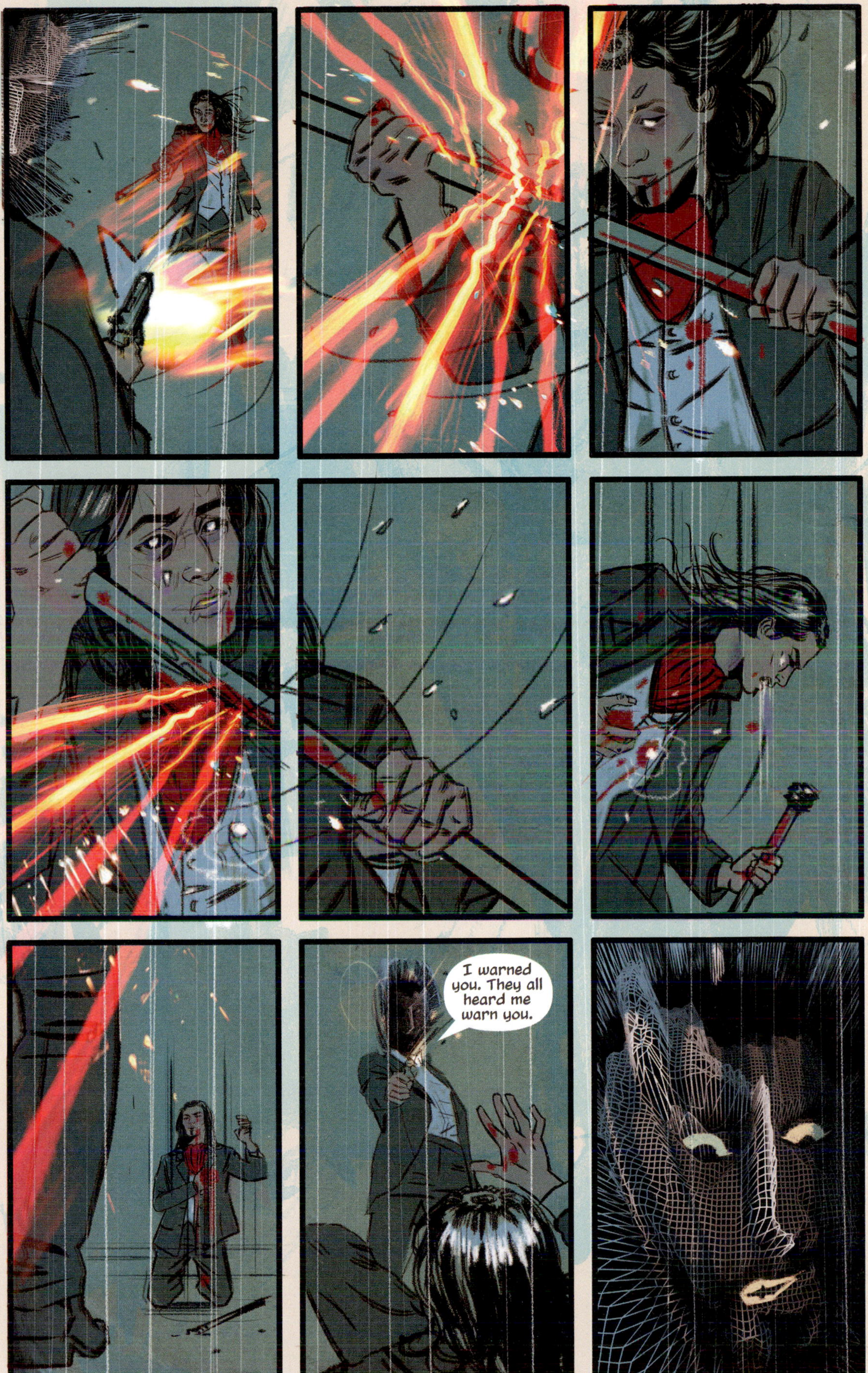
I warned you. They all heard me warn you.

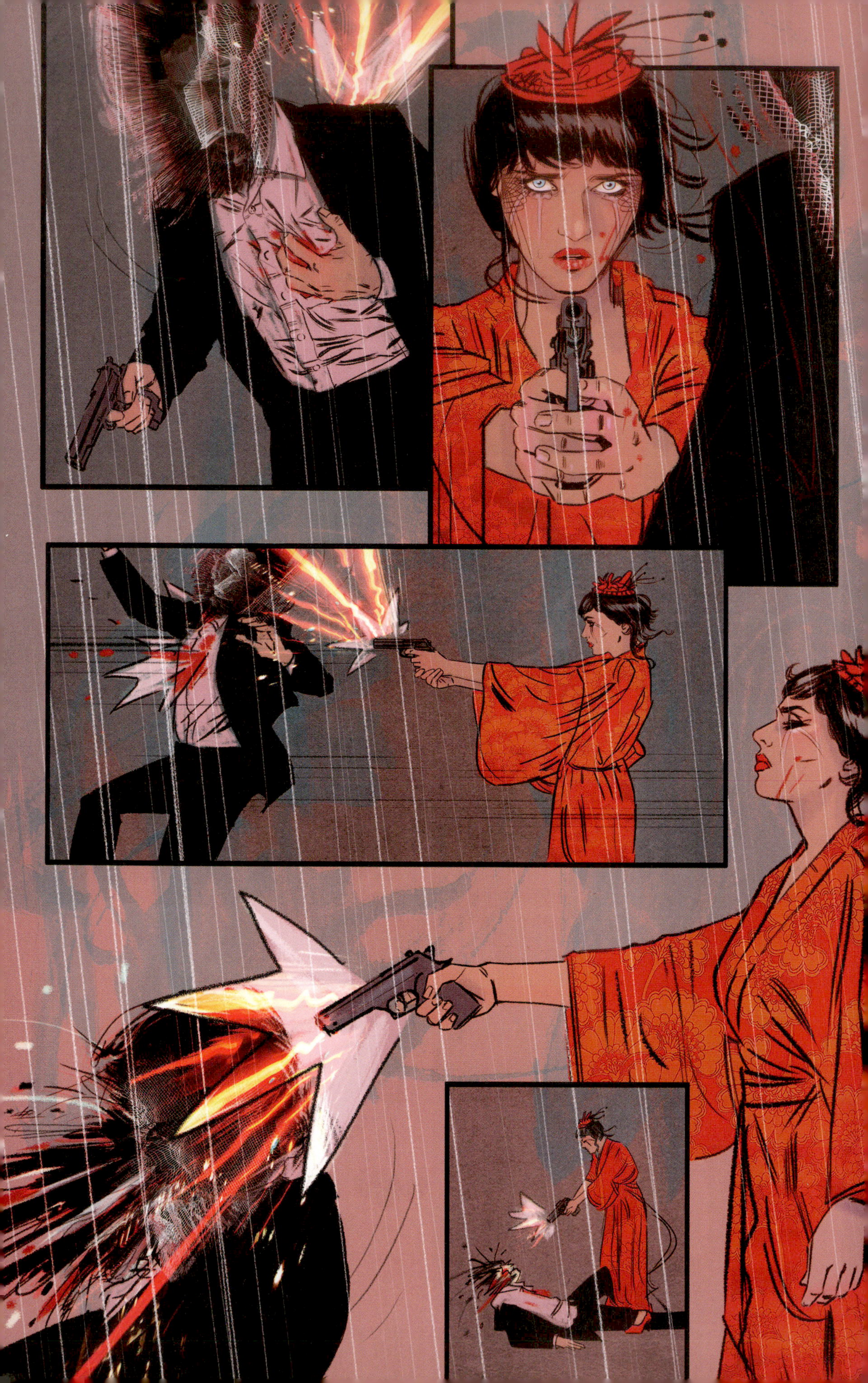

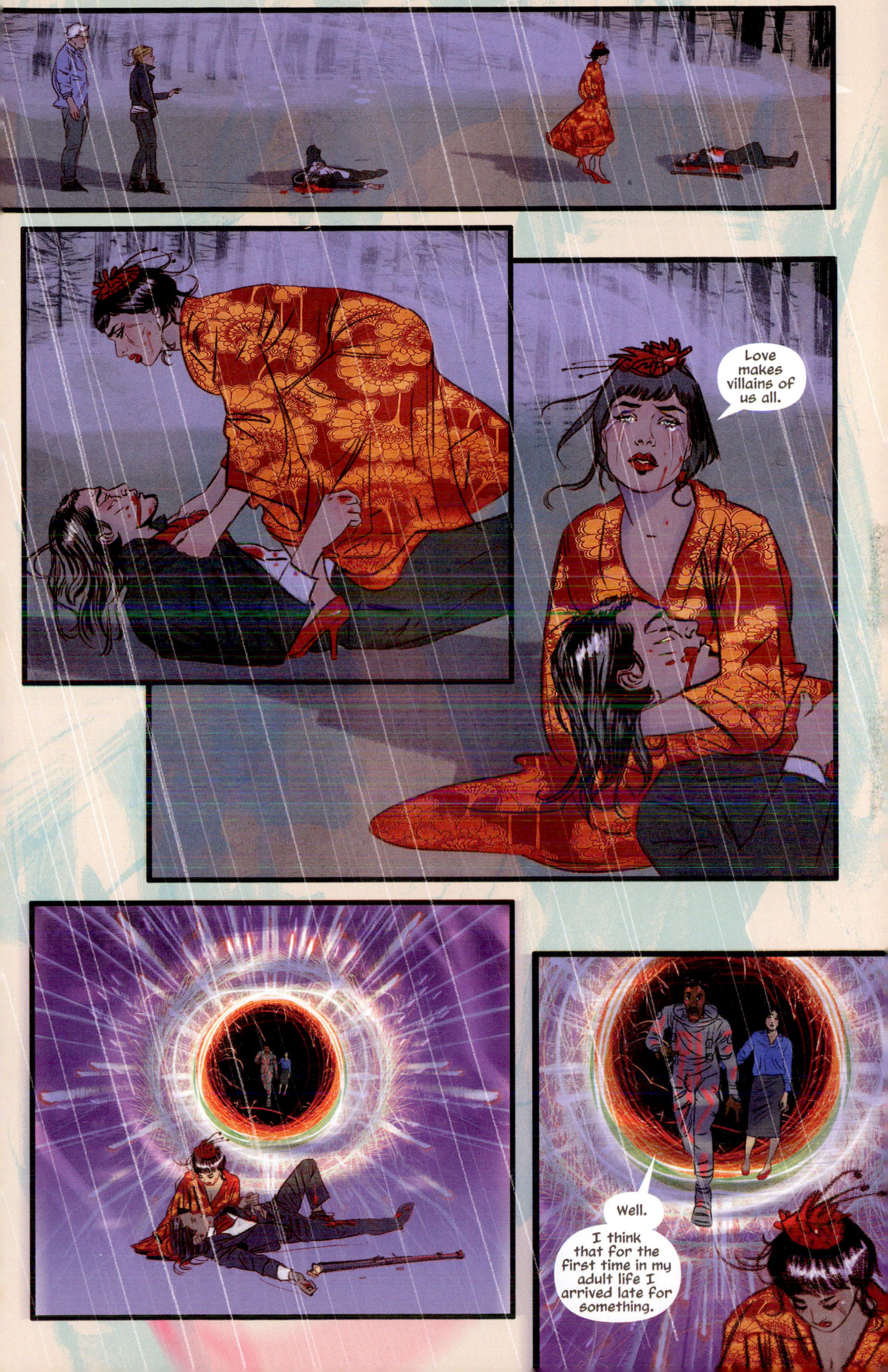
Love makes villains of us all.
Well.
I think that for the first time in my adult life I arrived late for something.

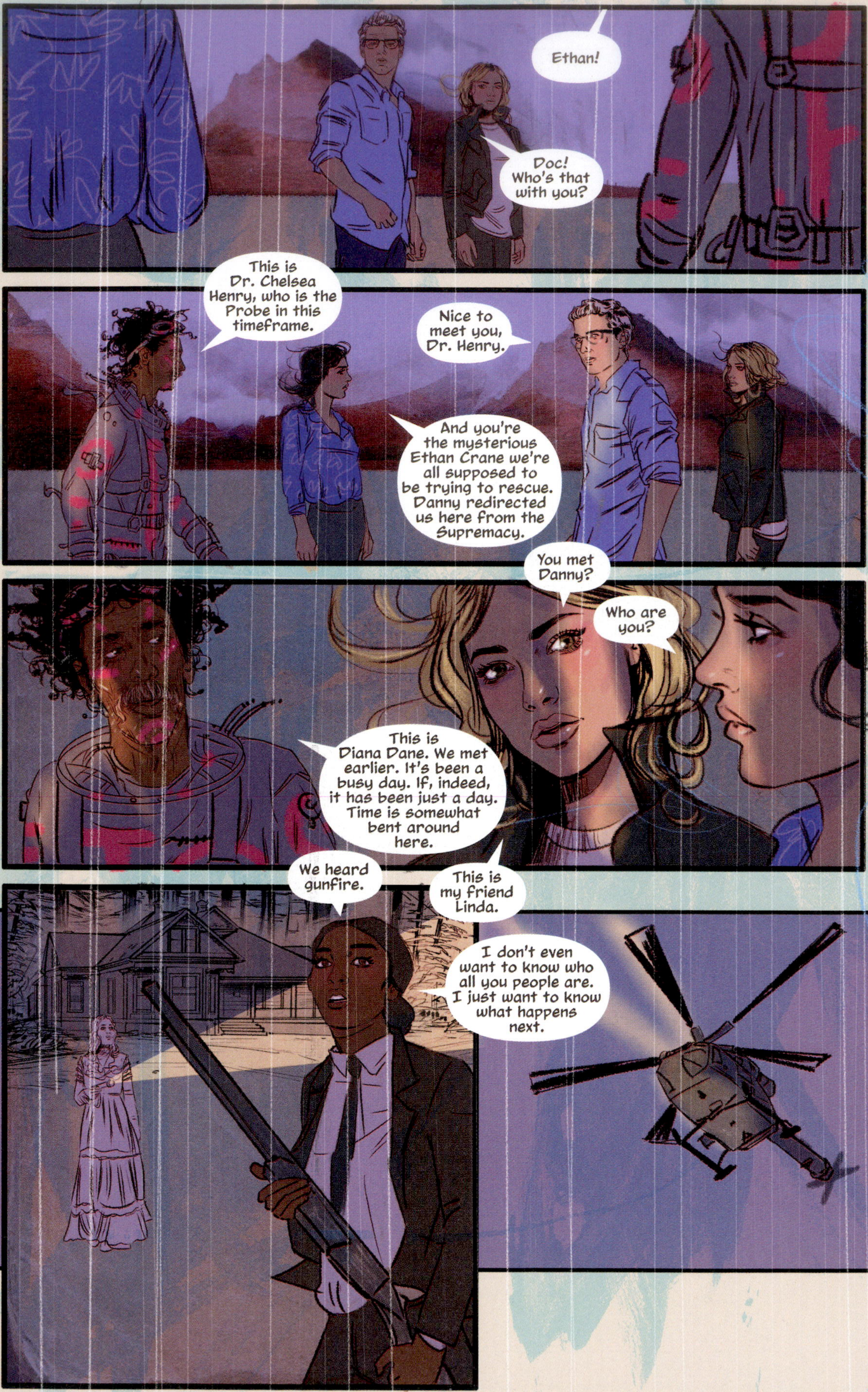
Ethan!
Doc! Who's that with you?
This is Dr. Chelsea Henry, who is the Probe in this timeframe.
Nice to meet you, Dr. Henry.
And you're the mysterious Ethan Crane we're all supposed to be trying to rescue. Danny redirected us here from the Supremacy.
You met Danny?
Who are you?
This is Diana Dane. We met earlier. It's been a busy day. If, indeed, it has been just a day. Time is somewhat bent around here.
We heard gunfire.
This is my friend Linda.
I don't even want to know who all you people are. I just want to know what happens next.

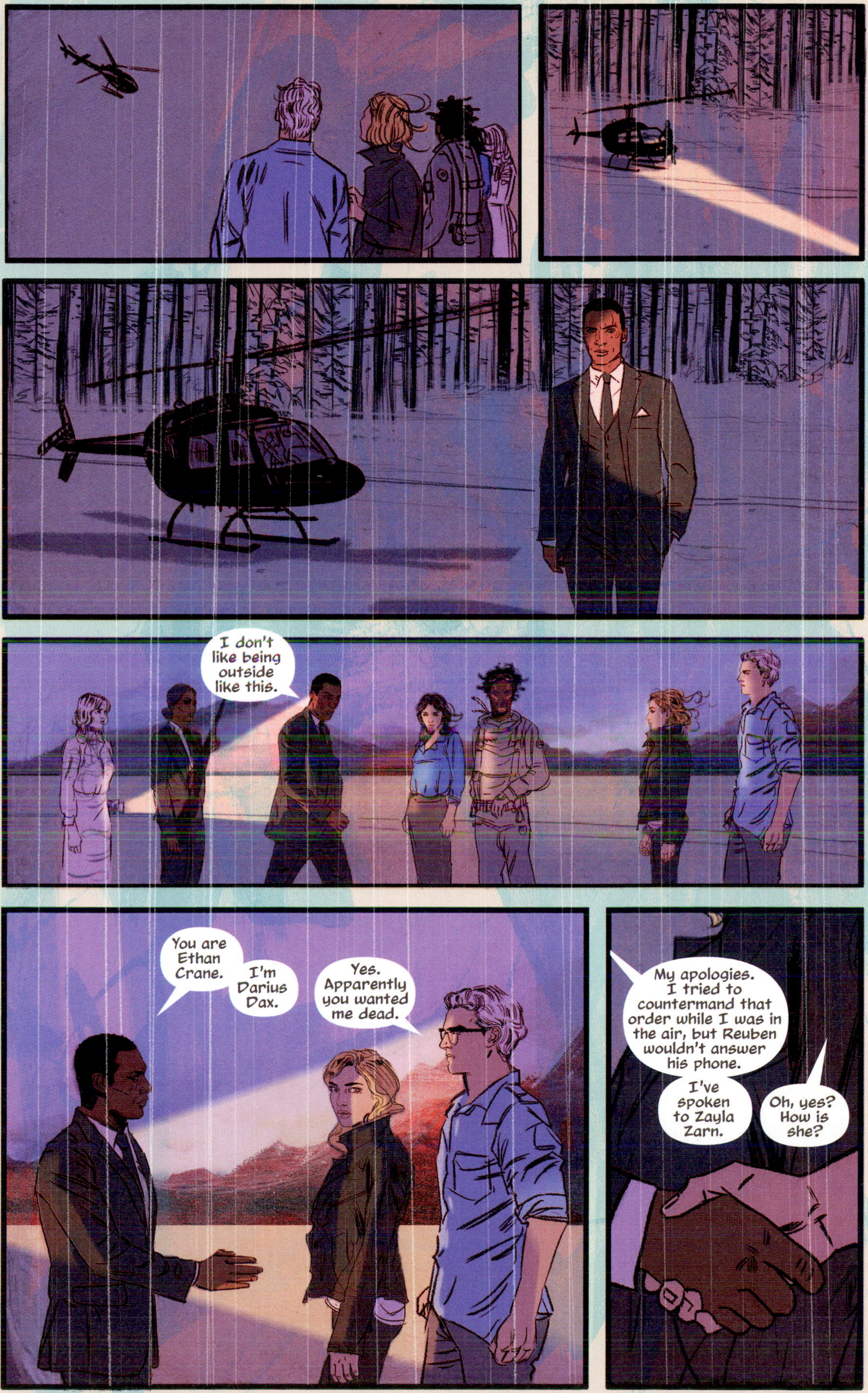
I don't like being outside like this.
You are Ethan Crane.
I'm Darius Dax.
Yes. Apparently you wanted me dead.
My apologies. I tried to countermand that order while I was in the air, but Reuben wouldn't answer his phone.
I've spoken to Zayla Zarn.
Oh, yes? How is she?

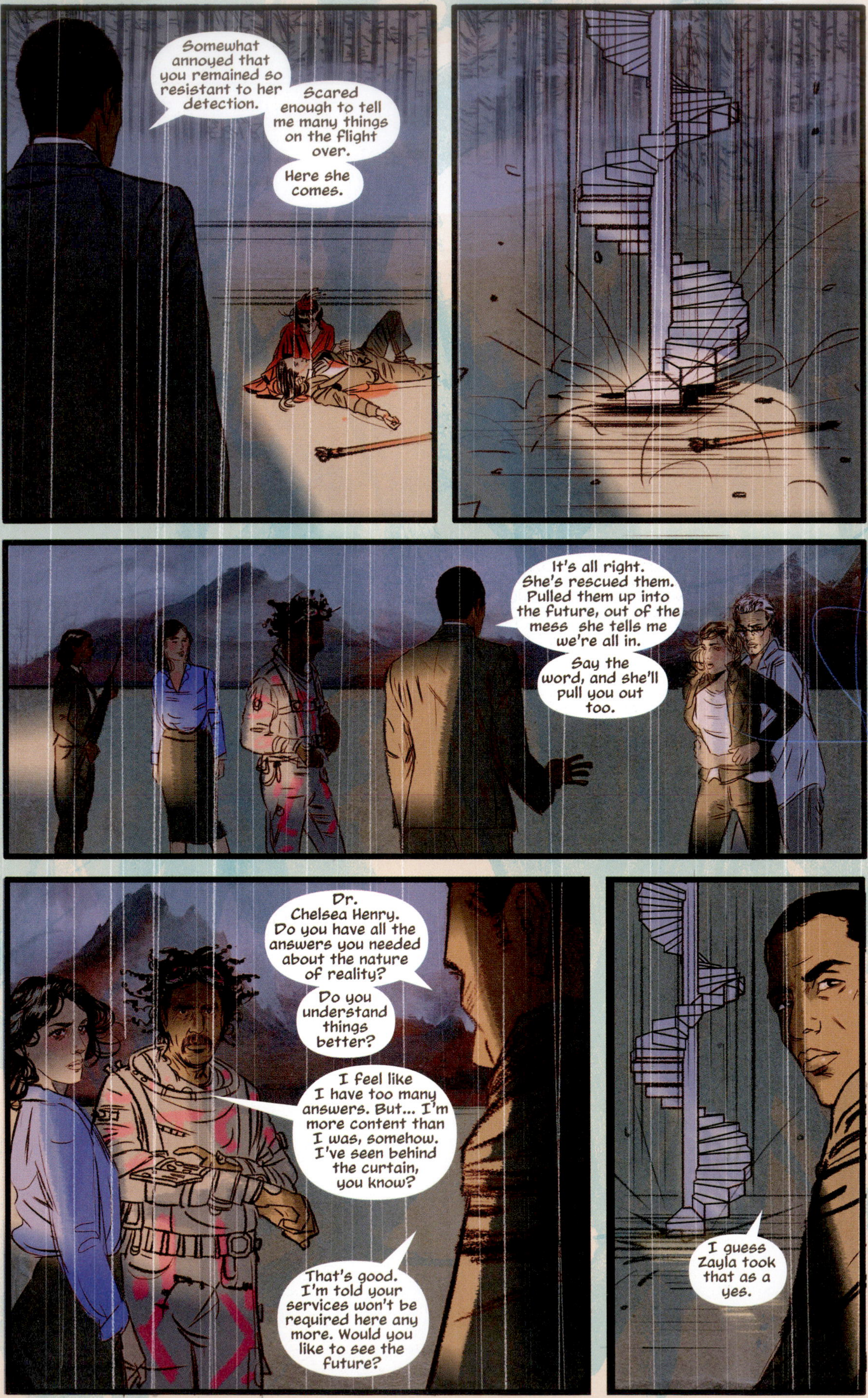
Somewhat annoyed that you remained so resistant to her detection.
Scared enough to tell me many things on the flight over.
Here she comes.
It's all right. She's rescued them. Pulled them up into the future, out of the mess she tells me we're all in.
Say the word, and she'll pull you out too.
Dr. Chelsea Henry. Do you have all the answers you needed about the nature of reality?
Do you understand things better?
I feel like I have too many answers. But... I'm more content than I was, somehow. I've seen behind the curtain, you know?
That's good. I'm told your services won't be required here any more. Would you like to see the future?
I guess Zayla took that as a yes.

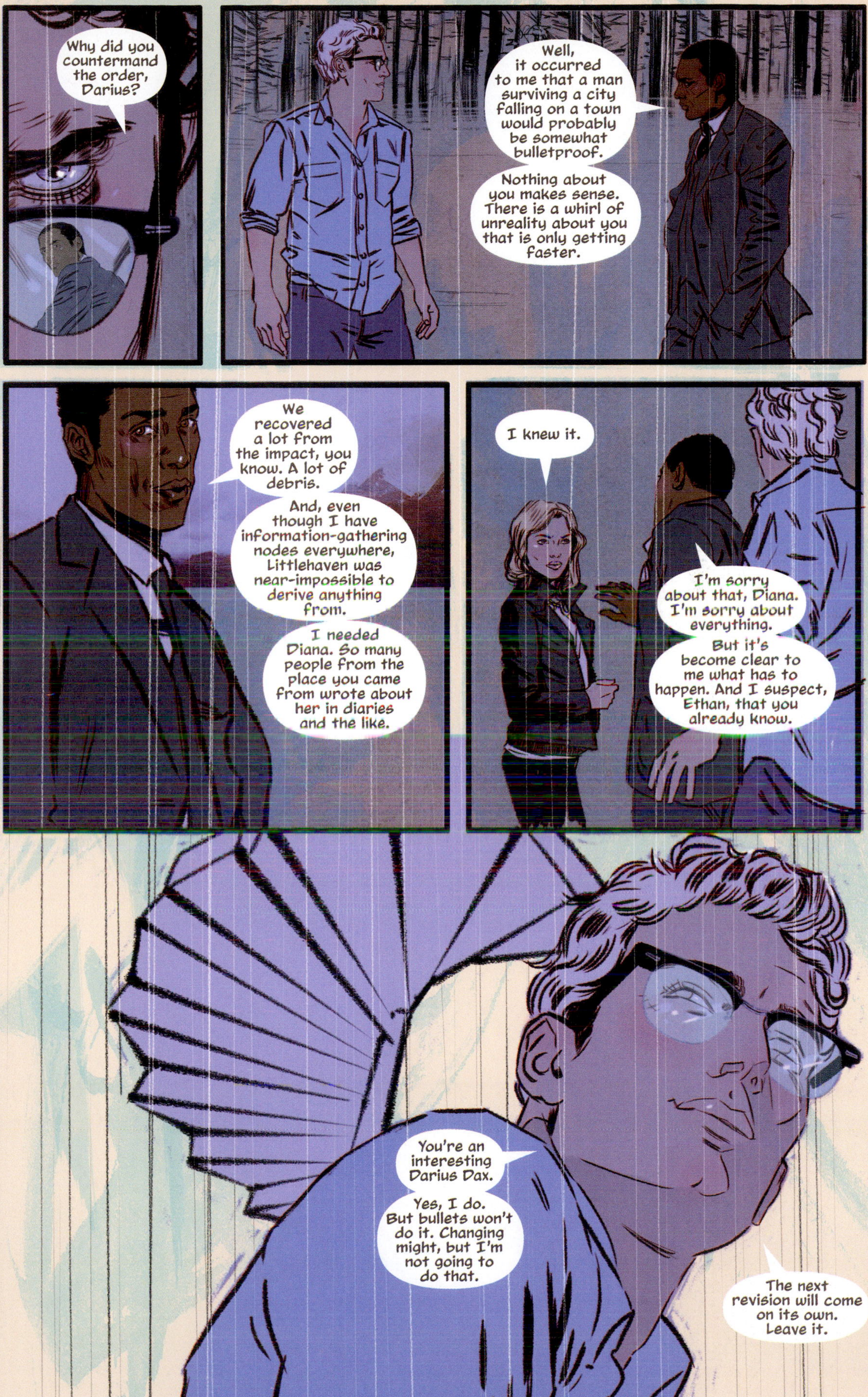
Why did you countermand the order, Darius?
Well, it occurred to me that a man surviving a city falling on a town would probably be somewhat bulletproof.
Nothing about you makes sense. There is a whirl of unreality about you that is only getting faster.
We recovered a lot from the impact, you know. A lot of debris.
And, even though I have information-gathering nodes everywhere, Littlehaven was near-impossible to derive anything from.
I needed Diana. So many people from the place you came from wrote about her in diaries and the like.
I knew it.
I'm sorry about that, Diana. I'm sorry about everything.
But it's become clear to me what has to happen. And I suspect, Ethan, that you already know.
You're an interesting Darius Dax.
Yes, I do. But bullets won't do it. Changing might, but I'm not going to do that.
The next revision will come on its own. Leave it.

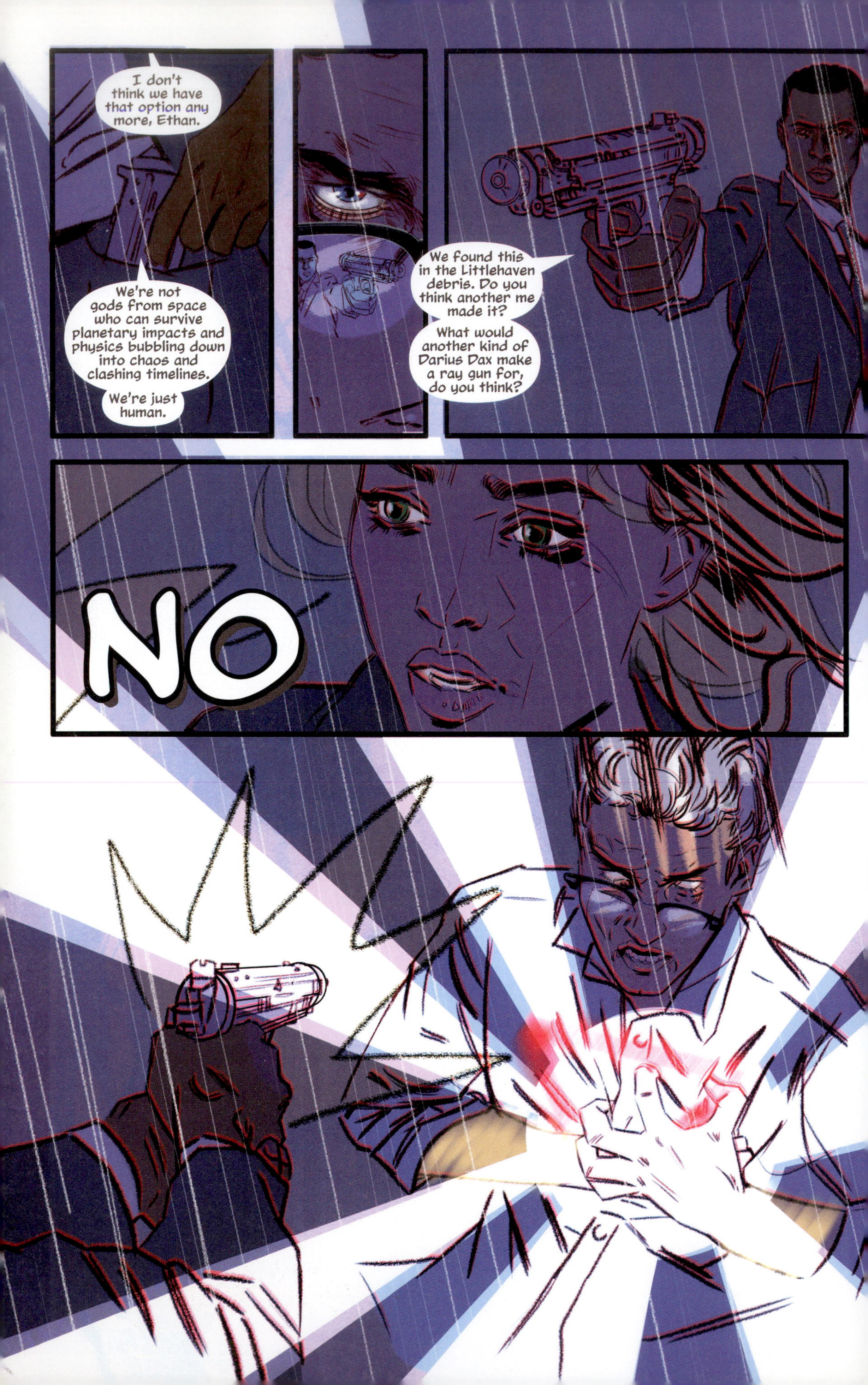
I don't think we have that option any more, Ethan.
We're not gods from space who can survive planetary impacts and physics bubbling down into chaos and clashing timelines.
We're just human.
We found this in the Littlehaven debris. Do you think another me made it?
What would another kind of Darius Dax make a ray gun for, do you think?
NO

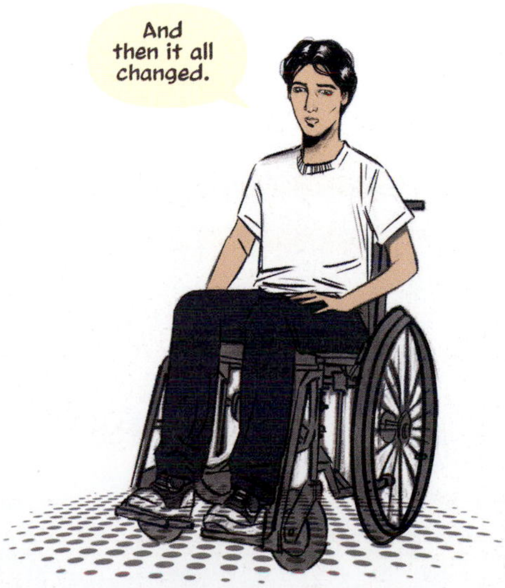
And then it all changed.

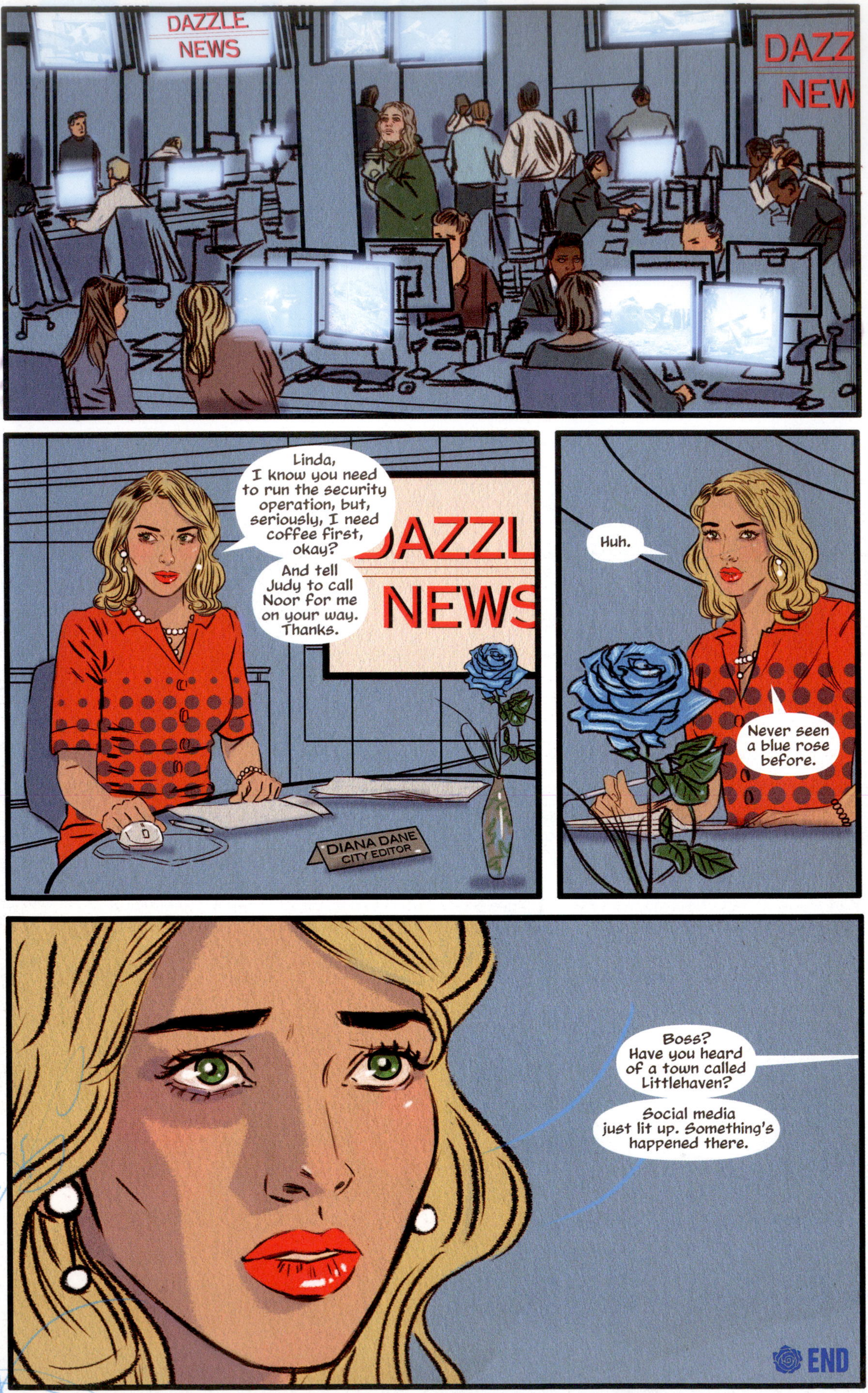
DAZZLE NEWS
DAZZ NEW
Linda, I know you need to run the security operation, but, seriously, I need coffee first, okay?
And tell Judy to call Noor for me on your way. Thanks.
DAZZL NEWS
DIANA DANE CITY EDITOR
Huh.
Never seen a blue rose before.
Boss? Have you heard of a town called Littlehaven?
Social media just lit up. Something's happened there.
END

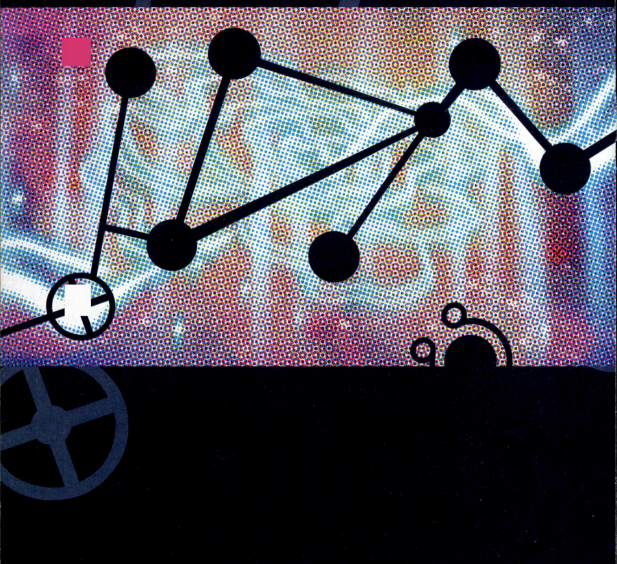